COMPROMISING POSITIONS

Emma's heart began to pound loudly at the feel of Max's light touch. "There's nothing confidential we need to chat about," she reminded him, feebly brushing his hand.

"Oh, no? Then why did you agree to meet me at the Artemisia? It was because you wanted to see me, wasn't it? Because you knew as well as I did that we needed to talk."

Emma had intended to shake her head resolutely and assure Max quite adamantly that there was nothing the two of them needed to discuss in private. Unfortunately, all she was able to manage was a single turn of her head toward the stairwell, a gesture that inadvertently resulted in her cheek being cupped in Max's palm, and that left Emma gazing up the stairs. Gazing up the stairs to find her future mother-in-law gazing back down at her.

THE
WEDDING

Elizabeth Bevarly

HarperPaperbacks
A Division of HarperCollinsPublishers

HarperPaperbacks *A Division of* HarperCollins*Publishers*
10 East 53rd Street, New York, N.Y. 10022

Copyright © 1993 by Elizabeth Bevarly
All rights reserved. No part of this book may be used or reproduced in any manner whatsoever without written permission of the publisher, except in the case of brief quotations embodied in critical articles and reviews. For information address HarperCollins*Publishers,*
10 East 53rd Street, New York, N.Y. 10022.

Cover photography by Herman Estevez

First printing: September 1993

Printed in the United States of America

HarperPaperbacks, HarperMonogram, and colophon are trademarks of HarperCollins*Publishers*

❖ 10 9 8 7 6 5 4 3 2 1

For Eileen Fallon and Carolyn Marino.
You guys should have lunch together more often.

And with much, much affection and appreciation for
the writers in Kentucky who make all the difference:
Katherine Bernardi, Lucia Clinch-Reimer, Lynn
Gray, Valerie Holcomb, Annie Jones, Teresa
Medeiros, Mary Morrow, Linda Ray, Patricia Rice,
Jan Scarbrough, Vicki Theobald, Jill Weathers, Kim
Whalen, Glenna Wilding, and especially Valerie
Kane and Sharon Wheat. You all are great friends.
Thanks for helping me through some rough times.

From this moment forward, your wedding will become the focal point of your very existence, usurping all else in your thoughts and activities. It is simply a fact in a woman's life that when she becomes engaged, she is necessarily preoccupied by thoughts of her wedding. But do not despair. With the proper planning, there's absolutely no reason why your wedding day cannot be the most supremely sumptuous, accurately arranged, elegantly executed day of your entire life. Just follow my easy-to-read guidelines, and everything will move along perfectly. And by all means, do enjoy yourself. It is your wedding, after all.

—ALISON BRIGHAM
Alison Brigham's Guide to Your Wedding

1

A woman's proposal may come in many forms, both spontaneous and well-planned. However, in Alison's opinion, the traditional way is the best way. With the man on bent knee, ring—and heart—in hand, solicitous and uncertain until the end. It simply makes for a much better presentation.

—ALISON BRIGHAM

"*I love you, Emma Hammelmann.*"

Emma glanced up from the Norton critical edition of the selected works of Edith Wharton to find Taylor watching her intently. She peered at him from beneath long black bangs and smiled. "I love you, too, Taylor Rowan. What brought that on?"

Taylor adjusted his glasses and then swept his dark hair off his forehead. It was a familiar gesture, one that made Emma feel content. She would be defending her master's thesis at eight o'clock that morning, just over six hours away, and right now Taylor's presence beside her at her parents' kitchen table was reassuring. He was reading a voluminous tome she knew had something to do with his law studies. When he flipped it shut, she looked over to read the spine and caught the words *Uniform Commercial Code*.

"You getting tired of finals?" she asked him.

Taylor nodded wearily. "You bet."

"If you're like this now, I hate to see how you're going to be before the bar exam. I might have to leave town for a few weeks."

"Please, Emma, that's still two months away. And then there will be more months of waiting to see if I passed. Don't make me think about it now. And don't you dare leave town. You're going to have to quiz me on my torts and briefs."

"Ooh, I love your briefs. And your torts just send chills down my spine. Anyway, don't sweat it." She paused. "Hey, I'm not looking forward to my orals tomorrow, either, but look at me." She stretched her arms out wide and groaned with satisfaction, bringing the letters that read "Georgetown University" taut across her chest. "I'm not worried. Once my orals are over and I have my master's that's when I'll start to worry. Because what exactly I'll do with an advanced degree in American literature, I'm not quite sure yet."

"I thought you were going to write that Great American Novel you keep talking about."

"I will. Eventually." Her smile became mischievous. "I'd suggest we pound the pavement together in search of employment, but since you already plan to go into practice with that fascist father of yours . . ."

"He isn't a fascist, Emma, and you know it." Taylor removed his glasses and rubbed his eyes. Emma knew he was feeling annoyed. "To you, anyone who's a member of the Republican party or the Daughters of the American Revolution is a fascist. If you had ever spent any amount of time with my family, you'd realize they're not complete ogres. Not all of them, anyway."

"I know they're not *complete* ogres," she teased. But Taylor didn't look amused. "All right, they're not ogres at all. They're too refined for that. But you can't deny that the few times I have been to your house, your parents have been less than warm toward me."

Taylor offered her a bland expression. Without his glasses, his brown eyes looked even darker. "Emma, they behave that way toward everyone. Even each other. It's nothing personal. You'll get used to it."

"Why would I want to get used to it?" she asked quietly, trying to quell the nervousness she felt. She was pretty sure she knew what was coming next.

"Because . . ."

Taylor took a deep breath and released it slowly. He left his glasses on the table and reached for his jacket, which was hanging on the back of the chair beside him.

"I, um . . . I have something I want to give you," he said, fumbling first in one pocket and then the other. When he still couldn't find what he was looking for, he jerked his jacket from the chair and tried the inside pocket. For a moment he panicked, then relief washed through him as his fingers closed over a small box covered in pearl gray velvet. He'd spent months looking for just the right ring. It would be just his luck to have dropped it somewhere in the mall.

"I thought . . ." he began. "That is, if you think it's a good idea . . . I mean, I know you do . . . at least, I hope so . . ."

Taylor sighed and told himself to stop behaving like a jerk. He and Emma had been seeing each other for more than five years, and the subject of marriage wasn't exactly something he was bringing up out of the blue. They'd talked about it. Sort of. And they'd pretty much agreed they were going to get married. Eventually. All that was left was to make it official. And usually a ring and a proposal went along with that.

Emma was sitting perfectly still, her hands atop her book, braced together in the church-and-steeple fashion of a game he recalled from his childhood. Taylor smiled at the appropriateness of the gesture and slowly pulled himself back together.

He began again. "What I'm trying to say is . . ."

Recalling suddenly that he'd intended to do this thing right, he shoved his chair away from the table and dropped down before Emma on one knee. She laughed a little uneasily as she turned to face him.

"Did you lose something?" she asked.

Taylor shook his head. "No, I've found something. Something I honestly never thought I would. Someone with whom to share the rest of my life . . . if she'll have me. Emma, I love you, and nothing would make me happier than for you and I . . . you and me . . ." He made a restless gesture with his free hand to include them both. "For us . . . to get married. So . . ."

He finally opened the tiny box in his palm to reveal a single, perfect, half-carat emerald perched atop a filigreed gold ring. "The color reminded me of your eyes," he said. "I wanted to go for a full carat, but I figured you'd never go out in public wearing something that big. You're not an ostentatious person. That's the only reason I can figure you'd spend so much time on a guy like me."

When Taylor finally looked up to meet Emma's gaze, he saw that her eyes were filling with tears. He smiled as he asked softly, "So what do you say? Will you marry me?"

Emma's laughter joined with her tears as she reached for the box Taylor held out to her. "Oh, Taylor," she said quietly, "you're so corny." She threw her arms around his neck and kissed him. "Of course I'll marry you, you sentimental fool. How could I resist?"

"I love you," he said again as he buried his face in her neck and kissed the warm, fragrant nape exposed by her short hair. "I really, really love you."

Emma pulled away only far enough to stare into his eyes. "I love you, too, Taylor. And I can't wait until we're married."

He took the box from her fingers and retrieved the ring from its resting place, then pressed the emerald against his lips before taking Emma's left hand in his own. Slowly, carefully, he slid the ring down over her fourth finger. It fit perfectly.

"If you don't like it, we can exchange it," he said. "If you want something different—a diamond instead of an emerald, or a setting in silver or something—I'll understand."

Emma studied the green stone that flashed and winked at her beneath the bright fluorescent light overhead. "It's perfect, Taylor. . . . It's so beautiful," she whispered, her tears welling up again. "How can you think I'd want to return a gift like this?"

He smiled once more, relieved that she approved of his selection. Emma smiled back and leaned forward to kiss him again. And again. And again.

Taylor's proposal hadn't come as a great surprise to Emma. For more than two years, they had occasionally spoken of getting married someday. But they'd agreed it would be best to postpone serious discussion of marriage until they had both earned their degrees. And now that they were about to achieve the latter, why shouldn't they discuss the former? Soon Taylor would be going to work in one of the oldest, most illustrious, most conservative law firms in Washington, D.C.—one that had been founded by his great-great-great-God-knows-how-many-greats-grandfather—and the next item on his agenda would naturally be an appropriate wife. And although Emma hadn't yet decided what precisely she would choose for her career, at least she would be finished with school.

Why shouldn't marriage be on Taylor's mind? Emma asked herself. She couldn't deny she'd been thinking about it, too, especially over the past several weeks. She just hadn't been sure how to broach the subject. But Taylor had taken care of that for her. His proposal tonight had been like him—sincere, affectionate, and touched with humor. As usual, he had said just the right thing, just the right way.

But something else occurred to Emma now as she studied him, something that put her just a little bit on edge. Of course she loved Taylor outrageously, but she had never much thought of herself as married to a conservative attorney. Being seriously involved with a student—even a student focused on corporate law—was one thing. Being married to a full-fledged corporate suit was quite another.

"What's the matter?" Taylor asked. "Don't you think this is a good idea? We've been dating since you were a freshman. I'd think five and a half years is sufficient time to decide whether or not you want to marry someone."

That was certainly true enough. Emma knew Taylor better than she knew anyone, and was sure he felt the same way about her. They'd both seen each other at their worsts—more times than she liked to think about—and still managed to love each other. They'd become so close as time had passed, there were times when she actually thought she could tell what he was thinking. They had nearly everything in common. They'd been in love for years.

And, as hard as it was to believe, they never, ever, fought. Well, except for that once, Emma amended, when they'd argued over Tina McDermott. But that had been two years ago—ancient history. Simply put, Emma Hammelmann and Taylor Rowan were a perfect couple. They should be married.

There was just one tiny little problem.

"You realize of course what this involves?" she asked. "We'll be permanently uniting the House of Rowan with the House of Hammelmann. It could be a little tricky."

Taylor smiled, and Emma could have sworn there was something behind it other than happiness. As if he were anticipating with relish the fireworks that would surely result at the comingling of their families. "Yeah, I know," he said.

"Blue blood joining with blue collar?" Then, recalling her mother's heritage, she added, "And bluegrass?"

"Uh-huh."

"Designer wear combining with hardware? I mean, can you actually picture your mother's bridge club and my mother's bowling team chatting over tea and Buds?"

Taylor raised his eyebrows. "It'll be the perfect arrangement," he said. "Your father can provide the garden supplies for my mother's garden parties."

"And your father will be claiming a new relation in the Hardware Czar." Emma sighed. "Gee, won't that be something to brag about at gatherings of the partners."

Taylor's smile became mischievous. "Wouldn't it be great?"

"It could completely disrupt the tenuous harmony of the universe as we know it," Emma said, only half-joking.

"I know."

"And that doesn't bother you?"

"Not in the least."

"You know, it might not be such a bad thing at that. Your family could use some loosening up. And God knows my family is just the group to do it." She looked at Taylor thoughtfully. "You sure you weren't adopted? You're absolutely nothing like anyone else in your family."

"Rogue gene."

Emma gazed at the shiny new ring on her left hand and sighed deeply. "Jeez, we're going to get married."

Taylor grinned, and if Emma hadn't known better, she would have sworn he was absolutely glowing with satisfaction. She was aware, however, that Rowans weren't generally the type to glow about things.

"But, Taylor, if it's all right with you, I'd rather not

have some huge, obscene, flashy wedding. I'd like it to be small and intimate, maybe twenty-five guests—just immediate family and very close friends."

"No problem. I couldn't agree more. We can have the wedding over the summer—the end of July maybe, right after the bar exam—with just a few friends and family. Nothing beyond that. The smaller the better as far as I'm concerned."

Emma nodded, nervously twisting the unfamiliar weight on her left hand. A simple, intimate celebration of their union shared with the people they loved most in the world—that was exactly what Emma wanted the wedding to be. And Taylor's assurance that that was exactly what he wanted, too, was good enough for her.

2

The groom may wish to inform his parents of his intentions in advance, or, in the spirit of wonder and celebration, may want them to be as surprised and excited as his intended. In either case, his parents should be as overjoyed by the news as he is himself. And of course, how could they not be?

—ALISON BRIGHAM

"Don't forget, Lionel, we have dinner with those Hammelmann people tonight." Francesca Rowan gazed at her husband's reflection in the mirror above his dresser, if not at her husband himself. "You will remember for a change, won't you?"

Lionel tied his modest striped silk tie into a perfect windsor knot and pretended not to hear his wife. He had a very full day ahead of him and was trying to recall at exactly what time he had which meeting. An eight-thirty appointment with Charlie Malcolm at the Enodyne compound to discuss one of the company's new acquisitions in India, then an eleven-thirty lunch at Horsefeathers with a potential new client named . . . what was his name again? Gordon? Grant? No, Godfrey.

Godfrey Carruthers. The afternoon would be tied up entirely with Edgar Parsons and that asinine lawsuit the other man had somehow managed to get himself into. And then, he hoped, an early dinner with Susan. In between his appointments there were a host of other problems requiring his attention if he had time, but God only knew what the day held beyond that.

"Lionel?" Francesca repeated.

He swiveled his head to the side enough so that he could glance at his wife, then returned his attention to getting dressed. "What is it?"

Francesca smoothed out a nonexistent wrinkle in the paisley silk robe that so exquisitely complemented the tailored silk pajamas beneath. She hated it when her husband ignored her like this. "The Hammelmanns have invited the girls to come along, too, so it makes me think something dreadful is about to happen." She paused to collect herself before continuing. "More specifically, it makes me think Taylor and Emma are . . . are going to announce a wedding engagement or some such thing."

Oh, yes, Lionel recalled then. He also had an engagement with Peter Flannery at four. Without acknowledging Francesca's statement, he lifted a glass of freshly squeezed orange juice from the silver tray their housekeeper, Margaret, had left on the table by the patio doors fifteen minutes before.

"Why would that be so dreadful?" he finally asked. "Emma's not such a bad sort."

Francesca sighed melodramatically. "Yes, but you know how the other Hammelmanns are. I just thought when Taylor married it would be into a . . . a higher caliber of family than that. Like Catherine did when she married Michael."

"Michael's father works for a newspaper," Lionel pointed out. "A liberal newspaper."

"Yes, but at least it's a successful newspaper, one that's been in circulation for generations. And Michael's father is the executive editor. *And* need I remind you that Michael's grandfather is the publisher. Your son, on the other hand, may be about to join us with the Hardware Czar. Don't you remember those terrible commercials of his that run during the evening news?"

Francesca shuddered for effect as she recited, "'Hi, I'm Laszlo Hammelmann, Hammelmann Hardware. Home improvements got you thinking you haven't got a prayer? Come to Hammelmann Hardware. Yard work giving you a scare? Come to Hammelmann Hardware.' It's absolutely awful, Lionel, the man can't even rhyme well. I would never have linked 'prayer' with 'hardware.' I would have chosen something like . . . like . . . 'Working on the stairs?' or 'Housework only fair?' or something like that."

Lionel sipped his orange juice and said nothing.

Realizing she would get no further reaction from her husband this morning, Francesca simply said, "Don't forget about the Hammelmanns."

"I'll remember."

"Cocktails at six o'clock," Francesca went on, "and dinner at seven." The rest of what she said was mostly for her own benefit. "I do hope Taylor and Emma get there before we arrive this time. The last time we were forced to be alone with the Hammelmanns, and Desiree went on and on about how much her life had changed since Laszlo had become such a successful purveyor of hardware. That's the word she used, too, 'purveyor.' Now where would she have learned a word like that?"

"It's a perfectly good word," Lionel said absently.

"Yes, but she's from a little nothing town in Kentucky. Honestly, I don't know that I could stomach another tale about how her family had to eat possum when her father wouldn't let them kill the roosters he raised for cockfighting. Really, how horrible."

After draining the last of his juice, Lionel said, "At least you didn't have to listen to a long-winded sales pitch about mulching mowers and chain saws. Christ, I don't even use those things. Hammelmann should have been talking to the gardener."

Francesca sighed and studied her husband. Lionel was as handsome now as he'd been the day they married. His skin was permanently tanned and lined from so many summers on the boat, and his full head of hair had whitened beautifully over the years.

She lifted a hand to her own hair and wondered if she should have an auburn rinse applied the next time she visited Kenny, to cover the gray that was fast overtaking the dark brown. It would subtract years from her appearance. Really, what was the point of spending thousands on cosmetic surgery when she balked at coloring her hair?

"Well, regardless of what happens, I've already thought of a way for us to excuse ourselves as soon after dinner as is politely possible," she said. "We'll simply tell Desiree and Laszlo we have an early morning engagement." She paused, waiting for some kind of response from Lionel, and when she didn't receive one, continued as if she hadn't noticed. "It bothers me, the way this invitation for all of us came out of the blue. After our last disastrous experience at the Hammelmanns', I would think they'd be as uneager to see us again as we are to see them."

Lionel remained silent, but Francesca thought he nodded his agreement.

"I hope Desiree makes something a little less . . . folksy this time," she added. "You'd think now that they have money she'd invest in a first-rate cook."

This time Lionel grunted his agreement as he looked at his watch. The Enodyne compound was a good thirty minutes' drive from his home. He'd better get going if he was to make his appointment with Malcolm on time. He placed his empty juice glass beside his empty coffee cup on the table, ignoring the rest of his meal.

Francesca frowned. "Skipping breakfast again, are we,

Lionel? Neglecting our nutritional needs in favor of some other needs, hmm?"

Lionel bent to pick up his briefcase, ignoring his wife's comments.

"Breakfasting with that tart, Susan, again? Or is there a new tart on the menu?"

Lionel sighed. "Jealousy doesn't become you," he said. "And I thought we agreed years ago that this was a topic not open for discussion."

"No, I believe *you* decided that years ago, Lionel."

"At any rate, draw in your claws."

Reluctantly, Francesca chose not to pursue her attack. Aggression was so unbecoming in a woman. Let Lionel go on thinking she was such a good little wife for allowing him his playmates, she told herself. She was such a good sport. Pushing thoughts of her husband's extramarital activities away, Francesca turned to a more important topic.

"Wear your dark gray suit. I think that would be most appropriate for tonight. I'll see if I can't get Adrienne into a dress for a change."

Lionel clicked open his briefcase and tossed a sheaf of papers from his nightstand inside. "I'll try to be home by five-thirty," he said as he left the room without a farewell.

"No, try to be home by five!" she called after him, certain he had heard her but not so certain he would comply.

Once Lionel was gone, Francesca felt as she did every morning when he left—bored, listless, and eager for something different to do. She sat down at the table and lifted the lid on her breakfast. Virtually every morning for the past thirty-six years, Margaret had brought a silver tray equipped with breakfast for two into the master bedroom of the Rowan home. Virtually every morning since a twenty-year-old Francesca, still giddy from a honeymoon in Havana, returned with her new husband to the Capitol Hill townhouse the two of them had inhabited as newlyweds. Today, of course, they lived in the legendary Georgian estate in Alexandria that had been built by the first Rowan to set foot on American soil. But Margaret was still bringing them breakfast, even after thirty-six years.

And so much had happened during all those years. Births and deaths. Private schools, birthday parties, polo lessons, cotillions, graduations . . . And now her son was about to embark on a career in commercial law, just as his father had thirty-six years ago. In so many ways, all those changes had simply brought them full circle. Somehow, this realization made Francesca feel a little melancholy.

A light tap on the door brought her attention back to the present. "Come in," she called without rising.

"Are you finished with your breakfast, Mrs. Rowan?" Margaret asked as she entered the bedroom. She was tall and slender, with hair that had been silver for as long as Francesca could remember.

"I haven't finished yet, Margaret, but Mr. Rowan has. You may take his things."

"Yes, Mrs. Rowan."

Throughout the many phases of their lives, there was one thing that hadn't changed at all in thirty-six years. Lionel had never once taken the time to sit down and enjoy a leisurely breakfast with his wife, not even on the weekend. If it wasn't work, it was a business trip. If not a business trip, then golf with his cronies—at least, he always said he was playing golf.

Now, as their housekeeper was about to remove his plate, Francesca couldn't help but be a little curious about it.

"Just a moment, Margaret," she said as she stayed the other woman's hand with her own.

"Yes, Mrs. Rowan?"

Reaching across the table, Francesca lifted the silver dome off of Lionel's charger. Beneath it, the plate was empty and squeaky clean. She eyed Margaret suspiciously. Margaret wove her fingers together behind her back and looked away, noticing a cobweb in the corner of the ceiling that she would have to clear away after Mrs. Rowan left for the day.

"How long have you been bringing in Mr. Rowan's breakfast this way, Margaret?" Francesca asked as she replaced the dome.

Margaret offered her employer the most dazzling smile she could manage. "Isn't that the strangest thing? Driscoll must have been asleep on the job this morning to have sent Mr. Rowan's plate up empty."

"How long, Margaret?" Francesca repeated.

Margaret sighed in resignation. "None of the cooks since Bailey has made breakfast for Mr. Rowan for more than a month."

"I see."

"It's . . . it's kept the housekeeping budget down, though," she said. "Some."

Francesca nodded absently. "Mm." She pushed her chair away from the table. "You might as well take my things, too. I'll have an early lunch at the club."

"Yes, Mrs. Rowan."

Lionel probably was breakfasting with that tart, Susan, Francesca thought with a frown as she watched Margaret depart. Why should things be any different now than they'd ever been? Before Susan it had been that tart, Vivian. And before Vivian, that tart, Michelle. That would take Lionel's affairs back seventeen years, when Francesca had first discovered unequivocal evidence of her husband's romantic interludes with other women, in the form of two plane tickets in his underwear drawer. She had no idea who his mistresses had been before then, but she did know Lionel was at least monogamous in that he kept only one woman at a time.

Francesca sighed and pushed her troubling thoughts away, and went to take her shower. As she did every

Thursday, she would play bridge at the club that afternoon, and afterward she would go for her tennis lesson. Of course she knew perfectly well how to play tennis— had learned years ago—but ever since the club had hired that new pro, Jason, with his blond hair and blue eyes and splendidly youthful physique, Francesca had decided she simply had to take some refresher courses.

On her way out of the bathroom she paused at her dresser and pulled open her extensive lingerie drawer. She would wear red for Jason today, she decided. It would surprise him.

Smiling to herself, Francesca began to hum. If the afternoon went along as usual, she thought with a little smile, perhaps Jason would have one or two surprises for her, as well.

3

The bride's family will surely be delighted by news of the impending nuptials, but will have a number of new considerations to face, always in conjunction with the bride herself. The size, expense, and scope of the wedding will be of primary consideration. However, regardless of what the bride decides, the bride's family should be supportive of her decision in whatever way is possible within their means. She is, after all, the bride.

—ALISON BRIGHAM

"*Good morning, sweetie,*" Desiree Hammelmann sang out to her husband as he strode into their bedroom from the adjoining bath.

Laszlo Hammelmann was sixty-one years old, barely topped five-six, weighed in at one eighty-seven, and had lost the bulk of his medium brown hair more than fifteen years ago. But when he stepped out of the shower wrapped in nothing but a flowered towel, with tiny droplets of water clinging to the hair on his chest, arms, shoulders, and back, Desiree still shivered like the sixteen-year-old she'd been the first time she'd laid eyes on him in his father's hardware store. Laszlo had been so handsome back then. And as far as she was concerned, that hadn't changed one bit.

"Morning, Desi," he mumbled into her dark hair before kissing her soundly on the mouth. "Thanks for bringing in my coffee," he said, nodding to the mug on the nightstand.

"You're running a little late, and I know how you always like to get to the store on time."

"Even after forty-two years, you can still read my mind."

"And that's the way it should be between a man and his wife."

She tugged the belt of her red satin robe a little more snugly around her ample waist and sat down on the bed. Laszlo whipped off his towel, smiling at Desiree's squeal of delight, and went to the dresser to retrieve a pair of boxer shorts adorned with images of power tools, a Christmas gift last year from his only daughter. He sat on the bed long enough to gulp down his coffee and then finished dressing for work. Hammelmann Hardware was having its biggest sale of the year, the "Spring into Summer House and Garden Extravaganza," and Laszlo had a big day ahead of him.

"Don't forget," Desiree said as he knotted the bow tie at his throat and shrugged into a well-worn cardigan, "Emma and Taylor will be here at five-thirty, and Taylor's family will be here at six for dinner." After a meaningful pause, she added, "I think we're going to be hearing wedding bells in the future. I think Emma and Taylor are going to announce their engagement tonight."

Laszlo broke into a smile. "It's about time. They should have gotten married a long time ago. Emma's what? Almost twenty-four years old? And Taylor . . . twenty-seven if he's a day. By his age, I'd been married eight years and had three sons."

"I remember," Desiree said with a grin.

Laszlo turned to gaze at his wife. "And then later on,

we had a nice surprise with Emma. Taylor Rowan should someday be as lucky a man as me."

Desiree blushed. "Well, as much as I love Taylor, I'm not sure my daughter could ever be as blessed as me in the husband department."

Laszlo leaned down and kissed her again. "Forty-two years, Toots, and still going strong."

Desiree nodded. "That's so true."

They had everything they'd ever wanted, she reflected. Four beautiful children, a business that had grown beyond their wildest dreams, a nice, roomy house in the suburbs . . . and best of all, they still had each other.

"You know, it just doesn't seem like we've been married for forty-two years," she said. "I look at the kids and see how big they've grown, how good they've done with their own families, and it feels like they should be friends of ours, not our children. Do you ever feel that way, Laszlo? Like we should still just be starting out?"

"Nah," he told her, swiping the air carelessly with his hand. "You couldn't pay me a million bucks to go back to the way things were. We got a good life. And it took a long, long time to get here. I don't want to go back to just starting out."

"Well, me neither. But sometimes . . . I don't know. Just forget it."

Laszlo took her hand and lifted it to his lips. "Desi, honey," he said. Her eyes met his. "You remember when we were still renting that dinky little house in Jefferson Heights, after my old man had his stroke and I had to take over the shop? I'd come home from work every night about ten or eleven, sometimes even twelve, and you'd always be up waiting for me. Remember that?"

Desiree smiled. "Of course I remember. I could never go to sleep unless you were there in bed with me."

Laszlo nodded. "Sometimes you'd be sitting in the kitchen with Joey or Eddie or Vick in your arms, feeding them or rocking them back to sleep after they woke up with a bad dream. And I was always so tired from working all day, always so damned tired. . . . I wanted to sit up and talk to you, share the day's events with you, find out what the kids had been up to. . . ."

His voice trailed off as he became caught up in the memories, until Desiree leaned forward and brushed back a thin, damp lock of his hair.

"I promised myself on nights like that," he continued, "that someday we'd have the kind of life where we could take the time out to enjoy each other. And now we have that." His kissed her on the lips. "The last few years have been magical. And when I retire, and Joey and Eddie take over the business, it'll be even better. No way could you make me ever go back to the way it was when we were young. No way."

"You're an amazing man, Laszlo Hammelmann," Desiree said with a broad smile. "A truly amazing man."

And he had turned out to be one heck of a businessman, too, she thought. With his father's blessing, Hammelmann Hardware had gone from a single brick storefront in Jefferson Heights to a chain of sprawling, independent warehouses that spanned five states. Two of their boys had gotten married and had children of their own, and if and when Vick and Emma married and started their own families, Desiree and Laszlo would be able to enjoy even more grandchildren.

Now it looked as if her daughter had been bitten by the love bug, Desiree thought as she swallowed the last of her coffee. The wedding should be a big one, she decided. Emma was their only daughter, after all. All of their friends from the old neighborhood would come, as well as their new friends in McLean. And of course everyone in both of their families, hers and Laszlo's. They'd also want to include a number of the Hammelmann Hardware employees. She mentally tallied the number—more than a hundred easy for the Hammelmann side.

Naturally Emma would have friends she'd want to invite, too, schoolmates and childhood buddies and some of the girls from all those social causes she worked for. The Rowans would probably have at least that many on their roster. . . . Hmm. . . . This was going to take some planning.

But that was all right. Desiree had lots of ideas.

As if he could tell by her expression what she was thinking, Laszlo said, "Now, Desi, I don't want you to be putting any pressure on the kids, all right? If they want to get married, they'll get married. If they don't want to, they won't. They don't need us pushing them."

"Oh, don't worry. I know that. But I also know how those two are together. You mark my words. We're gonna be hearing an announcement tonight."

Laszlo finished his morning preparations and kissed his wife goodbye. "I promise I'll be home early today. I wouldn't want to miss this evening for anything. Even if I do have to listen to dry old Lionel talk about whatever it is he does for a living. Law or something, isn't it?"

Desiree treated her husband to a scolding expression. "You know he's a lawyer. Taylor's going into practice with him."

"Well, as long as Taylor doesn't wind up as starched and pressed as his old man, I guess I won't mind."

"Talk about starched and pressed, Francesca looks like she'd snap in two and blow away if she bent over at the waist." Desiree shook her head. "When they came over before, I thought for sure that woman smelled something bad all night long. It was just that look she had on her face, remember? I kept worrying that the toilet was backing up or that I'd forgotten to change the cat box or something."

"Everything was perfect last time," Laszlo assured her. "I wouldn't do anything different tonight. Now, I have to go."

Desiree rose to follow him downstairs where she could

see him off in her usual morning fashion. She waved from the front door until his black Cadillac had disappeared from view, then started back up the stairs to take her bath. Her bunco club was meeting at her house that afternoon, something she had overlooked when she'd agreed to Emma's request that they have the Rowans over to dinner that evening. Still, she wouldn't have put off such a gathering of the two families any longer than necessary. If Desiree Hammelmann's little girl wanted to announce her engagement tonight, then nothing was going to stand in the way. She smiled. Now if she could just do something about Vick.

4

It is not at all unusual for a young couple to experience some misgivings concerning what they are about to do. But rest assured in the knowledge that there are two of you to face any obstacles that may arise, two of you to do battle in the face of adversity. Almost always, two can overcome what one cannot.

—ALISON BRIGHAM

    Emma paced restlessly across her bedroom floor and gazed once again out the window overlooking the Hammelmanns' front yard. The view from her room was a peaceful one of the street below, offering a panorama of spacious, nearly new, nearly identical brick houses that stretched like a beaded necklace down turns and twists as far as the eye could see. Moderately expensive cars were parked in circular driveways or in front of yards expertly kept by a number of local landscaping firms. Her own father, of course, tended the Hammelmann yard himself, because as he said, who would have faith in a Hardware Czar who couldn't tell a shovel from a spade?

    Now, however, Emma noticed none of her peaceful surroundings, because tonight she had too many other things on her mind.

She heard the sound of a car in the driveway below and saw Taylor's aged compact pulling to a stop. She hoped that just because he was going to be a corporate suit now, he wouldn't change his mode of transportation to something nauseatingly trendy and upscale. Emma had lost her virginity in that little car. It was a memory she'd cherish forever. When Taylor got out and approached the house, Emma ran downstairs and yanked the front door open for him. Before he could say a word, she threw herself against him, wrapping her arms around his neck in a hug so fierce she nearly knocked the breath out of them both. Taylor hugged her back, burying his face in the warm skin that joined her shoulder to her neck, then raised his head to kiss her softly on the cheek.

"Hi. I missed you, too," he said, chuckling.

Without pulling away, she said, "I'm scared about telling everyone tonight."

Taylor hooked his arms loosely around her waist and settled his chin on the top of her head. "Are you worried about what our families are going to say when we tell them we're getting married?" he asked. "Or are you worried about getting married, period?"

Emma remained silent. How was she supposed to tell Taylor she was worried that his family was going to completely humiliate hers this evening? What if the difference between their background was a sign of something else wrong between them? What if she and Taylor weren't suited to each other as much as she thought they were? She wondered further as panic began to seize her. What if their feelings for each other didn't run as deeply as she suspected? And what if once they were out in the world together alone they began to realize how incompatible they really were? Maybe this marriage wasn't such a great idea after all, she started to think. What if it didn't work out? What if something went wrong?

When Emma didn't answer him right away, Taylor's stomach knotted. He supposed it was normal for Emma to feel frightened about what they were planning to do. Hell, he wasn't exactly fearless himself where the thought of getting married was concerned. He only hoped what the two of them were experiencing now was a simple case of jitters and nothing more.

"Emma? Are you . . ." God, he didn't even want to think about it. "Are you having second thoughts?"

He felt her sigh deeply against his chest, and when she pushed herself away from him, he reluctantly let her go.

"I don't know," she said. "I wasn't before. Everything was fine until a few minutes ago, then suddenly . . ."

Taylor framed her face with his hands, gazing intently into her eyes as if he might find the answers to his questions there. Instead he only saw Emma's confusion, her anxiety, her fear.

"Come on." He took her hand.

Taylor led her to what Desiree called the rumpus room, sat her down on the couch, and went to the bar to fix them each a drink—their usual, Scotch for himself, club soda for Emma. When he returned to hand her the glass, he saw her perched on the edge of her seat, clutching a throw pillow to her chest. She looked so unhappy at that moment, all he wanted to do was pull her into his lap and say soothing things. But he knew Emma wasn't the kind of woman who took to sitting in a man's lap, and when soothing was necessary, she generally liked to do it herself. Still, Taylor reminded himself with a smile, at times like those, she always at least let him think he was helping.

"Okay, what's wrong?" he asked as he gave her the drink and sat down beside her.

Emma sipped her club soda, nervously rattling the ice around in her glass with her finger. When she looked up and saw his concern, she smiled and surrendered the throw pillow to lean into him instead.

"It's not that bad, Taylor," she said. "I promise. I guess it just hasn't sunk in yet . . . the fact that we'll be married in a couple of months. I mean, I don't care how easy it is to get a divorce nowadays, marriage just seems so . . . so terribly permanent . . . so utterly inescapable, you know?"

Taylor nodded, rubbing his cheek against hers. "Yes, it does. But then, that's kind of the point."

She smiled at him. "And you're so wonderful, so perfect for me. If there's such a thing as my ideal match in the world, you're definitely it."

He lifted his glass to his lips, focusing on the smoky fragrance of the liquor instead of the pounding in his heart and head. "I hear a 'but' coming," he said quietly.

Emma sighed. "But I'm only twenty-three years old. I've lived in my parents' house all my life. I've never really had the opportunity to get by on my own."

Taylor chuckled softly after he tasted his drink. "Oh, Emma, I think you do pretty well getting by on your own. You've experienced a lot more than most people our age. Hey, you're about to get your master's degree, you've traveled all over the country, and you're always involved in some social cause. Hell, you were even arrested once at a pro-choice rally. How many twenty-three-year-old women can claim that on their permanent records?"

Emma laughed at the memory. "And the fact that I'm a jailbird doesn't bother you?"

"Of course not. Why should it?"

"Well, what if some of your legal colleagues find out? Wouldn't it embarrass you?"

Taylor laughed too. "Emma, who cares? I would think they'd all be damned impressed I'm married to a woman who would go that far to stand up for what she believes in."

Emma leaned over to kiss him on the cheek and remembered what it was that had made her fall in love with Taylor Rowan to begin with—his ability to be so even-minded about everything. Somehow it was a perfect complement to her more . . . spontaneous personality.

And besides, her arrest had all been a misunderstanding anyway. She'd had no intention of actually *using* the fire extinguisher she was pointing at the policeman. It had all worked out for the best, though, because when the incident had been photographed by one of those radical left-wing publications Taylor's father loved to go on and on about, she had written an article for them chronicling the experience. It was the first literary sale Emma had ever made.

"So now that we have your wide experience in the world well established, what is it that has you so worried about getting married?" Taylor asked.

Emma was honestly unable to pinpoint exactly what was bothering her. So she simply voiced one of the many thoughts that had been troubling her since they'd made their decision to marry.

"I'm just not sure what kind of wife I'll make for a corporate lawyer."

Taylor's relief was almost tangible. "Is that all?"

Emma stared at him. "Taylor, I can't envision myself pouring dry martinis garnished with olives and little plastic swords and serving hors d'oeuvres to dozens of people who have invaded my home wearing dark suits and cocktail dresses."

Taylor laughed. "Hey, don't worry about it. My mother will be happy to recommend all the poshest caterers. You won't have to lift a finger."

Emma set her soda down on the coffee table, braced her elbows on her knees, and buried her head in her hands. "Oh, I'm just so confused. Part of me wants us to just keep going on the way we have been, and part of me wants you to take over every aspect of my life."

Taylor placed his glass next to hers, draped an arm around her shoulder, and pulled her back against him. Settling his other hand on Emma's rib cage just below her breasts, he bent his head close to her ear and whispered. "You realize of course that when we're married we won't have to work around the comings and goings of Max to have a little private time. Hey, he's been a swell roommate and all, but never the best where his timing is concerned."

Emma recalled the countless occasions when Max's

activities had interrupted her romantic evenings with Taylor or prohibited them altogether. "Well, that's true."

"When we're married, living in the same house, we can have sex any time we want," Taylor said. Leaning forward, he kissed the side of her neck softly, then nibbled gently on her earlobe. Gradually he moved his hand until it was settled fully over her breast, then ran his finger lightly over the peak. He smiled when Emma released an almost incoherent little sound and arched against his hand. "But," he whispered in her ear, "if we just keep going the way we always have been, we may never find any time to be alone together again."

Emma turned in Taylor's embrace to meet his gaze, wishing they could just forget about dinner and escape somewhere for a nice romantic diversion. Of course, she thought, Max would probably be home, and that would sabotage any chance they might have to make love.

"Well, then," she finally murmured, "in that case, I guess we'll just have to get married. Even if it does mean uniting the Rowans with the Hammelmanns forever."

Taylor held Emma's gaze for a long time, thinking about her final words. The more he thought about what she'd just said, the more sense her anxiety seemed to make.

"You know, I think what's really bothering you has nothing to do with the wedding we're planning or your feelings about us," he said. "And it has everything to do with the coming together of our families."

Emma pulled back slightly. "Is it that obvious?"

He nodded. "'Fraid so. In fact, I think all the fears you're experiencing right now have nothing to do with your feelings for me. You're just worried about the prospect of bringing our families together."

Emma knew she couldn't deny his assertion, but she said nothing, just continued to gaze at Taylor.

"What's to be scared about?" he asked her. "They

probably all already suspect what we're going to say tonight. Why else would we request the presence of every member of our families under one roof?"

"I know, but what if they're not happy about us getting married?"

"Are you crazy?" Taylor laughed. "Your parents will go through the roof, they'll be so happy. Your mom has been dropping hints for the last four years."

Emma smiled uncertainly. "I know," she repeated. "But your folks may not be quite as overjoyed."

"My folks never get overjoyed," he reminded her. "It isn't civilized to become overly emotional, you know. They'll be pleased, though. They like you."

Yet the tone of his voice couldn't mask the fact that he wasn't quite as strong in his conviction as he would have liked, and they both knew it. It wasn't so much that his parents disliked Emma herself as it was that they simply wanted to avoid mingling with commoners whenever possible. Emma's parents were probably about equal to Taylor's where personal assets were concerned. But the Rowans had been rich since America was in diapers, their wealth refined and mellowed with age. The Hammelmann money, on the other hand, fairly reeked of newness as if it were cheap perfume, a dime store specialty called Eau de Nouveau. The Rowans embraced everything that was old—old wealth, old houses, old social mores. For Desiree and Laszlo Hammelmann, the newer something was, the better. There was nothing the two families had in common.

"I can't help but keep remembering the last time your parents visited," Emma said, recalling the night more than two years ago, during the Christmas holidays. She and Taylor had just started talking seriously about marriage and had decided it was time for their parents to get to know each other. "And how your mother made fun of my mom's cooking."

"No, no, my mother wasn't making fun of your mom's

cooking," Taylor assured her. "She just, uh . . . she just mentioned how she thought it was really clever that Desiree made the cornbread look like little ears of corn."

"It's this iron cornbread mold my mom has," Emma said. "You pour the batter in, and when it cooks, it looks . . . like . . . little ears of . . . corn." She stopped when she realized how hysterical she was beginning to sound. "Anyway, it won't be any better tonight. Mom's of the opinion that when guests come, you cook them enough food to feed a small sovereign nation, and where she comes from, that means farm food. Your parents won't be getting the chateaubriand they're used to."

Taylor smiled. "Don't worry about it. They hardly ever eat chateaubriand anymore. Driscoll and Margaret have taken them off red meat. Now it's mostly coq au vin."

"Taylor . . ."

He kissed her once more, quickly on the lips. "Will you stop it, Emma? Quit worrying. We're adults, for God's sake. We're not asking our families for permission. We're just telling them of our plans because we think it might be nice for them to know about the fact that we'll be married and sharing the same address."

"But—"

"Everything will be fine."

Yet when Emma looked past Taylor and out the window behind him, she saw her leather-jacketed brother, Vick, pulling up the driveway on his Harley hog right in front of Lionel and Francesca's sleek, black Jaguar. And somehow her faith in Taylor's reassurances began to slip.

5

When mingling the groom's family with the bride's for the first time, try not to overdo your expectations. In many instances, this will be the first time certain family members have met, and one or two mishaps are naturally likely. Simply try to avoid topics of contention such as politics, religion, and fashion. And never forget that well-placed discretion is the better part of courtesy.

—ALISON BRIGHAM

The remaining guests arrived quickly, almost as if choreographed to interfere with and annoy one another. As Emma gazed out at the collection of Hammelmanns and Rowans making themselves comfortable in her parents' living room, she felt her stomach knot even tighter. What a motley crew, she thought. This comment was the most benign one she could offer under the circumstances.

Striding as confidently as she could into the living room, Emma adopted her most dazzling smile in an effort to make her future mother-in-law feel welcome. "It's nice to see you again, Mrs. Rowan."

Francesca had been discreetly absorbing her surroundings, arching her brow at the way the wall-to-wall carpeting was a different color in every room and how the knick-knacks and decorations on the walls seemed to favor an owl motif. She had been recalling what interior decoration heathens her host and hostess were when she turned an ear to the delicate strains of one of her favorite piano compositions. Francesca frowned. What on earth was Schumann doing at the Hammelmann's house?

"Mrs. Rowan?" Emma asked again.

Francesca spun around to find her son's girlfriend extending her right hand formally in greeting. Never one to commit a social faux pas, she brushed her fingers quickly against Emma's before dropping her hand back to her side and wondering aloud if Emma might be so good as to fix her a Manhattan.

"Uh, certainly," Emma replied, her smile faltering only the tiniest bit. "Mom's in the kitchen putting the finishing touches on dinner, but I'll be right back."

When Francesca turned to her husband to utter one of any number of critical observations about their surroundings in general and the Hammelmanns in particular, she was forced to curb her tongue, as Laszlo was fast approaching the couple.

"So, Lionel," he said when he reached them, clapping a hand on the other man's shoulder in the familiar masculine form of address. "Long time no see. How's the law business going?"

"Quite well, thanks, Hammelmann," Lionel replied.

"It's corporate crime you do, isn't it?" Laszlo asked, furrowing his brow as he tried to recall his last encounter with Lionel Rowan, one that had taken place more than two years ago.

"It's corporate law I practice, yes," Lionel corrected him. "More specifically, commercial law."

"Right. That's what I meant. I guess with all this savings and loan and Wall Street stuff going on, you got a lot to keep you busy these days, huh?"

Lionel sipped his cocktail and replied mildly, "Actually,

that's not exactly what I . . . never mind." A deep discussion about his legal practice was the last thing Lionel wanted to get involved in with Laszlo Hammelmann. God only knew how a man who sold sledgehammers for a living would interpret jurisprudence.

"You know, I got a cousin who's a lawyer," Laszlo said when the conversation threatened to drag. "Rudy Hammelmann. He does injury cases. Ever heard of him?"

Lionel feigned a ponderous expression. "Rudy Hammelmann," he repeated. "Rudy Hammelmann . . . let's see. Might I have run into him at the Supreme Court building?"

"Search me. Though he does take on some pretty tough cases. He's got this one going now with a guy who worked at a health club and got his"—he glanced quickly at Francesca, then lowered his voice as he continued—"got his . . . you know . . . family jewels . . . caught in a Nautilus machine. It was a freak accident, really, but Rudy's trying to get a couple hundred Gs for the guy. And, hey, if anybody can do it, Rudy can."

Lionel studied Laszlo for a minute, trying to recall if he'd ever had a conversation quite like this one. He decided quickly that no, he had not. "I'll keep an eye out for him in the future. Perhaps he and I can have lunch together sometime."

"I'll tell him to keep a lookout for you," Laszlo said with a smile, lifting his beer in the air to seal the bargain.

Emma returned with Francesca's Manhattan, praying she'd made it correctly. She'd had to consult the Mr. Boston guide, having no idea what went into such a creation. Taylor's mother thanked her politely as she took the cocktail and sampled it, and Emma waited anxiously for her future mother-in-law's reaction. After filling her mouth, Francesca paused with a curious expression on her face, and Emma wasn't sure if she'd swallow the drink or spit it back into her glass. For a moment she suspected Francesca wasn't sure, either. Evidently good manners won out, however, because Francesca gulped rather awkwardly.

"Oh, dear," she whispered when she was able to speak again.

"Too much Angostura?" Emma asked timidly.

"Perhaps just a bit."

"A dash didn't seem like enough, so I added a shot."

"I see," Francesca said as she placed the drink on the nearest flat surface. "Perhaps I'll just let the ice melt a little. Then it should be fine."

When Emma heard Taylor call her from the other side of the room, she gratefully excused herself to escape to more familiar territory. She found Taylor introducing her brothers and their wives to his sisters and brother-in-law.

"I don't think you've met Catherine's husband, Michael," he said to Emma when she joined the group. Catherine was older than Taylor by six years and had been married to Michael Conner for ten.

"Yes, Michael was elsewhere when you came to the house for Thanksgiving," Catherine said. She uttered the word *elsewhere* as if she meant a crack house or bordello. "The biggest family holiday of the year and Michael simply had to fly to New York for a meeting."

"Catherine, must we go into this *again*? It was a perfectly legitimate meeting with a big client," Michael said.

"Oh, yes. That big client who thinks any man who's saddled with a wife and family will go nowhere in the business world."

"It's only his personal philosophy, Catherine, it has nothing to do with his relationship with me. Look, how many times do I have to tell you—"

"And you remember Adrienne, of course" Taylor went on.

Catherine and Michael continued to bicker but had the decency to keep their voices down as they did so.

At twenty-three Taylor's other sister was the same age as Emma, but somehow Emma had always considered the other woman infinitely younger. Adrienne had started college when Emma had, but after five years had yet to declare a major, unable to make a choice between political science and fashion design. For now she called herself a liberal arts major, and that seemed to keep her parents satisfied.

"Nice to see you again, Emma," Adrienne said.

Emma was relieved to hear a friendly greeting. She had begun to think a huge, hairy mole had popped out on the end of her nose when she wasn't looking.

"And I don't think any of you have met my brothers and their wives," she said. "Catherine, Michael," she began, hoping to defuse what was fast becoming a rather heated debate between them. "This is my brother, Eddie, and his wife, Felicia."

"Charmed, I'm sure," Felicia said with a nervous smile.

Emma waited to see if her sister-in-law would curtsy, but either Felicia considered such an action too formal even for the Rowans or else she forgot. It had been enough, Emma decided, that Felicia had worn a hat and gloves for the affair, no doubt having been coached by Desiree to wear her very best.

"And this is my brother, Joey, and his wife, Diane."

The couples murmured awkward greetings and then fell silent.

"What a lovely dress, Diane," Catherine said in an effort to restart the conversation. "What kind of fabric is that exactly?"

"Organdy," Diane replied.

"My, my, my. You don't see organdy too often these days on adult women, do you?"

"Oh, you like it?" Diane asked, delighted. "I wore this in my cousin's wedding and had it shortened. See? You really can wear these dresses again."

Catherine wrinkled her nose in what Emma was certain was an unfelt smile. "It's lovely," she said again.

Diane's smile grew broader.

As she watched the exchange between her family and Taylor's, Emma recalled his claim to a rogue gene in the Rowan DNA and couldn't help but wonder if perhaps she might have received something similar from the Hammelmann gene pool. It wasn't so much that her family embarrassed her sometimes as it was . . . Emma sighed. No, it was precisely that her family embarrassed her sometimes. And at the moment, when she was trying to make as favorable an impression on her future in-laws as possible, she felt defeated before the fight had even begun.

"And this," she finished off as she grabbed the arm of a man who was quickly brushing by them, "is my brother, Vick."

Vick was far and away Emma's favorite brother. Brooding and sarcastic, Vick Hammelmann worked on cars at a local garage, moonlighting now and then as a bartender in a club owned by one of his friends. Although all of the Hammelmann children resembled one another in coloring, twenty-nine-year-old Vick was as wild and dangerous-looking as his older brothers were ordinary and inconspicuous. And, as usual, tonight he brought a certain aura of adventure to the family gathering. None of the other Hammelmanns ever quite knew what Vick was going to do.

"Vick, these are Taylor's sisters, Adrienne and Catherine, and this is Catherine's husband, Michael."

"Yo, Adrienne," Vick said, a crooked grin twisting his mouth.

Adrienne smiled back, staring at him as if he were a choice loin in the butcher's window.

"And yo, *Catherine*," he added as his eyes took in Taylor's older sister. "Very nice to meet you."

Emma could tell her brother liked what he saw when he looked at Catherine. And apparently, so could everyone else. Michael wound his arm around his wife's waist before she could stray and pulled her to his side.

"And I'm Catherine's husband, Michael," he said, repeating Emma's earlier introduction.

Vick nodded briefly in his direction. "Hiya, Mike."

"Michael," the other man corrected him.

"Whatever." Ignoring Michael, Vick took Catherine's hand in both of his and began to lead her away from the group as if none of the others was there. "Say, Cat, you like motorcycles? Ever seen a two-stroke engine before?" he asked her. "Mine's huge—twelve hundred cc's. Makes me go . . . faster, harder. I could, uh . . . I could show it to you if you want. It's right outside."

"As a matter of fact, Mr. Hammelmann," Catherine said, happily disengaging herself from Michael's arm, "I *haven't* ever seen a two-stroke engine before. It sounds rather . . . exciting. Would it be too much trouble for you to show me yours?"

Vick's grin broadened as they moved toward the front door, and his voice dropped even lower when he said, "No trouble at all. And please . . . call me Vick."

Emma looked at Taylor, who just shrugged. Michael evidently wasn't amused by the scene, however, and followed his wife and Vick outside with petulant pleas of "Catherine, this isn't funny, now come on. . . . Catherine? Catherine, please . . ."

With all the introductions finally concluded, the cocktail hour progressed much as Emma had suspected it would, filled with tension and anxiety and a number of uncomfortable silences. And that atmosphere predominated over the dinner table as well.

As the families took their seats opposite each other, it occurred to Emma they were like two warring factions about to engage in combat. Like generals, Laszlo and Lionel each sat at one end, and like lowly soldiers about to be taken prisoner, Taylor and Emma were trapped in two chairs beside each other somewhere in the middle.

"What was it you called this dish again, Desiree?" Francesca asked her hostess suddenly during one such uncomfortable silence, her soft voice sounding like a booming cannon in the otherwise quiet room.

"Fried country ham with redeye gravy," Desiree said proudly. "My cousin Noble slaughters his own hogs, cures the meat himself, and sends us a beautiful country ham every Easter. This year Laszlo took me and the kids to Sizzler for Easter, so the ham's been hanging down in the basement, just waiting for a special occasion."

Emma watched Francesca's fork pause just short of entering her mouth. "But Easter was more than a month ago. Hasn't this meat been refrigerated? Is it still safe?"

Desiree made a face and waved her hand toward Francesca as if she'd made a wonderful joke. "Country ham just gets better with age. Trust me."

But apparently Francesca was not the trusting type, Emma thought, because as soon as was discreetly possible, she replaced the ham on her plate and lifted a forkful of something else.

"And this?" she asked. "What did you say this was?"

"Cheese grits," Desiree told her. "Try some of that corn casserole, though. White corn, green beans, Ritz crackers, sour cream . . . you'll love it. I'll write down the recipe for you before you leave. It's *very* easy."

"And you made the cornbread look like little ears of corn again," Francesca murmured. "How sweet. But tell me, Desiree, doesn't it concern you, all the fat and cholesterol this meal contains?"

"Mother," Taylor began, his voice edged with warning.

"Well, I'm concerned about your father's blood pressure, dear," Francesca whispered loudly back.

Desiree shook her head. "All that cholesterol hype is exaggerated," she stated knowledgeably. "Where I come from, cholesterol is one of the four basic food groups, and none of us turned out any worse because of it, did we, Laszlo?"

Laszlo took a hearty bite of ham and smacked his lips in satisfaction. Emma sank a little in her chair. "I've never felt better," he announced. "Sure, my cholesterol is three-ninety-five, but if a man can't enjoy his dinner, what's the point in living anyway?"

Emma thought she saw Lionel nod his head in silent agreement at that, but she wasn't sure.

The remainder of the dinner hour passed in much the same way, with what little conversation that took place focusing on harmless topics such as food, the weather, lawn care, and Oprah's guests last week. Over coffee and Desiree's famous chess pie, when trivial subject matter became more and more difficult to find, Emma caught Taylor's gaze and nodded meaningfully.

Lifting the fragile china coffee cup in his hand, Taylor tapped the side with his fork to put an end to the nearly nonexistent conversation. As each family member turned his or her attention toward the sound, Taylor took a deep breath and said, "Emma and I have an announcement to make." He glanced over at Emma, who silently dipped her head once again in encouragement, then continued, "We've decided—"

"You're getting married!" Desiree shouted gleefully, throwing her hands into the air as she rose from her seat. Without further confirmation, she rounded the table and tugged her daughter up out of her chair, then embraced her in a hug. "Congratulations, sweetie!" she cried loudly into Emma's ear. "Let's see the ring."

Emma lifted her hand obediently for Desiree's inspection, wondering where her mother's tactfulness had gone.

"Oh," Desiree said with little enthusiasm. "It's not a diamond. It's . . . it's an emerald."

Emma smiled. "Taylor said he chose an emerald because it reminded him of my eyes. Isn't that sweet, Mom? Isn't it romantic?"

Desiree turned Emma's hand so that it caught the light from the chandelier above the table. "Well, you know, sweetie," she said quietly, but unfortunately not quietly enough, "you've got pretty big eyes. Much bigger than this."

"Mother!" Emma jerked her hand away. "It's a beautiful ring. I couldn't have chosen better if I'd gone with Taylor myself to pick it out."

"Maybe you should have," Desiree muttered, not quite under her breath.

Emma looked at Taylor apologetically, and saw that his mouth was half open, as if he was still about to utter their announcement even though Desiree had already made it for him. Before he could say a word, however, Desiree turned her attention to him, and without releasing Emma, included Taylor in the embrace.

"My new son-in-law," she said, kissing him on the cheek and then hugging the couple close. "Oh, I'm just so excited, I could explode. I don't know who to call first."

Everyone else at the table remained seated and silent, except for Laszlo, who grinned contentedly as he watched the scene unfold. "Desi," he began gently, "don't you think you might want to let the kids verify for sure that they're getting married before you start offering congratulations and calling all the relatives?"

"Well, it's true, isn't it?" Desiree asked Emma. "Even without a diamond."

Emma nodded, hoping her mother would eventually drop the subject of her ring. "Yes. We're getting married."

Desiree beamed. Laszlo smiled. Francesca paled. Lionel sipped his coffee. Everyone else murmured congratulations and asked the obligatory questions about their plans.

Emma reached for Taylor's hand to reassure herself and described their intentions. "We want to be married at the end of July, and, Mr. and Mrs. Rowan, if it wouldn't inconvenience you too much, we'd like to have the wedding at your house, in the garden . . . weather permitting, of course."

"In which case we'd like to move the wedding inside,"

Taylor added, "and have it in the garden room. What do you think, Mother?"

Francesca, who had remained silent until now, gazed at her son in somewhat stunned confusion. "I . . . we . . . that is . . ." She blinked three times in succession, as if invoking a magic spell to reinstate her vocabulary, and then said, "Will it be large enough to accommodate a wedding party?"

Emma nodded. "Oh, certainly. We won't be inviting more than fifteen or twenty people."

"Fifteen or twenty?" Desiree repeated.

Emma looked over at her mother warily, not liking the tone of voice she'd heard. It was the way her mother had always sounded just before putting her foot down. "Yes, fifteen or twenty. Neither of us wants the wedding to be a big affair, Mom. We'd just like to have the immediate families and a few friends."

"But that's impossible," Desiree said with a laugh. "Why, the guests for our side of the family alone are going to come to more than a hundred and fifty people."

"A hundred and fifty people?" Emma repeated with a gasp. "You're planning on inviting one hundred and fifty people to the wedding?"

"For our side, yes." Desiree tucked a hand into the pocket of her dress and extracted a sheet of paper Emma recognized as her mother's best stationery. "I've made up a quick list, but I'll probably remember more later. Of course, Taylor's family will probably have at least as many as we have, too. Won't you, Francesca?"

Francesca opened her mouth to respond, but all that emerged was a hastily muttered "Well, you see . . . I'm not quite sure."

Emma stared at her mother in disbelief. "Mom, we just announced our engagement thirty seconds ago, and you've already made up a wedding guest list? Of one hundred and fifty people? You can't be serious."

Desiree smiled. "And, Emma, there's no way we can have an event of this size planned by July. You and Taylor are going to have to bump the wedding back to, say, November."

"November?"

"At the very earliest." Desiree thought for a minute. "In fact, why don't we make it the last Saturday in November? That way all the relatives who come in from out of town can get here early for Thanksgiving. That would be perfect. I'm sure Reverend Ballard can perform the ceremony, but we're going to have to find a florist, a photographer, a caterer, musicians, not to mention a reception hall large enough for everyone to fit. The American Legion Post might be big enough. . . . No offense, Francesca," she added hastily. "Not that I'm sure your house wouldn't be a beautiful place to have the wedding—of course I wouldn't know for sure because you've never invited us over—but I think with this many people, we're just going to have to find someplace a bit bigger, don't you?"

Francesca remained silent, as Desiree's question didn't seem to require a reply.

Emma took a deep, fortifying breath and plucked the piece of paper from her mother's extended hand. The small, intimate nuptial celebration she had planned to enjoy in July had suddenly become the Macy's Thanksgiving Day Parade. She scanned name after name after name on the list. All she and Taylor had done was tell her mother the two of them were going to be married, and now suddenly Emma was holding a guest list of gargantuan proportions, representative of the Hammelmanns on one side of the family, the Broussards on the other side, and a number of her father's employees, most of whom Emma had never met before in her life. One hundred and fifty people in less than five minutes. If she didn't put an end to this right now, she was going to find herself walking down an aisle at JFK Stadium.

"Mom, this is way too many people. Taylor and I just want a small, private ceremo—"

"Oh, Emma, you know that will be impossible. You

have dozens of cousins in this area alone, and I'm sure everyone from back home will want to drive up."

"But—"

"You're our only daughter, sweetie. After all the weddings we've had in this family, no one would forgive us if we let you slip off and get married on the sly."

"It won't be on the sly, Desiree," Taylor began to object. "We'll have the immediate families."

"But my sister and brothers, and Laszlo's sisters and brothers, and all their kids—except for Virginia, of course, because *she* wanted adventure instead of children— would feel very left out." Desiree hooked her arm through Taylor's and steered him toward the living room, beckoning the others to follow. "Weddings are a very big deal in both the Hammelmann and Broussard families," she continued. "Everyone gets involved, everyone goes a little crazy, everyone has a lot of fun. And," she added with a conspiratorial wink, "you wind up with a lot more loot than you would if you just had some little quiet ceremony. You realize, of course, Taylor, that Laszlo is the oldest of eight kids. Think about it."

Emma heard Taylor faltering over his next words, trying to invoke a good reason why they should stick with the plans the two of them had already made. She knew he would be helpless against the efforts of her mother, so she quickly took her mother's other arm and joined them.

"Mom, we don't want to go through all the hassle and long wait of a big wedding," Emma said. "We just want to get married and get on with our lives. So we only want the bare necessities. Besides, all that expense for something that's only going to last a few hours is just plain silly."

"Oh, pooh," Desiree said. "The expense is worth it. Besides, I'll take care of everything. Francesca can help me." Over her shoulder, Desiree added, "Can't you, Francesca? It will be fun. We'll finally get to know each other better."

Francesca was, of course, less than anxious to get involved, but propriety prevented her from voicing her

misgivings out loud. So instead, she cited a hastily conjured hectic social calendar, explaining that autumn was
the busiest time of the year for such events.

"In November alone, I have several engagements at
the Kennedy Center, a fund-raiser for the Leukemia
Society, and a luncheon at the White House. The First
Lady's Children's Advocacy network, you know."

"Oh, that sounds like fun," Desiree said. "Well, in that
case, I can do all the planning and make all the arrangements, and then Emma can just give everything her
okey-dokey." She winked at her daughter as she added,
"Maybe we can get that nice accordion combo who
played at Eddie and Felicia's wedding."

Emma bit her lip to keep from chuckling out loud.
That thought alone ought to make Francesca rethink her
busy schedule.

"Well, perhaps I could rearrange a few things,"
Francesca said.

"Mom, no accordions," Emma stated.

"Okay, okay. It was just a thought."

Behind Emma and Taylor and their mothers, Emma
heard her father slap Lionel on the back in congratulations, heard Lionel's choked grunt of surprise in response.
The two men were as different from each other as a
power hedge clipper was from a mouth-blown crystal
brandy snifter. She shook her head and wondered yet
again if what she and Taylor were about to do wasn't perhaps some kind of weird, cosmic joke the two of them
were playing on Mother Nature.

She looked at her mother and Francesca and sighed
wearily. This was going to take some doing. Her mother
wasn't easily talked out of something once she set her
mind on it, and Emma knew it might take days this time
before she could bring Desiree around to her way of
thinking. But the wedding was *her* wedding, Emma
reminded herself. Her wedding and Taylor's. *They* were
the ones who would decide how, when, and where the

ceremony would take place. *They* were the ones who would make the final decisions. That was all there was to it. Desiree would just have to understand that.

The wedding would be in late July, at Taylor's house, with just the immediate families and a few friends as guests. Emma would wear a simple, tea-length ivory dress with a single white lily tucked behind her ear and a bunch of baby's breath tied with ivory ribbon as her bouquet. . . . Or maybe a white ankle-length dress with a wreath of lily-of-the-valley for her headpiece and a cascade of white roses and sweetheart ivy. There would be a string quartet to provide the music . . . or maybe a brass ensemble . . . a judge to perform a civil ceremony, and as little else as possible. Simple. Understated. Inexpensive. That was what Emma and Taylor wanted for the wedding. And that, she assured herself once and for all, was exactly what they were going to get.

"Oh, Emma, I just had a great idea," Desiree exclaimed, spinning around. She gazed toward the ceiling, enjoying some far-off vision no one else could yet see. "What do you think about a champagne fountain? And maybe, right after you and Taylor say 'I do,' we could release a hundred white doves into the air."

Emma sighed. The wedding would be exactly what *they* wanted it to be, she repeated firmly to herself over and over as if she were reciting a mantra. Exactly what they wanted it to be . . . exactly what they wanted it to be . . . she hoped.

6

A bride's choice for her maid or matron of honor should be someone in whom she can place her absolute trust and to whom she can reveal her innermost secrets. Not necessarily because a bride has a number of confessions to make, but because she must have a friend in whom she can confide when her choices become difficult. Choices concerning gowns, food and beverage, and even honeymoon plans can try significantly on a bride. A good maid of honor helps alleviate some of the stress.

—ALISON BRIGHAM

"It was a nightmare, Patsy," Emma told her cousin and best friend the following Sunday. "I don't know what ever made me think I could bring the two families together without upsetting the gods."

Patsy chuckled and handed Emma another clothespin. The two of them had been out shopping with little success to find a dress for Patsy to wear under her college graduation gown. Underneath Patsy Hammelmann's full figure was a reed-thin woman dying to wear something skintight and slinky. Since nothing they'd found in her size was quite what she had in mind, Patsy had gradually grown depressed.

So when Emma had realized how close they would be to Taylor's Georgetown apartment, she suggested they kidnap her fiancé and drive to Rock Creek Park to enjoy the warm spring afternoon and, she hoped, cheer Patsy up.

Instead of Taylor, however, the pair had stumbled upon a mountain of dirty clothes. Feeling restless and edgy and the need to be productive somehow, Emma had decided to make an unusually selfless gesture and do her fiancé's laundry. Now, as the dryer in the basement of Taylor's apartment building hummed and spun the last of Taylor's underwear dry, Emma pinned a pair of striped silk boxer shorts on the line and sighed heavily.

"God, do I really want to do this, Patsy?"

"What? The laundry? I'd say it's too late to be worried about that. We're almost done."

"No, I mean the whole marriage thing."

"Oh. Well, don't you think it's kind of late for that, too? You've already said yes."

"I know." Emma reached toward the pile of clothes she'd been reluctant to put in the dryer. "But until Taylor and I got engaged, I don't think I ever honestly thought about what it meant to be married, you know? Now that I have, I just don't know if marriage is going to be all it's cracked up to be."

Patsy sighed wistfully. "I don't know what you're so worried about. I'd love to get married. Weddings are so beautiful. All that white and pink . . ."

"There will be absolutely no pink in the wedding," Emma insisted. "I'm not a pink kind of person."

"No, but I am," Patsy told her, annoyed at her cousin's intrusion into her bridal fantasy. "White and pink," she continued on in her dreamy voice as if Emma hadn't spoken, "and all that organ music. You get to be the center of attention for an entire day with the man of your dreams drooling all over you. People give you gifts and money. You get to eat cake and those little pink mints and catered food to your heart's content. And best of all, you don't have to clean up anything after the party's over. You get to go to a hotel and have sex all night without worrying what about your parents would think. If you ask me, that's probably what heaven is like. One big wedding.

"Besides, Emma," she continued, returning to her usual no-nonsense tone, "you and Taylor have been dating since you first started college. I mean, how could you *not* think the two of you would wind up married after all this time?"

It was a good question, Emma thought. She took another clothespin from her cousin and thought of a time when her mother used to spend two or three afternoons a week hanging up the Hammelmann laundry in their own basement. Back then they hadn't been able to afford a dryer, despite her father's benefit of buying wholesale. Even as a child, Emma had helped her mother do all the traditionally female household chores. Her early introduction to such tasks had probably been instrumental in making her shun them in her adult life. Yet here she was, not even married yet, doing Taylor's laundry. Did some kind of madness come over women as soon as they decided to marry? she wondered. Some weird throwback to a more primitive time, before they knew better?

"I don't know," she finally replied. "Before I met Taylor, I just didn't think I would ever get married. I always saw myself growing up to write incredibly well-received novels and being the toast of the international publishing community. I'd live in London and wear berets and drink Campari and make love with every desirable man I met. I'd be totally and uninhibitedly free."

She sighed heavily. "I guess when I used to fantasize about being married to Taylor, I thought about us doing all the things outside of normal everyday behavior— traveling, socializing, going to parties, celebrating Christmas and Thanksgiving, and having summer picnics together. I never really considered things like . . ." She indicated the clothespins clutched in her fingers. "Well, like laundry. But here I am hanging up Taylor's underwear. It's just not what I ever envisioned for my future."

Patsy tried to sound reassuring. "But there's a lot more to being married than laundry, Emma. There will be socializing and holidays and fun stuff like that. Just like there will be coming home from work worn out and pissed off and wanting to be left alone. You just have to work around times like those. Nobody said it was going to be perfect. Or easy."

Emma stared at her cousin thoughtfully. The two of them were the same age—only three months had separated their births—but otherwise had little in common, despite their deep affection for each other. Patsy had long, blond, curly hair, blue eyes, fair skin, and a personality Emma could only describe as conservatively wild. Her father ran a laminator for a packaging company in suburban Maryland, and her mother worked as a waitress in a diner near their home. Patsy had earned her nursing degree the hard way—working two jobs while attending a local community college—and she would start working in neonatal intensive care at the end of the summer. There were no big surprises in her future, nothing for which she would be unprepared. Patsy Hammelmann was well organized, no-nonsense, and perfectly practical about life.

"I wish I could be more like you," Emma said suddenly.

Patsy stared at her cousin in frank amazement. "You gotta be nuts. Why on earth would you want to be like me?"

"You're so well organized. You never question anything that happens to you, you never worry about what you can't change. Whatever happens to you happens to you, and you just shrug it all off like it's no big deal."

"Isn't that the way everybody reacts to things?"

Emma laughed. "I wish. I feel like I'm always totally out of control. Here I am at a major turning point in my life, and I don't feel like I've consciously planned any of it. I question every decision I've ever made, sometimes years after the fact, and I worry about everything. There's no way I'm going to make it through the wedding without having a nervous breakdown."

"You'll be fine, Emma," Patsy assured her. "Marriage to Taylor will be easier than you think."

"It's not so much that I want it to be easy necessarily," Emma said. "I just want it to be . . . I don't know . . . right. Does that make sense?"

Patsy nodded. "Does it feel right?"

Emma gazed uncertainly at her cousin from over the clothesline. "Usually."

"But sometimes it doesn't?"

"Sometimes."

Patsy studied her intently for several moments, then asked, "Emma, you know what your problem is?"

Emma shook her head. "No. What?"

"You think too much."

Emma stared back at her cousin, bewildered. "I think too much? I *think* too much? And that's supposed to be a malady?"

"Well not for somebody like Einstein, no. But you and me, Emma . . . we ain't Einstein. Look, Taylor's a great guy. You guys have been together for years. If he wasn't someone you wanted to spend a lot of time with, don't you think you'd have realized it by now?"

"Patsy, 'a lot of time' is one thing. The rest of my life is a completely different matter."

Emma could see that Patsy was about to offer another comment but was distracted by the next item she pulled out of the clothes basket to fold.

"Whoa, whoa, whoa . . . what the hell is this?" She held up an extremely skimpy article of clothing that vaguely resembled a man's undergarment, patterned with bright orange and black tiger stripes. "Where did you bag this baby, Frederick's of Nairobi?" She laughed, trying to measure the ample crotch with her fingers. "Gee, I didn't realize Taylor was so . . . so . . . Oh, baby."

"It's not Taylor's," Emma mumbled, feeling her face heat with an uncharacteristic flush. "It must be Max's. It probably got in by mistake."

Max Bennett had been Taylor's best friend since childhood and his roommate since they had started college. He was also slated to be the best man at the wedding, while Patsy would be Emma's maid of honor.

"Max's?" Patsy raised her eyebrows. "Oh, so I guess you should know firsthand just how 'oh-baby' he is."

Emma flushed more deeply, and she felt herself grow hot all over. "Patsy, I thought we had an agreement that we wouldn't talk about that anymore."

"I know. I'm sorry. But you know, all things considered, you might want to reevaluate that little experience you and Max shared . . . what's it been, about two years ago?"

"A year and a half."

"Right. I mean, you will be getting married soon, Emma. And Max is going to be the best man. If there's any kind of . . . you know . . . unsettled business between the two of you, you better deal with it now or forever hold your peace."

"There is no unfinished business between me and Max," Emma assured her. "That was one night that never should have happened. And it wouldn't have if Taylor hadn't lied to me about being out with Tina McDermott."

"Mm-hm," Patsy murmured. "Whatever you say, Emma."

"It's true. If Taylor had been home that night the way he was supposed to, Max would have had no reason to take me out for a drink and console me. And we wouldn't have wound up, you know, at the . . . uh . . . the Captain Willie B. Schmidt Motel."

Patsy made a face. "Yeah, the least Max could have done was take you to a better place. I mean, I know the Willie B. is popular with the students—low rates, no questions asked, and all that—but I thought Max had better taste than that dive. Was it as bad as they say?"

"Patsy . . ."

"Are there really nonstop porno movies on TV and handcuffs connected to every bed?"

"Patsy . . ."

"Okay, I'll shut up. All I'm trying to do is make sure everything is cool between you and Max now."

"Everything is cool," Emma said. "We both knew what happened was a mistake as soon as it was over. And we never did anything like that again."

Patsy looked away before asking, "Are you planning on telling Taylor about it?"

Emma's eyes widened in shock. "God, no. Why would I tell Taylor?"

"I don't know. Just maybe that it's not such a good idea to go into a marriage with a big secret like that coming between you."

"It isn't coming between us."

"You sure?"

"I'm sure."

"Okay, if you say so." Patsy uttered a sound of longing and clutched the briefs to her heart. "Oh, God, Max is such a hunk. Now *there's* a guy I could easily consider being married to." She lifted his briefs for her inspection again and smiled. "I've always wanted to get this close to his underwear. Can I keep these?"

Emma made a grab for them. "Of course not. We'll put them back on the floor where we found them."

But Patsy was already stuffing them into her handbag. "I think not. A woman doesn't come across a trophy like this every day, you know."

"It isn't a trophy unless you removed them from him yourself," Emma pointed out.

Patsy shook her head. "A minor detail at best."

Surrendering to the nervous chuckles she felt bubbling up inside, Emma shook her head and decided no one would be hurt if Patsy happened to covet a pair of Max's underwear.

"I hope you and Max's underwear are very happy together," she said.

"Thanks. I'm sure we will be." As Patsy reached for another item from the laundry basket, she asked in an offhand tone, "So, Emma, just how . . . you know . . . 'oh-baby' . . . is Max exactly?"

"Patsy!"

"Oh, Emma, don't be such a prude. It's a perfectly understandable question, a perfectly healthy curiosity."

Emma smiled wistfully as she remembered that one night at the Willie B. "Actually, it's funny you should choose the word 'healthy.'"

Patsy leaned forward with interest. "Oh, yeah?"

Emma nodded.

"Pretty healthy, is he?"

"Very healthy."

Patsy smiled. "Oh baby."

While Patsy chattered on about Max and his intriguing wardrobe, Emma folded Taylor's boring white T-shirts and boring white cotton jockey shorts. Inevitably her thoughts returned to the wild underwear her cousin had claimed for her own, and she couldn't help but smile with the recollection of the night she had spent with Max.

When she realized where her thoughts were heading, however, she pushed the inappropriate memories away, wondering instead how Taylor would look in a set of similar briefs. That thought made her laugh out loud, and when Patsy looked up curiously, Emma could only shake her head and laugh even more until tears stung her eyes. Oh, God—Taylor in tiger-striped underwear? Really, it was just too, too funny.

Yet if that were the case, Emma wondered as she sat down in the middle of the basement floor to laugh some more, why did she feel so much like crying instead?

7

*A number of out-of-town guests will of course
be attending your wedding, and a bride can
only be expected to do so much to accommodate
them. Certainly they should be made to feel as
welcome and as involved in the wedding plans
as possible, but all in all, it might be best if you
leave them to their own devices. You are, after
all, the bride, and have so much else to concern
you. And your guests will surely be able to see to
their own needs.*

—ALISON BRIGHAM

More than two thousand miles away from where
her nieces were laughing about men's underwear, Virginia
Hammelmann sat alone at the bar in a tiny beachfront
establishment all the tourists knew as The Yellow Swan
but which was known locally simply as Paloma's. If she
bothered to turn around, she would be witness to a magnificent view, a huge fiery sun dipping low behind a
string of green islands rising out of the sea.

The first time Virginia had observed those massive green
bumps amid a vast pool of blue, the sight had made her feel
more content than she'd ever been in her life. But she had
seen so many Caribbean sunsets these past thirteen months.

And after reading over the letter in her hand for the third time, the rum and tonic sitting on the scarred, stained bar before her frankly offered more comfort than the scenery. It was a letter from Emma dated nearly three weeks ago that had arrived while Virginia was out on the open sea, and it had been waiting for her return at Paloma's.

"Paloma," Virginia said to the ancient-looking woman behind the bar who was filling a gallon milk jug with something red and sweet-looking, "it seems my favorite niece has decided to get married."

Paloma put down the bottle of red liquid, picked up another one filled with yellow, and tipped its contents into the jug as well. "That's nice," the other woman said in slightly accented English. "You know, my great-granddaughter Bianca was married last month. It was a beautiful wedding. Her husband is an idiot, though. It's too bad."

Virginia nodded absently. "I met the man Emma's going to marry at Christmas a few years ago. She seemed to like him very much, and I got the impression he was a decent enough sort. Still, I'm surprised she'd decide to marry so young. She hasn't even had a chance to get out and see the world on her own yet."

"How old is she?"

"Twenty-three."

"Bianca was only nineteen when she married."

"Still a child," Virginia said, though it wasn't clear whether she was talking about Paloma's great-granddaughter or her own niece.

Paloma picked up a bottle of green liquid and added that to the jug too.

"What on earth are you making?" Virginia asked when she finally realized what the other woman was doing.

Paloma chuckled and replied, "Rocket fuel."

Virginia laughed too. "Something to get the tourists in the mood, eh?"

"The last man who drank some of this accidentally left me a twenty for a tip."

"Sounds like one of the guys off my boat," Virginia muttered.

Of course it wasn't actually *her* boat, but the one on which she had been employed as a bartender since shortly after her arrival in the Caribbean over a year ago. Since then, Jack Kramer, the owner of the luxury charter yacht *Mephisto*, had moved his home base of operation three times—probably to keep ahead of the tax man, Virginia figured. Jack was something of a shyster. But, she added to herself with a dreamy little smile, he was truly phenomenal in the sack.

Her qualifications for the job had been nearly nonexistent when she'd applied, but Jack had been desperate, and they'd hit it off pretty well that first night. He had cited her experience as a waitress in a Paris bistro twelve or fifteen years ago, and as a cabaret singer in Rio de Janeiro some time before that, as sufficient for the job, and then they had sealed the deal with a drink and a dance.

Immediately prior to her arrival in the Caribbean, Virginia had been working as a blackjack dealer in Monaco, but her résumé was virtually as long as her life had been. Come to think of it, she realized suddenly, at forty-eight years of age, she had probably held about forty-eight jobs, all as varied and unconnected as she could manage.

Virginia sighed and sipped her drink, gazing at the woman behind the bar who looked like she was probably twice Virginia's age. "Hey, Paloma, how long have you and Desmond been married?"

Paloma glanced up from the task that had claimed her attention, gazing at the ceiling as she mentally tallied the number. "Let's see now . . . sixty-seven? No, sixty-eight years."

"Wow."

Paloma shrugged and went back to creating her potent

concoction. "That's not so many. My mother and father were married for eighty-two when my father passed away."

"Eighty-two years?" Virginia repeated incredulously.

"Yeah. Still spoke civilly to each other, too."

Virginia couldn't imagine spending that amount of time with one human being. She herself had never embraced any desire to be married, despite a number of proposals she had received over the years, some of them actually serious. Not that she didn't like men. On the contrary, men were quite possibly her favorite animal. She just couldn't imagine keeping one for more than a few years. They demanded too much attention, and they were very difficult to housebreak. Their care and feeding alone commanded around-the-clock supervision.

"You know, it's weird," she said after another idle sip of her drink. "I always kind of thought Emma would grow up to be like me."

"How's that?" Paloma asked.

"I don't know. A vagabond, an adventurer . . . caught up in that lone-wolf, nonconformist, individualistic kind of mystique that usually only grabs hold of a handful of people."

"Are you all of those things, Virginia? Sounds like a lot for one woman to be all by herself."

Virginia made a face at her. "Not that I'm suggesting you'd understand what it means to be a free spirit, Paloma. There's an awesome amount of responsibility that goes along with the label, you know."

Paloma nodded. "Sure. Like what?"

"Well . . . travel for one thing. You've always got to be on the go. I've seen more of the world than ninety-nine percent of its population. All seven continents, Paloma. Even Antarctica."

"That's nice."

Virginia lifted her drink, pondering the way the sunlight danced in the pale gold rum. "Yup, I've seen more, done more, lived more, and had more fun than anyone I know."

"And what else have you got?"

Virginia studied the other woman suspiciously. "What do you mean?"

Paloma didn't answer.

"Oh, I get it," Virginia said with a nod. "This is the part where I'm supposed to feel bad because I don't have the husband or the house or the kids or the minivan. This is where I throw my hands up in anguish, bang my head against the bar, and shout, 'Woe is me, my life is incomplete because I'm a single woman pushing fifty without a bank account or retirement plan.' Is that what you're waiting for, Paloma? Because if it is, you ain't gonna see it."

Paloma began to wipe down the bar and asked, "You're pushing fifty? I didn't realize you were that old."

"Very funny. Let me tell you something, Paloma. Not everybody wants to leave behind a legacy. Children aren't for everyone. Just because I happened to be born with a uterus doesn't mean I'd be a good mother."

"It doesn't have to be children, Virginia," Paloma said. "But everybody wants to know they've touched a life or made a change somewhere. That they've made a difference. Otherwise, what's the point?"

"Oh, hell, I've touched a lot of lives," Virginia said. "I just got kicked out of most of them afterward."

Paloma looked at her doubtfully. "Haven't you ever been in love?"

"No."

"Hasn't anyone ever loved you?"

Virginia shook her head. "Not that I know of." When Paloma frowned at her, she relented somewhat. "All right, all right. There have been the amorous liaisons along the way, I'll grant you that. But none of them has been particularly heart-wrenching, okay? They were nice little diversions while they lasted, but they weren't the stuff of fabulous forties films.

"Besides, what have you and Desmond got? You've worked all your lives for some squat little bar and a lopsided hovel on some dinky little island at the edge of nowhere that eludes even the retirement junkets."

"But we're happy," Paloma told her.

"Well, so am I."

"Okay, okay. I'll leave you alone."

"Thanks," Virginia muttered. "I appreciate it." After another sip of her drink, she added softly, "I just can't figure out why Emma's in such an all-fired hurry to attach herself to another human being. I mean, what's so great about that path of eternal union anyway?"

Virginia glanced down at the letter in her hand, recalling all the correspondence she had received from Emma over the years, ever since the little girl had learned how to write. If Virginia had ever had a daughter, she would have wanted her to be just like Emma—strong-willed, independent, outspoken. She liked to think that Emma had turned out that way partly because of her own influence. Not that Virginia had actually been around Emma all that much, but the two of them had exchanged letters frequently, and Virginia had managed to visit her brother Laszlo and his family at least once a year. Every time she had, she and Emma had made sure to make at least one outing together alone, to talk about all the important things that constituted girl talk. Woman talk, as Virginia had come to insist it be termed when Emma reached her teens. And now Emma was truly a woman in every sense of the word, fully capable of making a decision such as whether or not she wanted to marry.

Maybe she ought to go up to McLean for a visit, Virginia thought, to check all this out and make sure Emma wasn't being talked into something she didn't want to do. How long had it been since she'd seen Laszlo and Desi and the kids, anyway? A year? No, surely not that long. Yet when she thought back, Virginia realized a lot more time had passed than she thought. She was way overdue for a buzzing of the Hammelmanns of McLean.

"You know, Paloma," she said. "I think once this next charter is over, I'm going to call it quits on the old *Mephisto*. I'll be getting sunstroke if I'm not careful. And a year is long enough to spend at a job, don't you think?"

"I think that you have a fear of settling down."

Virginia stared at the other woman for a long time before replying, "Oh, great. I wasn't aware you had a degree in psychology, Paloma, but I thank you so much for your analysis. What do I owe you?"

Paloma laughed again, looked at Virginia's empty glass on the bar, and said, "Two-twenty-five. The drink, however, is on the house."

Virginia reached into her pocket for three bills and two quarters and set them on the bar beside her glass. "What a bargain. Up in the States, people pay hundreds of dollars for such a brilliant diagnosis. I should know. I paid a shrink myself for years."

"And what did he tell you?" Paloma asked as she scooped up the money and dropped it into a metal lockbox.

"He said I have a fear of settling down, and he could help me over it for a hundred dollars a session, three sessions a week minimum."

Paloma shook her head. "You should have come to me a long time ago."

Virginia sighed and turned to gaze at the islands on the horizon. "Yeah, maybe I should have at that."

Without awaiting a reply, she turned to leave, making her way slowly down the beach to where *Mephisto* was anchored offshore. It was a gorgeous yacht, the kind Virginia wished she could own herself someday. A number of sailboats and motor yachts were anchored out in the bay. Water lapped at the shore with a languid, almost exhausted rhythm, and people waded ankle-deep through the warm current.

As she walked, she repeated to herself all the assurances she had just made to Paloma. She loved the way she lived. She had left home almost thirty years ago and never looked back. She did things the way she wanted to, when she wanted to do them. So why did she feel so empty inside sometimes? Why from time to time did she still experience this almost desperate fear that she had so much left to achieve before she could call her life complete?

By the time she reached the Zodiac tied up on shore and turned it back out toward where *Mephisto* was anchored, Virginia had talked herself into a better mood. When she saw Jack waving to her from the bow of the boat with a drink in his hand, she told herself again she was living exactly as she wanted to live, in precisely the manner she had chosen years ago.

But maybe she would go to McLean for a little visit anyway. She missed Laszlo and Desi and the kids, not to mention all her other siblings and their families. But of them all, Virginia especially missed Emma. Her niece was about to embark on something that would irrevocably change her life. Surely she'd want her Aunt Virginia there to share in her hopes and anxieties, wouldn't she? Emma needed her, even if maybe no one else did.

Virginia decided she'd just finish up with this next charter and head on home for a while. It was funny how she always thought of Laszlo and Desi's house in McLean as home, even though she'd never spent more than a month at a time there. But it would be nice to see everyone again, she decided as she pulled up alongside *Mephisto* and threw Jack a line. It would be nicer still, she added to herself, if it was in fact her home.

8

*Sad to say, a bride may often find herself faced
with a few spoilsports who do not react favorably to the announcement of her wedding.
Unfortunately, we live in a time in which marriage is no longer celebrated as the ultimate rite
of passage it once was, and people of poor
breeding may consider you fair game for their
own opinions or experiences of failure. However, fear not. You and your groom know that
the ritual you are about to undertake is the ultimate affirmation of your love for one another.
Let no outside influence ever change that.*

—ALISON BRIGHAM

"*Well, Francesca,* it seems as if the two of us
have been roundly beaten yet again."

Francesca studied the woman seated opposite her at the
table and frowned. Elaine Garret was her partner in this
rubber of bridge, but not a particularly good player.
Francesca doubted the two of them would win at all today.

"Well, at least we have time for a little break," Celia
Davenport, seated to Francesca's right, remarked further.
"And what a perfect opportunity for Francesca to tell us
more about this girl Taylor is marrying!"

"Yes, Francesca, do tell," Marie Stokes said. She was the fourth member of the quartet playing bridge at the Crosscreek Country Club as they did every Thursday afternoon.

Exactly four weeks had passed since Taylor had stated his intention to marry Emma Hammelmann, and Francesca was still reeling from the announcement. Her worst fears about the family her son was about to unite with his own had been more than realized. Accordion music, she recalled again, unable to contain her shudder. And to insinuate that the ring Taylor had selected and presented to their daughter as a gift wasn't big enough. What had Desiree expected, the Hope Diamond? Francesca's strategy at the moment was simply to hope that maybe if she ignored the Hammelmanns they would just go away.

"Taylor's fiancée is actually quite lovely," she said as she absently watched Celia collect the cards and arrange them in two meticulous stacks. "She's received her master's degree in literature and has had her work published in a number of nationally known publications."

"Oh?" Celia asked, clearly interested. She was, after all, the editor of *The Crosscreek Chatter*. "Which publications?"

Francesca was quite certain that her future daughter-in-law's extremely liberal views would go over at the Crosscreek Country Club as well as fine jewelry worn before 6:00 P.M. So instead of naming every radical extremist rag she could think of—the ones where Emma would no doubt submit her work—she simply replied, "You know, I'm not sure exactly which ones, but they are quite well known."

"Is she the same girl Taylor brought to the club Christmas party last year?" Marie asked.

"Yes, she is."

"Oh, I remember her," Elaine chimed in. "She was wearing those . . . unusual . . . boots, wasn't she?"

Francesca had been hoping no one would remember that.

"The ones that came up way past her knees?" Celia asked.

"Almost to her hemline," Marie said.

"Oh, my, yes, she was a lovely girl," Elaine said with a forced smile.

"Emma Hammelmann is something of a . . . a free spirit," Francesca explained. "Marches to a different drummer, you know. That sort of thing."

"She's the one Taylor started dating after he broke up with Helen McDermott's daughter, Tina, isn't she?" Elaine asked.

"Taylor and Tina dated for a long time," Marie remarked. "They were quite the couple among the younger set here at the club."

"They went to the high school prom together," Celia added. "And dated almost all through college."

"Now *Tina*," Elaine went on, "*she's* a lovely girl."

"And her parents are the nicest people," Marie agreed. "Pillars of the community, both of them. Steven just developed that new heart-surgery technique, Helen chairs the local Cancer Society. And I hear their youngest, Mark, is up for a Rhodes scholarship. Quite a remarkable family."

"Francesca, what does Emma's father do?" Celia wanted to know.

Francesca had known the question was coming, but dreaded it nonetheless. "He's . . . um . . ." She supposed she could claim Laszlo was from some obscure line of Eastern European royalty. He was, after all, the Hardware Czar. But of course, everyone at the club would sooner or later learn every little detail about Taylor's impending nuptials, so she might as well tell them all now. "He's in hardware."

"Computers?" Elaine asked, curious because her husband imported them.

"No," Francesca answered slowly, "more like . . . rakes, shovels, garden hose . . . light bulbs . . . toilet plungers. . . ." Oh, dear God, was her son actually going to go through with this? she asked herself. How could Taylor do this to them?

"Ooohhh," the other three women said in unison, nodding their heads in understanding.

"He's quite successful," Francesca assured them. "He has stores in five states."

"Wait a minute," Celia said. "Emma Hammelmann. As in Hammelmann Hardware? Her father is the Hardware Czar? The one on late-night television?"

Francesca smoothed back her hair with all the dignity of a queen as she responded, "Yes. That's the one."

"Ooohhh," the others replied.

The four women remained silent for several moments without further conversation, until Celia began it again by asking, "Might we know Emma's mother from her involvement in any of the local charities?"

Francesca studied the results of her morning manicure as she replied quietly, "I believe she mentioned that she spends most of her free time with her bunco club and her bowling league."

"Ooohhh."

Another round of silence ensued, until Marie interrupted it by asking, "You will be having the reception here at the club, won't you?"

"I offered the club facilities to the Hammelmanns, of course," Francesca said. "But I believe they've opted to hold the reception at the American Legion Post near their home."

"Well, perhaps you can talk them out of it," Elaine said, patting Francesca's hand.

Francesca sighed as she realized one of her cuticles was already forming a hangnail. "Perhaps."

Two counties away in suburban Maryland, Desiree was playing games as well, enjoying her usual Thursday afternoon bunco club at her sister-in-law's house. She liked it best when they met at Laszlo's sister Lillian's house, because Lillian always managed to find the absolutely nicest gifts for under five dollars to give as prizes. Desiree didn't know how the woman did it, but one time, she had even found a crystal clock to give as a prize. Lillian said the secret was finding the clearance tables in the big department stores and waiting for the days when they had additional percentages off. Desiree thought she must know when every store in the metro area had a sale.

"Bunco!" Ruby Marks shouted when her roll of the dice revealed three fours. "Bunco, bunco, bunco!"

"All right, Ruby," Eleanor Delaney said, "we heard you the first time. Sheesh. Give the woman one good roll and she goes through the roof. Lillian, you got any more of that sour cream cake left? I want the recipe."

"Here," Lillian said, handing Eleanor a piece of paper. "I Xeroxed it, because I knew everybody was going to ask for it."

"I want one, too," Desiree said, reaching for the recipe. "Laszlo will love this. What did you use? Just a regular bundt pan?"

Lillian nodded. "Just a regular bundt pan."

"Very convenient," Desiree said.

"Very," Eleanor agreed.

"So, Desi, what's going on with the wedding?" Ruby asked. "You haven't said word one about it lately."

Desiree sighed and reached for the dice on the table. "Well, Emma and I aren't quite seeing eye to eye on a lot of things, so we're still pretty much up in limbo at this point."

"Daughters are so uncooperative when it comes to their weddings," Eleanor said. "Marianne nearly drove me nuts when she got married. They usually come around, though. They know their mamas know what's best."

Desiree nodded. "I think Emma's beginning to realize that."

"You stand firm, Desi," Lillian told her. "Emma's a nice girl. She'll do the right thing."

"You're so fortunate, Desiree, that she's marrying a professional man," Ruby said. "My Cindy's husband, Lester, has been looking for work ever since they closed the chemical plant. I don't know what they're going to do. And with the baby coming in September . . ."

"It will be nice to have a lawyer in the family," Lillian said. "They're like plumbers. You just never know when you're going to need one."

"Emma will never have to worry whether she'll have someone there to take care of her," Eleanor added. "And won't it be nice, they can start a family right away, because they don't have to worry so much about money."

Desiree raised her eyebrows. "Well, you know Emma. She says they're not going to have kids for a long time. She wants to establish her career first."

"What career?" Ruby asked. "I thought she majored in English."

"I know," Desiree said. "But she wants to be a writer. And she says it will take a long time for her to do that."

"What's the big deal?" Eleanor asked. "She writes a book, they publish it. She wants a career, she's got it. Then she can start having kids."

"Well, I wish you would talk to her, Eleanor, and explain all that," Desiree said. "I can't seem to get anywhere with her."

"Tell her to call me."

"Anybody ready for another game?" Desiree asked as she rattled the dice. The other women took their seats again.

"What's Taylor's mother like?" Lillian asked.

Desiree smiled as she searched for the right words. "Francesca? She's okay, I guess. A little uptight about things, but I think that's because of the way she grew up. I feel kind of sorry for her. Very upper-crusty, country club crowd, that kind of thing." She tossed the dice and smiled. "Oh, goody. A one. In fact," she went on, "they offered Laszlo and me the use of the Crosscreek Country

Club for the reception if we wanted, but I think we're going with the American Legion Post."

"Oh, Desi, don't," Lillian told her. "Take them up on it. We can see the inside of the old Legion Post any day of the week, but how often would we get into the Cross-creek Country Club?"

"Yeah, I'd love to see that," Ruby said.

"I bet it's gorgeous," Eleanor agreed. "And the food would be out of this world."

"Are you serious?" Desiree couldn't believe it. "You'd really want to go inside that snooty club?"

All three women exchanged glances and then admitted they did.

Desiree shrugged and reached for the dice once again. "Well, maybe we will have it there. They'll cater it, too, so that'll be one less thing to worry about getting together."

"And the wedding's going to be in November?" Lillian asked.

Desiree recalled the little disagreement she had had with Emma that morning just before coming to play bunco. Emma still insisted the wedding would be in July. Desiree, however, knew better. "The wedding will be on the last Saturday in November," she told the other woman. "And of course you're all invited."

9

There will be occasions during the hectic plan-
ning of your wedding when you and your
groom cannot seem to find a single minute to be
alone together. Therefore, make every effort to
steal a few private moments. And take it from
Alison, this is a tip any bride would be wise to
follow after the wedding has become little more
than a memory.

—ALISON BRIGHAM

"*Your father would kill you if he saw you now.*"
Emma leaned over on the blanket and popped a red
grape into Taylor's mouth, laughing when he tried to consume her finger along with it. It was a beautiful late-June
day, and Emma and Taylor had taken advantage of it by
meeting for lunch near the edge of the Tidal Basin,
beneath a shady tree and well away from the crowds of
tourists choking the Mall. The basket she had brought
with her now contained only the remnants of their
lunch—cheese rinds and strawberry crowns, half a loaf of
French bread and a small handful of grapes. Taylor's
expensive suit jacket lay in a crumpled heap on the grass
beside them, and the Hawaiian print silk necktie Emma
had given him as a birthday gift hung unfettered around

his open collar. At the moment, he looked about as much like a conservative law clerk as George of the Jungle did.

"Why would my father kill me?" he asked as he picked up the wine bottle and topped off their glasses.

"Well, sneaking away for a romantic, secluded lunch with your girlfriend when you should be slaving away at your desk," Emma said. "It's not very professional."

Taylor lay back with his head cradled in the palms of his hands. "You're not my girlfriend anymore," he reminded her. "You're my fiancée. Besides, hell, this is nothing my father hasn't done on a dozen occasions this year alone."

Emma leaned back on one elbow beside him and brushed his hair back from his forehead. She felt so good just being here alone with Taylor, she wondered why she still fretted from time to time about getting married. "Your father and mother sneak off for romantic lunches?" she asked. "I never thought they seemed the type."

Taylor had closed his eyes, enjoying the feel of Emma's fingers stroking his forehead. Now he opened them to gauge her reaction as he said, "No, not my father and mother, my father and his girlfriend."

Emma's hand halted in its gentle caress. "Your father has a girlfriend?"

Taylor nodded.

"How come you didn't tell me before?"

"For some reason, it didn't seem necessary."

Emma bit her lip, weighing this new information. "So how come you're telling me now?"

Taylor shrugged. "Now it does."

"Does your mother know?"

"I don't know. I figure she must if I do. I don't see how she could be married to him for thirty-something years without at least being suspicious."

When Emma sat up, Taylor rose, too. He smoothed his hand over her short hair, tracing her nape before bending to place a kiss there.

"Emma, I want you to know up front that I certainly don't approve of my father's affairs."

"Affairs?" she asked, turning to look at him. "Plural? As in more than one? How did you find out about all this?"

Taylor sighed. "I'm not sure when I first started putting two and two together, but the signs have always been there. My father's had a girlfriend for as long as I can remember, but it hasn't always been the same one."

"That's awful."

"That's my father. Look, I know it's not something to be proud of, but I think you have a right to know what kind of family you're marrying into."

Emma sensed his anxiety. "I'm not marrying your family, Taylor. I'm marrying you. And I know you'd never do what your father is doing. You're too decent for that."

Taylor smiled. "It has nothing to do with decency," he said. His eyes never left hers as he lifted her hand and pressed it to his lips. "It has to do with the fact that I have you. Forever. And you, sweet Emma, are my very heart and soul. Why would I look elsewhere when I already have everything I want . . . everything I *need* . . . right here?"

Emma smiled back. "Beats me."

Taylor circled her waist with his arm and pulled her close, and they sat in comfortable silence as they watched a day-sailer skim lightly over the waters before them. The wind picked up, barely touched with a coolness that reminded him of autumn, and inevitably, Taylor thought back on the first day he had met Emma Hammelmann.

It had been late October, right around midterms. He had been a senior, not quite the big man on campus, but he'd allowed himself to feel that way now and then. She'd been a freshman, still unaware of where everything was on Georgetown's main campus, and she'd stopped him in front of the library to ask where she might find the bursar's office.

Taylor recalled that for a moment he hadn't been able to answer her. Her black hair had been long then, nearly to the center of her back, and she'd been wearing a black beret shoved low over her forehead. Her flowing black coat had hung open over a black dress and black boots, and all he'd been able to do was wonder why such a harmless-looking woman was dressed like a terrorist. Instead of making her look formidable, her outfit had only enhanced the softness of her features, the utter gentleness so evident in her huge green eyes. Ultimately, it had been her eyes that so entranced him. This woman couldn't have hurt a fly, let alone blown up an airport.

The more Taylor had tried to give her directions, the more confused they'd both become, until he'd finally offered to walk Emma to her destination himself, knowing he would miss the first half of his business ethics class if he did so. He hadn't cared. Because the moment Taylor had gazed into Emma Hammelmann's seemingly bottomless eyes, he had known somehow that the two of them would be together forever. Suddenly his long-standing, intense relationship with Tina McDermott was forgotten, and before he knew it, he was asking Emma to a party at the frat house the following night. He'd get out of going with Tina, he told himself in a fit of optimism. Never mind that Tina's father was a hulking six-foot-four, former Golden Gloves champion who could conceivably beat the hell out of him if he hurt his little girl, as Mr. McDermott had been wont to threaten to do. All Taylor had wanted that afternoon was to get to know Emma better, and asking her to go out with him as soon as possible had seemed the best way.

She had turned him down, telling him with a nervous smile that her mother wouldn't allow her to go to fraternity parties for fear that her daughter might get gang raped. That had been Taylor's first insight into the complicated psyche of Desiree Hammelmann. And much to his great fortune, it hadn't been his last.

"What are you thinking about?" Emma asked, bringing an end to his silent reflections.

Taylor grinned. "I was thinking about the first time we met."

Emma gazed at him happily. "So was I."

"When you said you wouldn't go out with me."

"Hey, there was a perfectly good reason why I couldn't," she reminded him.

"Yeah, you thought I would jump you the minute I had you alone." He laughed.

Emma shook her head. "No, my *mom* thought you would jump me the minute you had me alone. She warned me about you randy frat guys. She said all you wanted was sex, sex, sex."

"That had nothing to do with being in a fraternity."

"Well, anyway," she went on, "it all worked out in the long run, didn't it? I did go out with you the next time you asked—"

"That you did."

"—and kept going out with you, even after Tina McDermott started stalking us."

Taylor laughed harder. "God, I'd almost forgotten about that. You're a hell of a woman, Emma."

"More woman than Tina will ever be."

"I guess that's why she finally gave up and left us alone," he said.

Emma knew Tina's surrender had little to do with recognizing Emma's undeniably superior womanhood. More likely, Tina's loss of interest came when she started dating a Marine. Still, the somewhat complicated relationship between Emma and Taylor and Tina had been touch-and-go for a while, but Emma had finally walked away victorious. And now she was about to make the ultimate commitment to the man she had won. She looked at Taylor again and decided the journey had been well worth it.

"So," she asked, "did Mr. McDermott ever beat the hell out of you like he promised he would?"

Taylor glanced at his wristwatch, began to straighten his necktie, and then reached for his jacket and shook it out. "I think he telephoned my father and tried to call him out, but no, Mr. McDermott never laid a hand on me."

Emma nodded. Maybe the McDermotts were a decent sort after all. "Do you want to invite them to the wedding?" she asked, teasing him.

Taylor stood and fidgeted with the knot of his tie, fingered his hair back into place, and settled his glasses on the bridge of his nose. "Let's not push our luck, shall we?"

Emma rose, too, brushing her palms over Taylor's jacket in an effort to smooth out the wrinkles. He was back to looking like a corporate attorney now, she thought wistfully, except for the grass stains on his little tush. With a mischievous smile, she decided not to mention them. "Okay. But it could have been interesting."

"The wedding is going to be interesting enough without the added stimulus of Tina and the McDermotts," he told her. "Let's just try to get through it as best we can, all right?"

"Well, since you put it that way," she said, "there are still a few things we have to talk about where the wedding is concerned."

"Such as?"

"Mom says we have to get registered somewhere so people will know what we want in the way of gifts."

"But we're not having enough guests to warrant that, are we?"

Emma hedged. "We-ell, no, but Mom says there will still be people who want to get us something when they hear."

Taylor grimaced. "Do I have to go, too? Can't you do that by yourself? I trust your judgment."

"Taylor . . ."

"I'll think about it."

Emma frowned at him.

"What else is there?"

"You haven't picked out a tuxedo yet."

"That's because you haven't picked out a dress."

Emma sighed. "That's because my mom refuses to look in any of the stores I like. Just pick something in black that will go with anything."

"All right," Taylor said, working at the knot of his tie to straighten it. "What else?"

Emma dropped her gaze to her feet. "We-ell, there's just one . . . tiny . . . little . . . problem. But nothing I can't handle."

"What's that?"

She took a deep breath. "My mom is telling everyone that the wedding's going to take place the last weekend of November."

Taylor smiled. "Then won't they all be surprised to hear we've been married four months when they show up?"

He bent to kiss her, his lips still tasting faintly of the cabernet wine. It was a nice kiss, Emma thought, a comfortable kiss, a familiar kiss. It was a kiss that was meant to reassure her, and it did.

Together, they gathered the remains of their lunch and packed it back into the basket. When they were done, Taylor lifted it into his right hand as he took Emma's with his left. Hand in hand, they made their way slowly back to the metro in quiet conversation.

As they each awaited separate trains, Taylor inquired about Emma's plans for the afternoon.

"I've got a few job interviews lined up."

Taylor lifted his brows in interest. "Oh? Anything that looks like it might pan out?"

"I don't know. I'm beginning to think I'll never find anything to really suit me. Of the three interviews today, one is for a proofreader, one is for an editorial assistant—read secretary—and one is for a junior copywriter. Not bad for an advanced degree, huh?"

Taylor kissed her lightly on the forehead. "Something will turn up."

Emma nodded. "I just hope something turns up soon."

The lights on the platform before them began to flash, announcing the impending arrival of a train. As they waited to see whose it would be, Taylor turned to Emma.

"I realize this is kind of a touchy subject, but you know it's no big deal if you don't find a job right away. I'm making enough at the firm for us to live comfortably."

"No big deal?" Emma was surprised by his comment. "It's not a question of money, Taylor. It's a question of self-worth. What's the point of my having gone to school for five years if I'm just going to sit around twiddling my thumbs?"

"Emma, any education is never wasted, regardless of what you choose to do with it."

"Well, I choose to put my degrees to use. I intend to find a job."

The steady whine of the approaching train made it difficult for her to hear Taylor's next comment, but she got the gist of it from his expression as he uttered his final words, something about starting a family right away.

Well, this was certainly a new development, Emma thought. Although both had reached some vague agreement in the past that they wanted to have children at some equally vague point in the future, this was the first time Taylor had suggested doing it right away.

Before she had a chance to respond, the train emerged from the tunnel—the blue line, traveling to Taylor's destination. He handed Emma the basket and quickly kissed her good-bye. "Just think it over, okay?"

She watched dumfounded as his train pulled away from the platform, wondering when he had started feeling particularly paternal. She was still pondering his behavior when the orange line made an appearance from the same tunnel, and then she pushed her troubled thoughts away as she hurried to beat the throngs of tourists to a seat.

10

Perhaps the most exciting part of planning for your wedding will be your quest for the perfect bridal gown. Opt for the gown that you like, one that speaks to you alone, one that shouts to the world what kind of bride you are. And while you're out shopping, don't forget to stop by the bridal registry of your local department store. The staff there are remarkably well informed and can aid you in selecting just the right items to get your future household off on the right foot.

—ALISON BRIGHAM

"Mom, *this dress costs* almost two thousand dollars."

"So?"

Emma shook her head and turned back to look at herself in the mirror. It was the last Saturday in July, she reminded herself needlessly for perhaps the tenth time that afternoon, the day that was supposed to have been her wedding day. But instead of dressing for her wedding that afternoon, Emma was still out shopping for a gown. Still out shopping, she reflected, because she had all the time in the world. Her wedding wouldn't be taking place until the end of November.

The dress she was wearing at the moment was in no way similar to the calf-length, soft white number she had originally planned to wear. No, this one was of stark white satin that fairly screamed of her nonexistent purity, with huge muttonchop sleeves dipping nearly to her fingertips. The entire concoction dripped with bugle beads, seed pearls, and luminous, nearly invisible sequins, a combination Emma was certain made the bodice of the dress fully bulletproof.

"So, with two thousand dollars, Taylor and I could furnish our living room instead," Emma replied in response to her mother's question.

Although, now that she thought about it, it was kind of a nice gown, she decided, in its own . . . excessive . . . way. All those beads did provide a certain decadence to the concoction, and it was kind of fun being all sparkly this way. Still, she reminded herself firmly, the gown was nothing at all like the simple dress she'd initially had in mind—even if it did catch the light so perfectly when she twirled around.

"Try it with that princess veil," Desiree said, ignoring Emma's objection. "The one with the little pearl tiara on it."

Emma wrinkled her nose at the thought, trying to resurrect her earlier conviction that she would *not* look like a puff pastry for her wedding. "Mom, don't make me throw up. If I wear that I'm going to wind up looking like Princess Di."

"And what's so terrible about that? You're much prettier than she is, anyway."

Emma rolled her eyes, torn between wrapping her fingers around her mother's throat or throwing her arms around her instead. "Yeah, but look how Diana's marriage turned out."

"Vicious gossip," Desiree muttered as she smoothed out the long train on the dress and tugged at the cascades of lace that Emma was beginning to fancy looked like giant moth larvae scattered about her feet. "Nothing but lies to sell bad newspapers and trashy books. Oh, miss!" Desiree jumped up and pushed aside the curtain to the dressing room in an effort to summon the saleswoman. "We'd like to try that veil on the mannequin in front, please. And maybe you have one or two more that you like yourself and could recommend, hmm?"

"Mom, I'm not wearing that veil," Emma insisted, tugging viciously at the high, lacy collar of the gown. "And I'm not wearing this dress," she announced decisively. "I look like something from a nightmare Hugh Hefner would have after eating too much birthday cake."

"Bite your tongue," Desiree whispered.

Emma reached behind herself to yank at the zipper. "I'm sorry, Mom, but this just isn't me. I like that dress we saw in the window of Woodie's." She shoved the gown down around her ankles and stepped out of the froth of white. "I think we should go back and get that one."

Desiree leapt to her feet to gather up the cast-off gown and replace it on its hanger as if it were a priceless painting. "That was a cocktail dress, Emma. You can't wear that to get married in."

"Why not?" Emma reached for her blue jeans and tank top and pulled them on once again. As she tucked in her shirttail and buttoned her fly, the feel of softly worn denim against her skin made her feel like herself once more. She ran a hand quickly through her bangs and adjusted the huge, hammered metal earrings that had looked so incongruous with the fluffy wedding gown. She promised herself she wouldn't let her mother rope her into something like that again.

"You just can't, that's why." Desiree gazed at her daughter's transformation and sighed hopelessly. "Oh, sweetie. For a minute there, you looked like an absolute princess."

"Mom . . ." Emma protested. "I don't want to be a princess."

Desiree shook her head in disappointment. Seeing Emma reflected back at her in bridal white from the five mirrors in the oversized dressing room had filled her with so many memories she had almost lost her breath—little Emmaline as an infant, the first time the doctor had placed the baby in her arms, Laszlo standing beside her weeping more tears than Desiree had wept herself.

"No, I don't guess you do want to be a princess," Desiree said softly. "I should know that by now. But at least you're a daughter. And I always wanted a daughter," she added as she sifted again through the half-dozen dresses Emma had tried on, gazing wistfully at each one. "Mind you, my three boys have given me more joy than a mother deserves, but . . ." She reached out to brush her bent knuckles gently over Emma's cheek. "There's just something about a little girl. Your father and I didn't think we were going to be able to have any more children after Vick. And when I found out I was pregnant again, six years after having him, Emma, I knew, I just *knew* I was going to have a girl."

Emma smiled at her mother. "I know, Mom. You've told me this story before."

And just as she always did, Desiree finished it. "And what a girl you turned out to be, Emma. You've grown up to be a woman I would never have expected. Your spirit, your drive, your beauty . . . You know, you get all that from your Great-Grandmama Broussard. My Grandmama Emmaline was a woman completely ahead of her time. She just couldn't wait for the rest of the world to catch up. I guess I learned a long time ago to let you go your own way and hope for the best. I know my daughter is smart enough to know right from wrong and good from bad." She sighed and kissed Emma on the cheek. "I only wish my daughter was also a little more cooperative."

"Oh, Mom." She kissed her mother back. "Can we go get some lunch now?" she asked as she drew the strap of her purse over her head, making it clear that there was nothing for them here at Faye's Bridal Shoppe.

Desiree glanced down at her watch. "We're supposed to be meeting Francesca in about fifteen minutes to get you and Taylor registered."

Emma felt a headache threatening. "Why can't Taylor and I just do that by ourselves?" she asked. "I mean, it seems kind of unnecessary for you and Mrs. Rowan to be there."

"Sweetie," Desiree began, trying to sound patient and tactful, "if Francesca and I aren't there, the two of you will wind up registering for all the things you don't need, and none of the things you do."

"Well it's just china and stuff, isn't it? Not that I feel like we need all that much anyway."

"Oh, you say that now," Desiree warned her, "but you just wait. When you and Taylor have children, you're going to be happy you have nice things to celebrate special occasions. Besides, there's a lot more than china and crystal that you two need. I've been to Taylor's apartment, remember? The only flatware he has are those combination fork-spoons that come from Kentucky Fried Chicken."

Emma made a face, but she had to laugh at the accuracy of her mother's assessment. "Hey, he has a couple of plastic knives, too. He isn't a complete barbarian, you know."

Desiree laughed and pushed aside the fitting room curtain to find the saleswoman standing there with her arms full of cascading white netting sparkling with even more beads and sequins.

"Oh, thank you, dear," Desiree said apologetically, "but my daughter has decided she'd rather look like a cocktail waitress for her wedding. So now we'll be looking for a dress at Miniskirts-R-Us."

"Mom . . ."

"Come on, sweetie. We don't want to keep your future mother-in-law waiting."

However, by the time they traversed the mall, stopped to use the ladies' room, and detoured to pick up a bottle of mineral water and a cup of coffee in the gourmet section of the big department store, they were in fact a bit late. When at last they found the bridal registry, they discovered Francesca was already there waiting for them, seated in one of the plush chairs in front of the bridal consultant's desk, looking intently at her wristwatch and smoothing out nonexistent wrinkles from her skirt. Desiree could feel Emma tense beside her when she caught sight of Francesca, and she wished her daughter's future mother-in-law weren't such a stiff.

"Francesca!" Desiree greeted her loudly as she and Emma came up from behind.

Francesca stood graciously and nodded her head in greeting. "Desiree. Emma."

Emma paused awkwardly, then formally extended her hand. "Mrs. Rowan. I hope we haven't kept you waiting."

"No more than fifteen minutes," Francesca replied, taking Emma's hand briefly in hers.

"We were trying on dresses," Desiree announced in a voice that left no doubt she was still annoyed about Emma's refusal to dress like a member of the royal family. "But we didn't quite see anything we liked, did we, sweetie?"

"Actually, Mrs. Rowan, did you happen to go by Woodward and Lothrop and see a dress in the window that was—"

"So we'll be trying Springfield Mall this evening," Desiree interrupted her.

Before Emma could utter an objection, a woman who looked to be only a few years older than she introduced herself as Sheila-the-bridal-consultant and asked if she could help them. Desiree, Francesca, and

Emma responded in unison, each indicating her specific expectations, none of which had anything in common.

Sheila-the-bridal-consultant stared at them silently for a moment before offering, "How about if I just give you the basic form to get you started, and if you have any questions you can ask me or one of the salesclerks in any of the departments. We'll be happy to help in any way we can. I can go over our policies when you've decided what you like."

"That would be fine," Desiree replied.

"But I've been looking around, and I already know what I want," Emma told them.

"Of course you do, dear," Francesca said.

Desiree took the clipboard and registry form Sheila was extending toward Emma and unfolded the latter, which appeared to be a good two-and-a-half feet long.

Emma gasped. "I have to fill out all that? Both sides?"

"Don't you worry about a thing," Desiree said. "Francesca and I know exactly what you need."

"But, Mom—"

"You'll be wanting Limoges for your china," Francesca told her, looking over Desiree's shoulder at the long list of blank spaces that required filling. "Twenty-four place settings. Before you two arrived, I was inspecting the selection available, and I found one over here that's quite lovely, a Haviland pattern called 'Dammouse.'"

"But I—"

"It's absolutely splendid," Francesca said, ignoring Emma. "And quite traditional. It will be just perfect for you and Taylor."

"How much is it?" Emma asked Sheila.

"Four hundred and five dollars for the five-piece place setting."

"Four . . . four hundred and five?" Emma sputtered. "Dollars?"

"And Baccarat will be suitable for your crystal,"

Francesca added. "It is, after all, what Lionel and I have. 'Harcourt' is a lovely complement to 'Dammouse.' So you'll be wanting to register for that as well."

Emma glanced over at Sheila in silent question.

"One hundred and eighty," the bridal consultant said. "That's the price for the wine glasses. The water goblets are two hundred."

"She'll be wanting the champagnes, too," Francesca said. "Both flute and saucer. You never really know which ones you'll be using until the last minute. And the saucers are lovely for sorbet."

"They're also two hundred dollars," Sheila told them.

"Two hundred dollars?" Emma squeaked. "For one glass?"

"Well, of course there will be those who want to buy two," Francesca said. "One for each of you."

Desiree was busy scribbling Emma and Taylor's personal information on the registry form and didn't seem to be paying attention to the conversation. In a last-ditch effort to maintain some form of control, Emma said, "But there's a Lenox pattern I like. It's nice and elegant . . . very simple and . . . and fairly inexpensive. I showed it to Taylor and he liked it all right. Can't we have that?"

Francesca settled a proprietary hand on Emma's shoulder. "Emma, dear, forget about what Taylor likes. Rowans have always had Limoges, ever since Daniel Rowan first came to America with his wife from England. It's a tradition."

"But—"

"Lenox is good china, Emma," Desiree said suddenly. "And it's made in America. You know how important that is to your father."

"Yes, I'm sure it's lovely," Francesca said. "But Limoges is incomparable in quality and—"

"If Emma and Taylor like a Lenox pattern, Francesca, I think they should have what they want."

"Emma," Francesca began softly, tightening her grip on Emma's shoulder just the tiniest bit. Emma could tell she was making a supreme effort to be tactful but also had a very clear intention to usurp Desiree's power as mother of the bride. "You and Taylor will be doing quite a bit of entertaining after you marry. It's to be expected of a young attorney in Taylor's position. And it will be absolutely imperative that the two of you make a good impression. Take it from me"—she lowered her voice to a confidential murmur—"I've been exactly where you are right now. The members of Washington society are absolute predators. If I hadn't done things *just so* after Lionel and I married, I would have been a social pariah for the rest of my life."

Emma gazed at her future mother-in-law in horror, weighing this new realization heavily in her mind. *Good God*, she thought, *I am going to be like Francesca.* In the same position, that is. And married to a man like Lionel—professionally, anyway. A tiny explosion went off somewhere in Emma's midsection, its heat coursing through her body at an alarming speed.

For the first time, she fully considered the realization that after she married, she, too, would become a Mrs. Rowan. Emma didn't want to be like Francesca. She didn't want to have to worry about what kind of china went where or who noticed it. Maybe she should keep her maiden name. . . . Of course, surely Taylor didn't expect her to be like his mother, did he? He never would have gone out with her if he'd wanted someone like Francesca, would he? Unless. . . .

Unless he was hoping to change her after they got married. Lots of men did that, Emma reminded herself, a profound panic gripping her. They married a certain kind of woman only to turn around and try to make their wives just like their mothers. Was Taylor going to be like that? No, certainly not. He wouldn't know Limoges from Chinet, she reassured herself. And she'd already been to a number of parties with him and his law student friends. "Society" was the last word she would use to describe any of them.

"I'm putting you down for the pattern you like, Emma," Desiree said beside her, scribbling the word "Lenox" on the registry above the category marked *Fine China*. "What was the name of the pattern?"

"'Eternal,'" Emma replied quietly, the word sounding ominous in light of the situation.

Desiree scribbled some more. "Now we're getting somewhere." She then turned her attention to the *Fine Crystal* category and glanced over at Emma. "You know, sweetie, I saw a crystal pattern over here that I just adore. . . ."

Four hours later, Francesca was inspecting the quality of the sterling flatware and still insisting Emma should have gone with the pattern Francesca liked instead of the one Desiree had chosen, Desiree was still wandering through the housewares department collecting pamphlets on cookware, the registry list was still only half completed, and Emma was exhausted. She glanced over the registry list her mother had shoved into her hands nearly an hour ago, marveling at how little recorded there reflected anything she had wanted or liked, but she was simply too tired to protest any further.

She and Taylor would be lucky to receive a fourth of the items her mother and Francesca had written down, and many of the remaining products were total mysteries to Emma as far as usage was concerned. Did they actually *need* a duvet cover? she wondered. What was a duvet anyway? Whatever it was, there was a good chance they'd be receiving one, because Desiree had inscribed the number one beside it. Or had Francesca done that? There were so many marks on the list that Emma hadn't made herself, she couldn't begin to imagine what her future home would look like. At least they had allowed her to choose the colors of her decorating scheme—most of the time.

"I think we're going to have to come back next week to finish," Desiree finally said when she returned to where Emma sat as motionless as a mannequin.

Francesca joined them then, clutching two pieces of silverware, one in each hand. "Look, don't you think you should have *something* with a little decoration? The 'Golden Aegean Weave' has just a touch of gold accenting it that would match your china beautifully. The silverware you've chosen, Emma, just doesn't do your china pattern justice."

"Actually, that's the one my mom chose," Emma pointed out. "I thought that silver-plate pattern was fine. And it didn't cost three hundred and sixty dollars."

"You said you liked this one," Desiree protested, defending her choice. "If you don't, let's go look for something else. I only want you to get what you like, sweetie."

Francesca beamed, clearly delighted at having another chance to lobby for her favorite pattern. "Let's just set up your china and crystal together over on one of the tables, and we can see what works best."

Emma closed her eyes, wishing the entire afternoon were no more than a bad dream. "No, I can't do this anymore. I told Taylor I'd be over at his apartment an hour ago, and he must be frantic by now wondering where I am."

"Oh, no he isn't," Francesca said absently. "I called Lionel some time ago to let him know I wouldn't be home for dinner, and told him to call Taylor and tell him that you'd be a while yet, too."

Emma searched for an alternate escape route. "Then let's just do as Mom says and come back next week. At this point, I couldn't choose what I want for dinner, much less which cookie sheets are the best."

"Oh, we already decided that," Desiree said. "Baker's Secret. It's what I've been using for years. You'll love them."

"Fine," Emma muttered.

"But speaking of dinner, we should get something to eat," Desiree suggested. "How about the three of us going for some Mexican food? There's a nice restaurant not too far from the mall. If we get there before six, jumbo margaritas are half price."

"Dinner would be wonderful," Francesca agreed. "I haven't eaten since this morning."

Emma was quite confident that even a healthy dose of tequila wouldn't be enough to help her maintain her fragile grip on reason if she were forced to spend more than five more minutes with her mother and future mother-in-law. So instead she said, "I have a lot to do this evening. Why don't the two of you go alone? You haven't really had the opportunity to spend much time together, and you can talk about all the plans you have for the wedding."

Desiree nodded. "That sounds like a great idea. What do you say, Francesca? You like margaritas?"

"No, not particularly," Francesca said. "But if they can create a suitable Manhattan, consider me included."

"They have a big bar," Desiree told her. "I'm sure they do other things besides margaritas. I had a good banana daiquiri there once."

Emma excused herself as discreetly as possible from the two women, promising her mother she wouldn't be late. She returned the clipboard to the bridal consultant, saying that the three of them would be back to finish her list next week, and then departed as quickly as she could before her mother or Francesca remembered something incredibly important they'd forgotten. Like which bath mat would last longest, or which pasta grabber grabbed pasta best.

She needed to see Taylor, to talk to him and hear his reassurances that this marriage business was the right thing to do. No, Emma corrected herself immediately. She already knew marriage was a good thing. But she was beginning to think it was just too bad that marriages had to be preceded by weddings.

11

Many couples enter marriage with the less-than-comforting knowledge that their parents are virtual strangers. But now is the time for that to change. Your wedding will provide the perfect opportunity for your mother and the groom's mother in particular to get to know each other better. Who knows? By the time you and your groom become wife and husband, your mother and mother-in-law may be your two best friends.

—ALISON BRIGHAM

"So, Francesca, here we are, alone at last." Desiree licked the salt along the rim of her glass before taking a deep swallow of her margarita. With a contented sigh, she settled back in her chair. "Nobody does margaritas like these guys. This is just what I need after a day like today."

Francesca nodded, sipping her Manhattan. "It has been a rather demanding afternoon."

"Those bridal registries sure have changed a lot since we got married, haven't they?" Desiree said. "Back when Laszlo and I got married, there was one little shop in the neighborhood where everyone went to register, and strictly for china, crystal, silver, and linens. There was no place on the card to mark for VCR and personal computer, I can tell you that. Nowadays, these kids can ask for *everything*."

"I wasn't allowed to register," Francesca said. "Lionel's mother didn't think it was dignified. She had the butler pull down two huge trunks from the attic filled with the things that had belonged to Lionel's grandmother and grandfather and passed them along to us."

Desiree was impressed. "That must have been wonderful, getting things with so much sentimental value attached."

"It would have been nice if the things had had something in common with the decor I wanted," Francesca muttered. "As it was, we had to paint the dining room and kitchen colors I never would have chosen. Of course, that was before Lionel's father passed away and his mother went to live in Florida, and we moved into the big house. Now, of course, *everything* in the house is exactly as it was in his grandfather's time." She took another swallow of her drink and stared at a point somewhere over Desiree's right shoulder. "There are days when I'd pay a hundred thousand dollars for a first-rate sledgehammer and shovel, so I could just—"

Suddenly Francesca remembered where she was and with whom she was speaking, and she set her drink back down on the table. "Of course, the house doesn't really belong to me. Everything in it will be Taylor's someday. The girls will get some of the pieces, of course, but . . . It isn't my house."

Desiree wasn't sure, but she thought her dinner companion sounded a little resentful. She was surprised to hear the other woman say her house wasn't her own. Even though Desiree's house was technically in Laszlo's name and not her own, she wouldn't for a second think of it as not belonging to her, too. And as for Francesca's having received her husband's grandmother's things,

Desiree would have loved anything she might have received from either Laszlo's grandmother or her own. But both the Hammelmanns and the Broussards had come from pretty humble beginnings, so beyond the occasional pitcher or vase, there was little in their home that had been there before their own wedding.

"So how long have you and Lionel been married?" Desiree asked.

"Thirty-six years. You and Laszlo?"

"Forty-two years last February. We were married on Valentine's Day less than a year after we graduated from high school. Laszlo had gotten drafted, and we were afraid he was going to be sent over to Korea, so we decided on the spur of the moment to get married. It was all very last-minute, because we didn't have time to make any plans. We got on the telephone a week before and called as many friends as we could, and a few of our family members in the area were able to make it. The ceremony and reception together didn't last much more than an hour. Then we went off for a whirlwind honeymoon in Atlantic City. We had three days alone together before we had to come back to Maryland. Then I watched Laszlo get on a train taking him to God only knew where."

She paused for a moment, as more memories assailed her. "I was so sure I'd never see Laszlo again. I was positive something terrible was going to happen to him overseas. But Laszlo got lucky. Instead of being shipped off to Korea, he spent most of the war in La Jolla."

Francesca smiled back, reluctantly charmed by the account. Desiree's story sounded like something from an old movie, so much more romantic than her wedding to Lionel, despite the grandeur of her own affair. She was about to take another sip of her drink when Desiree interrupted her with a question.

"How did you and Lionel meet?"

Normally Francesca would never share her personal

history with a virtual stranger, but she reminded herself that the woman seated across from her would be her son's mother-in-law in a few short months, and therefore, alas, would essentially become family. Besides, she realized much to her surprise, feeling mellowed by the effect of her Manhattan on an empty stomach, trading tales with Desiree was oddly . . . enjoyable.

"Lionel and my brother, Collins, roomed together at Georgetown when they were law students. I drove down from Bryn Mawr with a few of my sorority sisters to visit one weekend, and when I met Lionel, I was immediately captivated. He was so handsome, so charming. . . ." Francesca, too, smiled at the recollections tumbling through her mind. "He used to be a blond, you know."

"Really?"

Francesca nodded. "I always loved Lionel's hair. Of course," she continued after a moment, "dating one's brother's friend meant we never had a moment of privacy, but back then it didn't seem to matter. It seemed as if every weekend, Lionel was driving up to Philadelphia or I was coming down here. We made the rounds, all the best parties and the most prestigious social events. Everyone thought we were such a stellar couple. After six months we were engaged."

Francesca gazed unseeingly into the depths of her drink. "My mother and Mrs. Rowan made all the wedding plans. They simply told me where to be at what time, and I arrived on schedule." And little had changed after the wedding was over, she added to herself. Every time she'd turned around, one of the older women was telling her what to do. Until she and Lionel had moved into the big house, Francesca hadn't felt her life was her own. In many ways, even the move hadn't changed that.

"Funny how neither one of us really got to plan the big blow-out we wanted," Desiree said as she hailed the waiter and requested another round of drinks.

"Yes, isn't it?" Francesca said once the waiter had left.

The two women sat quietly, thoughtfully, for a moment before Desiree broke the silence.

"I was thinking of pink for the bridesmaids, what do you think?"

Francesca tried to contain her shudder. "Not for a November wedding. Claret, or perhaps a deep forest green, would be much more appropriate. And I think velvet would be a suitable fabric. Now for the men—"

"I think morning coats."

Francesca shook her head slowly. "The wedding is to take place at seven P.M., is it not?"

"That's what Emma and Taylor decided, even though I like afternoon weddings myself."

"For an evening wedding in autumn, one of this size, I'm afraid we must insist on black tie," Francesca said. "There's simply no alternative."

Desiree's interest picked up at this. "Oooh . . . They can wear tails!" she cried.

Francesca shook her head again. "Too much. Although I think it's perfectly appropriate for Taylor, since he is the groom after all, for the groomsmen to be in tails as well might be a bit too . . . too . . ." She had been about to say "too nouveau riche" but curbed herself just in time. "A little *too* formal," she said instead. "We don't want to overwhelm the guests."

"Well . . ." Desiree thought for a moment. "Maybe you're right. But we have to have little Joey and Rosie for the ring bearer and flower girl. Maybe he can wear tails."

Francesca abhorred the idea of having children in a wedding ceremony, but she capitulated to Desiree's wishes, because she realized that so far the woman had contributed nothing, and Francesca didn't want her to think she was usurping power. "They may be allowed a few modifications," she said.

Desiree pulled a much-folded piece of paper from her purse and scanned it quickly. "We still have a lot to go over," she said as the waiter placed fresh drinks on the table.

Francesca pulled out a tapestry-covered notebook and turned to a dog-eared page. "Yes, we certainly do. Musicians, florist, photographer . . ."

"It's a good thing Emma has us to help her out," Desiree said. "I don't know what she'd do without us. I only hope she appreciates us."

Francesca nodded. "She will, Desiree, she will. If not now, then someday. Now, I know a wonderful florist, recommended to me by the wife of a *very* prominent senator . . ."

Heads bowed over their notes, the two mothers went to work.

12

Your groom's choice of best man should be a complement to whomever you choose for your maid or matron of honor. And, like your maid or matron of honor, the best man should be a friend or relative in whom the groom can place his complete and utter trust. In many ways he will act as your groom's second, and should be as much a man of honor as your primary attendant is a woman of such.

—ALISON BRIGHAM

Instead of living near Georgetown's law school campus in Capitol Hill, Taylor and his roommate, Max, had opted for a one-hundred-year-old town house nine blocks from the university's main campus, four floors up, with, unfortunately, no elevator. The two childhood buddies had shared the apartment for almost seven years—throughout college and law school—and would continue to do so until the end of November. Emma hoped she and Taylor would be able to find another apartment close by, however, because she loved Georgetown. There was so much to do there. Taylor would have no trouble driving to and from his father's M Street firm, and if no work turned up for Emma in the near future, she figured she could always find something temporary in one of the numerous boutiques or restaurants nearby.

Her search for employment since graduation had yielded nothing, but then again she hadn't expected positions for people with masters degrees in English to be in abundant supply. She had managed to sell a handful of news articles and fiction pieces here and there, and had made a few hundred dollars over the past few months. But such income was less than substantial and certainly not reliable for the future. She reassured herself that Taylor was doing quite well, earning more than enough to support them both, and that he had a pretty secure future in the law firm—his father was the senior partner, after all. But Emma balked at having to rely on him alone. Surely something for which she was qualified and suited would turn up soon, she told herself confidently.

Yet when she arrived at Taylor's front door after leaving her mother and Mrs. Rowan to their dinner, Emma was feeling anything but confident. All she was able to manage in the way of knocking was a feeble scraping of her fingers against the aged, overly varnished wood. "It's me, Emma," she called out.

The door opened a moment later, but instead of Taylor it was Max who greeted her.

"Oh. Hi, Max," Emma said. Although she liked him very much, she never quite felt completely at ease around him, thanks to the awkward past they shared. These days they got along well enough; they just tried to stay out of each other's way as much as possible.

Now, as she studied Taylor's roommate, she marveled that she could be attracted to both men when they were so utterly opposite in their appearance and demeanor. Max was blond and blue-eyed in comparison with Taylor's dark good looks, and he was taller and broader and much more athletic. Whereas Taylor had entered college at the top of his class and stayed there, Max's grades had always been barely high enough to squeak by. And while

Taylor had chosen commercial law and would be practicing with a firm that represented big business and corporate giants, Max had chosen to study environmental law and hoped to work for an organization that would go after the very companies Taylor's firm would probably defend.

Like Emma, Max was still looking for a job. And, like Emma, he spent a lot of his free time working for a variety of political and social causes whose headquarters were located in the nation's capital. There had been a time, during their undergraduate years, when the two of them had found themselves working for a number of the same causes. But these days they tried to avoid such crossings of their paths whenever possible. It was just somehow easier that way.

"Is Taylor around?" Emma asked as she came inside.

Max closed the door behind her and leaned back against it. "No. When his father called to say you all had been held up, he decided to go to the gym to get in a couple of games of racquetball."

Emma gazed at Max curiously. He seemed to have something on his mind. "Oh. Okay. Well, maybe I'll just go look for him there, then. Thanks, Max."

She waited for him to move out of the way so she could leave, but he continued to lean against the front door with a thoughtful expression.

"Was there something else?" she asked.

When he didn't reply, Emma reached for the doorknob, turned it, and tried to pull the door open despite the obstruction of Max's big body.

"Emma, wait," he said finally, reaching out to touch her wrist. "Don't go yet. I need to talk to you about the wedding."

It could be a legitimate concern, Emma thought. Max was going to be Taylor's best man, after all. But something in his voice caused her dismay. "What is it?" she asked.

"I don't think you should have it."

Emma closed her eyes and felt a headache threatening again. "Considering the afternoon I've just spent, I'm inclined to agree. Maybe Taylor and I should just elope."

"No, that wasn't what I meant, either."

Emma opened her eyes and stared at Max suspiciously. "What are you talking about?"

"I think we should sit down." Max led her over to the couch in what passed for the living room. It was a hot evening, and the building wasn't air-conditioned. An aged fan with a chipped blade hummed in the window, offering little relief from the uncomfortable evening. The irregular whirring sound seemed unusually loud to Emma.

Max was wearing only brief shorts and a cutoff jersey to keep cool, and her gaze was reluctantly drawn to the play of muscles in his arms and legs as she followed him. It struck her again how utterly different he and Taylor were in their physiques. Max looked like such a jock, while Taylor epitomized the rumpled, brainy student. Certainly Emma had always considered Taylor attractive, even handsome, but there was a certain . . . rawness to Max that a woman simply could not ignore.

She was suddenly aware of a rivulet of sweat that trickled down her neck and lingered between her breasts. It really was hot tonight, she suddenly realized. When had the temperature soared? When she and Max were seated on the couch, he turned to gaze at her but still remained silent. Emma lifted her hands palms up to illustrate her confusion. "What?" she asked.

"I don't think you and Taylor should get married at all," Max finally said. His voice was quiet, calm, and very serious.

Emma stared back for a moment, wondering what had brought all this on. Of course she knew what Max was suggesting was ridiculous, but curiosity got the better of her. "Why not?"

"Because the two of you aren't suited to each other," he told her.

"Taylor and I are perfectly suited to each other."

"Not as suited as you and I are."

A great fist wrapped around Emma's insides and nearly squeezed the breath right out of her. "What are you saying, Max?" Her voice was barely more than a whisper.

He stared at her for a moment before replying, "I'm saying that I think you should give what the two of us had together a second chance."

Max held her gaze intently, and Emma's heart rate doubled. He was serious. He was actually suggesting that she call the wedding off. "Max, I thought we settled this a long time ago. What the two of us had together never had a first chance. It was just one night. It was nothing . . . a mistake . . . it never should have happened."

"It wasn't nothing to me," he said. "I've never been able to forget about that night. Every time I see you, I think about it." He paused for a moment, as if weighing his next statement carefully. "I love you, Emma."

"What?"

Max hurried on. "I've loved you ever since you and Taylor started seeing each other. And you've felt something for me, too. I know it. You can't deny that you've always been attracted to me. That night never would have happened if you hadn't felt something, too."

"Drunk, Max. That's what I felt that night—drunk. What happened between you and me—"

"We made love, Emma. Twice."

"We had sex, Max. There was no love involved. And it only happened because I was mad at Taylor for going out with Tina McDermott behind my back, and you and I were *both* too drunk to know any better."

"I wasn't all that drunk that night, Emma."

"Well, I was."

Neither one spoke for a moment, but only continued to gaze at the other as if facing an opponent. Then, before Emma realized what was happening, Max leaned forward and cupped his palm behind her neck, pulling her slowly toward him.

"Think about it, Emma," he murmured so low she had to strain to hear him. "Remember what that night was like. It was incredible. It was hot outside . . . like it is tonight."

"Max, don't . . ."

"You were wearing that white dress . . . like something from the last century."

"I . . . I don't have it anymore. I gave it to one of my cousins."

"And you smelled . . ." He inhaled deeply, still pulling her forward until her forehead was settled gently against his. "You smelled like you do tonight."

Emma inhaled deeply too, hers a ragged, unsteady breath, then wrapped her fingers around Max's big biceps in an effort to push him away. She felt weak, though, as if the heat of the evening had completely sapped her strength. All she could do was squeeze his arms, an action Max must have thought was an invitation, because suddenly he was pressing his mouth against hers.

It wasn't a demanding, overpowering kiss. It was like the first one they shared two years ago—tentative, searching, coaxing, as if he were uncertain as to how she would respond. Max brushed his lips softly against Emma's, urging a response from her she knew she simply should not offer. Still, it wasn't such a bad kiss, she decided. She remembered, too late, just what a good kisser Max Bennett was.

"I love you, Emma," he repeated as he pulled slightly away. "Don't marry Taylor. Just give me a chance."

The mention of Taylor's name was exactly what Emma needed to jolt her to action. Immediately she pulled away, scooting quickly into the corner of the couch, as far away from Max as she could manage.

"Max, I love Taylor. I'm *marrying* Taylor. You and I spent one crazy night together. Okay, it was great," she conceded helplessly. "But it could never amount to anything more than one crazy night."

Max was clearly running out of patience. "Can you sit here and look me in the eye and honestly say you don't still think about that night sometimes, too? Think about it fondly and wonder what it would be like between the two of us again?"

No, Emma realized reluctantly, she couldn't honestly tell him that. She did indeed still think about that night with Max from time to time, even almost two years after it had happened. And she still entertained warm thoughts about what it would be like to make love with him again. With his heat-inducing smile and a body that suggested he was capable of exhaustive creativity in his sexual technique, Max Bennett epitomized the dream lover. Even beyond that, he and Emma had so very much in common—their politics, their musical and literary preferences, their outlooks on life in general. Max could be a magnificent partner, she realized uncomfortably. He was the man of every woman's fantasy.

Yet, for some reason, Emma had fallen in love with Taylor, not Max. And if she were asked to identify exactly why she had chosen him, she knew she'd be hard-pressed to provide a solid explanation. One thing was certain, however—Taylor was her reality, the man with whom she wanted to spend the rest of her life. Reality, not a fantasy like Max. Fantasies could never be real. Could they?

Emma realized she could provide no answer to that question right now. Max gazed at her expectantly, and she could feel that he knew what kind of war was raging in her brain. It probably was similar to the one he'd been experiencing himself for the past two years.

"Oh, Max, why didn't you say something sooner?" she asked him almost desperately. "Why did you wait until . . ."

"Would it have made a difference?"

Emma shook her head in an effort to clear it. "I don't know. Maybe . . ."

"Maybe what?"

Her breathing then came in quick, almost helpless gasps, but she was unable to say a word. Without a look back, she leapt up and ran for the door, yanking it open until it crashed against the wall, and ran out into the hallway without closing it. All she could think was that she had to find Taylor. But all she could hear was Max's voice calling her name.

$\underline{13}$

Weddings provide an opportunity for everyone to reflect back over his or her own married life. This journey down memory lane creates a welcome diversion for anyone involved firsthand in the planning of your wedding. Often, it leads to a reenergized approach to married life.

—ALISON BRIGHAM

Francesca gazed stoically at the man seated across from her at the dinner table, trying to figure out when exactly her relationship with her husband had gone careening off a cliff. The first few years of their marriage had been blissful enough. Lionel had been attentive, loving, and charming, and the two of them had gone out constantly to every kind of function imaginable. Thinking back now, Francesca decided it must have been when she had become pregnant with Catherine that things between them had begun to go awry. Back then, she hadn't been comfortable attending social functions after she began to show. She'd felt awkward and frumpy and unattractive, and no one then had manufactured attractive maternity clothes to wear socially. As a result, she had missed an entire Washington season.

But Lionel hadn't. With her encouragement, he'd gone

on to make appearances at all the parties without her, always with suitable escorts like cousins and elderly matrons, of course. There had been nothing wrong with his behavior, Francesca reminded herself now. Nothing *socially* wrong, anyway. But would a man who truly loved his wife have gone out to enjoy himself without her? she wondered. Especially when she was pregnant with his child?

After Catherine's birth, Lionel had gradually started to grow more distant. He'd been a decent enough father to the children, had never treated them with a heavy hand, and had attended all the appropriate academy functions and sporting events. But Francesca couldn't recall a single incident in which Lionel had taken one of the children out by himself, one on one—not even Taylor, his only son.

She realized, though, that the distance between her and Lionel wasn't solely his fault. She had seen him slipping away from her all those years ago, yet she'd done nothing to try to pull him back. And once she'd discovered that he was seeing other women, she hadn't thought it would be dignified to fight for him. Men would enjoy their little dalliances, she would tell herself on the occasions when she found herself feeling blue. Then she would remind herself that, in the end, Lionel always came home to her. And Francesca would try to take comfort in that fact, if in little else about her husband's activities.

Now she wondered if Lionel did indeed come home to her in the end. After all, when was the last time he had really been at home? Yes, here he sat across from her at the dinner table, eating his meal and speaking to her. But was Lionel honestly there with her, or were his thoughts somewhere else, someplace other than his home, a place where they stayed most of the time now? Would there ever be a time in her life again when she didn't have doubts?

"Lionel," she said softly, crossing her silverware carefully over her plate.

He didn't look up from the latest issue of *The Harvard*

Law Review that had arrived in the mail that afternoon, but made a receptive sound.

"I hate to say this," she continued, "but I think we should throw an engagement party for Emma and Taylor."

"All right."

"After all, they announced their intent to marry two months ago. Everyone at the club is beginning to wonder about the Hammelmanns. As much as my social instincts recoil at the thought, we really should introduce them to our friends."

"That's fine."

When he continued to read his journal without acknowledging her further, she tried another tack.

"Lionel?"

"Hmm?"

"Look at me."

Her request must have startled him, because he did exactly as she asked.

"I thought we could have the party the last week in August here at the house," she went on, folding her napkin to place it on the table beside her plate. "We can have the close relatives, some of our friends from the club, and a like group the Hammelmanns might want to include."

Lionel's expression was puzzled, as if he had no idea why his wife was telling him these things. "Fine."

Francesca knew she had him bewildered, so she went ahead and made her final announcement. "And I'd like you to help me organize the event."

"I beg your pardon?"

"I think you and I should plan this party for the children together."

"Can't Margaret and Driscoll take care of the particulars? Better yet, why don't you hire a caterer?"

Francesca squared her shoulders and prepared to do battle with her husband. "Because unless you've forgotten, Lionel, Taylor is our son. And we've done nothing for him in years except sign our names on checks to cover his tuition and college expenses." Feeling suddenly as if she would explode if she didn't move around, Francesca rose from the table and began to pace the length of the dining room. "Remember after we married how we used to throw parties at home once a month?"

Lionel had the decency to put down his magazine and watch his wife's restless movements, all the while wondering if perhaps she was finally going mad. "Of course I remember."

"Do you know how long it's been since we threw a party here?" Francesca demanded.

Lionel shook his head slowly. "I don't recall. It hasn't been that long."

"It was Adrienne's eighteenth birthday, Lionel. More than five years ago."

"So?"

"So why don't we entertain anymore? Why don't we go out together anymore? Why . . . why for God's sake don't we even *talk* anymore?"

Lionel watched his wife cautiously for a long moment before responding to her assault. Good God, what had gotten into her? One minute they'd been enjoying dinner together, and the next she had gone off on a verbal rampage.

"We're talking now," he pointed out.

"This isn't talking, Lionel." Francesca came to stand at the corner of the table beside him. "This is arguing. This is fighting. This is not a conversation—it's a confrontation."

"Only because you're turning it into one."

Francesca slowly leaned forward and flattened her palms against the table, lowering her head until her face was level with Lionel's. "Do you realize," she said softly, "that you don't even address me by my name anymore? Not even when we make love, which incidentally occurs about as often as we talk."

"You're being silly."

"Say my name, Lionel. Just once. Say, 'You're being silly, Francesca.'"

Lionel drew an impatient breath. "You're being silly. . . ." He faltered for a moment before adding quickly, "Francesca."

Francesca nodded. "There, you see? It feels funny to say my name, doesn't it? It's not like 'Susan' or 'Vivian' at all, is it? No, your wife's name causes you some difficulty, doesn't it, Lionel? *Doesn't it?*"

Lionel rose slowly from his seat, causing Francesca to straighten to her full height as he did so. He towered over her by a good five inches, but she did not back down. Instead she met his gaze intently, waiting for an answer.

"What in God's name has gotten into you?" he finally asked.

It was a fair question, Francesca thought, one she wished she could answer. She only knew that in having dinner with Desiree the evening before, hearing the other woman speak with such obvious affection for and devotion to her husband, Francesca wondered why she didn't enjoy similar emotions with her own. It wasn't fair. It wasn't fair that Desiree Hammelmann, a nobody from nowhere who had come into the good life by luck, experienced a joyful union with a man who clearly adored her, while Francesca Taylor Rowan, who had been bred and groomed for this life, should wind up so damnably miserable. What good was it all if she couldn't enjoy it? And why didn't he love her the way he once had?

A sudden, almost debilitating loneliness came over Francesca then, and she felt the fight go out of her. She sighed. "I'd just like for you to help me plan this party for Taylor and Emma, that's all," she said quietly. "Is it too much to ask that you play some active role in your son's engagement?"

"Of course not," Lionel said, his own voice softening at her sudden acquiescence. "But I'm very busy at the office right now. I don't have time to plan parties."

Francesca lifted her chin and stared at her husband. "Well, make time, Lionel. Because soon our son will be too busy for us, too. And I won't sit around when I'm eighty wishing I'd done more while he was still ours."

"I can't—"

"You will."

And with that, Francesca spun on her heel and left the room. Lionel fell back into his chair and watched her leave, feeling a mixture of relief, confusion, and wonder. He had forgotten how his wife's eyes could flash when she was angry, had forgotten that once she had been an indomitable force to deal with.

He recalled the first time he had seen her, when she had been taking her brother to task because he had forgotten their mother's birthday. Lionel had been amazed that such a small woman could be so forceful, and when his roommate had introduced him to Francesca, he had felt the wind knocked right out of him because she was so beautiful, too.

It had been a long time since Lionel had entertained memories about his youth. A long time since he'd entertained memories about Francesca. He was distressed to realize it did feel awkward saying, or even thinking, her name. Why was that? He'd once thought her name the most melodious sound his ears could hear. Of course, he'd been little more than a boy then, besotted by young love. Much like Taylor was now, he supposed.

Lionel thought of Emma Hammelmann fondly. He had no doubt why Taylor had fallen in love. And although Lionel didn't know Emma well, he'd seen immediately that in many ways, she was much like Francesca had been at that age—strong, fiery, opinionated, unwilling to cede to anyone as long as she knew she was right. It must be the destiny of the Rowan men to marry such women, he thought. So why then did most of the Rowan men find other women in addition to their wives to occupy their time? Something told Lionel that in Taylor's case, there would be little question of fidelity. He and Emma were clearly devoted to each other and had no intention of ever going their separate ways. And for the first time in his life, Lionel began to wonder when he and Francesca had begun to stray apart.

It was too long ago to remember, he decided, and too long ago for him to start trying to make amends now. Still, it wouldn't hurt to help her plan an event for Taylor and Emma, would it? The wedding plans were obviously beginning to cause her some strain. That could be the only reason for her odd behavior this evening. If something as insignificant as hosting an engagement party could soothe Francesca and make her feel better, then the least he could do was go along with it. His schedule wasn't all that hectic. With a little minor rear-ranging, he could swing a couple of nights at home with his wife. He resolved to have his secretary do something about it in the morning.

Looking down at his watch, however, Lionel realized he'd better get moving if he was going to be on time tonight. Susan was expecting him precisely at eight. And she wasn't a woman who would tolerate being placed second.

14

Bridal fairs, shows, and expos have increased dramatically in popularity in recent years, something of a mixed blessing, in Alison's opinion. Although these events do organize a variety of merchants and merchandise under one roof, they tend to take the fun out of the challenge and search for the perfect wedding accoutrements. The hunt is, after all, part of the nuptial tradition.

—ALISON BRIGHAM

"Emma! Hurry up! We're going to be late!"

Emma lay on her back in the middle of her bed, staring at the ceiling and wishing she were anywhere but there. Her mother and Mrs. Rowan were about to drag her off to a bridal expo, an event Emma would have sworn she had told them she was planning to attend with Patsy. Every time she undertook to orchestrate some aspect of the wedding by herself, either her mother or her future mother-in-law stepped in with a proposition that they thought was even better.

Emma had embraced such hopes for her nuptial celebration and had been so excited about making the arrangements just so. Yet her happiness at joining her life with

Taylor's had gradually been dissipating into so much aggravation generated by the looming specters of the mothers. One more afternoon with them might just do her in.

"Emma! Come on!"

"You'd think by now they'd have it planned down to the last detail," Emma muttered to no one in particular. It was, after all, already August.

"Emma!"

"Coming!"

She forced herself to rise from the bed, shoved her feet into grubby sneakers, and reached lethargically for her purse. She took her time trudging down the stairs, trying to stretch the activity over as much time as possible. Not paying much attention to where she was going, Emma nearly plodded right over her Aunt Virginia before she actually saw her. The moment she realized the obstruction in her path was her vagabond aunt, however, Emma's mood became considerably lighter.

"Aunt Virginia!" she shrieked before throwing her arms around the other woman. "When did you get here?"

Virginia Hammelmann hugged her niece fiercely and laughed. "About fifteen minutes ago. How you been, kiddo?"

Emma hugged her again and then pushed herself away enough to get a good look at her aunt. "God, you look incredible! What a great tan! When did you go blond?"

"Believe it or not, this time the color's natural. Spend enough time down in the Caribbean sun, and this is what happens to your hair. You look wonderful, too, Emma," she added. Ah, to be that young again, she thought. She ruffled her niece's bangs affectionately. "All grown up and getting married. I can hardly believe it. I guess congratulations are in order. So . . . congratulations."

"The wedding, yeah," Emma replied with little enthusiasm. "Thanks."

Virginia lifted her brows in surprise. "You don't sound too excited about getting married."

"Oh, I'm very excited about getting married. So excited, it should have happened a month ago. I'm just growing less and less thrilled about the wedding that Mom and Mrs. Rowan are planning for November."

Understanding gradually began to seep into Virginia's tired mind. Hers had been a long trip from the islands, with Jack Kramer's curses for jumping ship on him ringing loudly in her ears the entire way. Men were such jerks. It wasn't as if the two of them had anything special, for God's sake. He just hated the fact that she'd been the one to end it instead of him.

Virginia was glad she'd come home. She hadn't realized how much she'd missed her family until the taxi had pulled away from the curb and she'd seen Desiree open the front door of the Hammelmann home with welcoming arms. It was even better to see Emma, even in the face of a little adversity.

"So the mothers are getting you down," Virginia said. "Maybe you and Taylor should elope. Families can be a real pain in the ass sometimes."

"Is that why you spend so little time with yours?" Emma asked, smiling.

Virginia smiled back. "I'm crushed, *crushed*, that you would say such a thing. You know I left home because I crave adventure and romance. And the Hammelmanns are notoriously lacking in both."

"Except where you and I are concerned." She and Virginia had decided this together years ago.

"Except where you and I are concerned," her aunt agreed.

Desiree bustled in then with her car keys jangling ominously, gazing at Emma with unmistakable intent. "We're going now," she said. "No more excuses."

"But Aunt Virginia's here, and I haven't had a chance to talk to her. Why don't you and Mrs. Rowan go alone? Patsy said she could go with me tomorrow, so we'll just go on our own then."

Desiree rolled her eyes. "Emma, you know we can't make any decisions without you there. Don't be silly."

Emma's gaze traveled quickly from her mother's face to her aunt's. "This from a woman who has already decided how many bridesmaids I'm to have, what color they'll be wearing, which music will be played before, during, and after the ceremony, and what food will be served at the reception. Of course, I did get to choose the maid of honor," she added. "From a list of five nominees."

Desiree dismissed her daughter's comments with a wave of her hand. "Don't listen to her, Virginia, she's overreacting. Francesca chose the color of the brides-maids' dresses. Now, come on, Emma. Virginia will be staying with us until after the wedding, so you two will have plenty of time to talk."

"Come with us," Emma said to her aunt as a final plea.

"Where are you going?"

"Something called 'The East Coast's Biggest and Most Complete Bridal Expo.'"

Virginia shook her head and laughed. "No way, kiddo. Absolutely not."

"Please?"

By now Desiree was tugging on the sleeve of her daughter's T-shirt.

"Uh-uh," Virginia said. "I'll dance and drink wine at your connubial celebration, my dearest niece, but you know how I am when it comes to things matrimonial—I want as little to do with them as possible."

"But—"

"Have fun," Virginia concluded as Desiree practically pulled Emma out the front door. "We'll visit when you get back."

"But, Aunt Virginia . . ." Emma made a face at her aunt, envying her freedom and independence. "One of these days," she called out, "you'll meet a man who sets you spinning on your ear, chomping at the bit to get married. Just you wait, Aunt Virginia! Then you'll be sorry! And don't come crying to me when it happens!"

Virginia waved goodbye to Emma and Desiree, then closed the door behind them. The day she met a man who could make her think about marriage was the day she checked herself into the mental ward, she thought. There wasn't a man alive who could make her give up her freedom.

"It'll never happen, Emma," she replied to her niece, knowing she couldn't hear her. "Never in a million years."

Hefting up her two well-traveled duffel bags, Virginia took the stairs two at a time and headed down the hall to the bedroom she always used whenever she came to visit. A little sleep was what she needed right now, she told herself. She would never need a man.

The East Coast's Biggest and Most Complete Bridal Expo sprawled over more than five acres at the Capital Center, and by Emma's estimation, there must have been about three and a half billion people attending. Most were female, she noted with little surprise, accompanied by a few hapless males who seemed utterly lost in their surroundings. The younger, more bewildered of the men were of course mostly grooms, while the older men with shocked and harried expressions were no doubt fathers of the brides who were just beginning to realize what a large chunk of their bank accounts their daughters' weddings were going to cost them. Mostly, though, there were brides and mothers of brides. Lots and lots of mothers of brides, Emma realized. Perhaps more of those than the brides themselves.

Desiree and Emma had picked up Francesca at her house, and Emma had politely surrendered her front seat to her future mother-in-law, making herself comfortable in the back. Now she was still effectively in the back seat, trailing along behind the two older women as they stopped at every booth to inspect its wares, dismissing most of them as insufficient for their needs, collecting a card or order form from a handful of the vendors.

Emma marveled that something as harmless as a wedding could generate such incredible revenue. Everywhere she looked, she saw booth after booth of photographers, florists, caterers, musicians, disc jockeys, singers, limo drivers, cake bakers, hat makers, shoe tinters . . . anyone who could make a buck off of the lifelong union of two people. What would happen to the economy if people stopped getting married? she wondered. It would probably collapse. Maybe she could write a story about it and sell it to one of the numerous bridal publications that seemed to be littering the Hammelmann home these days. Hmm . . .

"Sweetie, taste this."

Her mother's voice took her away from her story outline, and Emma looked up to find a large glob of icing on the end of a little plastic spoon less than an inch away from her mouth. She pushed her mother's hand away.

"Mom, you know I don't eat sugar."

"It's got artificial sweetener, Emma, try it. You'll like it. Mrs. Weinstein here says it's a recipe she developed herself. None of her cakes has sugar. I thought it would be perfect, since you got on this health kick of yours and don't eat sugar."

"Actually, Mom, artificial sweetener is even worse than sugar," Emma said. "I'd rather—"

"Sweetie, taste it."

Obediently, Emma opened her mouth as if she were a two-year-old all over again and allowed her mother to insert the spoon. Vanilla. And not too bad, she had to admit.

"It's good, but in spite of not eating sugar, I figured for the wedding cake, we'd have the real thing. And chocolate for the flavor . . . if that's okay."

"Mrs. Weinstein does chocolate," Desiree said. "And I kind of like the idea of a sugar-free cake. Laszlo's sisters are all putting on way too much weight lately, and you know they're going to be eating more than their share at the reception, so maybe this is the best way to go, hmm?"

"But there's still an awful lot of ground to cover here, Mom," Emma pointed out. "There are probably lots of other cakes to sample. I know you and Mrs. Rowan must have tons of things to do, so maybe Patsy and I could come back tomorrow . . . just the two of us . . . and make the final decisions."

Desiree dismissed her daughter's suggestion with an indulgent smile. Francesca, who was sampling another flavor, held out another spoon to Emma.

"Try this one, now," she said. "It's amaretto."

Emma complied, feeling more and more like an infant with every passing moment. "That's good, too," she said after swallowing.

"Here, one more," Desiree said. "This one is hazelnut."

Emma stared at the spoon in her mother's hand for a moment, and suddenly all of her feelings of frustration roared up to greet her in a rush—frustration at being treated like a child, frustration at still being unemployed, frustration at her inability to put thoughts of Max behind her where they belonged, and frustration at having completely lost control of her own wedding plans. Letting her anger get the better of her, she recoiled from the spoon Desiree was holding and snapped, "Jesus, Mom, I can feed myself."

Desiree jerked back her hand before Emma could take the sample and glared at her daughter. "Don't you dare use that tone of voice with me, young lady. And don't you *ever* take the Lord's name in vain in front of me again, is that clear?"

Christ, when had she reverted to a toddler? Emma wanted to shout. She was an adult woman about to be married. She held an advanced degree and had seen more than one piece of her writing published in a national magazine. In many ways, she carried more experiences under her belt than her mother did. So why was she suddenly being treated like such a child?

"Mom, you're embarrassing me," she said when her mother refused to back down. "What's Mrs. Rowan going to think?"

But her mother would not be moved. "She's going to think her son is about to marry a tramp if you don't apologize, Emmaline."

Emma's mother hadn't spoken to her this way in years—not since she was a child. She knew better than to argue. "I'm sorry, Mrs. Rowan," Emma said quietly, unable to meet the other woman's gaze. "I shouldn't have sworn that way in front of you."

Francesca was polite enough to pretend she hadn't heard a thing but accepted Emma's apology graciously.

"Now, Mrs. Weinstein says she makes a marvelous French cream vanilla or Dutch chocolate cake that go very well with any of these icings. Which do you like best, Emma?" Desiree asked a little more calmly, handing her daughter the spoon this time so she could taste the icing herself. "You should be the one to decide. This is your wedding, after all."

Emma placed the spoon obligingly in her mouth, but at this point anything would have tasted like cardboard to her. "This is fine," she told them. "The hazelnut is fine. With whatever cake you think is best."

"If you want chocolate, we can order chocolate," Desiree said. "But how about we alternate a layer of vanilla with a layer of chocolate?"

"Fine."

Desiree turned back to the woman behind the table to place an order for the cake. Emma waited patiently while her mother and Mrs. Rowan dictated the particulars. Yes, they would need enough for four hundred people, but nothing too flashy, although those little plastic cupids were awfully cute. And the swans. And oh, what was that, a little miniature fountain that fit on top of the cake? That might be nice, too. Emma heard her mother ordering more and more decoration and felt herself losing what little control she might have fooled herself into thinking she had left. Then she heard Francesca interject that a simple floral arrangement to repeat the pattern found in the girls' bouquets might be nice for the cake.

"Real flowers?" Desiree asked.

Upon Francesca's nod, Desiree decided she liked that idea even better.

For much of the afternoon, Emma found herself repeating the episode at the cake booth. First her mother would suggest one thing, then Francesca would suggest another. In no time, Emma would find herself clashing with both of them, insisting fruitlessly that she wanted to go back to the original plan and abandon all these unnecessary and expensive frills. Desiree would then stroke her daughter's hair, and Francesca would pat her hand, each of them convinced that *she* knew what was best, and Emma invariably wound up agreeing to something she did not want.

By the end of the day, heavily laden with brochures and order forms, the three women retreated to inspect their booty. It was an impressive haul, one that would require days of pondering. As they walked to the car, chattering incessantly about all the wedding wonders they had just discovered, Emma decided all she really wanted to do was get some sleep. Or run away to Abu Dhabi. Or run away to Abu Dhabi and get some sleep. Instead, she let her mother put her in the backseat with promises of a stop for hot fudge sundaes on the way home. And, still feeling like a recalcitrant child, that seemed to Emma the most logical thing to do.

15

A bride need never worry whether or not her wedding is "enough." Regardless of the size, formality, or price tag of the affair—something that Alison is certain you know by now is irrelevant—your married life will sustain itself not upon how it was introduced to the public, but upon how well you and your groom can keep the spirit of your vows alive.

—ALISON BRIGHAM

"I think Emma's getting wedding jitters."

Laszlo glanced up from one of a number of hardware supply catalogs stacked by his side of the bed and frowned at his wife. "Already? But the wedding is still three months away."

Desiree shrugged and capped the bottle of red nail polish, blowing on her fingertips as she spoke. "I know, but . . . you should have heard . . . the way she spoke to me . . . at the expo today. And in front of . . . Francesca, too."

"I'm sure she didn't mean what she said, whatever it was."

"Probably not," Desiree said after another puff of air over her hands. "But she hasn't . . . acted that way since . . . she was going through puberty . . . and you remember how bad . . . she was then."

Laszlo dropped the catalog into his lap as he watched his wife curl her fingers toward her and blow on them some more. Desi had always had the most beautiful hands he'd ever seen, with long, slender fingers tipped by perfect crimson ovals.

"You were going through the change back when Emma was going through puberty," Laszlo reminded his wife with an affectionate smile. "You were both hell to live with. More than once, me and the boys talked about leaving home to let the two of you duke it out by yourselves."

Desiree nudged him playfully with her shoulder. "Hormones. It was all hormones. Emma was getting them while I was losing them. No wonder we fought all the time back then." She began to shake her hands vigorously to accelerate the drying process. "Anyway, I think she's got the jitters bad."

Laszlo went back to his reading. "Well, it's to be expected. Getting married is a big deal. Even bigger now than it was when we got married."

Desiree nodded. "Kids are too hard on themselves today. When they think about getting married, they worry, 'Will I still love this person when I'm sixty?' and 'Have I really done everything I want to do before I settle down?' and 'What if he or she gets fat or bald or something?' They plan their kids down to when it's most convenient to take time off from work, and sometimes they don't have them at all. Choices. That's the word that keeps coming up all the time nowadays. Whether or not to get married. Whether or not to have kids. Whether or not to pursue a career. Whether or not to stay married."

She laughed, a rich, rumbling sound so unlike the gentle laughter of most women. Laszlo smiled. He always loved to hear Desiree laugh. Fortunately for him, it was something she did often.

"The only thing you and me worried about was

whether we'd have chicken or beef for dinner," she continued. "Who would have thought back then we had choices?"

Laszlo chuckled. "It was easier for us, I think. When we got married, we didn't even know what tomorrow would bring. There was a war going on, my father was about to lose his shop . . . who knew from one day to the next whether we'd even have enough money to get by? Emma and Taylor are going into this marriage without money problems or concerns about their futures, and the world is a lot more stable now than it was then. But I think they have a hell of a lot more to worry about than we did."

Desiree sighed. "I guess you're right. I guess it is only normal that Emma would be jittery. Taylor probably is, too."

Laszlo reached across the bed and covered Desiree's left hand with his. "They'll be fine, Desi. Things won't go smoothly all the time, but those two love each other very much. They'll be fine."

"I know." She twined their fingers together. "I just can't help but keep worrying about Emma. I guess I'll never stop, even when she's been married ten years and has kids of her own."

"And you know what?" Laszlo asked.

Desiree shook her head silently.

"I don't think she expects you to stop."

Desiree brightened. "You don't?"

Now Laszlo shook his head. "I think whatever happened between the two of you today was just her way of letting you know she didn't want you to get too far away from her. Maybe by acting like a child, she was trying to remind you that in a lot of ways, she's still a little girl who needs you."

Desiree liked that explanation. "Maybe you're right."

They sat in silence for some moments, smiling a secret smile at each other. Desiree's fingers tightened their hold on Laszlo's, and with her free hand, she reached over to gently rake her freshly painted nails lightly up his naked torso.

"So, Laszlo, the store opens late tomorrow, doesn't it?"

Laszlo rolled onto his side, the sheet dipping dangerously low on his naked hips. Desiree's heart began to beat faster, and her skin grew warm as she turned to face him.

"Tomorrow's Sunday," he said. "So the store won't open until noon."

He reached over to cup Desiree's hip in the palm of his other hand. Slowly, deliberately, he skimmed his fingers along her thigh, pulling back the sheet as he went. When Desiree lay before him in nothing but a skimpy little piece of purple satin, her breasts appearing larger because of her reclining position, his pulse rate doubled.

"Why, Desi?" he asked, his voice low and husky. "What did you have in mind?"

"Oh, not much. I was just thinking that maybe you could stay up a little late tonight."

Laszlo's smile grew wicked. "Maybe I could."

She walked her index and middle fingers across the bed until they reached the hardware catalog that had fallen onto the mattress between them. Tossing it deftly over her shoulder, she smiled, then leaned toward Laszlo to switch off the lamp on his night stand. He did likewise, leaning toward Desiree to switch off the matching lamp on her side, a motion that brought their bodies flush against each other. The room was thrown into darkness then, and the couple embraced, igniting a passion that only sparked brighter with each passing year.

The last thing Desiree remembered thinking before Laszlo's caresses sent her tumbling over the edge was that her husband had been right. Once Emma was married to Taylor, she was going to be just fine.

16

In order to marry in a church, the bride and groom will usually be required to undergo counseling from a member of the clergy. This is a common practice for most denominations and certainly should not be looked upon as a suggestion that a couple are incompatible or unable to make their own decisions. Rest easy in the knowledge that you and your groom have made it this far together. For heaven's sake, what could someone as benign a clergyman possibly say or do to disrupt your plans?

—ALISON BRIGHAM

"It was nice of you to meet with us on such short notice, Reverend." Emma shook hands with the Reverend Mr. Robert Ballard and tried to smile. She hadn't quite recovered from the trying afternoon she'd spent with her mother and Mrs. Rowan yesterday, and now she was expected to be on her best behavior for a man of the cloth. "And to make room on your schedule to marry us in November. I'm sure that must be a very busy month for you, what with the holiday season coming so soon after. I guess Christmas is a big one for you, isn't it?" Emma wished she could do something about her tendency to ramble incessantly whenever she felt nervous.

"Yes, Christmas is a biggie, but not as big as Easter," Reverend Ballard replied. "That's what's it's all about, you know."

"I guess that's true."

Reverend Ballard was the Hammelmann's minister from the suburban Maryland church the family had been attending for decades, though Emma herself had gradually stopped when she had become interested in more secular pursuits. But because what Emma had intended to be an intimate wedding at home was rapidly becoming *the* social event of the D.C. area season, it was going to be impossible to have the gathering in the Rowan garden. Or even Madison Square Garden, for that matter, Emma thought.

When Francesca had suggested that Emma and Taylor marry at the Rowans' church, Desiree had quickly countered that the bride's church would be a more appropriate choice. Emma had then pointed out that she hadn't attended any church for more than five years and that neither she nor Taylor harbored any desire for a religious service, anyway. Both mothers, horrified by the idea of a civil ceremony, had hastened to make a compromise: The wedding would be held at the Rowans' church but would be presided over by the Reverend Mr. Robert Ballard of the Hammelmanns' house of worship. Each family had then sent in generous donations to the other church, thus making certain the arrangement would be to everyone's liking.

Unfortunately, now that they were to be married in the church, by the church, and for the church, Emma and Taylor had discovered it would also be necessary to be "counseled" by their clergyman—something they both considered completely unnecessary. After almost six years together, there was little mystery left in their relationship. One might even argue there was too little. Counseling seemed a bit silly, and certainly at this point they would learn nothing about each other they didn't already know.

Now, as Emma and Taylor sat opposite Robert Ballard in his small chamber crammed with religious publications, faux biblical artifacts, and other inspirational paraphernalia, Emma could feel her palms sweating. It wasn't that she didn't believe in God or that she had reservations about the holy aspect of life. She simply felt religion should be a personal, individual thing, a philosophy extending beyond an organization of people. She knew Taylor felt essentially the same way, though he continued to attend church services occasionally with his family. It kept his mother off his back, he said.

They really should have stood their ground a little more firmly, Emma thought as she gazed at the man opposite her with the bland smile and shiny face. She and Taylor should have insisted on a civil ceremony. Of course, they should have insisted on the much smaller ceremony they'd wanted, too, she reminded herself. And while she was at it, Emma decided, she should have insisted on the wedding gown she really wanted instead of the whirlwind of white lace she and her mother had ultimately ordered. Why were she and Taylor such pushovers where the wedding was concerned? she kept asking herself. Why didn't they just put their feet down?

Because, as Emma and Taylor were quickly learning, the moment an adult offspring announced he or she was to be married, his or her mother ceased to think of him or her in terms of "I'm so impressed with the man or woman you've become," and began the backward slide toward "But you're still my little boy or girl."

"Now, then, Emma, your mother tells me the ceremony will be taking place at Johnson Memorial," Reverend Ballard began. "That's a lovely church. A wonderful place for the wedding. And the service I have planned will be equally beautiful, I promise. Here's a copy for each of you."

He handed Emma and Taylor a script of the ceremony, complete with their roles as bride and groom and his as emcee. Emma flipped idly through the booklet's pages, wondering if there would be a point where she could take a bathroom break, because surely this service would last ten hours. She caught Taylor's eye and could tell he was thinking the same thing.

"Naturally we can make a few changes in the text if you think it's necessary, but most couples find this service more than adequate for their needs. But before we get down to the particulars about the service, I need to ask you a few questions."

Emma straightened in her chair for what was to come next: the counseling part. Her sisters-in-law had prepared her for this, the intimate, personal questions the clergyman would ask her and Taylor, questions that could be potentially damaging to their relationship. Felicia had said her minister had even wanted to know her opinion on the upcoming presidential campaign. Emma was glad she was not getting married in an election year. But she'd done her homework and was ready to voice her opinion and quote statistics on any subject matter he might bring up—morality, sexual freedom, women's rights. . . . Name your poison, she commanded him silently, because I am ready. Emma gripped the arms of her chair and waited.

"How many attendants will you be having in the wedding?"

Emma looked at Reverend Ballard blankly. Attendants? What did they have to do with morality and sexual freedom? "Uh . . . six," she responded, feeling a little confused. "I mean . . . twelve with the groomsmen. Fourteen if you count the flower girl and ring bearer."

Reverend Ballard made a notation and then looked at her with a warm smile that put Emma on edge. Her grip on the arms of the chair became white-knuckled. Clearly that question had just been the warm-up, something to lull her into a false sense of security. *Now* would come the hot topics of discussion, something she could sink her teeth into.

"The names of the maid of honor and best man?"
Reverend Ballard asked.

Emma felt even more bewildered. "Uh . . . Patricia
Hammelmann and Max Bennett."

"Maximilian," Taylor corrected her.

"What?"

"Max's full name is Maximilian."

"It is?"

Taylor nodded.

"I never knew that."

Reverend Ballard made the proper notations on his
form. Emma relaxed a little, content in the knowledge
that he simply wanted some basic information he would
need for the marriage certificate. Clearly Felicia and
Diane had simply had to suffer through clergymen who
were busybodies. Reverend Ballard seemed like a pretty
easygoing guy.

"Emma, what is your date of birth and your social
security number?"

She supplied him with the information, and then he
turned to Taylor with a request for the same from him.
After scribbling a few more notes, he turned back to
Emma.

"Now then, Emma, how do you feel about abortion?"

Emma snapped forward in her chair, all her ready
arguments and statistics now flown out the window.

"What?"

"Abortion. What's your opinion?"

"Why?"

"Well, if you and Taylor were to find yourselves in the
situation of say . . . an unwanted pregnancy . . . how
would you react?"

Emma thought for a moment before replying. "In a
case like ours—when we're married, financially secure,
and have supportive families—I'd definitely want to
have the baby, and naturally I'd hope Taylor would too."

"Ah. Very good." Reverend Ballard smiled some more

and scrawled something on the notepad before him.

Emma was relieved she had apparently given him the response he wanted to hear. However, because of the way she'd grown up, with politics and social issues the stuff of everyday conversation, she felt compelled to voice a strong opinion when she had one.

"Overall, however, I feel family planning is a matter of personal choice. A choice involving no one but the pregnant woman, her doctor, and in some situations, the father of the child," she said.

Reverend Ballard looked up from his notes. "So you think abortion is an acceptable practice?"

Emma tried not to be too smug. "Certainly I think it should be an available option for all women, a right that shouldn't be impeded by the government or a few overzealous self-professed morality groups."

"I see. Taylor? What are your views?"

Taylor looked at Emma for a moment and then turned his attention back to Reverend Ballard. "Honestly?" he asked.

"Well, of course."

"Frankly, I'm against it."

"*What?*" Emma exclaimed. "You never told me you were anti-choice."

"You never asked."

"Well, you're so impartial about everything else, I just assumed you were."

"Well, I'm not. I don't think women should have abortions. It isn't right."

"Not even in extenuating circumstances like rape or incest or the mother's health?"

"Well . . ."

"Taylor, I can't believe you'd be so narrow-minded about—"

"Emma, Taylor," Reverend Ballard interjected. "We're all entitled to our opinions. The good Lord did endow us with brains to consider all the facts, after all. Some of us view the facts in one way, while some of us view them in another. And that's what this session is about. To illustrate the fact that we can all get along despite our differences of opinion."

"Taylor and I don't have any differences of opinion," Emma muttered. She glared meaningfully at her fiancé as she added, "At least I didn't think we did."

"Now then," Reverend Ballard went on, "on to the subject of fidelity. Emma, what would you do if you discovered your husband had engaged in sexual relations with a woman other than yourself?"

I'd nail his butt to the wall, Rev, what do you think I'd do? Emma looked at Reverend Ballard cautiously, wondering if it was a trick question. "I'd leave him," she said decisively.

"You'd *leave* me?" Taylor asked incredulously, bending forward in his chair, turning to face Emma more fully. "You'd leave me just for having an affair?"

"What do you mean *just* for having an affair? The whole point of marriage is to unite with one other person, forsaking all others and all that. Sleeping around is the most insidious thing a man can do to his wife."

"Oh, right," Taylor said. "Worse than lying to her?"

"What do you think having an affair is? It's lying."

"No, it isn't."

"Yes, it is."

"Emma, Taylor," Reverend Ballard said in his singsong, placating tone of voice. "We have a number of things to go over today."

They ended their disagreement with the unspoken understanding that they would pick up where they'd left off later.

"All right, Taylor, what would you do if you discovered Emma was having sexual relations with a man besides yourself?"

Emma tried not to squirm as Taylor considered his answer.

After a moment, he replied, "Well, naturally I'd feel

hurt and betrayed, and it might take a long time for us to work through it, but eventually I'd forgive her."

"You'd forgive me? Just like that? You wouldn't care?"

"Well, of course I'd care. But I'd still forgive you."

"Why?"

"What do you mean why?"

"I wouldn't forgive you," she said.

"I know," he snapped. "You'd leave me."

"You'd better believe I would."

"Emma, Taylor, please . . ."

They ceased their argument once again, again maintaining a silent understanding to finish it later. Reverend Ballard sighed and made a few more notes.

"Money," he continued. "How important is it in your relationship?"

"Not at all," Taylor replied immediately.

"Very," Emma replied at the same time.

Reverend Ballard made more notes. "Sex—"

"Very important," they both said at once. For the first time since arriving, Emma and Taylor were able to look at each other and smile. "Very, very important," they added with a laugh.

Reverend Ballard sighed again, scribbling furiously on his notepad. "I can see we have a lot to do," he said, not entirely under his breath. "Quite a lot to do."

Some time later, Emma and Taylor still sat in their chairs, completing a "test" Reverend Ballard had asked them to take. At the top of the page were the numbers one through ten, one standing for "strongly disagree" and ten standing for "strongly agree." Down the side of the page were a number of personality descriptions which the couple were—independent of each other—to match to their own characteristics. For example, where the personality trait stated was, "I go to pieces whenever the slightest thing goes wrong," Emma reluctantly made a tiny dot beneath the number eight. Where the trait described the test-taker as one who had strong leadership skills, Emma dotted number three. When she and Taylor had both finished, Reverend Ballard took their tests back and connected their dots with a red marker, then held both papers up for the couple to see. Emma slumped back in her chair and stared in disbelief. Where Taylor's lines zigged, her own zagged, where his zagged, hers most definitely zigged. The two red lines on the pages before her couldn't have been more opposite if they'd been held up to a mirror.

She propped her elbows on the arms of her chair, dropped her head into her hands and muttered sullenly, "We're never going to get out of here."

Reverend Ballard smiled and suggested, "Why don't we just make an appointment for next week, shall we?"

With Saturday evening traffic as bad as ever on the Beltway and in town, it took Taylor and Emma nearly an hour to get back to Washington. The mood in the car was less than buoyant, and the conversation was for the most part absent. Emma did a good job of pretending to concentrate on the creeping flow of cars surrounding them as she drove, and Taylor fiddled with the radio in an effort to find an apparently nonexistent station. Finally, when Emma could no longer tolerate the erratic gaps of static and garbled talk of disc jockeys, she reached over and switched the radio off.

"Hey, I was listening to that," Taylor objected.

"And it sounded great, too," Emma muttered.

Taylor leaned back and tugged his seat belt viciously into place. "You know, you've been pissed off about something all day, and I wish you'd just say what it is and get it out in the open."

Emma stared at him in disbelief, only turning her attention back to the traffic at the honking of another motorist.

"Something? Taylor, I'm pissed off about everything."

"What are you talking about?"

"I'm talking about what we just went through with Reverend Ballard."

"What about it?"

"Are you deaf? Didn't it bother you how quickly we disagreed on so many things?"

"We quickly agreed on a lot of things, too," he said. "We can't see eye to eye on everything."

Emma sighed. "I know. But . . ."

"But what?"

She shook her head in confusion again, a gesture she was beginning to find familiar. "Nothing," she said, unsure how to explain the sudden onslaught of agitation swirling around in her brain.

"We should talk about it," Taylor said softly.

"There's nothing to talk about."

"There's everything to talk about, Emma, we—"

"Just forget it."

For a moment, Taylor did as she instructed, but he just couldn't let it go yet. "You know, you've been doing this a lot lately," he started up again.

Emma's fingers tensed on the steering wheel. "Doing what?"

"Starting a fight with me and finishing it by yourself."

"I have not been starting fights with you."

"Oh, yes you have. But you haven't carried any of them through to their potential conclusion."

Emma pushed her fingers through her bangs, growing more and more exhausted with every passing minute. "Taylor, I do not want to have this conversation. I'm tired and I want to go home and relax for a little while before we go out."

"See? You're doing it right now."

Part of Emma knew he was right, but they had been disagreeing all day long, and she didn't want to end their day with an argument. So she simply remained silent, willing Taylor to do the same, all the while growing more and more anxious about the ever-widening chasm between them.

When they finally crossed Key Bridge back into D.C., Taylor asked Emma to drive him to the law library instead of taking him back to his apartment.

"But it's Saturday night. I thought we were going to see *The Cabinet of Dr. Caligari* at the Smithsonian," she reminded him.

He hung his head, unwilling to look at her as he said, "Yeah, well, I have some work I need to do on a case my father assigned to me this week. I didn't think we'd be so long with Reverend Ballard today. Now I'm going to have to work on this case for the rest of the weekend."

"But—"

"Sorry, Emma."

She was going to object further but decided it might be best if they did spend some time apart. Maybe that was the problem, she thought as she drove through the gradually darkening streets of Capitol Hill. Because of the wedding plans, they'd been spending more time together than they usually did. It was only natural that they'd get on each other's nerves. A couple of days away from each other might be just what they needed. Still, as Taylor got out of the car at the library, Emma couldn't help but remind him of something.

"You know, we always promised each other we'd never put our jobs before our relationship. Of course, I still don't have a job. . . ."

Taylor smiled sadly. "Yeah, well . . . we also always promised we wouldn't *let* each other put our jobs before our relationship, either."

"Yeah, I guess you're right. Well, don't work too hard."

"Don't worry."

There was an awkward pause before Emma asked, "Will you call me tomorrow?"

"I'll be pretty busy." When he saw her expression, he added, "I'll try."

He closed the door behind himself, slamming it a little harder, perhaps, than was necessary. Emma watched him climb the stairs toward the library, wondering what was happening to them.

The wedding, she reflected morosely. She was beginning to think weddings could end perfectly beautiful relationships.

17

If by chance you should find yourself worrying overmuch about aspects of the wedding that seem not to be going quite right, do not keep your concerns bottled up inside. Describe your anxieties to your maid of honor or another trusted friend or relative. Almost always, talking about your troubles minimizes their impact. And take it from Alison, worrying profusely does nothing for your complexion.

—ALISON BRIGHAM

Taylor worked relentlessly during the week that followed and was unable to spend much time with Emma, so she used those days to visit with her aunt and to ponder the repercussions of everything that had been happening of late. As she lay on the rumpus room sofa one night after dinner, trying to concentrate on a new book she'd been anticipating for weeks, she realized she'd read the same page three times without knowing what it said. Dropping the book face down on her chest, Emma surrendered to her troubled thoughts.

How had so many aspects of her life become so utterly beyond her control lately? she wondered. The only truly good thing that had happened since she and Taylor had announced their decision to marry was the arrival of her aunt. Virginia, who ordinarily turned the Hammelmann household upside down when she visited, suddenly seemed to Emma like the one beacon of normality amid the storm-tossed ocean of insanity.

Emma lifted two fingers to pinch the bridge of her nose, wishing that just once, a plan she intended for the wedding would go the way it was supposed to. Perhaps she should talk to someone about all her misgivings where the wedding was concerned. In fact, a chat with her aunt—the one nonpartisan member of the wedding planning—might just help.

As if conjured up by Emma's thoughts, Virginia strode into the room with a glass of red wine in one hand and the current issue of *TV Guide* in the other.

"Oh, I'm sorry," she said when she saw Emma sprawled along the length of the sofa. "I didn't think anyone was in here. Championship wrestling is coming on. Billy 'the Bruiser' Bernicky is up against Ugly Poi tonight. . . . Should be a good match." When Emma continued to lie motionless with her arm thrown over her eyes, Virginia went on. "I was going to watch it in the living room, but Desiree has *La Traviata* on in there. I guess I could watch it upstairs in my room, it's just that the TV screen is much bigger in here. Stereo sound and all that."

Emma finally lifted her arm above her eyes and studied her aunt dubiously. "Championship wrestling? Billy 'the Bruiser' Bernicky? Ugly Poi? Just how long were you out in the sun down there in the Caribbean, Aunt Virginia?"

Virginia seemed embarrassed. "It's a guilty pleasure. All those big, sweaty men in tights . . . grunting and groaning . . . rolling around on the floor. What can I say? I'm as susceptible as the next woman."

Emma sat up on the couch and abandoned her book to the end table.

"What are you reading?" Virginia asked, craning her neck to see the title.

Emma lifted the book for her aunt's inspection. It was *Alison Brigham's Guide to Your Wedding*.

Virginia nodded and reached for the book to flip through it. "Alison Brigham . . . she's the one who does all those fancy-schmancy entertainment videos, isn't she?"

"That's the one."

"So you *do* actually care about this wedding you're planning after all."

Emma smiled. "Guilty as charged."

Virginia placed the book carefully back on the end table, then took a seat on the sofa beside her niece. "I suspected as much. You might pretend to be out of sorts about it, but you can't fool me."

Emma slumped back against the sofa. "I just don't know what to do, Aunt Virginia. Every time I turn around, Mom and Mrs. Rowan are looking over my shoulder, both of them contradicting each other and totally at odds with what I want."

"And just what is it that you want?"

Emma took a deep breath and studied her aunt closely. It had been so long since someone had actually asked her such a question that she had to think for a moment before she replied. "I just wanted the two of us to have a nice wedding, then for us to get on with our lives."

"Mm-hmm. Okay, that's a start." Virginia sipped her wine. "Maybe the two of you *should* elope."

Emma chuckled without mirth. "What, and miss what Mom assures me will be the greatest event of my life— except for the births of my children, of course."

"Is there *anything* about this wedding so far that you like?" Virginia asked.

Emma thought for a moment. "Well . . . I guess my wedding dress isn't *too* bad. It's got a little more frou-frou on it than I originally wanted, but it *is* a nice dress."

"Anything else?" Virginia prodded.

"I thought Mom's suggestion that the bridesmaids

walk in to the 'Promenade' from *Pictures at an Exhibition* was a nice touch."

Virginia nodded. "And?"

"And the tuxedos Mrs. Rowan recommended for the men are really very elegant."

"Anything else?"

Emma sighed impatiently. "The reception at the country club ought to be pretty nice. What's your point, Aunt Virginia?"

Her aunt lifted her hands palm up in a gesture of surrender. "No point, kiddo. I'm just thinking that maybe there's more bothering you right now than your impending nuptials, that's all."

Emma leaned her head back to stare unseeingly at the ceiling. "Since when have you been such a psychic?"

"It doesn't take ESP to see that you haven't been yourself lately." Virginia sipped her wine again. "You want me to fix you a drink?"

Emma nodded. "Scotch. Neat."

"See what I mean? You never used to drink the hard stuff."

Virginia went to the bar and then returned to the sofa with a drink for her niece. She had observed Emma consuming hard alcohol on exactly three other occasions: after Desiree had been in a rather serious car accident several years ago, when Laszlo had wound up in the hospital after going ten rounds with an EKG a few Christmases before, and when she'd discovered Taylor had gone out with another woman behind her back. On all three occasions, Emma had feared she was about to lose someone she loved above all else in the world. Virginia wondered exactly what—or who—her niece was afraid of losing now.

She narrowed her eyes suspiciously as Emma slugged back nearly half of the Scotch, and then asked, "You want to talk about it?"

Emma swirled the remainder of the liquor around in her glass and then reluctantly shook her head. "No. It's a little bit of everything, I guess. The stress of the wedding, not being able to find a job, Taylor talking about having kids right away, Max suddenly telling me he's madly in love with me and thinking I should marry him instead of Taylor—"

"*What?*"

Only at her aunt's gasp of surprise did Emma realize she'd spoken her thoughts aloud. She downed the rest of her drink in one gulp and set the glass atop her wedding book. "It's nothing," she assured Virginia as she rose to leave. "He'll get over it by the time the wedding rolls around." *I hope*, she added silently to herself.

Virginia started to speak again, but Emma cut her off.

"Just don't say anything to anyone about it, Aunt Virginia, okay?"

"Sure. Whatever you say, Emma. But, really, if you need to talk . . ."

Emma nodded. "Oh, I'm sure I will," she muttered as she turned to leave. "But it will probably wind up being to the men in the white coats."

She and Taylor never should have announced their intentions to marry, she decided once she was safely alone in her room, even though she knew she was far too late in making that particular observation. They should have just taken off for some romantic destination and tied the knot in secret. Then Emma's stomach wouldn't be tied in knots over the wedding she wasn't even sure she wanted to have anymore. And then maybe Max would have kept his stupid mouth shut.

Emma realized suddenly that Max's disturbing revelation of a month ago was what really bothered her most right now. His confession of love had been followed up by a number of telephone calls requesting that she meet him somewhere to talk. On each of those occasions Emma had insisted they had nothing to talk about, and then had promptly gone in search of Taylor to reassure herself and keep thoughts of Max at bay.

The few times she had run into Max at Taylor's apartment, she had done her best to ignore him and hustle her fiancé out to wherever they'd planned to go. Unfortunately, even thinking of how much she loved Taylor now didn't prevent Emma from remembering the way Max had made her feel at one time. She tried to tell herself she was being silly, blowing it all out of proportion—that night with Max two years ago and the single kiss they'd shared several weeks before. Unfortunately, Emma wasn't so certain that such was the case at all.

She went into the kitchen and opened the refrigerator, restlessly searching for something to eat even though she wasn't hungry. When she glanced away from the unappetizing contents in the fridge and saw the telephone on the wall beside it, her restlessness turned into a desire to get out of the house. Maybe Taylor was home and they could go to a movie. Maybe she just needed a little diversion from everything else. Yes, that was it. She would give Taylor a call.

However, deep down, as she punched the familiar phone number, she was hoping it would be Max who answered.

18

*As the bride, you will, for the most part, have
little contact with the best man. However, as a
matter of courtesy, try to make yourself available to him should he request direct assistance
from you. It would be the polite thing to do.*

—ALISON BRIGHAM

The *Artemisia Café* was just one of many eclec-
tic Georgetown watering holes sustained by the numerous Washington universities, this one frequented mostly
by literature and humanities students. On Saturday
evenings the proprietors served up poetry readings along
with pasta and Pinot Noir, Ferlinghetti being among the
most popular. At one point in the café's recent past,
someone had suggested the owners install a karaoke
machine—and now that individual was no longer welcome at the Artemisia. It was the kind of place Emma
Hammelmann loved but Taylor Rowan avoided at all
times. And that was precisely why Max had chosen the
café for this occasion.

When he'd picked up the phone the night before to
hear Emma's voice, he had hoped she was calling to talk to
him. But of course she'd asked for Taylor instead, and
when Max had told her he wasn't there, Emma had started

to say goodbye. Not one to let a good chance slip away, he'd quickly said her name and had been surprised and encouraged when she didn't hang up right away. With some fast talking and gentle coaxing, Max had finally convinced Emma to meet with him just so they could talk.

Now as he sat at a table in the back of the restaurant, running his thumb nervously up and down the side of his beer to erase the cool condensation collecting there, he wondered if she was really going to show up. She was already fifteen minutes late, and he was getting anxious. He had finished his first beer and ordered a second when he looked up to see her coming through the door.

The sun was beginning to set over the buildings across the street, its rays nearly blinding as they spilled through the windows of the Artemisia. Max could only see Emma's dark silhouette pause inside the door, and he wasn't sure whether she was looking for him or had seen him immediately but was reluctant to approach. She wore a thin, sleeveless dress of a color he could not distinguish, and the light shining through it contoured her body beautifully. Max licked his lips nervously and waited to see what she would do.

Slowly, Emma entered the café and let the door swing closed behind her. When she arrived a few feet away from his table, he stood up too fast, knocking his chair over as he did so. The clatter was jarring in the otherwise quiet room.

"Hi," he said, ignoring the sound.

"Hi," Emma replied softly.

"I wasn't sure you'd come."

"Neither was I."

"I'm glad you did."

"I'm not sure I am."

They gazed at each other for a long moment, each waiting to see what the other would do. Finally Emma pulled out the chair opposite Max's and sat down—right at the very edge of it, he noted, as if poised to flee at any moment. Max righted his own chair and sat as well. He remained silent while the waiter came to take Emma's order. At first she requested club soda, then as the waiter turned away, she seemed to quickly rethink her situation and asked for a glass of chardonnay instead. Only after her drink had been served did Max finally speak.

"We need to talk," he said.

Emma sipped her wine and nodded. "I'll say we do."

"Have you thought about all the things I said to you?"

Emma sighed. "I've barely been able to think about anything else."

"And?"

"Max, you've got to put this crazy idea about the two of us out of your head. Nothing good will come of it. I'm marrying Taylor. I *love* Taylor."

Max stared at her in disbelief. "You won't even give me a chance?"

"There's no point to it."

His eyes met hers. "You can honestly say you don't have any feelings for me."

Emma's gaze strayed away from Max's, and she focused on some point over his left shoulder. "Yes."

"Now look me in the eye and tell me that."

Her eyes met his again briefly before she looked down toward her glass of wine. Max slowly pushed his hand across the table to cover hers, gripping her fingers tightly when she tried to pull away.

"Emma?"

For a long time she couldn't respond. When she finally looked up at him again, her chin was trembling, and her eyes were about to overflow. As two fat tears tumbled down her cheeks, something inside of Max slowly began to unravel. She still cared about him, he realized. She did. There was no way she could deny it.

"If you don't think the two of us have a chance," he said softly, "then why did you agree to meet with me today? It was because you wanted to see me."

"No, it wasn't," Emma said. "It was because I wanted to set the record straight with you once and for all."

"Then why are you crying?"

Emma looked up and let out a ragged sob, then lifted her free hand to cover her eyes. Before she could stop herself, she began to cry in earnest. "Because all I wanted was to get married to Taylor and get on with my life with him. Now suddenly, my life isn't my own anymore. I'm doing things I never thought I would do, saying things I never thought I would say. . . . My mother wants one thing, Mrs. Rowan wants another, my aunt is telling me to elope, and now *you* . . . you're telling me I should leave Taylor altogether and be with you. And all *I* want—" Her words were halted by another strangled sob. "All I want, as if anyone cared anyway . . . God, at this point, all I want is to be left alone."

Max released Emma's hand and reached into his pocket for a handful of bills, dropping them onto the table without looking at them. "Come on," he said as he took her elbow and gently pulled her out of her chair, "we're getting out of here."

Once again, someone was telling her what to do, Emma thought. She might as well just surrender to Max's insistence, because by now she was simply too exhausted to argue. They left the Artemisia and entered the heavy pedestrian traffic on the sidewalk outside, Max running interference with Emma in tow. They didn't stop until they'd made it to Max's car, parked along a side street in front of a busy parking garage. He hustled Emma inside and started the engine, but instead of driving away, he simply switched on the air conditioner and turned in his seat to face her.

"Are you all right?" he asked.

Emma nodded, wiped at the last of the tears she had finally gotten under control, and mumbled, "Uh-huh."

"You're sure?"

"Yes."

This time Max was the one who sighed, running his big hands restlessly through his hair. "We're supposed to be talking, but I don't know what to say."

"Say you made a big mistake about thinking you were in love with me and that you'll leave me alone to try and survive the wedding on my own."

Max smiled at her choice of words. "Survive the wedding? Isn't that kind of an odd way to put it? Shouldn't you be enjoying the wedding?"

"Evidently, brides don't so much enjoy their weddings as they do . . . endure them."

Max's smile faded. "I won't say I made a mistake, Emma. I do love you. And I will do my best to win you back."

"Win me back?" she asked. "You never really had me, you know."

"Yes I did." Max reached across the seat and brushed back her bangs before cupping her jaw in his palm. "You were mine for a few hours once. All mine. Taylor wasn't with us at the motel that night—that was just you and me. The way it should be. The way it could be again, Emma, if you'll just give me one more chance."

He curved his hand over the back of her head and leaned forward, pulling her face toward his.

"God, you're so beautiful," he whispered. "So unbelievably beautiful. . . ."

This time when Max kissed her, there was none of the solicitude nor uncertainty of the first time. Now he made his intentions and desires quite clear. As he covered her mouth completely with his, trying to possess her with every caress, Emma could only go limp. She was tired of fighting people, tired of worrying about whether she was doing the right thing. She would be lying to them both if she said she was no longer attracted to Max, if she said didn't want to kiss him. Why shouldn't she steal a little pleasure for herself? She wasn't married to Taylor yet. And this would only take a moment.

But as Max continued to kiss her, pulling her from her seat in the car to settle her in his lap, Emma realized her pleasure was far outlasting a moment. Only when a group of teenagers passed the car with hoots and catcalls at their behavior did she finally realize how far she was about to allow things to go. Immediately she disentangled herself from Max's embrace and scrambled back into her seat, where she gasped for breath and groped for some semblance of coherent thought.

"I'm sorry," Max said. "I didn't mean for it to go that far. Not here. Not yet."

"That shouldn't have happened," Emma told him. "And it won't happen again."

"Emma," he said with a nervous laugh. He gripped the steering wheel tightly before shoving into first gear, then gazed at her once more before he pulled out slowly into the long line of cars constituting the late afternoon rush hour. "Don't you see? Of course it's going to happen again. And it'll keep happening, because we still have feelings for each other."

"Max . . ."

"Look, let's have some dinner, and then go someplace a little more private."

The way she felt right now, Emma knew the last thing she should do was find herself alone in some secluded rendezvous with Max Bennett. What she needed was to be by herself somewhere to sort out her thoughts and figure out what was going on. Oh, God, she thought as she dropped her head into her hands. What she needed was therapy.

"No, Max, I don't think so," she finally said.

"Emma, come on, we still need to talk."

"Look, just drop me off at the Foggy Bottom metro station and I'll find my way from there, okay?"

Max sighed in exasperation. "Emma . . ."

"And after that, Max, don't call me again unless you need to talk to me about the wedding, all right?"

"It's not going to go away just because we aren't together. Not even after you're married to Taylor. I want you, Emma. I love you. And like I told you before, I won't give up."

"You know, you talk like I'm some trophy for you to win away from Taylor."

"That's not what this is about and you know it."

Emma stared at Max for a long time, studying the hard line of his jaw and the fierce way he held onto the steering wheel. "Are you sure about that?"

He glanced over at her quickly, his eyes full of some emotion Emma couldn't quite name. "Of course I'm sure. How can you even ask that?"

How indeed? Emma thought. Max had said he loved her, several times. But why had he waited until now to tell her? And why couldn't she bring herself to believe him? Worst of all, why, dammit, did she find herself somehow wanting to think his declaration was true?

"Just take me to the metro," she said. "And I'll take it from there."

Emma was opening the passenger-side door before Max had even pulled to a stop near the busy entrance to the metro. But before she could extricate herself completely from the little car, he circled her wrist lightly with his fingers and tugged her back down.

"I'll see you Friday," he told her.

"Oh, no you won't."

"What, you're going to skip your own engagement party? I don't think Mr. and Mrs. Rowan will be too happy about that. They're going to a lot of trouble, you know."

Emma frowned. She had forgotten the party was this Friday night. "Forget about me, Max. I'll be with Taylor that night. And for all the nights to come after it."

"Not if I can help it," Max vowed as he released her.

Emma slammed the car door behind her, and Max watched her disappear down the escalator into the bowels of the Washington metro system. *Not if I can help it*, he repeated to himself.

19

Often, the groom's family will offer to throw the newly engaged couple a party in order to announce their impending nuptials. Such a party may take many forms, but all share one thing in common: They establish the bride and groom as a unified front for all to see and provide an opportunity for everyone involved in the wedding plans to get to know everyone else a little better. Oh, Alison does so love a party.

—ALISON BRIGHAM

More than two hundred years ago, Daniel Rowan, the very first Rowan to come to America, arrived with his wife, Marian, in Washington, D.C., to establish a private legal practice. These Rowans soon discovered, however, that city life did not appeal to them. So with the ample family fortune Daniel had brought with him to the New World, he built an expansive estate in what was then rural Alexandria. The huge Georgian mansion, listed in the national registry of historic homes, had remained in the family for seven generations, passed down through the eldest sons. It would someday pass to Taylor and Emma, and then to their eldest son. It was an instruction set down in Daniel Rowan's will two hundred years ago, a codicil that each recipient of the home had to agree to place in his own will in order to occupy the estate.

That must be the reason, Emma decided, why such houses were called *mansions* and *manors* and given names like *Manderley*. Now, as she approached the big house where her engagement party was no doubt already in full swing, seated beside her aunt in the back seat of her parents' car, she looked at the house as if seeing it for the first time. Ultimately, in the years to come, she would live in that house, surrounded by Rowan memorabilia and Rowan antiques. It was where she and Taylor would spend their golden years. By then their children would be grown and gone, and they would return home on holidays with the Rowan grandchildren.

It was strange for Emma to think of becoming a grandmother someday. Although Taylor had been talking less than he had before about starting a family right away, there was no doubt that the two of them would eventually have children. What would she be like as an old woman? Emma wondered. What would Taylor be like as an old man? She tried to envision herself and Taylor in the roles of Francesca and Lionel Rowan, but no matter how hard she concentrated she was unable to imagine them as anything other than the twenty-something couple they were right now.

What would they be like as they aged? she wondered. How would their attitudes change over the years? Would they be able to meet all their goals? Would they still love each other after fifty years of marriage? Or would they wind up like the elder Rowans—distant and civilly unloving?

Emma decided she hoped Taylor wouldn't fall prey to his ancestor's archaic dictates but rather would refuse the terms of the will where the house was concerned. Who knew when the last loving couple had occupied it? Let some other unsuspecting Rowan have it. It was kind of a scary house anyway, and it was probably haunted—if not by conventional ghosts, then certainly by hundreds of years of conservative behavior and outdated tradition. It wasn't exactly the type of environment in which Emma wanted to raise children. She tried not to think about the fact that her future husband was a result of just such an upbringing.

"Wow," Virginia whispered under her breath beside Emma as they drew nearer the floodlighted brick wonder. "Nice digs. I knew you were marrying into money, kiddo, but *this* . . ." She thought for a moment before asking, "Will all this come to Taylor after his old man buys the farm, or will you have to squabble with a bunch of malcontent relations for dibs?"

"Virginia!" Desiree exclaimed from the front seat, mortified by the question. "What a terrible thing to ask."

"Oh, come on, Desi, you can't tell me you haven't wondered the same thing yourself a time or two."

"Well, I would never talk about it, that's for sure," Desiree said. "Especially in front of Emma."

"Yes, all this is supposed to come to Taylor eventually," Emma told her aunt and mother. "If he doesn't want it, someone else in the family gets it. I'm not sure of the particulars."

"Why wouldn't Taylor want it?" Virginia asked.

"I don't know. It's kind of a relic. Taylor and I have much more contemporary tastes."

Virginia wanted to ask more but decided her niece's lack of enthusiasm was a result of more than her decorating tastes. Instead she leaned back in her seat and marveled at the life-style Emma was about to enter.

Living the way she had over the past few decades, Virginia had enjoyed a number of experiences on the fringe of opulence and old money, but she'd never been thrust into the center of things as she was about to be at the party tonight. To put it simply, although she'd often *worked* in various capacities at swanky functions, Virginia had never been a *guest* at one. It could turn out to be an interesting evening.

As if Desiree had heard Virginia speak her final thought out loud, she turned around in the front seat and said, "Virginia, don't do anything to embarrass us tonight."

Virginia adopted her best *who-me?* expression. "Embarrass you guys? Me? What have I ever done to embarrass you?"

Laszlo glanced in the rearview mirror as he made the final turn around the fountain gushing in front of the Rowan home. "Well, there was that Christmas dinner I threw for my suppliers where you jumped out of the cake wearing a red and green bikini with jingle bells—"

"Oh, come on, Laszlo," Virginia chided her brother. "That was more than twenty years ago. And besides, you said your suppliers gave you some great deals after that, remember?"

"That's beside the point," Laszlo grumbled.

"And the Fourth of July, at George and Ruthie Milton's anniversary party in Florida?" Desiree added. "You gave new meaning to the song *Moon over Miami*."

Emma laughed. "Oh, Aunt Virginia . . . you didn't!"

Virginia had the decency to look sheepish. "It was the mid-seventies," she said. "Everyone was doing it."

"Not in church parking lots, they weren't," Desiree chided.

"That was a long time ago," Virginia pointed out. "I've mellowed since then."

Laszlo made a derisive noise as he pulled the car to a stop behind a number of others, and left the key in the ignition for the valet.

Inside, the Rowan house was buzzing with people, most of whom were strangers to Emma. She occasionally glimpsed one or two familiar faces who were friends of Taylor's, and of course there were the Rowans themselves. She was thankful when Taylor emerged from the crowd and approached them, kissing her softly on the cheek in greeting. Behind him, she saw Max watching them with a wistful expression before he ducked out of the room.

"Laszlo, Desiree," Taylor said as he shook his future father-in-law's hand and embraced his future mother-in-law. "And Virginia," he said as he extended his hand toward her. "I'm sorry I haven't been able to see you sooner. . . . I've been very busy at work this month. I can't believe two years have passed since the last time I saw you. Emma's been keeping me apprised of all your recent adventures, though."

Virginia smiled and took his hand, shaking it robustly before pulling him forward for a quick hug. "All of it heinous lies and vicious rumor, I'm sure."

Taylor eyed her curiously. "You know, there's something I've always wanted to ask you about."

"Shoot."

"Were you really working at the Watergate the night of the break-in?"

Virginia laughed. "Look, I explained all that business about the broom closet and the janitor to the Feds. They were perfectly satisfied that I was in no way implicated. I was a registered Democrat, for God's sake."

Taylor nodded.

"Anyway, congratulations and best wishes to the both of you on your impending nuptials," Virginia went on. She put her arm around Emma's shoulders. "Be nice to this woman or I'll cut your heart out. She's the best there is."

Taylor gazed at Emma for a long moment before he responded quietly, "I know."

Emma tucked her arm through his and reached for Virginia's hand. "Come on, Aunt Virginia, I want to introduce you to the rest of Taylor's family."

The trio found Francesca and Lionel quickly enough in the living room amid a group of well-dressed, professionally coiffed, expertly manicured men and women whom Taylor's father introduced as "members of the club." In the kitchen, they located Taylor's younger sister, Adrienne, helping the hired waiters fill glasses with champagne. Taylor's other sister, Catherine, was complaining about having to help Francesca with the hosting responsibilities, rushing from room to room to make certain everyone else was having a good time, even if she was unable to enjoy the evening herself. Apparently Michael was in one of the guest rooms watching a baseball game with some of Taylor's friends. Emma decided not to bother looking for him. Virginia wouldn't like him anyway.

For the most part, Virginia found the Rowans to be rather a stiff bunch of people, far too formal and stuffy for her tastes. She couldn't help but wonder if Emma would be truly happy in their midst. Of course, her niece wouldn't be marrying Taylor's entire family, but still, she wouldn't be able to disassociate herself from them completely.

Inevitably, as Virginia wandered through the Rowan house admiring everything in sight, she found herself drawn to one of the many bars, this one set up in a large room with big windows. When the bartender handed her the drink she requested, Virginia gazed at it blandly for a moment before sampling it. She bet the Rowans would be just the kind of people to throw a really swanky party at their gorgeous digs and pour cheap liquor to cut the cost. However, upon tasting her Scotch, Virginia's experienced palate told her she was drinking a rather expensive single malt, and her estimation of Emma's future in-laws rose a notch. Before she could taste her drink again, however, she was sidetracked by a man who joined her at the bar.

"Hi," he said, giving her a smile she could only call smarmy. "I'm Guy. Just Guy," he continued. For some reason, he made Virginia's palms feel greasy. "I'm an associate of Lionel's. Can I buy you a drink? A car? A house? Anything?"

Virginia smiled back at what she was sure he thought was a very droll line, lifted her full glass up for his inspection, and replied, "Thanks, Guy-just-Guy, but I already have a drink."

"Then maybe we could get in my car and go to my house."

Virginia sipped her drink again, pretending to consider his offer. "Gosh, thanks, but I really should get home soon. The doctor's supposed to call with my HIV test results tonight. I'm *pretty* sure they'll be negative. Maybe we could get together some other time?"

She could tell Guy wasn't quite certain whether she was being honest or not, but he apparently decided to take the safe route. "Yeah, maybe," he said as he began to back away. "Some other time."

Virginia wrinkled her nose at him flirtatiously, wiggled her fingers in farewell, and wandered into the next room, which she immediately identified as the library. It was a cozy, quiet room, making her feel at home right away. Inhaling deeply, she detected the faint, sweet aroma of old paper, a hint of last winter's burnt wood from the fireplace, and a softly lingering fragrance it took her a moment to identify as pipe tobacco. She leaned back and closed the thick, solid door behind her. The Rowan party had not yet breached the perimeter of this room, which made Virginia like it even more.

She carried her drink to the nearest chair, a leather Queen Anne, and was just about to heave herself into it when she realized it was already occupied.

"Hello," the man said as he looked up from a huge tome settled comfortably in his lap.

"Uh . . . hi," Virginia replied. "I . . . uh . . . I'm sorry. I thought the room was empty. I wasn't planning on throwing myself into your lap, honest."

The man was older than she was, dressed in a brown suit that was nowhere near in style, a striped bow tie, and loafers. He had thinning gray hair, a meticulously trimmed moustache, and the most beautiful blue eyes Virginia had ever seen. For a moment, she couldn't look away, but stared into his eyes as if she'd gotten lost in them. And then he smiled at her, a gesture that made his eyes seem even larger and more expressive.

"It's all right," he said. "I only came in here to escape the noise outside. I generally avoid Francesca's parties, but Taylor is my favorite nephew—in fact, he's my only nephew—and I didn't want him to think I was slighting him by not attending."

What a voice, Virginia thought, completely oblivious to what the man had just said because she was so busy being captivated by the way he had said it. His voice was like the cognac he cradled in the palm of his hand—dark and mellow, warm and intoxicating. She suddenly found herself wondering what his hands would feel like on her skin.

"Uh . . ." she began again. She moved away to sit in the chair opposite his, hoping that by putting a little distance between herself and the man, she might also unscramble her brain waves.

"Are you a friend of the bride or a friend of the groom?" he asked.

"The bride," Virginia told him, admiring her quick recovery of her vocabulary. "I'm the bride's aunt, Virginia Hammelmann."

"Eliot Browne," he said, closing his book to place it on the side table between them.

Eliot rose and approached Virginia to enclose her hand in his. His grip was firm, but his hand was soft. She wondered if he was a lawyer, as all the men in Taylor's family seemed to be. After a perfunctory shake of her hand, he backed up to reseat himself, in the process tugging on Virginia's fingers because she hadn't yet released his. An awkward moment passed before she realized what she was doing. It was only when Eliot tugged on her hand again that Virginia realized her transgression. Immediately, she jerked her hand away, an action that caused Eliot to take an unsteady step backward. Virginia laughed nervously as Eliot retreated to his chair, and he smiled.

"We seem to be a bit out of sync," he said.

"Story of my life."

"So you're Emma's aunt."

Virginia nodded. "One of several. But she likes me best."

Eliot grinned. "I don't doubt it for a moment."

He took in the woman seated across from him, from the dark gold curls tumbling past her shoulders to the boxy blazer and baggy trousers she wore. She could have been one of his postgrad students in the English department at GW, he thought. But then again, perhaps not. Surely this woman would choose as her topic of study a twentieth-century writer like Flannery O'Connor or Anaïs Nin. She would probably run screaming in horror from medieval studies, particularly Middle English literature, his own private passion.

"And you're Taylor's uncle," she said. "But your last name is Browne, so you must be Francesca's brother."

"Brother-in-law, actually," Eliot corrected her. "I was married to Francesca's sister, Sarah."

"Was?" Virginia asked, hoping her sudden, rather intense interest in this man wasn't *too* obvious.

"My wife passed away three years ago."

"Oh, I'm so sorry."

"Thank you. As am I."

Virginia didn't know what else to say. Finally, she continued with the first thing that came into her head. "It's nice, isn't it, to see the kids getting married. Do you have any children?"

Eliot nodded and sipped his cognac. "Two children, and two grandchildren."

Virginia was surprised. "You can't possibly be a grandfather. You're far too young." He probably wasn't much older than she was, and she was certainly too young to be a grandmother. Which of course she would never be, since she had no children.

But some of her nieces and nephews had children, she realized, and that made her a great-aunt. But she was only forty-eight, Virginia tried to reassure herself. She didn't want to be a great anything. Except maybe a great pool player.

"And you are much too kind," Eliot replied. "I have two grandsons—twins—Graham and Bryan. They're five years old. Would you . . ." He paused a moment, wondering if he would sound too awfully boastful—like the proud grandfather he knew himself to be. "Would you care to see a picture?"

At that moment, Virginia decided Eliot Browne had to be the cutest man she had ever met. A grandfather, she marveled. She didn't think she'd ever been attracted to a grandfather before. Yet here was a man who had captivated her from the moment their eyes had met. And he was a grandfather. Imagine that.

"I'd love to see a picture," she said.

Eliot reached into his jacket pocket and retrieved his wallet, unfolding it for Virginia's inspection. Realizing she was too far away for him to hold it out for her, he rose from his chair and went to stand beside hers, placing the wallet carefully in her hand.

"This is Bryan on the left," he said, "and Graham is on the right."

"They're fraternal twins," Virginia remarked, noting the vast differences in the two boys' appearances. "Graham looks quite a bit like you."

"Yes, he takes after his father—my son, Spenser, resembles me. Bryan takes after his mother's side of the family."

"They're both very handsome."

"Yes, they are, aren't they?"

Eliot was leaning over Virginia's left shoulder, and she realized it was he, and not the library, who smelled faintly of pipe tobacco. It was a nice aroma, she decided, sweet and spicy and somehow reminiscent of a winter's day. All of a sudden, she wanted to get to know Eliot Browne a little better.

Virginia didn't realize she was having a similar effect on Eliot. Much to his surprise, as he stood over her, he actually found himself gazing down into Virginia Hammelmann's blouse. He was shocked at himself. He'd never been one for salacious leering, but suddenly Eliot Browne, professor of Middle English literature and expert on Chaucer, was fascinated by the wisp of sapphire blue lace that lay mere inches below Virginia's shirt collar. And her perfume . . . Whatever it was, it made Eliot think of New Orleans and saxophones on a hot summer night. It was odd, really. His appreciation for jazz was quite limited. He generally enjoyed a good Gregorian chant or perhaps a nice Renaissance piece.

"Do you have any plans for the rest of the evening?" he heard himself ask Virginia, uncertain when he'd chosen to speak.

She signed a little unevenly before responding, "Not a one."

"Would you . . . would you care to go out for a cup of coffee or something?"

"I'd love to."

20

There will be times when members of the wedding party do not necessarily see eye to eye on what you as the bride have decided. Avoid ripples of resentment by delegating responsibilities and activities. You are the bride. And there is absolutely no reason why you can't have things exactly the way you want them to be.

—ALISON BRIGHAM

It took *Virginia* only a few moments to find Emma and inform her of the evening's new developments. Trying to be as evasive as possible, she revealed to her niece only that she would be leaving the party early and had arranged a ride home, so Emma and her parents shouldn't worry about her. Also, she said as she tried to beat a hasty retreat, they shouldn't wait up for her.

"Hold on there, Babalooie," Emma said as she curled her fingers around Virginia's upper arm to halt her aunt's escape. "What's his name?"

Virginia tried to affect a puzzled expression. "What's whose name?"

"The guy you're leaving with. He isn't a Rowan, is he, Aunt Virginia? Just tell me he isn't a Rowan. With two of us infiltrating the family, it could be mass chaos."

Virginia sighed and wove her fingers together nervously. "Well, he isn't a Rowan *exactly*."

"His name?"

"Eliot. Eliot Browne."

Emma's mouth dropped open in astonishment. "Uncle Brownie? You're leaving with Taylor's Uncle Brownie?"

Virginia looked at her niece blankly. "Brownie? He told me his name was Eliot. He actually allows people to call him 'Brownie?'"

Emma nodded, regarding her aunt thoughtfully. "Are you sure you know what you're doing?" she asked. "I mean, do you know what kind of person Brownie is? Do you know what he does for a living?"

"He teaches at George Washington University," Virginia answered, proud she could offer some scrap of information about the man she had just met minutes ago. Normally she knew very little at this stage of the game.

"Do you know what he teaches?"

"English."

"Medieval studies," Emma said. "With an emphasis on Middle English literature. That's the big snore in literary circles."

"Yes, well . . . literature isn't exactly what we have on our minds right now." Virginia turned to leave.

"Aunt Virginia . . ." There was a note of caution in Emma's voice.

Virginia made a face at her. "I only meant that we have other things to talk about. Over coffee." Then she feigned shock. "Why, Emma! I'm appalled at you. Whatever could you think I was talking about?"

"He's widowed, you know."

Virginia sobered, suddenly feeling defensive for some reason. "I know."

Emma continued to gaze at her aunt, marveling that of all the eligible men at this function, Virginia had managed to lock onto the one who was without question least suited to her way of thinking and philosophy of living.

"What's wrong?" Virginia asked her.

"I'm just trying to picture the two of you together."

Virginia grinned. "How do we look?"

"Oddly enough . . . not too bad," Emma heard herself say, and was surprised to realize it was true.

Virginia kissed her niece hastily on the cheek. "Like I said, kiddo . . . don't wait up."

"Have fun."

Emma followed her aunt out to the hallway where she saw Taylor's Uncle Brownie waiting by the front door. He angled an arm casually around Virginia's waist and opened the door, gesturing that she should precede him, then followed her out into the night.

Emma was about to turn when she caught sight of her brother Vick and Taylor's sister Catherine completely caught up in some seemingly fascinating conversation. When Catherine threw her head back to laugh at something Vick had said, Emma saw her brother lean forward, as if to sniff Catherine's neck for a hint of her perfume. Emma could only shake her head in disbelief, wondering what kind of madness must be overtaking them all.

"Emma," a voice whispered from behind.

Emma turned to find Patsy scanning the crowd furtively.

"I haven't seen much of you tonight," Emma told her cousin.

"I've been shamelessly scoping out the groomsmen," Patsy said. "You know, with one or two exceptions, Taylor has a very nice-looking family. You guys should have pretty cute kids."

"That's a long way off."

"Did you, uh . . ." Patsy glanced down at her watch to affect an uninterested pose. "Did you notice that Max Bennett is here?"

At her cousin's offhand comment, Emma's heart

began to race wildly. Just the mention of his name had her jumping, she realized unhappily. She had to stop fretting over Max. "I think I saw him once or twice," she said, pleased that her voice reflected none of the turmoil she was feeling. "Why?"

Patsy tugged nonchalantly at the top of a strapless sundress that was far too tight for her, then casually tangled her fingers behind her back. "Oh . . . you know . . . I just thought maybe it was time the maid of honor and best man got something going, that's all."

"Got something going?"

"With the wedding preparations, I mean," Patsy quickly clarified. "You know."

"So why are you telling me?"

A waiter passed them balancing a tray laden with drinks, and Patsy snaked out a hand to grab one. She took a long gulp, grimaced, gasped, and then coughed a couple of times. "Oh, jeez, I hate gin. It gives me terrible hangovers." She placed the glass gingerly on a side table. "So much for false courage."

"Patsy . . ."

When Patsy began to cough again, Emma patted her gently on the back. Her cousin had a bad habit of bringing up the subject of her tryst with Max every now and then, and Emma had a feeling this was about to be one of those times. Then a new thought struck her, and she froze.

If she'd told Patsy about her experience with Max, what was there to have kept Max from telling one of his friends about it? Worse than that, what if, in an effort to "win her back" now, Max threatened to spill his guts to Taylor sometime before the wedding? Emma's head began to pound when she considered the possibility.

With one final cough, Patsy cleared her lungs and regained her voice. "So I thought maybe you could tell me a little more about Max before I make a fool of myself. I mean, hey, you've known him intimately, after all."

Emma cringed and glanced around nervously. "Will you keep your voice down?"

"Sorry."

"What did you want to know?"

"I want to know whether or not he has a serious girl-friend right now."

"I . . . I don't think so, Patsy. I mean, there's no one I can think of who's . . . who's *serious* with Max right now. Not that I know of, anyway."

"And you, uh, you wouldn't mind if I made a play for him?"

"Why would I mind?"

"Well, the two of you were . . . you know . . . after all."

Emma sighed impatiently and glared at her cousin. "Patsy, as I've told you a million times, that only happened once, and it was two years ago, and I never cared that deeply for Max to begin with."

"So you don't mind?"

"I don't mind." It might even get him off my back, Emma added to herself.

Patsy beamed. "Great. Wish me luck."

"With you, Patsy, he doesn't stand a chance."

Patsy squeezed her cousin's arm in excitement, and Emma leaned back against the stairwell and sighed. The wedding was becoming more and more like a Molière farce. Then she turned to see Taylor approaching her with Max right behind him and amended her literary allusion. No, not a Molière farce. More like an Orwellian nightmare.

"Or something out of Kafka," she said under her breath.

"What?" Patsy asked.

"Nothing," Emma mumbled, focusing her attention on the two men. "Now what?"

"Max and I are going on a beer run," Taylor said when he was within speaking distance.

"A beer run?" Emma asked. "Your mom hired a caterer who ran out of beer?"

Taylor grinned, and Emma detected a certain note of pride in his voice as he said, "I'll have you know my mother and father arranged this party for us all by themselves."

Emma was impressed. "No kidding."

"Hence the fact that we're almost out of beer."

Max grinned too. "Yeah, Mrs. Rowan thinks that just because Taylor's friends have all graduated and are respectable esquires now, we've stopped drinking beer and started imbibing martinis. She can't fathom the concept of white-collar workers consuming blue-collar brew."

"Do you want to come with us?" Taylor asked.

"I'll come," Patsy said, her eyes raking over Max's body as if he were a fish to fry.

Emma shook her head. "Probably one of us should stay here, Taylor, since it's a party in our honor. So I won't go."

"Well, then I'll stay here and keep Emma company," Max offered.

Emma scowled at him. "No, that's all right, Max, you go ahead. In fact, why don't you and Patsy go so that Taylor and I can both stay here?"

She saw Patsy nod vigorously at her suggestion, but Taylor was quick to cancel the plan.

"Max didn't bring his car," he told them. "He came with me. Look, it's no big deal. Patsy and I can go. Right, Pats?"

"Yeah, okay," Patsy muttered. "I guess so."

"We won't be long," Taylor added, jingling his car keys. "Be back before you know it."

Emma watched helplessly as her fiancé and her best friend left, abandoning her to the clutches of Max Bennett. Despite the house full of people, she somehow felt as if she'd never been more alone in her life. As Taylor and Patsy disappeared through the front door, Emma whirled around again, glowering at Max.

"You did that on purpose," she snapped.

Max looked at her as if he had no idea what she was talking about. "Did what? Drank every beer in the house just so I could contrive some excuse to be alone with you? Hey, Emma, I like beer as much as the next guy, but come on."

"You know exactly what I mean, Max, and we are *not* alone," she told him, looking over her shoulder anxiously, as if to reassure herself. "There are a lot of people around, so don't try anything funny."

Max leaned forward, his voice cool and coaxing as he spoke. "Emma, you can rest easy knowing that whatever I might try with you—and whatever you might allow me to get away with—would be anything but funny. Erotic, probably, arousing, definitely, but certainly not funny."

She blew out an impatient breath that stirred her bangs, falling back against the stairwell. "You've got to stop this," she said.

Max leaned forward even more to rest his bent arm above her head, bringing his body into closer contact with hers as he did so. "Stop what?"

Emma's eyes widened at the feel of him so close to her, and she quickly pushed him away. "This," she whispered crossly. "This . . . this familiarity you keep trying to maintain. What if someone saw us like this?"

"What if someone did?"

"They might get the wrong impression about us."

"Or they might get the right one."

"Max, don't start, please."

He settled his hands on his hips and stared down at her for a long time without speaking. She could tell by the way the muscles in his throat worked above his loosened necktie and open collar that he was agitated. She didn't think she had ever seen Max dressed in a suit before. His clothing tonight was so similar to what she normally saw on Taylor that it made her feel somewhat uncomfortable. As long as the two men were separate entities in every way it was easier for her to keep her troubled feelings in check. But now suddenly everything felt jumbled up and confused. She wasn't sure what she was feeling.

"You know, we never did have that confidential little chat we were supposed to have," Max told her as he reached out a hand to brush at a nonexistent piece of lint on her shirt above her right breast.

Emma flinched at Max's light touch. "That's because there's nothing confidential we need to chat about," she said, feebly brushing his hand away.

His eyes met hers as he lifted the hand she had pushed away and gently thumbed back a stray lock of her hair. "Oh, no? Then why did you agree to meet me at the Artemisia? It was because you wanted to see me, wasn't it? Because you knew as well as I did that we needed to talk."

Emma had intended to shake her head and assure Max quite adamantly that there was absolutely nothing the two of them needed to discuss in private. Unfortunately, all she was able to manage was a single turn of her head toward the stairwell, a gesture that resulted in her cheek's being cupped in Max's palm, and that also resulted in her gazing up the stairs. Gazing up the stairs to find her future mother-in-law gazing back down at her.

It suddenly occurred to Emma how compromising her position with Max must seem, but she was too startled to do anything but stare back at Taylor's mother. Out of the corner of her eye, she saw Max look up to discover the presence of Mrs. Rowan too, and for just an instant the three of them seemed frozen irrevocably in time. Then Emma felt him seize her wrist with uncompromising fingers and pull her away from the stairwell. She allowed herself to be led through the Rowan house in what seemed like an endless maze, as she was too caught up in worry and confusion about what Mrs. Rowan might or might not think to wonder where Max was taking her.

Only when it came to her attention that the two of them had come to a breathless halt, with Max towering over her and holding her close, did Emma stop to assess her situation. She decided almost immediately that it wasn't good.

They were in the pantry, and quite alone. There was no light in the tiny room save the L-shaped line of white creeping in where the door remained slightly ajar, scarcely enough to make out indefinite shapes of canned goods and bottled condiments. The air smelled faintly of garlic and Tabasco, and before Emma realized what was happening, Max was cradling her breast with one hand as he pulled her collar aside with the other to kiss her neck.

"Max, stop it," she whispered.

"No," he whispered back.

He pressed himself against her more insistently, forcing Emma back against a row of shelves that dug painfully into her back. Instinctively, she pushed herself forward, an action that served only to drive her more fully into Max's embrace. Interpreting her gesture as one of surrender, Max pulled her close and began to kiss her in earnest.

It was a magnificent kiss. Even though Emma knew it was crazy and improper to allow him such a liberty, she just couldn't quite make herself tell him to stop. Nor could she quite keep herself from kissing him back. Max was a forbidden fruit—tempting, luscious, offering her physical delights unlike any she'd ever experienced with Taylor. That one night she'd spent with Max had been the most erotic adventure Emma had ever had the pleasure to undertake. He had been a phenomenal lover, and now he was offering her the chance to repeat that night. Max wanted her. And, God help her, Emma had to admit that a part of her still wanted Max.

As their embrace grew more heated, went further past

the boundaries Emma knew were falling fast, Max covered her hand with his and pushed it down to the buckle of his belt. When she uttered a hesitant sound, he kissed her more deeply, then dipped their hands lower, rubbing their fingers roughly over the hard ridge of flesh that strained against the zipper of his pants. For one wild moment, Emma allowed the caresses to continue, then she jerked her hand away.

"Stop it," she gasped. "Max, we have to stop it."

He looked down at her, his breathing heavy and irregular in the darkness, yet he continued to hold her loosely in his arms, which still prevented her from bolting through the pantry door, as her instincts commanded her. Even without the benefit of light, Emma could tell he was angry.

"Why?" he demanded.

An awkward moment passed while Emma tried to gather herself enough to sound effective when she spoke. "Because I'm marrying Taylor," she said finally. "I love Taylor."

Max laughed softly, without humor. "That's starting to sound like a litany, Emma. You keep saying how much you love Taylor, yet here you are, groping me in a dark closet at your fiancé's parents' house."

Emma slapped him. Even as she was doing it, she knew she was reacting like some outraged starlet in a bad melodrama, but she didn't know what else to do. Max's hand went up to cover his cheek, but he smiled.

"Touched a nerve, did I?" he asked.

Emma looked pointedly at the hand that was still curved over her breast. "You've touched a lot more than a nerve, Max," she muttered through gritted teeth. "And I'd appreciate it if you'd let me go."

Instead of heeding her request, Max pulled her close again. Emma began to push him away, but at the sound of voices in the kitchen, Max pulled back of his own accord. One of the voices was Taylor's. The other was

Patsy's. Their words were unintelligible, but Taylor said something that made Patsy laugh.

That sound was followed by footsteps approaching the pantry, then by the creak of hinges as the pantry door slowly began to open. As the thin line of white light outside began to grow wider, Emma's heart began to pound more fiercely. She pushed Max to the other side of the pantry, waiting to get caught in a compromising position she hadn't even been instrumental in creating.

Then as suddenly as the door had begun to open, it fell closed again.

"Nuts," Emma heard Patsy say on the other side. "I just remembered I left my purse in the car. Taylor, you're going to have to put these pretzels and stuff away."

Emma swallowed hard. Oh, great.

"Just leave it on the counter," she heard Taylor's voice clearly. "We're going to be using it before the end of the night, anyway. Let's get back to the party. I need to see how Emma's holding up."

Emma sighed as Taylor and Patsy left the kitchen, then flattened her palm against the pantry door to let herself out. But Max covered her hand with his, twining his fingers with hers to keep her from leaving.

She turned to face him one final time. "For the last time, Max, leave me alone. It's bad enough that you probably have Mrs. Rowan thinking there's something going on between the two of us on the sly. If she didn't already think the worst of me, I'd try to explain to her that there's nothing between me and you." Emma's voice dropped along with her gaze as she added, "But she probably wouldn't believe me. She'd probably misconstrue my effort to explain as an admission of guilt."

"Sounds to me like you're already feeling guilty," Max said, curling his fingers around the back of her neck. "Guilty because I still turn you on," he whispered near her ear. "Guilty because you still want me . . . because you still have feelings for me."

"I don't have feelings for you," she insisted, pulling away from him once again. "Except maybe feelings of total confusion." She started to push the door open again, but Max stopped her.

"Emma, wait."

She stared at him sullenly but didn't make an effort to leave.

"You have a decision to make," he said softly. "Me or Taylor. Who's it going to be?"

Emma sighed in frustration, lifted her hand as if to make a point, then dropped it futilely to her side. "I've already made my decision."

Max curled his finger under her chin and tipped her head back so that she would meet his gaze in the dim light. "Have you?"

"Of course I have."

"Then who's it going to be?"

Instead of answering his question, Emma pulled her chin out of his grasp, pushed open the pantry door, and walked away. She kept on walking until she was safely back among the crowd of well-wishers who were attending the party tonight to celebrate her engagement to Taylor. Taylor, she said to herself firmly. It was Taylor she loved, and Taylor to whom she owed an obligation. Not Max. Emma helped herself to a glass of wine from a passing waiter, took a hefty sip, and then planted herself firmly on the sofa in the living room. The moment Taylor made an appearance, she would affix herself to her fiancé for the rest of the evening. With any luck at all, Patsy would make good on her promise to go after Max, and then Emma knew Max would have more than enough to keep him occupied for the remainder of her nuptial celebration.

Occupied? Emma thought. Hell, once Patsy got through with him, Max would be lucky if he made it to the wedding at all.

21

Anyone who has ever been married can tell you that the journey upon which you and your groom are about to embark is not only the ultimate act of commitment, but also the ultimate act of faith. To place oneself in the care and keeping of another is to risk one's very soul. Yet it is this supreme trust that will keep you and your groom so very much in love. Never take such trust for granted. And never consider it anything less than omnipotent.

—ALISON BRIGHAM

"*So then the martian* says to the bartender, 'Oh, yeah? Well, neither was the mailman, but he was delicious!'"

Desiree chuckled at the punch line of Laszlo's standard party joke, even though she'd heard it a hundred times over the last forty-odd years. It was a timeless story that still brought laughs, and tonight was no exception. Even Lionel managed to crack a smile. Only Francesca seemed not to have enjoyed it, Desiree noted as she watched the woman sip a martini on the other side of the room. But then that was no big surprise, was it?

The Rowans' friends seemed like nice enough people, Desiree thought as she studied the guests once again.

One or two of them carried that same bad-smell expression that Francesca had raised to an art form, but for the most part they were okay. That Celia Davenport was a real talker, though. Country club this and country club that. Desiree had hardly been able to shut her up long enough to get a word in edgewise.

"My goodness, Desiree," Celia began again when the laughter had died down. "That husband of yours is certainly amusing. And what a charmer."

Desiree smiled. "Yeah. Laszlo's one of a kind, all right. He's a member of that dying breed—decent guys. You don't find too many of them anymore."

Celia nodded. "So true, I'm afraid. So true."

"Excuse me, for a minute, Celia, will you?" Desiree asked suddenly. "I just now remembered something I need to ask Francesca about the wedding."

"Certainly. I'll stay here and see if I can't coax your husband into telling us another one of his delightful stories."

"He's got a million of 'em. Don't get him started or we'll be here all night. I've always said my husband could have been a real comedian if he wanted. He's always been ten times funnier than Alan King or Ernie Kovacs or any of those guys."

As she crossed the room to where Francesca had tucked herself modestly into the corner of the love seat, Desiree heard Laszlo begin another joke, the one about the three-legged dog who came to town looking for the man who shot his Paw.

"Great party, Francesca," she said as she sat down onto the tiny sofa beside her hostess.

Francesca looked up quickly, feeling a little fuzzy-headed and surprised to discover she was no longer alone. "Oh. Thank you, Desiree. Yes, it is going nicely, isn't it?"

"Everyone seems to be having a good time. It was nice of you and Lionel to do this for the kids."

Francesca shrugged. "Lionel and I should have done something like this for Emma and Taylor a long time ago. It's just that both of us have been so busy lately."

She took another swallow of her drink and tugged at the hem of her skirt, unable to prevent her gaze from wandering toward her husband. Lionel had been playing the role of lord of the manor to the hilt tonight, she thought, chatting amiably with everyone in attendance. To his left was Laszlo, telling yet another joke, and to his right was a young, auburn-haired woman Francesca didn't recognize as anyone from the long list of guests to whom she'd sent out invitations. Evidently her husband knew the woman well, however, because he hadn't left her side all night.

"Well, Lionel's been busy, anyway," Francesca amended quickly. There was a touch of resentment in her voice. "Of course it isn't just lately that Lionel's been busy. He's been busy for the last thirty years of our marriage." She punctuated this statement with another hefty swallow of her drink, then became somewhat irritated to discover her glass was empty.

Desiree watched Francesca carefully, wondering how many martinis the other woman had tossed back so far tonight. "Francesca," she began, rattling the swizzle stick around in her amaretto sour, "you know, maybe it's none of my business . . . but we are going to be sort of related soon and everything . . . well, what I mean is . . ." She tried to sound casual as she asked, "Is everything okay? Between you and Lionel, I mean?"

When Francesca turned her attention from the empty glass in her hand to Desiree, it was with what she hoped was a veiled expression. Then, closing her eyes, she lifted a hand to her temple and rubbed furiously. God, her head was throbbing. Just what kind of talk had Desiree heard about her and Lionel? she wondered. And how could Desiree have heard that talk unless the source had been some bigmouth from the club? And if it was someone from the club, then that meant the talk was going on right now inside Francesca's own home by people who were enjoying her hospitality. Those predators, she thought bitterly. They circled like vultures, waiting for misfortune to befall someone else, hoping the suffering of others might alleviate some of the misery they felt themselves.

Francesca opened her eyes. Goodness, that was dramatic thinking. She rather liked that.

"You've been talking to Celia, I see," she said.

Desiree looked confused. "Well, yeah, but not about you and Lionel."

Francesca nodded. "I guess that's understandable. Randy Davenport runs around on his wife more than anyone else's husband does, so Celia probably wouldn't be spreading rumors like that. They would hit too close to home."

"Francesca . . ." Desiree began again, "I don't think—"

"Paulette Davidson, then. She's envied my position on the Crosscreek entertainment committee for some time now. Or maybe Doreen Parker?" Francesca began to study her friends one by one, wondering which of them had stabbed her in the back this time.

"Francesca, nobody's been talking about you," Desiree assured her. "I just couldn't help but notice that you and Lionel don't seem to spend a lot of time together, talking, I mean. Of course, if I'm out of line, you just let me know."

"You're out of line, Desiree." An awkward silence ensued for a moment before Francesca relented. "But not entirely off-base."

"Do you want to talk about it?"

Francesca sensed her sincerity, and her voice was much more benign as she shook her head and said, "No, not really."

The two women sat in silence for some minutes, Desiree sipping her drink and Francesca sullenly staring out at the crowd of people making themselves comfortable in her home. As she scanned the occupants of the room, her gaze inevitably came to Laszlo. Her first instinct was to bypass her son's future father-in-law, but something made her hesitate. For the first time, she inspected him closely, trying to imagine what he must have looked like forty-two years ago when Desiree had decided to marry him. If she tried very hard, Francesca could just make out the remnants of a very handsome, if somewhat short, man. He'd probably had a full head of dark, wavy hair then and considerably less girth . . . nice brown eyes and a truly sweet smile. He had probably laughed as frequently then as he seemed to laugh now. Francesca smiled in spite of herself. All in all, Laszlo Hammelmann must have been quite an eyeful at one time. No wonder Desiree had fallen in love.

"Desiree," Francesca began, still inspecting the other woman's husband, "since we're in the position of asking personal questions tonight—as you yourself pointed out, we are going to be family, after all—would you mind if I posed one to you?"

"Sure, Francesca. What do you want to know?"

"Clearly Laszlo was at one time a very handsome man—"

"He still is," Desiree was quick to point out.

"Yes, of course. But at one time, he must have drawn the ladies' eyes quite frequently."

Desiree smiled at the memories crowding into her head. "Oh, yeah. He was a real looker back when I met him. Every girl in the neighborhood wanted to go out with Laszlo. Not only was he the handsomest guy around, but he had a future in his father's hardware business. Not an easy combination for a woman to overlook."

"Certainly not."

"So what's the big personal question you wanted to ask?"

Francesca decided she'd clearly had far too much to drink tonight, otherwise she would never have been so presumptuous to ask the question burning in her brain. However, her curiosity finally got the better of her, and she asked Desiree, "Has Laszlo ever strayed?"

Desiree looked confused. "Strayed?" she repeated after a moment.

Francesca nodded. "Has he ever . . . you know . . . had an affair with another woman?"

Understanding finally dawned, and Desiree began to laugh. "*Laszlo?* Have an *affair?*"

Francesca nodded again, a little more vigorously. "Yes. Has he?"

"Of course not. What a silly question."

"Are you sure? You're awfully quick to deny that such a thing is possible. Married men have affairs all the time, you know. The vast majority of husbands have been with women other than their wives."

"Maybe so," Desiree said. "But not Laszlo."

"But how do you know?"

Desiree stared at her hostess in frank amazement. It wasn't so much that Francesca had asked such a question—after all, she'd started this whole thing herself by putting her nose into Francesca and Lionel's business. No, what startled Desiree was the question itself. The thought of Laszlo looking for sexual satisfaction or anything else in the arms of another woman was just plain . . . crazy. He wasn't the kind of man who would do something like that. Not that he didn't take a healthy interest in the opposite sex. He waited impatiently for the *Sports Illustrated* swimsuit issue like other guys, and the boys down at the hardware store bought him the new lingerie calendar for his office every year. But an affair? What a loony idea.

"I don't know how to put this, Francesca," Desiree began, "but I just *know* he hasn't. It sounds kind of like a cliché to say it, but Laszlo and I made vows to each other forty-two years ago. And a big part of those vows was that we would be faithful to each other. It's just not in Laszlo to go back on a promise. But more than that . . . I mean, forgetting about it being immoral or any fear that he might get caught . . . Laszlo loves me." This was the only reason she could think of that would explain her complete certainty in her husband's fidelity. "It's just that simple. He doesn't feel a need to make love to other women."

Francesca inhaled deeply, expelled the breath slowly, and for some reason wanted to cry. Perhaps it was as simple as that after all. Maybe there was no one thing that had caused Lionel to grow more and more distant from her with each passing year—no one thing that could be fixed. Perhaps it was simply that the two of them didn't love each other as they once had.

"You thinking of going after my husband, Francesca?" Desiree asked playfully, trying to lighten the mood.

Francesca paled and was about to reassure Desiree that she would never, ever, go after another woman's husband—there were limits, after all—but then realized Desiree was simply making a joke. So she smiled and leaned back against the sofa, letting her gaze wander toward the man in question once again.

"Although the temptation is certainly strong," Francesca said as her smile broadened, "I guess I'll let you keep him."

"Thanks."

"But be sure to keep blinders on him, Desiree," she said. "Because men like that don't much exist outside of dreams anymore."

"Oh, I wouldn't say that. Look at your son. Taylor represents a whole new generation of good guys."

Francesca shook her head. "No, my son is as much an exception as your husband is. There just must be something about the Hammelmann women that appeals to men like Taylor and Laszlo. Maybe if I play my cards right you might let me in on your secret."

Desiree smiled. "What secret? I don't have a secret. You want to keep a marriage happy? All you got to have is love for your man." She arched her eyebrows sugges-

tively. "And maybe a nice little see-through black neg-
ligee . . . and a bottle of good Chianti . . . and a copy of
Johnny Mathis' greatest hits." Suddenly a new thought
struck Desiree. "Say, Francesca, you and Lionel ever been
to Atlantic City?"

22

      Two weeks after the Rowan party, Virginia was
the one lying on the sofa in the Hammelmann rumpus
room, thumbing idly through Laszlo's latest issue of *Field
and Stream* without much interest, feeling restless and
wishing something would happen. She always felt this
way when she was forced to wait for something, and waiting was all she seemed to have been doing lately. Eliot
had said he would call, she reminded herself as she had
every day for the last two weeks. He had promised. Yet
she had heard nothing from him since she'd gotten into a
taxi outside his front door fifteen days ago.

    After leaving Emma's engagement party, Virginia and

Eliot had indeed stopped for coffee and a chat, at a tiny, smoke-filled Georgetown establishment decorated with nothing but a crippled blue neon sign that said "Aristotle's." For some reason, Virginia hadn't been surprised to discover that Eliot loved Greek food, because she loved it, too. Although their differences in character certainly outnumbered their similarities, they agreed on those things that were most important—food (Greek, Thai, and well-prepared Caribbean), spirits (well-aged single-malt Scotch), music (whatever was available) and personal philosophy (essentially, live and let live). Agreement on these four subjects, Virginia was quite certain, was the foundation upon which every solid relationship began.

Afterward, instead of going home with Eliot to explore more intimate avenues—which was what had lingered at the forefront of Virginia's mind all night— they had gone to his home to talk some more. It had been one of the most enjoyable evenings she had ever spent with a man, sitting opposite him with a cup of espresso and later a mellow whiskey, doing nothing more than shooting the breeze.

Virginia couldn't remember the last time she'd done that—gotten to know a man by talking to him. In retrospect, she had thought perhaps that's why she hadn't liked very many of the men she'd met in recent years— because she hadn't taken the time to converse with any of them. Later, however, when Eliot didn't call her as he'd promised he would, she had begun to remember the real reason she didn't like most men. They simply couldn't be trusted. Now, fifteen days later, she was still inclined toward that way of thinking.

Until she heard the phone ring.

Then Virginia regressed to a breathless adolescent, waiting, waiting, waiting to see if the phone was for her. As she listened to the approach of footsteps, muffled and unidentifiable thanks to the carpeting, she sat motionless until she saw Emma's head pop around the door. At her niece's breezy, conspiratorial smile, Virginia smiled back.

"Oh, Aunt Virginia," Emma sang out, "there's a phone call for you."

Virginia rolled off the couch and tossed the magazine onto the coffee table, taking her time to stretch in an effort to affect an air of nonchalance.

"It's a boy," Emma added, her smile broadening.

Virginia fluffed up her curls with a careless shake of her head, and stood up.

"It's Brownie."

Virginia strode from the room, wondering not quite under her breath why a fifty-four-year-old man, a scholar no less, would allow himself to be addressed by the name of a popular dessert.

"Thank you," she said a little more clearly as she and Emma parted ways near the kitchen. She waited until her niece was out of range to pick up the receiver and say, "Hello?"

"Virginia? It's Eliot."

"Eliot?" She turned the word into a puzzle for his benefit, mumbling it over and over quietly as if she didn't know anyone by that name.

"Eliot Browne?" he added.

"Oh, *that* Eliot! The one who was supposed to call me two weeks ago."

There was an almost inaudible sigh on the other end of the line, and she could imagine him standing in his study, waiting for her to finish what he probably thought would be a petulant tirade.

"I'm sorry," she said, leaning against the refrigerator, bunching up the phone cord in her fist. "Let me try again." She cleared her throat and went on carelessly, "Oh, hi, Eliot, what's new?"

Now she could visualize him smiling, his blue eyes flashing as he swept his hand over the gray hair that was fast receding to the back of his scalp.

"I'm sorry I didn't call earlier," he said "I've been . . . it's been rather a hectic two weeks for me, and—"

Virginia was quick to interrupt him. "You don't owe me any apologies or explanations, really."

"Actually, I do, but they're not to be made over the telephone." He paused a moment before asking, "Are you free tomorrow evening? I know it's short notice and all, but—"

"What did you have in mind?"

She heard him sigh again, almost as if he felt what he was doing was pointless. "There's a guest lecturer at American University. Someone you've probably never heard of before talking about something you probably have absolutely no interest in knowing more about. But it would mean a great deal to me if you'd . . . if you'd like to accompany me."

Virginia's heart kicked up the funny rhythm that only Eliot seemed capable of stirring in her, and she glanced down at her shoes, marveling that she had actually been nervously shuffling her feet while talking to him. "All right," she said almost shyly. "I'd love to."

Eliot emitted a sound of relief. "Wonderful. I'll pick you up at seven, if that's acceptable."

"Seven is fine." She gave him directions to the Hammelmann house, then stopped him before he had a chance to hang up. "Eliot?" she began slowly. "What exactly does one wear to a university lecture?"

This time there was a long pause before he answered her, and Virginia had the distinct impression that he was weighing his response very carefully. Finally he said quietly, as if the words had to be drawn from him, "I think one should wear . . . as little as possible."

"Professor Browne, you have a lovely navel."

Virginia rubbed her cheek lightly over Eliot's bare torso, kissed the part of him she had just complimented, then snuggled closer to his warm body.

"Why, thank you, Ginnie. I don't suppose anyone's ever told me that before."

Virginia could feel him chuckling softly and smiled. He'd been right about the lecture. She couldn't remember who'd been speaking or what the man had been talking about. However, this evening had brought with it a new experience of another kind. Until an hour ago, Virginia had never made love with an academic. All in all, the experience had been quite—dare she say it?—educational. Although Eliot Browne wasn't the handsomest man she had ever met, nor really the most interesting, nor even the most charming, Virginia had to admit that he was without question the sexiest. She didn't know what made him so, but from the moment she had seen him sitting so complacently in the Rowan library, she had scarcely been able to think about much else other than how he would be in bed.

And now she knew. He'd been wonderful.

"You know, Ginnie," he said, his voice little more than a gentle caress in the darkness surrounding them, "there was a reason why I didn't call you right away, after promising you I would."

Virginia shifted so that she could look at his face, her head resting on his shoulder, her hand spread open over the center of his chest. Beneath her palm she could feel his heartbeat, a slow, steady thumping that made her feel at peace.

They lay on the couch in his Georgetown condominium, surrounded by what Virginia considered all the accoutrements of an English professor who had been on his own for a while—books, manuscripts, the odd snifter of brandy and scattered bits of uncollected tobacco, and a huge, beastly-looking tabby cat named Chaucer.

Eliot had started a fire some hours before at Virginia's request, despite the seventy-five-degree temperature outside. She had suggested they simply set the air conditioner at sixty-two in order to keep things comfortable.

Now the dying flames of the fire in the fireplace reflected the blaze still stirring within her, a warm glow and steady heat, banked but not yet extinguished. With a simple touch, the fire could begin again at any moment, and with further encouragement might possibly burn out of control.

"And what reason was that?" she asked him softly.

Eliot didn't answer for a moment, but instead tightened his arms around her waist to bring Virginia closer. How did one go about describing a fear? he wondered. Especially a fear one didn't understand oneself? That first evening he'd spent with Virginia Hammelmann had set his mind to spinning until he didn't know which end was up, and he wasn't sure if he'd ever come down to earth again. She was beautiful and sensual, smart and funny, and arousing as hell. Women like her were rare, and they simply didn't take an interest in sedate, dry old men like him. Yet here he was cradling the most exquisitely curved derriere in his palm, wondering if he might suffer a major coronary in making love to Virginia again.

"I didn't call you," he told her quietly, "because I was afraid."

At this, Virginia squirmed in his embrace until she was lying fully atop him, staring him down with a puzzled expression. "Afraid of what?"

Eliot sighed. "Of this," he said, indicating their naked, entwined bodies. "And of you."

"Me?" Virginia asked. "Why on earth would you be afraid of me?"

He wound a strand of her hair around his finger, loving the way the shimmering tresses managed to catch and dance with what little light could be found in the room. Then as he released the rowdy curl, he tried to explain.

"Ginnie . . ." Eliot paused when he realized what he had to tell her wasn't going to be easy.

"Chaucer is staring at me," Virginia said suddenly, as

if sensing Eliot's need to stall. She looked over his head at the big cat who gazed down at them from his perch atop a bookcase. "Why would he be staring at me like that?"

Eliot seized what he saw as the perfect opening for his explanation. "I suppose it's because Chaucer has never seen a naked woman before."

When Virginia looked back at Eliot, her expression was puzzled, but she said nothing.

"Until tonight, Ginnie, I'd only made love to two women in my entire life. A woman in college to whom I was practically engaged, and then my wife, Sarah."

Virginia's eyebrows arched in surprise. "I'm the first woman you've been with since . . . since your wife's death?"

"Yes. The first in three years."

"Why didn't you tell me before now?"

"Because," he told her with a devilish smile, gently squeezing her warm flesh, "something tells me you've not been out of circulation for quite that long."

Virginia smiled back. She might as well be honest. "No, I haven't been out of circulation since 1961."

Eliot sighed and skimmed his hands slowly up and down the smooth skin of her back. Virginia fairly purred in contentment, arching like a cat who's been too long without affection.

He spoke again into the darkness in a voice that sounded calm, sober, and perhaps a little sad. "Which leads me to suspect that you've had more than two partners before me."

"Considerably more." Virginia wasn't about to lie or feel guilty about her past.

Eliot wrapped his arms around her shoulders as if fearing she might try to leave him. "Therefore, I was afraid if you knew how inexperienced I was, you might . . . I was afraid you wouldn't find me . . . exciting enough for you."

Virginia looked at him incredulously. "And that's why

you didn't call me? Because you didn't think you were exciting enough?" She dropped a hand to his hip, raking her fingers slowly over his thigh and between his legs until she found the part of him she was looking for. Immediately he came to life again, and her heart raced with anticipation. Even Jack Kramer hadn't been able to resurrect himself that quickly. "Oh, Eliot, believe me," she said. "You have absolutely nothing to worry about there."

Her words reassured him somewhat, and he gasped at the heat that shot through him when she touched him in just that way. "No?"

Virginia grinned and leaned up to trace his ear with her tongue. "Uh-uh," she whispered, gliding a finger slowly over his shoulder to make lazy circles on his chest. "You're a wonderful lover. And I love that little thing you do with your moustache."

Eliot blushed. "Really?"

She moved her hand between his thighs again until she made him gasp. "Really."

Eliot squeezed her gently, trying to ease the trembling he felt winding its way through his body. He rolled on the couch until their positions were reversed and Virginia was beneath him, then dragged his fingers along her thigh and up her rib cage until he could circle the bottom of her breast with the curve of his thumb and forefinger. She really did have the loveliest breasts, he thought. Quite beautiful, actually. "There was one other thing that concerned me about us, Ginnie."

Virginia sighed contentedly at the heavy weight of him atop her and between her legs. She arched her body upward toward him, circling his waist possessively with her arms. "Can't we talk later, Eliot?"

"I just want you to know that the moment I saw you at Lionel and Francesca's that night, I felt something I hadn't felt in many years. And it startled me, the immediacy of it, the irrationality of it, the . . . the incredible *strength* of it."

Virginia tilted her head to one side, looking like a small bird who was considering whether or not to gobble up its meal. "What, Eliot? What was it you felt?"

He rubbed his palms over her breasts, circled her throat gently with his fingers, and then traced her cheekbones with his thumbs before burying his hands in her hair to pull her face close to his. "Desire," he said in a hoarse whisper before kissing her. "Pure, unadulterated desire."

Despite having dated no one since Sarah's death, Eliot had certainly received offers, both subtle and blatant, from women of his acquaintance, yet he had never been interested in other women. None of them had come close to making him wonder whether he might be able to start his life over with someone new. His wife's death had left him feeling a remarkable absence in his life, a void he hadn't felt could be filled by someone else. And perhaps it couldn't—not in the way Sarah had managed to fill it. However, as feelings of desire overcame him again, Eliot began to suspect that there might be a way to . . . to put a cover over the emptiness somehow. A way to patch it, so to speak.

"I can't seem to stop wanting you, Ginnie," he whispered as he ended the kiss. "And I'm afraid you'll leave after all is said and done, and I'll be left here wanting you forever."

Virginia stared at him for a long moment, shocked to realize that for the first time in her life she had absolutely no idea what to say. Somehow she felt as if she had lost control of the situation, a feeling she couldn't ever remember experiencing. She kissed Eliot deeply and shifted their bodies again in an effort to put herself on top once more. Instead of achieving her goal, however, she simply succeeded in rolling them both off the couch and onto the floor. The force of the impact caused a log to shift on the fire, and the blazes shot up anew, warming the darkness surrounding them.

"Don't use that word where we're concerned, Eliot," she said, kissing him with an almost desperate need.

"What word?"

"Forever. Whatever you say to me, don't ever say forever."

"But—"

"Shh."

Their passion built slowly this time, with nowhere near the wild intensity of their first encounter. Their initial joining had been explosive, as if it were the result of emotions kept at bay for too long. This time they wanted to prolong their enjoyment, each wanting to explore exactly what it took to make the other squirm in delight and cry out in ecstasy. Virginia had just discovered what was necessary to make Eliot do just that when there came a rapid, ceaseless pounding at the front door. At first they ignored it, or perhaps didn't even hear it, but when the knocking was followed by shouts of "Father! Father!" they had no choice but to discontinue their activities.

"Good heavens," Eliot said as he sat up and leaned against the couch. "That sounds like my son, Spenser."

"Daddy? Was that you groaning? Is everything all right?"

"And that sounds like my daughter, Gwyn."

"Uh-oh," Virginia muttered. "I, uh . . . I don't suppose you've told them about me, have you?"

Eliot chewed his lower lip thoughtfully for a moment. His hair was frantically mussed, his cheeks pink from his heightened arousal, and he looked like a man who was on the verge of achieving a sexual fulfillment like none he'd ever known. "No, I hadn't quite gotten around to it yet."

"Why do you think they're here?"

He frowned. "Hmm . . . I suppose now, looking back in hindsight, that leaving the phone off the hook all this time wasn't such a good idea."

Virginia tried to tame her own hair, but knew such an

effort was futile. Eliot was nothing if not extremely physical in his lovemaking, and he did so enjoy her hair. "How long has it been off the hook?" she finally asked.

He glanced up at the clock on the mantle. Four-seventeen A.M. "About seven and a half hours. You know, they've been this way ever since I experienced that mild infarction shortly after Sarah's death. It was nothing, really, but the children have become terribly overprotective of me as a result. Panicking at the drop of a hat."

"Father!"

"Daddy?"

The words were followed by more pounding, then the scrape of a key in the lock. Virginia and Eliot smiled at each other, then reached for whatever was closest to provide cover for themselves. Before they were modestly draped enough for company, however, the front door burst open, and in tumbled a man and woman in their twenties or thirties who Virginia thought looked like very nice people. At first the four of them only stared at each other in silence. Then Eliot remembered that he was the nearest one there to a host, and he smiled as he rose from the floor, clutching at the sweater he'd scarcely had time to wrap around his midsection. Fortunately, he had managed to get the long side in front.

"Spenser, Gwyn, I'd like you to meet someone."

"Hi, kids," Virginia said, lifting her hand for a wave. The action pushed the afghan in which she had wrapped herself down over one shoulder, and she tugged on it until she was safely covered once again. "I'm Virginia Hammelmann. Your father's new squeeze."

23

Because of the stress and frustration that unfortunately come naturally with planning one's wedding, a bride and groom may find themselves at odds over a variety of decisions they must make. Fortunately, these decisions are not so all-consuming as to effect global change. However, they may seem so to the couple involved. Simply do your best to keep the lines of communication open. Speak frankly and frequently about whatever concerns you. You may even learn more about each other than you knew before.

—ALISON BRIGHAM

"We have to start looking for a place to live soon."

Emma nodded at Taylor's statement, but silently continued to scan the classifieds in search of a job. The two of them sat side by side on Taylor's sofa one Sunday morning in late September, sharing sections of *The Washington Post* and a pot of strong coffee. Bits of baguette and croissant crumbs were scattered over chipped plates on the floor below them—all that was left of the breakfast Emma had picked up at a nearby bakery on her way over.

Although she had circled a few possibilities for employment she wanted to investigate further, most of the choices left a lot to be desired. She had finally decided to give herself a deadline in her job search. If she hadn't found a position for which she was educationally suited by the time she and Taylor married, then she would settle for something else upon her return from their honeymoon.

Surely with the onslaught of the holiday season, retail positions would be plentiful, she thought. Or perhaps there might be some word-processing work in one of the numerous offices in town. And if all else failed, she was confident that she'd be able to find a job at a restaurant. Waiting tables probably appeared on all of the best writers' résumés, she figured.

"Emma? Are you listening?"

It took a moment for the words to sink in and for Emma to realize Taylor was speaking to her. "What?" she asked as she glanced up from the newspaper.

Taylor sighed as he gave the real estate section a vigorous rattle and dropped it onto his lap. "I asked whether you wanted to live in town or in the suburbs."

"Oh, definitely in town."

"Definitely?"

Emma nodded. "Sure. Isn't that what you want? I think we're both better suited to city living. Your job is here in town. And with any luck at all, I'll probably wind up working in town. Every time we go out, it's to someplace here in the city."

Sensing a deep discussion about to come on, she folded her section of the newspaper carefully and placed it on her lap. "I mean, how much time do we ever spend in the suburbs aside from my parents' house anyway?"

"That's true," Taylor said. "But things will be different after the wedding."

Emma narrowed her eyes. "Different in what way?"

"Well . . ." Taylor began, shifting his gaze to some point above Emma's head. This wasn't a good sign as far as she was concerned. Whenever he lost eye contact, it meant he was about to say something he knew she wouldn't like to hear. "We'll be a married couple, for one thing."

"So?" Emma dreaded whatever would come next.

"So . . ." He shrugged. "So married couples should live in the suburbs."

"Why?"

"Because then they have houses to paint and lawns to mow and backyards to barbecue in."

"And why would they want all that stuff?"

"Because, Emma, all that stuff is what married couples do."

Emma gazed at Taylor curiously wondering what was going on in that cute little head of his. "That's silly, Taylor. You've never painted a house or mowed a lawn in your life. And when have you ever known your father to barbecue in the backyard?"

"Your father does all those things."

"My father owns a chain of hardware stores. It's a prerequisite for his job."

"Yeah, well, other fathers who don't own hardware stores do all those things."

"Taylor," Emma began, trying to remain patient despite her discomfort with the route the conversation was taking, "you're not a father."

"Not yet." He dropped his gaze to watch his fingers tug at a tear in the sofa. "But I will be someday."

Not this again, Emma thought. She sighed and then decided it would probably be best to face this discussion now. "Taylor, what's gotten into you with this fatherhood kick?"

"What do you mean?"

"I mean every time I turn around lately, you're talking about having kids."

"I haven't been talking about it any more than usual," he said, sounding more than a little defensive.

Emma shoved a hand through her bangs. "I remember once, maybe three and a half years ago, we rented 'Bedknobs and Broomsticks.' And during that one scene where the kids are being so obnoxious, you turned to me and asked, 'Do you want to have kids someday?' And I turned back to you and said, 'Yeah, sure. Why not? Someday.'" She paused for a moment. "Until a few months ago, Taylor, that was the only time in the entire history of our relationship I can recall you ever talking about having kids. But for some reason lately, you're suddenly trying to get yourself nominated for the Father of the Year award. What I want to know is why?"

Taylor was silent for some moments, still unable to meet her eyes. "I don't know," he finally said. "It's just that when I think of marriage, I start to think about kids, too. One follows the other, right?"

"Usually, but not always. And hardly ever immediately following the wedding."

When Taylor eventually looked up again, his expression was adamant. "I want to have kids, Emma."

"So do I. But not right away. Someday."

"Then what's wrong with moving to the suburbs now? It'll be one less thing to worry about later, when someday arrives."

Emma was about to voice another objection when she heard a muffled sound from down the hall and paused. "I thought you said Max was going to be camping on the Chesapeake this week."

Taylor shook his head. "He found a job Friday with some group called Citizens for a Cleaner Country, and they want him to start tomorrow, so he decided to put his trip off for a while. Now what are your big objections to living in, say, Arlington or Silver Spring?"

The sound down the hall grew louder and nearer.

"Can't we talk about this later?" Emma asked.

"Emma, we're getting married in two months. If we're going to buy a house, it better be quick."

"We could rent first. For a while. There are always apartments available in D.C."

Taylor waved off her suggestion. "Renting is a waste of money when it isn't necessary. And it isn't necessary for us. My parents are going to be handing us a tidy sum of money after we get married—"

"How do you know?"

"Because they gave Catherine and Michael twenty-five grand for a wedding present."

Emma's mouth dropped open in disbelief. "Twenty-five thousand dollars?"

Taylor apparently didn't consider the sum an overly large amount. "Sure."

Emma furrowed her brow anxiously. "But all my parents are going to give us is a washer-dryer combination."

Taylor clearly didn't understand what the problem might be. "That's all right. That's something we need, too."

"Do we really need twenty-five thousand dollars?" How were her parents supposed to compete with that?

"We do if we're going to buy a house in the suburbs."

Emma had finally reached the end of her patience. She picked up the section of newspaper from her lap and threw it onto the floor with a vicious motion, rose from the couch, and spun around to glare at Taylor with her hands clenched into fists on her hips. "Taylor, will you please shut up about a house in the suburbs?"

Taylor got up too, with slow, deliberate grace. He tossed his section of the paper atop the one she had thrown down, and glared back at her. "Emma, I want to buy a house in the suburbs."

"And I want to live in the city."

Emma was about to tell Taylor he was behaving like a big, overgrown baby, but Max chose that moment to shuffle into the room, and she was halted in her speech by his appearance. He was clad in a ragged, plaid flannel bathrobe, his hair tangled in irregular spikes, one tube sock shoved down around his ankle, the other tugged up to his knee. He stopped briefly to consider the scene unfolding before him and then continued to amble toward the kitchen.

"Actually, Taylor," he said as he went, "city life has a lot to offer. You'd probably choke to death in the suburbs. Hell, look at what it's done to your father. Lionel used to be an interesting man."

Without looking away from Emma, Taylor said, "Stay out of this, Max."

Emma was helpless to keep her eyes off of Max. She hadn't seen much of him since the Rowans' party, and now she followed his every movement as he went to the nearest cabinet and withdrew a box of Cheerios and dumped a good portion of it into a bowl. Some bounced out onto the counter, and when he splashed the cereal liberally with milk some of that went over the rim of the bowl, too. Max ignored the mess, intent on reading the back of the box while he ate, slurping noisily as he leaned against the counter with one foot rested atop the other. Every now and then a tiny stream of milk dribbled down his chin, and he wiped it away with his sleeve.

God, had she actually once made love to such a creature? Emma wondered. And had she actually been entertaining an occasional thought lately about what it might be like to wake up next to Max every morning? What could she have been thinking?

"All right, Taylor, look," she began again quietly as she turned her attention back to her fiancé. "I have no objections to buying a house. But let's look in the city and the suburbs and see if we can't find a happy medium somewhere." She lowered her voice even more and turned her back to Max. "Besides, I think the city is a great place to raise kids. There's the Smithsonian, the

Library of Congress, a million children's events going on all the time, and they're only a metro ride away."

"You guys already talking about having kids?" Max said, his mouth still full. He stopped in midcrunch. "Emma, don't tell me you're already pregnant!"

"Not that it's any of your business, Max," she snapped over her shoulder, "but no, I'm not pregnant. Not yet, anyway," she added deliberately, hoping to remind him that she *had* chosen Taylor.

"Emma, look," Taylor said. "We need to decide—"

"Taylor, I don't think this is the time to talk about it."

"But—"

"No buts," Emma insisted. "We'll talk about it later."

Max scraped the last of his Cheerios from the bottom of the bowl and reached for the coffee pot, splashing some in a mug with about as much grace as he'd managed with his cereal. "You know, you guys sure have been fighting a lot lately," he said. "You used to never fight. Now it seems like once a week you're at each others' throats over some little insignificant nothing. Why do you think that is?"

Emma and Taylor continued to stare at each other in silent combat, but Max's question lingered in the air like a crisp echo.

"I don't know," Taylor finally said. "But we were doing fine until we decided to get married."

"Then maybe you shouldn't get married." Max enunciated his words with a little more clarity than was really necessary.

Taylor kept studying Emma, but his quiet, steady reply was directed toward Max. "That way you could have another shot at her, right, Max?"

When no one spoke out to correct him, Taylor emitted a single, unhappy chuckle. Then he turned away from Emma and walked to the front door, pausing only long enough to jerk his jacket from the coatrack. Emma wanted to call out his name and stop him, but by the time she found her voice, he had disappeared through the door.

Before the latch had clicked shut behind him, Emma rushed at Max, grabbed him by the lapels of his robe and shoved him back against the refrigerator. Coffee sloshed over the rim of his cup, resulting in an untidy brown stain on Emma's gray suede boot, but that was the least of her worries right now.

"What did you say to him?" she demanded, pressing her fists into Max's chest. "What did you tell Taylor about us?"

"Jesus, Emma, relax." Max was glad he'd finally managed to arouse some kind of reaction from her, but this . . . He looked down at the fingers curled over the fabric of his robe, at Emma's body pressed so firmly against his. This exceeded his wildest dreams.

"What did you tell him?" she repeated.

"Nothing. I didn't tell him anything."

Emma loosened her hold on him somewhat but didn't release him completely. Her voice was a little more subdued as she asked, "Then what was Taylor talking about when he asked about you having another shot at me?"

Max's confusion seemed genuine. "I don't know."

He began to reach past her, ostensibly to place his coffee mug on the counter, and then with little effort switched their positions so that Emma was the one being pushed backward and Max was the one holding her there. Before she realized what had happened, Emma was no longer the one confronting, but the one being confronted.

"What are you doing?" she demanded.

"Don't panic," Max told her softly. "I just want you to listen to me, and this is the only way I seem able to keep your attention."

Emma frowned but didn't try to move away. "All right, I'm listening."

Max leaned forward, holding her gaze steady with his.

After taking a deep breath, he vowed, "I never told anyone about the night we spent together. It was too personal, too . . . too special for me to share it with anyone but you. Taylor was the last person I'd tell. Do you believe me?"

She studied his face intently. His eyes never strayed from hers as he spoke, and his voice was level and confident. There wasn't so much as a twitch to suggest he was telling anything but the truth. "Yes," she finally said. "I believe you."

"However, I can't promise things are going to stay that way."

"What?"

Max smiled cryptically. "Yeah, I've been thinking. What do you suppose Taylor would do if he did find out about the two of us that night at the Captain Willie B. Schmidt Motel, hmm?"

"You wouldn't."

"Wouldn't I? All's fair in love and war, isn't that what they say?"

"This isn't love," Emma said.

"Maybe not to you. But to me, it could be war."

His statement puzzled her. "What are you talking about?"

"I've told you before that I intend to have you, Emma. Maybe if Taylor knew about us, that might expedite the process a little."

Emma pushed Max away. "Even if you manage to sabotage the relationship Taylor and I have, I would never come crawling to you."

"Wouldn't you?"

She narrowed her eyes. "God, you are so full of yourself. I don't know why I didn't notice it before. You're arrogant, spoiled, obnoxious . . ."

"And I really turn you on."

"You're crazy."

"And you're aroused."

Emma shook her head slowly. "You are unbelievable, you know that? And I'm getting out of here."

"Make the right decision, Emma," he said in a final warning, "or I might be forced to tell Taylor about our little rendezvous. And trust me when I assure you that I won't leave out a single detail."

Emma ignored his threat and pushed past him, moving hastily to the couch to retrieve her jacket. "I've already made the right decision," she said as she thrust her arms into the sleeves. "And nothing, *nothing,* is going to make me change my mind."

"We'll see," he called after her as she left the apartment in much the same manner as Taylor had only a few minutes before. "We'll see."

Although Taylor had a good five minutes' head start, Emma was pretty sure she'd have little trouble finding him, especially when she saw that his car still sat across the street from his apartment building. There was a small park less than a half-dozen blocks away where the two of them frequently strolled when they wanted to be alone, free from Max's intrusions. Taylor was there, just as she'd known he would be, seated on a bench near the entrance with his glasses off, his eyes closed, and his face turned toward the sun.

Emma sat down beside him, close enough so that their bodies were touching. For a while they sat in silence, neither verbally acknowledging the other. Around them, Georgetown awoke slowly, and a soft breeze ruffled the leaves overhead, leaves that were just barely touched by the golds and reds and browns of a fast-approaching fall. It was Taylor who finally ended the silence.

"I figured you'd be right behind me," he said softly, as if trying to preserve the tranquility of the day. "At least, I hoped you would be. I didn't think you would stay with Max."

Emma thought his statement curious. "Is this a test?"

she asked him. "Am I supposed to be choosing between you and Max? And if I am, did you honestly think I would react differently than this?"

"Maybe."

When Emma covered his hand with hers, he turned to gaze at her with solemn eyes. She hated to ask the question wandering through her brain, but she needed to find out how much Taylor knew about her and Max, needed to find out if she'd completely blown her relationship with him by succumbing to the stupid weakness and lousy judgment she'd experienced one night two years ago.

"What . . . what did you mean back at the apartment?" she asked. "When you asked Max if . . . if he wanted another shot at me?"

Taylor closed his eyes and bent his head back against the bench once again. For a long time, he didn't reply, and then he said quietly, "It's a long story, Emma."

Her stomach clenched into a knot, a reaction repeated in every organ in her body. "One that obviously includes me, too."

Taylor sighed. "Yeah. It includes you, too."

She waited for him to continue, and when it appeared he would not, she said, "So maybe I have a right to be let in on it."

"I think you already are."

Emma tried to remain calm, tried to reassure herself that Taylor didn't seem angry or upset with her. He just looked . . . tired, she thought. And maybe a little sad. "Taylor," she tried again, "please tell me what's wrong."

He sat up straight, entwined his fingers with hers, and looked her in the eye as he said, "I know about you and Max."

Stay calm, Emma told herself. *Don't panic*. "What about me and Max?"

He continued to study her, pausing for an agonizing moment before he continued. "I know he's always been attracted to you."

"That's all?" Emma cursed herself immediately for blurting out such a response.

"Isn't that enough? I mean, hell, he's always wanted to take you away from me if he ever got the chance. God knows he's made a point of letting me know it whenever he could. And I'm sure there have been times when he . . . when he's let you know it, too."

"What do you mean he's let you know it?" she asked.

"Oh, come on, Emma. I've seen the way he looks at you. I've seen the way he dances with you at parties and the way he always finds excuses to touch you. Every time you and I have a disagreement of any kind, Max is there to remind me how lucky I am to have you and that I'd better make amends if I want to hold on to you or he'll go after you himself. Christ, after that night I . . . I went out with Tina, Max wanted to beat the hell out of me."

"You and Max fought after that night?"

Taylor nodded and rubbed his eyes wearily. "We exchanged a few jabs at each other the morning after, yeah. He was furious at me for going out with Tina behind your back, and I was mad at him for . . ." He stopped abruptly and gazed into the sky again. "Look, it was nothing major. We got over it. It's not the first time we got into a fight."

"Oh, Taylor . . ."

He smiled at her then, a smile that was cautious and anxious. "Max has told you how he feels about you, hasn't he?"

Why lie? Emma asked herself. She'd been withholding one truth from Taylor for two years and felt bad enough about that. Why make matters worse than they already were? "Yes," she said softly. "He has."

"I thought so. And how have you responded to him?"

Boy, talk about a strange situation, Emma thought. She didn't know whether to feel relieved or frustrated. She suddenly realized that a big part of her wanted Taylor to know about the night she'd spent with Max, because she was tired of carrying the guilt and anxiety around with her. She should just confess to him right now what had happened two years ago, assure him it had only happened because she'd been jealous of Tina, and then maybe they could both try to put it all behind them. But there was another, bigger part of Emma that was terrified of losing Taylor if he discovered the truth. And that was the part that won.

"Taylor, you don't have anything to worry about where Max is concerned," she said. "Whatever Max's feelings are, Max is the one who has to deal with them, not you, not me."

Apparently that wasn't good enough for Taylor, because he asked more insistently, "But how do *you* feel about Max?"

Emma hedged. "I love *you*, Taylor. Nothing could ever change that." She was only half joking when she asked, "What's the matter? Don't you trust me?"

He smiled a little, but Emma could see he wasn't completely satisfied with her answer. "I trust your feelings for me enough to know that you love me and not Max. But sometimes . . ."

"Sometimes?"

"Sometimes . . . sometimes . . . I don't know. Forget about it, Emma. Forget I said anything." His expression wasn't quite as worried as he asked, "So I don't have to worry about you leaving me for Max?"

Emma shook her head. "Of course not." She smiled mischievously as she added, "He'll never make nearly as much money as you will."

Taylor laughed, and Emma felt the restraints around her heart and limbs loosen somewhat. Things were okay between her and Taylor again. But she still felt saddled by the looming specter of her night with Max, and the new possibility that he might expose it. She knew that she would eventually be forced to confront the truth, whether Max acted upon his threat or not.

She should confess to Taylor now, Emma told herself again. As long as there was this . . . this . . . lie between them—because Emma didn't delude herself into thinking it wasn't in fact a lie—she would never be fully able to deal with her guilt or her feelings for Max, nor be completely free from her fear that someday Taylor would find out what had happened.

And what if he hated her after uncovering the truth? He had told Reverend Ballard he would forgive her if she were unfaithful. But what if in fact he left her, as she'd threatened to do to him if he were ever unfaithful to her? What would her life be like without Taylor? How would she be able to stand it?

Taylor stretched his arm across the back of the bench and draped it over Emma's shoulder. "Just think," he said. "In two months, we'll be married. Then nothing will ever come between us again."

"Nothing is between us now, Taylor," Emma said, wishing her voice didn't sound so uncertain.

The smile on his face was not quite as bright as she knew it could be. "You're right, of course. I don't know what made me say it like that."

Emma nodded, recalling how she'd once told Patsy that she and Taylor knew each other so well, they were almost able to read each other's minds. She hoped, just this once, that she'd been overly optimistic in her assessment of their relationship.

24

*When selecting dresses for your brides-
maids, abide by the same rule you would
adopt when choosing your own gown—opt
for something you like, but consider something that will also display your attendants'
best attributes most favorably. With virtually thousands of styles to choose from, such
a task should not be difficult.*

—ALISON BRIGHAM

With the onset of October, plans for the wedding
began to get fully under way. For so long, Emma had felt as
if she were hanging in some kind of suspended time
warp—almost married . . . but not quite, big things coming
. . . but not just yet. Being an engaged woman had caused
her to feel like next to nothing at all—neither single nor
married, neither available nor taken, neither naive and
carefree nor mature and responsible.

After she and Taylor had announced their engagement, there had been the initial burst of excitement and
giddiness and harried making of plans. But once those
primary wedding particulars were out of the way, she'd
actually had little else to do but wait.

However, October brought with it a number of things

demanding Emma's attention. There was a dress to be fitted and a bridal registry to be updated. There were showers to be attended, relatives to be visited, invitations to be addressed. Lots and lots of invitations to be addressed. Even five years of composing papers for university requirements hadn't given Emma writer's cramp the way inscribing her wedding invitations did. And then there was all the confirming of all the reservations she and her mother had made over the summer. And then reconfirming.

One thing in particular challenged Emma—the question of what tokens of thanks to give her bridesmaids. Desiree had suggested jewelry, but Emma wanted something more unique, more unusual. A special gift that would be a keepsake of the wedding, yet not some tiny trinket the women would tuck away in a drawer and never look at again. Surely there must be something. She'd just have to keep her eyes open.

By the time the wedding invitations went into the mail at the end of October, Emma was already exhausted. So when her mother roused her from bed at eight one Saturday morning to take her to yet another dress fitting, Emma was too tired to protest.

"It'll be the last one," Desiree promised her. "Unless you start eating too much like you always do when you get nervous. If you do that, we'll have to have the dress let out again."

Emma groaned and made a vague promise not to stuff herself, then stumbled into the bathroom for a shower.

By the time she and her mother made it to the shop, Patsy and all the other bridesmaids were already there and dressed. Their gowns were made of a lush burgundy velvet, scooped low in front and sweeping down in back into a deep V whose apex was hidden beneath a broad satin bow of the same color. There was otherwise no decoration save a discreet satin piping along the neckline and around the edges of the long sleeves.

Emma, and not Francesca, had ultimately been the

one to choose the dresses, and she was still pleased with her selection. These dresses *could* be worn again. They would just need to be shortened a little bit, and maybe have the big bow removed. She'd taken great pains in choosing something simple and relatively unadorned so that none of her bridesmaids could find fault with her selection. And now as she observed them in their finery, Emma could not have been more pleased.

"Dammit, Emma, I told you not to pick this dress," Patsy said as Emma entered the fitting room. She tugged at the low-cut neckline. "I asked for something with a high collar. I look like Boob Woman here."

"And you know my back always breaks out when I get nervous," another cousin, Mindy Hammelmann, added. "I'll have my bare back exposed to everyone there." Then she addressed Patsy. "You're lucky. I'd rather look like Boob Woman than Zit Woman."

"And what's with this bow?" Felicia threw in. "It makes my butt look *huge!*"

"And the long, full skirt does nothing to add to my height," said Taylor's sister, Catherine, who was a scant five-three.

"Oh, will you all just lighten up?" Emma asked as the boutique's manager entered with her own gown. "Quit overreacting. Those are beautiful dresses. You guys look fabulous. Nobody's going to be looking at your various body parts, trust me. Now give me a hand here. I'm the bride, remember? And you're my attendants. You're supposed be attending to me and my every whim."

Patsy and Mindy exchanged dubious looks. "Yeah, right," they said in unison as they turned away. Felicia and Catherine quickly followed.

"Don't you want to see me in my dress?" Emma called after them.

They all continued on their journey, muttering something about going to check on their shoes.

"I'd like to see you in your dress."

Emma turned around to find Adrienne watching the byplay. "I suppose you hate the dresses, too."

"Oh, no. I think they're beautiful. Of course, I don't have big boobs or a back that breaks out or a huge butt, either. And I'm four inches taller than Catherine."

Emma laughed. "So that means you'll give me a hand with my dress?"

"Sure."

Emma's sister-in-law Diane came over to help, too, joining Adrienne in spreading open the gown until it was an ethereal circle of white on the floor. After Emma had stripped down to her underwear, she stepped inside and waited while the other women pulled the dress up and over her shoulders and went to work on the dozens of tiny pearl buttons that ran down the back of the dress from hips to neck. Desiree fastened the dozens more from Emma's wrists to her elbows. All the while Emma stood still in front of the mirror, marveling at the changes that came over her as the women performed these duties.

She had never fancied herself a particularly whimsical woman, nor did she consider herself one who would get especially caught up in ultrafeminine pursuits like dresses and ruffles and weddings. Yet here she was, practical, no-nonsense, down-to-earth Emma Hammelmann, on the verge of tears because she was now standing center stage in this incredibly beautiful bridal salon.

Every wall, every rug, every curtain, every fixture was pure white, with a huge crystal chandelier sparkling like a cache of diamonds above her. Jewel tones of amethyst, sapphire, emerald, and amber were splashed about the room like fine gems, in the form of gowns and flowers and frills. Emma would have sworn she was above succumbing to lace and bows and soft fabric. She would have pledged on her honor that she would never be moved by the rustle of ribbons or the shimmer of silk.

Yet she was helpless to stop her fingers from roving over every inch of her dress, and she couldn't prevent the sigh that slipped past her lips. Although there were no beads and pearls and sequins to weigh the dress down, it was decorated with a pattern of well-tatted lace across the bodice. The sweetheart neckline mimicked the sweep of the low waistline, and in the back, below the long row of buttons, was a bow reminiscent of the one on the bridesmaids' dresses.

It was a beautiful gown, Emma decided as she turned first one way and then another, trying to get the full effect from the six mirrors surrounding her. She was glad she'd let her mother talk her into choosing this one.

"Did we ever count how many buttons there were?" she asked.

"One hundred and forty-two," Adrienne replied as she slipped the last one through its loop just below Emma's hairline.

"We're going to have to make sure we all get to the church early on your wedding day," Diane said. "Just getting you dressed is going to take all afternoon."

Emma chuckled and tugged at her bangs. "Well, at least I we won't have to spend a lot of time doing my hair."

Desiree's head snapped up. "What do you mean?"

Emma ran her hand over her closely cropped hair. "There's not a whole lot I can do with it, Mom."

"Pooh," Desiree said. "I've made arrangements for Mr. Pierre to come to the church and do your hair before the ceremony."

"Mr. Pierre? But he's the one who does your hair."

"And has done it for thirty years," Desiree said proudly.

"And he does it the same way he did it thirty years ago," Emma reminded her. "That's okay, Mom. I can do it myself, honest."

"Don't be silly. Mr. Pierre is looking forward to it."

Emma wanted to object further, but Adrienne came forward with her headpiece, so Emma decided to postpone this conversation with her mother until a later date. The veil upon which Emma had finally decided was a simple Juliet cap covered with the same lace that decorated her dress. And because the train of her gown billowed out a good three feet behind her, Desiree had insisted the veil do the same.

All in all, Emma decided she liked the effect very much. It was festive without being obnoxious—quite clearly a wedding dress, but not an overly trendy one. Her gaze skimmed up beyond her dress, taking in the picture of herself as a whole. And suddenly, she couldn't quite believe her eyes.

"Emma, you look absolutely beautiful."

Desiree's voice was quiet, reverent, and when Emma looked over at her, she discovered her vision was a little blurred. At first she thought it was because her mother was crying. Then she understood it was because she was crying herself.

She glanced back at her reflection in the mirror, shaking her head in disbelief. "God, I do, don't I?" she whispered, sniffling as she quickly wiped away her tears. Never for a moment had Emma considered herself a beautiful woman. Attractive, yes, and sometimes, if she really worked on it, even pretty. But never beautiful. Never until today. "Sorry," she added hastily in reference to her tears, rubbing her nose vigorously. "It's time for my period. I always get hormonal at the end of the month."

And then her words hit her with their full impact, forcing her to realize something she hadn't thought about before. She did a quick mental tally, then checked and rechecked it. "Oh, no," she moaned as her tears came up from nowhere again. "I'm going to have my period on my wedding day! On my honeymoon!"

The other women clucked sympathetically and patted Emma's back, urging her not to worry about a thing.

"It happened to me," Desiree said. "And Laszlo was very understanding. Very anxious . . . remember, we only

had one weekend together before he went off to war . . .
but also very understanding. And in the long run it all
worked out, because we did manage a . . . an intimate
interlude together on the train coming back."

"But, Mom," Emma said before thinking, "it's only a
few hours from Atlantic City to D.C. Surely you and
Daddy weren't on a sleeper train."

Desiree smiled and tucked an errant curl behind her
ear. "No, we weren't."

"But—"

"I guess I should have had this talk with you a lot
sooner, sweetie. You don't really have to have a bed, you
know."

Emma colored as the other women began to laugh.
"Gee, Mom. I didn't know you and Daddy had it in you."

Desiree lifted her chin and arched her brows in mock
censure. "There's quite a lot you don't know about your
father and me."

Emma was about to ask another question of her
mother, but her sister-in-law's comment prevented it.

"Don't you worry about your period," Diane added. "I
was supposed to start mine on my wedding day, but I was
so nervous, I was almost three weeks late. For a while
there, Joey and I were afraid I might be—" She glanced
at Desiree, then quickly concluded, "Well, never mind.
All I meant was that maybe you'll be so lucky."

Emma sniffled once more and tried to smile. She
didn't know what had gotten into her to make her cry so
much lately. Who cared if she had her period on her
honeymoon? It wasn't as if she and Taylor were chomping at the bit to have sex because they'd never done it
before. But it would be a pain to be so inconvenienced
on a Caribbean cruise. She'd bought all those new
clothes to wear, and that skimpy little thong bikini she
still wondered if she'd have the nerve to put on. Not to
mention that sexy little red peignoir set she hadn't been
able to resist.

Emma sniffled once more and felt Desiree press a hanky into her hand. She blew her nose indelicately and sighed. "Oh, well," she said, "I guess it won't be the end of the world."

The four women were joined by the rest of the bridesmaids then, and all lined up to have their hemlines adjusted. Patsy, Mindy, Felicia, and Catherine had all gotten over their dismay at the way the dresses showed off some of their lesser assets. Now they got more into the spirit of things, cooing over Emma's dress, laughing at nuptial anecdotes provided by the already-married women in the group. By the end of the morning, all was well with the female members of the Hammelmann-Rowan wedding party.

As the group was about to break up in front of the store, Patsy made an announcement. "Mindy and I want to throw you a shower. Do you have anything going on the Saturday before the wedding?"

Emma shook her head. "No. The bridesmaids' luncheon is that Sunday, but I don't think we have anything planned for Saturday." She looked to her mother for confirmation, and Desiree shook her head. "That's awfully nice of you guys," she told her cousins, "but you really don't have to—"

"We want to," Mindy assured her with a mysterious smile. "Do you have any preference for what kind of shower? I know you've got a couple others going on."

A couple! Emma wanted to shout. Every time she turned around, someone wanted to give her a shower. "Well, let's see," she began. "Catherine and Adrienne are giving me an around-the-clock shower. Two of the attorneys Taylor works with are giving us a bar shower. Aunt Miriam and Aunt Miranda are giving me a kitchen shower. One of Taylor's aunts is giving me a miscellaneous shower—"

"So do you have a preference?" Patsy repeated.

"Not really," Emma told her.

"Anyone giving you a personal shower?"

Emma thought for a moment before she finally shook her head.

"Good," Patsy said. "That's what we'll give you. One week before the wedding. We'll send out the invitations next week."

"Hey, wait a minute, guys. What's a personal shower, anyway?"

Patsy and Mindy smiled, glanced at each other for a moment with expressions Emma could only liken to suspicious, then looked at Emma again. "You'll see," they chorused as they began to walk away. "You'll see."

$\overline{25}$

Wedding gifts will begin to arrive shortly after you mail your wedding invitations. Be gracious in receiving—write your thank-you notes immediately after opening a gift. And should you find yourself with duplicates— not at all uncommon, particularly if you're having a big wedding—by all means return one. But never tell a guest that his or hers was the gift you returned. In such instances, little white lies are by no means unforgivable.

—ALISON BRIGHAM

The gifts began to arrive very soon after the invitations went out. Less than one week after Emma and Desiree had dropped the four bundles of meticulously addressed envelopes into a mailbox, UPS began to make an almost daily stop at the Hammelmann house, usually with one or two boxes, occasionally with three. The first delivery record was set two Thursdays after the invitations were mailed, when Emma returned home from her weekly job search to find a whopping five boxes stacked outside the Hammelmann's front door.

She was already in a very good mood, having finally been victorious on the job front. But her happiness began to ebb somewhat when she realized that her mother was far more excited about the mountain of packages growing larger by the day in the living room than by her daughter's future career.

"I'll be working for a small weekly newspaper that's just starting up," she told her mother as they worked together in the kitchen to prepare dinner. "I'll have my own column, writing about social and political issues affecting women in America. This could lead to something really big."

"Congratulations, sweetie, I'm very happy for you. I'm also dying to find out what's in that big box from your Aunt Claudia and Uncle Leo. She told me what she was going to get, but she must have changed her mind, because sterling silver salad tongs wouldn't take up nearly that much room."

"I already have some great ideas for columns," Emma went on. "Proposed federally funded family leave and how it compares to its European counterparts, the skyrocketing cost of health care and what we can do to counteract it, whether or not high unemployment affects things like alcoholism and domestic violence . . . Of course, when I'm not working on my column, I'll be working on other facets of the paper—editing, proofreading . . . running the printer . . . getting everyone lunch . . . But that's okay," she concluded hastily. "I'll get a more rounded view of the paper as a whole."

"Sounds very interesting. There's also a package in there from a Marie Rowan," Desiree added. "Isn't that Lionel's sister, the one who runs the big bank down in the financial district? She has to be worth a bundle. I wonder what she got you."

Emma scraped the skin off the last of the carrots and began to slice them. "My salary won't be so great just yet, but the paper is still small and building itself up. When it catches on and starts generating more revenue, I should be able to get a raise. Or better yet, if somebody from *The*

Post or some other big paper reads my column, maybe I can start syndicating."

"Sounds like you're on your way, Emma. Now, I was just thinking maybe we could invite Taylor's parents—and little Adrienne, too, since she lives at home—over for dinner tomorrow night. Virginia will be home—oh, and maybe she could invite her new man-friend over—and that way you and Taylor could open your presents surrounded by family. Wouldn't that be fun?"

Emma scooped the carrots into a saucepan and wondered if her mother had heard a word she'd said. Probably not. Still, the important thing was she'd finally landed a job, one she could really sink her teeth into. Who cared if she was barely going to make minimum wage? It was a foot in the door, wasn't it? Right now she felt so relieved, even the thought of eating with the Rowans again didn't put her off.

"Yeah, Mom, it sounds like fun," she said. Then she had to stop and think about her remark for a moment. Because deep down inside, Emma suddenly realized to her surprise, that she meant exactly what she said. Dinner with the Rowans did sound like fun. She shrugged as she turned her attention to the salad. Maybe she would be able to enjoy the wedding after all.

The stack of boxes had grown enormous by the time Emma and Taylor sat down to open them the following night. During the time it took the group of eight to finish eating dinner, the UPS man had delivered three more to the Hammelmann's front door. There were big boxes and little boxes, some wrapped in brown paper, some in white. One or two had clearly been jostled around a bit and boasted scars of crushed corners and slashed cardboard. But all had one thing in common. All were addressed to Emma Hammelmann.

"How come none of the gifts has my name on it?"

Taylor asked as they took their seats in the living room.

"Because traditionally," Emma told him, "the gifts belong to me, not you. A little leftover custom of the prefeminist world, you know."

"One of the few things that worked to our benefit," Virginia added.

"Why don't I get any gifts?"

"Because nobody likes you," Adrienne said, contributing the obligatory little sister torment.

"Because you're the groom." Desiree chuckled. "You're supposed to be able to take care of yourself. As opposed to my poor, defenseless daughter who could never make her way alone in the world."

Emma made a face at her mother.

Desiree just laughed some more and added, "So you better think twice if you decide to divorce her, because all this stuff will come to her."

"Yeah," Emma said. "And you know how important you're going to consider fondue sets and cheese domes and electric knives and toaster ovens."

Taylor smiled. "Couldn't live without 'em. So I guess I'll just have to stay married to the woman who has 'em."

"Open that big one first," Adrienne ordered them.

"Adrienne," Francesca said, "let Taylor and Emma decide."

Emma and Taylor looked at each other and smiled. "The big one," they said in unison.

"It's from Claudia and Leo," Desiree told Laszlo. "It should be very nice."

Aunt Claudia and Uncle Leo had indeed changed their minds about the sterling silver salad tongs, Emma realized immediately upon opening the ungainly box, and had opted for a lamp instead. A big lamp. A big, obnoxious lamp, with scrollwork and curlicues and cherubs, in a shade of . . . coral—yes, that was definitely coral—unlike anything Emma had ever seen. The only thing she could think of that might begin to describe the color was that piece of flesh that hung down from the top of one's throat at the opening of the esophagus.

"It's a lamp," she said unnecessarily. Her comment was met by a looming silence from the others. "A lamp I don't think I remember putting on the registry list."

"Oh, you didn't, Emma, I did," Desiree told her. "I thought it was just gorgeous."

For a long moment, Emma only stared at her mother, then finally mumbled, "It is. It is . . . gorgeous. It's just . . . it's not . . . it isn't really going to match the decor Taylor and I have planned."

Desiree favored her daughter with her best disapproving expression and tone of voice. "Now you know your Aunt Claudia and Uncle Leo are going to come visit you in your new home, and the first thing they're going to look for is that lamp. You'll just have to find a place for it, Emma. That's all there is to it."

"How about the basement?" Taylor mumbled so that only Emma could hear.

"Now open the one from David and Ellen Cochran," Adrienne said. "They have terrible taste. I'm sure they bought you something really awful."

Gradually, what had begun as a tentative exploration of each of the boxes grew into a frenzy of torn paper and cardboard, with mountains of plastic bubble wrap and Styrofoam popcorn littering every spare inch of the living room by the time Emma and Taylor were through.

"Does the EPA knows about this?" Emma wondered aloud at one point, marveling at the amount of non-biodegradable material that went into the packaging of bridal gifts. "We should say something to Max. He can alert the Citizens for a Cleaner Country."

"Last one," Taylor announced as he settled a large, square package onto Emma's lap. "It's from . . ." He opened the card attached. "Stephanie Dryer. Is that a friend of yours, Emma?"

Emma shook her head. "Never heard of her. Mom?"

"No one on our side."

Taylor looked at Francesca. "Mother?"

Francesca was about to answer that Stephanie Dryer was no one she and Lionel had included on their list, but glanced over at her husband in time to see him squirm visibly in his chair. "Lionel?" she asked, amazed that she could keep her voice level. "Is she a friend of *yours?*"

Lionel looked quickly at his wife, then even more quickly away. "Ah, yes. Yes she is. She's a paralegal who's done some work for the firm. You met her at the engagement party."

"No, I didn't," Francesca said. "You must have forgotten to introduce us."

"Did I? How careless of me."

"Yes," Francesca said. "How careless of you."

The others watched the exchange with much interest and were clearly disappointed when Francesca didn't press the issue. Emma went back to opening the gift in her lap.

"Oh boy," she said without much enthusiasm when she'd lifted the lid. "It's more wine glasses completely unlike the ones we registered for."

"How many does that make?" Taylor asked Desiree, who had written down which gift came from which wedding guest.

"How many are there in that one?"

"Twelve," Emma replied.

Desiree did a quick count. "That makes sixty-eight all together."

Taylor smiled. "Guess we'll be doing a lot of large-scale entertaining."

"Guess we'll be taking most of them back," Emma corrected him.

"Oh, well," he said. "We only doubled up on a few things. Two blenders, two toasters, two wine racks. Look at all the china we got." He lifted one piece and turned it over and over in his hand. "A gravy boat, Emma. Someone actually bought us a gravy boat. Doesn't that make you feel like a grown-up? I mean, have you ever owned a gravy boat before tonight?"

She shook her head. "No, can't say that I have."

"This marriage stuff is great," he went on. "Everybody hugs and kisses you when they see you, people buy you presents and send you checks. We should have done this a long time ago."

Emma pulled him close for a hug. "Yeah, we should have." After a moment's thought, she added, "However, the down side is that now we're going to have tons of thank-you notes to write."

Taylor pulled away from her a little. "What do you mean *we're* going to have tons of thank-you notes to write?"

Knowing full well what was coming, Emma shook her head vigorously and said, "Oh, no you don't. You're not weaseling your way out of this. You're helping me write them."

"Hey, you're the writer, Emma. You can blow this off in no time."

"The gifts came from your relatives, too."

Taylor grinned. "Yeah, but they were all addressed to you. They're your gifts, remember?" He turned to Desiree for reinforcement. "Right, Desiree? Back me up on this."

Desiree tried to skirt the issue. "Well, *traditionally*—"

"Traditionally, Emma said, the gifts belong to her, not me, a leftover custom from the prefeminist world. So I don't have to help, right?"

"Wrong," Emma assured him.

"Actually, Emma, he may have you there," Virginia said with a smile.

Desiree nodded. "Laszlo sure didn't help me write the thank-you notes, did you, Laszlo?"

"That was your job," Laszlo replied.

"Lionel didn't help me, either," Francesca added.

"The world was a different place then," Lionel said.

"Everyone had specific roles to play, and women played the thank-you-note-writing role."

"My point exactly," Laszlo said.

"Emma . . ." Taylor's voice was pleading.

"Taylor . . ." Emma's voice was threatening.

"I'll lick the stamps."

Several hours later, after the Rowans had gone home and the remnants of dinner had been tidied up, Emma sat alone at the desk in her bedroom. Beside her was a stack of little white cards discreetly engraved with the words *Emma and Taylor Rowan*, and beside them an equal stack of little white envelopes addressed to the givers of tonight's gifts. Emma gazed sullenly at the roll of stamps. Like hell Taylor would lick them, she thought.

Picking up the first card in the stack, she glanced at the address on the top envelope and saw the names of Richard and Louise Gideon. Richard Gideon had been a friend of Taylor's father since college, a very distinguished criminal attorney with a national reputation. He and his lovely wife of six months—a woman Taylor had mentioned offhandedly was barely older than Emma—had gone to no small expense in giving the two of them a set of twelve soup or cereal bowls in their fine china pattern, a very generous gift indeed.

Dear Mr. and Mrs. Gideon, Emma began in a formal script that bore no resemblance whatever to her usual cryptic scrawl, *Thank you so much for the twelve beautiful soup/cereal bowls to match our china. Taylor and I just love them, and can't wait until we can enjoy them together.* She nibbled the end of her pen thoughtfully, then smiled as she continued, *They'll be especially handy for Taylor's usual morning repast of Froot Loops and Michelob. Again, thank you so much, and we look forward to seeing you at the wedding. Best wishes, Emma and Taylor.*

Smiling at the ease with which she had composed the

note, Emma folded it in half and tucked it into its envelope, humming as she licked the flap and sealed it. When she had affixed the stamp in its proper place, she doubled her fist to give it a good whack to make sure it would hold, then pounded it three more times, just to be sure.

Next on the list was Taylor's Aunt Marie, the banker, a very upstanding pillar of D.C. society, one of the first women to make inroads into the nation's financial community. Very upper-crusty, as Desiree would say. Emma smiled as she penned the words, *Dear Ms. Rowan*. She gazed ponderously at the crisp white card for a moment before writing, *Thank you so much for the gorgeous Baccarat vase. It's absolutely exquisite. And although Taylor has never given me flowers enough to fill it, perhaps someday another man will. Again, thank you so much, and we look forward to seeing you at the wedding. Best wishes, Emma and Taylor.*

Emma completed the same postal ritual she had performed on the first note, placed the second atop it, and then went on to the next name on the list. David and Ellen Cochran, two of Lionel and Francesca's oldest and dearest friends. They'd been responsible for a huge, olive green, marble ashtray shaped roughly like the state of Montana. Neither Emma nor Taylor had ever smoked in their lives. According to Adrienne, however, David and Ellen Cochran both smoked like chimneys. Francesca had called the ashtray an objet d'art. Desiree had called it impractical. This should be fun. Taking pen in hand, she began to write: *Dear Mr. and Mrs. Cochran . . .*

26

A side note: You may be surprised to discover love blossoming all around you as your wedding day approaches. Alison herself met Mr. Brigham when both were guests at the wedding of a mutual friend. Should such a relationship develop during your own celebration, be enthusiastic, and take pleasure in the knowledge that you were somehow instrumental in creating a match as loving as the one you share with your groom.

—ALISON BRIGHAM

Garlic, parsley, ground beef, tomatoes, mozzarella, ricotta . . . Virginia ticked off in her head the ingredients of the only culinary creation she knew how to make—lasagna. As she stood in the middle of the produce section of Giant Foods the following Monday afternoon, with one eye closed in concentration and the other fixed on a display of harvest-fresh vegetables, she knew she was forgetting something.

"Oregano, onions, parmesan . . ." she mumbled. " . . . *basil!*" she finally shouted out loud when she remembered, and then grinned sheepishly at the

other shoppers, who were startled by the suddenness
of her recollection.

"Uh, sorry," Virginia muttered under her breath to an
elderly woman behind her who clutched at her heart.
"It's been a while since I made lasagna."

Or anything else for that matter, she thought. As she
gathered a fistful of the herb in question and shoved it
into a plastic bag, Virginia tried to remember the last
time she had cooked a meal for anyone. It had been for . . .
Etienne? No, he'd always taken her out to eat. Jorge? No,
she hadn't liked him enough to ever invite him home
with her. Ah, yes. Luciano. She had cooked lasagna for
Luciano. And when he'd told her it wasn't nearly as good
as what his mama had made for him as a child, she had
dumped him. Maybe that was why she hadn't cooked for
anyone after that.

But now she was going to cook for Eliot. Actually,
Virginia recalled somewhat nervously, she was going to
cook for Eliot and his children. And their spouses. And
his grandchildren. Suddenly she wondered what the hell
she thought she was doing acting like Mama Leone. Trying to buy his family's trust by cooking for them, she
answered herself. Or maybe trying to bribe her way into
the family by cooking for them?

As she fingered tomatoes in search of just the right
ones, Virginia smiled, remembering the way Eliot always
squirmed when she touched his . . .

Well, never mind, she thought as she picked through
the pile. There would be time enough for thoughts like
that later. After the children and grandchildren were
gone. Perhaps she should buy a nice bottle or two of red
wine. . . .

She arrived at Eliot's apartment a little after four, an
hour before he was to get home from the university,
three hours before their guests were to arrive. Virginia
used the key he had given her to let herself in, carried
the groceries to the kitchen, and began to unpack them,

searching through his cabinets until she'd figured out what went where. That accomplished, she ventured to the living room to study Eliot's collection of music, marveling at the variety she found there. She bypassed the Tallis Scholars, the Chieftains, and Edith Piaf, finally settling on the sound track to Bizet's *Carmen*. She smiled when she recalled the night she and Eliot had made love to "Bolero" and decided the composition was overrated. The two of them had found much more fun with the "Toreador Song."

Virginia did her best not to think about how comfortable she was in Eliot's home. She tried to forget about how she now knew where he kept everything, how he'd trusted her enough to give her a key to his place, and how warm and fuzzy all that made her feel inside. When she began to think about how nice it would be to come home to this place every day, Virginia caught herself and made herself stop. Instead, she sang as she began to chop the onions.

"Hey, toreador-o, don't spit on the floor-o, use the cuspidor-o, what do you think it's for-o?"

When she couldn't remember the rest of the words, she began to hum.

That was how Eliot found her when he came home from work. His ears were exhausted from listening to his students fracture and mispronounce the Middle English version of *The Canterbury Tales* Prologue, his eyes hurt from grading forty-two blue book exams, his head still ached from the budget cuts meeting he'd had with the department head, and his heart felt heavy because he'd been missing Virginia all day. Yet the moment he closed the door behind him, lifted his nose to inhale the delectable fragrance of Italian food, and beheld the sight of Virginia Hammelmann taking over his apartment, all of Eliot's little discomforts miraculously went away.

She looked wonderful, her hair a riot of dark gold

curls tumbling about her shoulders, her lush body showcased by the man-styled, beaded vest, the short, slim skirt and high stiletto heels. Sarah would never have dressed in such a fashion, Eliot mused. His wife had worn tailored dresses in muted shades and sensible pumps, never anything that might draw attention to herself. Not to say that Sarah had been a shrinking violet. Quite the opposite. She had been strong in her opinions, resolute in her convictions, straightforward in the manner in which she approached life. She'd been a lovely woman. But so utterly different from the woman who stood in his home now.

So why had he fallen so helplessly in love with Virginia? Eliot wondered. What was it about her that left him sleepless most nights? Made him suddenly grin in the middle of his lectures at the salacious thoughts that paraded into his head? Caused him to completely forget he was a fifty-four-year-old grandfather who should know better than to become besotted by someone so completely wrong for him?

When Virginia glanced up to find Eliot watching her, her smile was radiant, her face a little flushed. Surely her reaction was a result of the heat in the kitchen, he thought, and not because he had come home.

"Hi," she said a little shyly when he didn't say anything first, and then looked back down into the saucepan she was stirring as if its contents held the secrets to the universe.

"Hello," he returned, still standing by the front door. He inhaled another deep breath. "It smells wonderful in here."

"I haven't started the lasagna yet. I'm still working on the tomato sauce."

"Homemade tomato sauce? You can buy that already prepared, you know."

Virginia smiled and looked up at him again. "I've

heard that. It comes in cans or jars or something, doesn't it?"

He nodded.

"Well, I wanted to make it from scratch."

"Why?"

"Because it tastes better," she told him. Then she added reluctantly, "And because I want to make a good impression."

"You've already made a good impression on me, Ginnie."

She fumbled for a handful of sage. "I know. But I want to make a good impression on your family, too."

"Why?"

"Because."

"Because why?"

"Just because, Eliot, okay?" She gritted her teeth at him playfully. "What is this, the third degree? Boy, see if I ever cook anything for you again."

Eliot smiled, thinking her reaction a good sign. She was nervous about meeting his family. She wanted to make a good impression. Surely if she cared about his family's reaction to her, she must care about him, too.

It had been Virginia's idea to invite his children and their families over for dinner one night. After their disastrous first encounter with his son and daughter, she had thought it might be best if she offered the first overture toward making amends. Eliot had been delighted when she had suggested hosting a family dinner. It seemed such a normal, everyday kind of thing to do, and it was a ritual normally performed by couples.

Finding her here to greet him when he arrived home made Eliot feel good. Knowing they would spend the evening as a couple made him feel ecstatic. He couldn't stop himself from wondering if he might ever be able to convince her to do this permanently.

He tossed his briefcase into the nearest chair and went into the kitchen to be closer to Virginia. When he leaned down to kiss her cheek, she turned her head so that he kissed her mouth instead. Immediately they both threw themselves into the kiss, Eliot burying his hands in Virginia's hair while she struggled to loosen his bow tie. She had just tugged it free from his collar when the tomato sauce she'd stopped stirring began to pop and splatter in the pan.

"Oops," Virginia mumbled as she pulled away, feeling as hot and agitated as the mixture she quickly began to stir again.

"I'll, er . . . I'll just go change, shall I?"

"Good idea," Virginia said.

Their guests began to arrive at exactly the time specified, first Gwyn and her husband, Roger, followed closely behind by Spenser and his wife, Amelia, and their twin sons. The two little boys instantly began to tear apart the living room, throwing pillows to the floor and upending whatever they could get their little fingers wrapped around. Then they went after the cat.

Adorable little bastards, aren't they? Virginia thought with a frozen smile. "Oh, boys," she said when Graham—or was it Bryan?—had Chaucer by the tail. "Leave the kittycat alone, won't you?"

"Oh, please don't correct the little ones," Amelia said when she heard Virginia's admonition. "Curiosity helps them grow. It's healthy for them to be adventurous this way."

"It will be healthier for them if they knock it off," Virginia said. "Chaucer has some mighty big fingernails. And he's not afraid to use them."

As if the big cat had heard Virginia, one of the boys yelped in pain and cradled one hand in the other.

"Chaucer scratched me!" he wailed, running to his mother for sympathy.

Amelia clucked and cooed over her son, assuring him

that the big, nasty pussy cat wouldn't hurt him anymore. "Brownie, could you please lock that animal up while the boys are here? He's absolutely vicious." Then a new thought seemed to strike her and she paled. "Good God, he has had his shots, hasn't he?"

"Yes, Amelia," Eliot said. "Don't worry."

He started toward the cat, but Virginia stopped him. "I'll take care of Chaucer," she said. "Why don't you open the wine?"

She picked up the oversized tabby and scratched him affectionately behind the ear. "Well done, Chaucer," she whispered as she brought him into the bedroom. "I'll save some lasagna for you."

Chaucer curled up on Eliot's pillow and licked his whiskers in anticipation.

"See you in a few hours," Virginia said as she closed the door behind her.

When she returned to the others, Eliot had served the wine and seemed to be having words with his son over something. The two of them stopped talking as she approached, thus confirming her suspicion that they had been talking about her.

"So, Eliot," she said, trying her best to be cheerful, "aren't you going to introduce me to the rest of your family?"

He smiled at her, a smile that was at once comforting and leering. Virginia smiled back. She couldn't wait until they were alone together. Whose dumb idea had it been to invite his family over for dinner anyway?

"Well, you've met Spenser and Gwyn," he began.

"Briefly," Virginia said, extending her hand first to one, then the other.

"And this is Gwyn's husband, Roger," Eliot continued, indicating a young man who looked to be half Virginia's age.

"I've heard a lot about you," Roger told Virginia with a huge grin as he vigorously pumped her hand. Funny, though, she thought, how he seemed to be speaking to her breasts.

"And this is Spenser's wife, Amelia," Eliot concluded, "and their two sons, Bryan and Graham, whose photographs I showed you at Francesca's party."

"Hello," Amelia said tightly. It occurred to Virginia then that everything about Amelia seemed tight. Tight features, tight expression, tight shoes . . . tight ass.

"Well, dinner still has a few minutes to go," Virginia announced. "Shall we sit down?"

The boys continued to hoot and cavort about the room while the adults made themselves comfortable, creating an almost impossible situation for reasonable conversation. When Virginia sat down on the sofa, Eliot took a seat right beside her, folding her hand in his. Virginia noticed that Gwyn and Spenser noted the gesture, the two of them exchanging wary glances before assuming bland expressions once again. She sighed. Obviously she wasn't going to fall for Eliot's family as quickly as she had fallen for Eliot, and vice versa.

"Virginia, my father tells me you've been working in the Caribbean," Spenser said, opening the discussion.

"Yes," she replied with a dazzling smile.

"On a charter yacht, no less," he added. "As a bartender . . . or something, wasn't it?"

Virginia didn't like his tone of voice one bit. He'd said the word *bartender* as if it were the oldest profession. Still, she tried to persevere. "Entertainment coordinator," she corrected him.

"Entertainment coordinator," Spenser repeated. "I see. Sounds . . . fascinating."

There, he'd done it again, Virginia thought. He'd made *fascinating* sound like *immoral*. "Actually, Spenser," Virginia said after a sip of her wine, "it was a real pain in the ass. The guy I was working for was a complete crook, and all his clients were the kind of people who had more dollars than sense, know what I mean? After a while, you start wishing some torqued-up maniac with an AK-47 would just come along and open fire on the whole excursion crowd."

The others gazed at her in silence for a moment, then Amelia asked, "And where are you working now?"

"I'm not," Virginia told them. Suddenly, she felt the almost uncontrollable urge to laugh hysterically out loud as she added, "I'm unemployed. And you know, I suppose you could even say I'm homeless. I'm staying with relatives in the area until my niece's wedding in a couple months, and then . . . who knows? Guess I'll be hitting the road again."

She felt Eliot's pressure on her hand increase, and when she looked over at him, found him staring back at her with a very curious expression. The timer went off in the kitchen then, and he seized the opportunity to yank her up off the couch and away from his family. When they were safely out of earshot, he spun Virginia around to face him and glared at her.

Virginia marveled at his expression. He looked absolutely betrayed. "What?" she asked. "What's wrong?"

"You didn't tell me you were planning on leaving after the wedding."

Virginia looked away, reaching for the oven mitts hanging over the stove and focusing her attention on retrieving dinner from the oven. She suddenly felt very nervous about something and wished Eliot would just drop the subject. "Well, of course I'll be leaving after the wedding," she told him. "Laszlo and Desi are great to let me stay as long as they do. But I can't depend on them forever."

"But—"

"I'll have to find a job somewhere," she continued. "And I'm not sure there's anything around here that will appeal to me."

"But—"

"A friend of mine is opening a bookstore in Alaska soon." She snatched up the pan with the garlic bread and shoved it unceremoniously into the oven. "And she mentioned that if I ever needed work, I could give her a call."

"Alaska?" Eliot said with a gasp. "*Alaska?*"

Virginia closed the oven door with a loud clatter. "Yeah, I hear it's a beautiful place."

"But I thought . . ."

Virginia pushed past him to open the refrigerator, reached in for the salad and dressing, and began to combine the two. "You thought what?"

She was hurrying from stove to counter to lasagna to salad and back again, trying her best to convince herself she hadn't a worry in the world. Eliot grabbed her by the shoulders to stop her hustle and bustle, forcing her to look at him fully.

"What?" Virginia asked. She gestured toward the food with her oven-mitted hands to stress the urgency of the activities he was preventing her from performing.

"Ginnie, I thought . . . I had rather thought you might stay for a while."

Virginia stared down at her hands. "Where would you get an idea like that?"

Eliot inhaled deeply and raked his fingers through his hair. "Because . . . because I thought perhaps you might want to spend more time with me."

Virginia looked up quickly, then cupped his cheek with a hand still enclosed in an oven mitt. "I told you before, Eliot, don't—"

"Don't ever say forever," he repeated. "I know that. But the least you could do is stay for a little while."

She wished she could. She really did. But staying here in town meant seeing more of Eliot. And the more she saw of Eliot, the less she wanted to leave. And Virginia Hammelmann was first and foremost a drifter, an adventurer. Eliot, on the other hand, was sedate, steadfast, and

most of all . . . secure. And security was the last thing
Virginia wanted or needed in her life. She was having
too much fun without it. At least she had been before . . .
before she'd met Eliot.

She sighed. "Look, Desi invited me to stay on after
the holidays, but I really can't impose on them much
longer than I already have. I can't stay with them past
Christmas."

Eliot studied her face for a long time, feeling more
helpless than he'd ever felt in his life. He couldn't lose
Virginia, he just couldn't. "Then perhaps . . ." He
paused for a moment. "Perhaps you could stay with
me."

Something twisted painfully inside Virginia at his quietly uttered offer. For the briefest of moments she considered it, weighing the differences between a life-style
she'd been enjoying for more than twenty years and the
prospect of uniting herself to one other human being for
the rest of her life. Wedlock was one state of being that
Virginia had always considered suitable only for suckers.
Freedom was the one determining factor for happiness in
her life—freedom and the fact that she was unhampered
by the likes of a man.

Now she was actually wondering what it would be
like to go the other way. She'd never done that
before—had never even questioned the way she lived.
Yet here she was in Eliot's kitchen, cooking for Eliot's
family and wondering what it would be like to spend
the rest of her life with him. How odd. How strange.
How completely unlike her. What could it possibly
mean?

Virginia lifted her other hand to his face, then leaned
forward to kiss him chastely on the lips. "Eliot, I—"

"Daddy? Virginia? Do you need any help in here?"
Gwyn rounded the kitchen door with Spenser hot on her
heels.

"We're fine, kids," Virginia told them, dropping her

hands back to her sides. "Just fine." With one final, longing look at Eliot, she turned around to open the oven door and remove the garlic bread, slamming it harder than necessary when she closed it again.

She blew an errant curl out of her eyes. "Everything . . . is just . . . fine."

27

In organizing her trousseau, a bride will often turn to her mother for assistance. Despite the free and easy times in which we live, one must not assume that a bride's knowledge of peignoirs and lingerie is necessarily extensive. If this is the case where you are concerned, do not be afraid to ask questions of your mother, future mother-in-law, or another close, married, female relative. Such inquiry may spare you minor embarrassment in the days—and nights—to come.

—ALISON BRIGHAM

"It truly amazes me what some women will wear these days."

Francesca fingered the long purple fringe decorating a green satin brassiere and wrinkled her nose in disgust. Desiree had invited her to go shopping for a gift for Emma's personal shower, along with her sister-in-law, Virginia, and the three women had spent the entire morning and afternoon wandering through virtually every lingerie department in the metro—D.C. area. So far Francesca had seen nothing she deemed appropriate for her son's new bride. Everything was either too revealing or too concealing, or, in this case, too tacky.

"You don't like that?" Desiree asked her. "I think the colors are kind of nice together."

Francesca eyed her doubtfully. "But the fringe . . ."

"It could be a very extrasensory experience," Desiree said.

Francesca considered the garment for a moment. "Well, since you put it that way, I suppose it does have its own certain . . . bizarre . . . charm. What do you think, Virginia?"

Virginia glanced over from a display beneath a sign that read, "Novelty Panties." "Looks okay to me. I'm still trying to figure out this little number here." She withdrew an extremely small garment from a rack of other extremely small garments in a variety of colors. "Crotchless panties with a whistle sewn on," she muttered. Then, in case the others hadn't been able to hear her the first time, she repeated loudly, "Crotchless panties with a whistle! Now what marketing genius came up with this?"

"Well, maybe that's a bit much," Desiree said. "After all, they would be very impractical, especially in cold weather. And I would think that whistle would show if you wore a tight skirt with them."

Virginia stared at her sister-in-law for a moment before responding, "I, um . . . I don't think they're supposed to be worn as an undergarment, Desi."

"Well what else would you wear them for?" Francesca asked.

Virginia tried to remember why she had agreed to this excursion in the first place. "Never mind," she said as she replaced the panties on the rack. "Maybe we should try another store."

Francesca scrutinized the green and purple brassiere one more time. "Perhaps we should."

They were about to depart when another item caught Desiree's eye.

"Oh, whoa, hold on a minute," she said as she crossed the small boutique to the New Arrivals rack. She plucked a pale yellow creation from the seemingly hundreds of pieces hanging there. The neckline dipped dangerously low in front and even lower in back, and it had spaghetti straps trimmed with a delicate white length of marabou. The front of the gown was beaded from top to bottom with dozens of tiny seed pearls and white sequins. And the rest of it was completely transparent. On the whole, Francesca decided, the gown was rather . . . loud. Like something one might see in a bad TV miniseries. And it was certainly far from appropriate for a twenty-three-year-old bride.

"This," Desiree said in a solemn, authoritative voice, "is beautiful."

Francesca and Virginia exchanged dubious glances.

"I don't think that's quite Emma's style," Francesca said softly. "It's a bit too . . . too . . ."

"Too frilly," Virginia said.

"Yes, that's it exactly," Francesca agreed, relief evident in her voice. "Too frilly. Thank you, Virginia."

"No problem."

"I wasn't thinking of this for Emma," Desiree told them.

Virginia looked from the gown to Desiree and then back again. "I don't know . . . it's not exactly you, Desi. You look better in bright colors."

Desiree smiled. "I wasn't thinking about it for me, either."

Virginia eyed her warily. "You can't possibly be suggesting I buy that thing. I never wear this kind of stuff." Although wouldn't Eliot be surprised if she showed up in something like that this weekend? she thought.

Desiree shook her head. "I was thinking about it for Francesca."

"*What?*" Francesca cried.

Desiree held the gown up in front of Francesca with a

satisfied nod of her head. "I know I originally suggested black, but this color suits you, and it's just racy enough that it will make Lionel go bonkers when he sees you in it."

"Desiree, you can't be serious." Francesca gave Virginia a nervous sidelong glance. "I couldn't possibly . . . I mean, that gown is . . . is . . . lovely . . . but I just don't think . . ."

"What are you talking about?" Desiree said. "You'll look great in it." She thrust the hanger into Francesca's hand. "Try it on."

"Oh, no, I don't—"

"Go on," Desiree encouraged her. "See how it looks."

Francesca turned to Virginia.

"Hey, go for it," Virginia said. "Can't hurt to try it on."

Outnumbered and too tired to protest, Francesca took the garment, handed Desiree her purse, sighed melodramatically, and stepped into the dressing room.

As she slipped out of her Evan-Picone separates and carefully arranged them on the pegs behind her, she surveyed the gown again. Perhaps it wasn't quite as bad as she'd first considered it. Although certainly more revealing than anything she owned, and infinitely more decorative, it did compel one to take notice. And the color was rather nice. She ran her finger over the fabric and was surprised to discover how silky and soft it was. Somehow, she had expected the texture to be rough.

"How's it going in there, Francesca?" Desiree called from the other side of the door.

"Almost finished," she called back.

"Say, Francesca?" This time it was Virginia's voice.

"Yes?"

"You know, I've been wondering. Francesca is kind of a long name. Has anyone ever called you Fran or Francie or Frankie?"

"Virginia," Francesca heard Desiree say. "Don't be rude."

"No," Francesca said as she slid the pale yellow gown over her head. "No one." She smiled, unable to help herself as she added, "Does anyone ever call you Virgie or . . . or Virgin?"

Virginia laughed. "No, not recently. Touché, Frankie."

Francesca smiled again as she straightened the gown, then turned to look at herself in the mirror. *Oh, dear,* she thought when she saw how much of herself was revealed. And she was still wearing her underthings. Very little was left for the imagination, and when she turned to view herself from the back, she gasped. Absolutely nothing left to the imagination there. She could never wear something like this. Lionel would be shocked.

Then with a little half-smile of anticipation, Francesca realized that was the whole point. Turning back to view herself again, she decided maybe this wasn't such a bad little piece of work after all. The marabou tickled where it brushed against her skin, and the pearls and sequins felt heavy and oddly erotic against her abdomen.

A few quick knocks on the door reminded her of Desiree's presence. "Come on, Francesca, let's see," she said as she tugged open the door.

"Oh, no, I don't think—"

Desiree let out a low whistle and smiled with satisfaction. "That's it," she said. "That gown is exactly what you need. You know, you got a nice figure, Francesca. I don't know why you don't show it off a little better."

Francesca turned first one way, then another, taking in the full effect. "Yes, I have, haven't I?" she murmured. "I don't know why, either."

The three women gazed at Francesca's reflection in the mirror, marveling at the way a single gown had seemed to completely transform her.

"You know, I think they had some of those crotchless panties in that color," Virginia said. "What size would you take, Francesca?"

"Medium," Francesca replied automatically. By the time she realized the significance of her response, Virginia had returned.

"I brought you a pair with a whistle," she said as she extended the panties toward Francesca. "I figured you might as well have a little fun. And what the hell . . . I think I might get myself a pair, too. Desi?"

Desiree closed the fitting room door to give Francesca a little privacy while she changed back into her clothes. "Did they have any in red?"

"I think so."

"Sure, I'll take a pair."

As the two women walked back toward the Novelty Panties rack, Virginia said, "They had one pair with a kazoo, too. Do you think Francesca would like that better?"

"Nah. We don't want to get her started off in the big leagues just yet. Lionel might have a heart attack."

Virginia nodded.

Desiree smiled. "So, I'll take the ones with the kazoo."

Francesca rejoined them, and the three women chattered aimlessly on their way to the sales counter to make their purchases. As they exited into the mall again, Francesca suddenly remembered something.

"Remind me that I want to stop by a record store on the way out," she told Desiree.

"What for?"

Francesca smiled. "A Johnny Mathis album."

"Oh, good idea. I got a nice bottle of Chianti at home I've been saving for a special occasion. You and Lionel are welcome to it."

"Why, thank you, Desiree. And by the way," she added, "in what hotel did you and Laszlo stay when you honeymooned in Atlantic City?"

Desiree sighed at her memories. "We had the honeymoon suite at the Cupid's Arrow Motor Lodge. Very classy back in 1951. Free bubble bath *and* they had a beautiful fruit basket waiting for us on our arrival. I can't guarantee it would be that nice today. Atlantic City has changed a lot."

"Yes, well, so have Lionel and I. The Cupid's Arrow Motor Lodge sounds like precisely what we need."

Virginia had been listening to the byplay with much confusion. "What on earth are you two talking about?" she asked the other women.

Desiree and Francesca shared a secret smile.

"Love, Virginia," Desiree said. "True love. Someday you should be so lucky to find it for yourself."

28

*Nowhere in the annals of history will one
find a more perfect example of feminine
bonding than that created during a bridal
shower. Other than the nail salon, this is the
last bastion of female camaraderie. Unlike
the bachelor party, which too often becomes
little more than an excuse for gross masculine misbehavior, a bridal shower centers
around games and gifts that promote style,
good taste, and graciousness.*

—ALISON BRIGHAM

Because of the number of guests who would be
attending Emma's personal shower, Patsy and Mindy had
been happy to accept Felicia Hammelmann's offer to
host the event at her big house in Falls Church instead of
the cramped apartment the two of them shared in
Adams-Morgan. Now, as Patsy and Mindy gazed at the
shower decorations, the two of them sighed in satisfaction with their handiwork.

The living room and dining room were strung with
crepe paper in pastel pink, yellow, lavender, and blue,
with balloons and fold-out paper wedding bells springing
from every available corner. From the light fixture above

the dining room table hung a massive paper swan with a cardboard cupid riding its back, and atop the table was an enormous array of treats—cupcakes speared with plastic hearts, petits fours decorated with tiny frosting roses, pastel mints, Hershey kisses in the Easter-colored foil wrappings (which Desiree had cleverly tucked away in the freezer the previous spring, just in case), and a huge sheet cake baked by Mindy's mother—Emma's Aunt Camellia—splashed with more pastel color and the inscription, "Emma + Taylor = ♥."

In the living room, the two women had set up and papered a large table for the gifts and a small table to hold the door prizes for the half-dozen games they had planned.

"It'll be the bridal shower to end all bridal showers," Mindy said.

"The mother of all bridal showers," Patsy agreed.

The guests—all thirty-seven of them—began to arrive right on time, the Hammelmann aunts and cousins outnumbering the Rowan aunts and cousins nearly four to one. Emma arrived a bit late, citing traffic from the city as her excuse, then took her seat in the chair of honor Patsy and Mindy had adorned with even more crepe paper and balloons. Emma struggled to remain calm as she looked out over the guests and saw aunts she hadn't spoken to in years, cousins whose names she could barely remember, and a variety of Rowan women she didn't even know. The only way she could tell they must be Rowans was by the way they were dressed—elegantly. She gazed down at her blue jeans and old, oversized sweater and sighed. How was she going to survive becoming a Rowan?

After the obligatory greetings and well-wishing, Patsy and Mindy took charge.

"All right, everybody, settle down," Mindy announced as she and Patsy began handing out tiny pads of pastel-colored paper. "We're going to start the games now, and the first one is called 'How Feminine Are You?'"

Emma groaned. She didn't like the sound of that one bit.

"This one was Aunt Desi's idea," Patsy added. "Mindy and I had nothing to do with it. Aunt Desi insisted."

Desiree waved a hand in dismissal but smiled. "I love this game. It separates the women from the girls."

"Now," Mindy continued, "everyone starts off with twenty points, and then you get to add or subtract points depending on how you answer questions. A perfect score would be one hundred. Everybody got it?"

"What kind of questions?" Adrienne Rowan asked.

"Well, now Adrienne, you'll just have to wait and find out with everyone else, won't you?" Desiree said. "Besides, look how pretty you look today in that nice flowered dress and high heels." At this point Desiree turned to stare pointedly at Emma, though her comment was clearly addressed to Adrienne. "You'll probably be the winner."

Emma sighed and ignored her mother's comment, focusing instead on the pen in her hand that read, "I Eat at Fogelman's Diner."

"Now, everyone write the number twenty at the top of your pad," Mindy instructed, "and as I ask questions and give or subtract points, you're going to have to do the math yourself. You're all on the honor system here, so don't disappoint me."

Everyone made the notations on the pads they'd been handed, and then Mindy began reading from a list of questions. "Question number one: Are you wearing a dress, skirt, or pants? Give yourself four points for a dress, two points for a skirt, and subtract three if you're wearing pants."

Emma subtracted three.

"Question number two," Mindy continued. "Are you wearing stockings or knee-high hose? Four points for the first, two points for the second."

"What if you're wearing socks?" Emma asked. She noted belatedly that her question seemed not to be a concern for anyone else present.

Mindy consulted her scoring sheet. "Subtract three points."

Emma subtracted three.

"Question number three," Mindy went on. "Are you wearing makeup?"

Emma subtracted three more points.

The questions continued for the better part of a half hour, covering a broad spectrum of unquestionably feminine requirements ranging from mascara to sleepwear to whether one's hair was curly or straight and whether one would choose to watch *South Pacific* over *Terminator 2*. Then Mindy instructed everyone to tally her score to see whose was highest.

"I've got seventy-six," Emma's Aunt Miranda said.

Taylor's cousin, Gwyn, announced that she had scored eighty-six.

"She cheated," Virginia said to Emma under her breath. "When I was coming back from the bathroom, I saw her give herself four points in the courtesy round, and that woman's manners are a negative three if they're anything at all. God only knows what other kind of creative scoring she concocted for herself."

"Aunt Virginia . . ." Emma muttered with a nervous smile. "I think she heard you. She's staring at us."

Virginia looked up to find Eliot's daughter gazing at her through slitted eyes, so she raised her hand in greeting. "I saw your father last night, Gwyn."

"Brownie?" Francesca asked. "I haven't seen him since the engagement party. How was he?"

Virginia circled her thumb and index finger in an "okay" gesture. "He was *great*," she said, pronouncing the word so that none of the women present would be able to doubt its sexual implication.

Francesca was about to say something else, but Mindy

interrupted with, "Okay, eighty-six. Gwyn has an eight-six. Can anyone do better than that?"

"I only got to forty-three," Patsy grumbled from the other side of Emma. "What did you get?"

Emma gazed sullenly at the final number on her page. "Negative thirty-two."

"Don't feel bad," Virginia whispered as she leaned closer. "I got negative forty."

"I have a perfect score of one hundred," Francesca announced.

Everyone oohed and aahed their admiration.

"Anyone else?" Mindy asked, glancing around the room.

"Of course, I didn't play since I was the one who suggested the game," Desiree said. "It wouldn't have been fair."

No one could claim she was more feminine than Francesca, so the first game went to Emma's future mother-in-law. At Mindy's encouragement, Francesca went to the prize table and selected a medium-sized gift in front, then unwrapped it to discover an oven mitt shaped like a giant lobster claw.

"I'll cherish it," she told them all as she tried it on.

"The next game," Patsy announced when everyone was seated again, "is one of mine. It's a memory game." She lifted an enormous tray which was stacked with a variety of items and covered with a piece of fabric to hide them. "Under this cloth are all the things that Emma and Taylor will need for their wedding night. You'll have sixty seconds to look at them, then I'll remove the tray and you'll have three minutes to write them all down from memory. Everyone ready? Gather close."

Everyone leaned forward in anticipation, and Patsy removed the cloth with all the flamboyance of a cheap magician. For a moment, no one said a word, because each was intent on studying the assortment of goods on the tray before them. Eventually, however, one or two began to snicker and chuckle, with an occasional "Oh my God." By the end of sixty seconds, most of the guests were down on their knees in front of the tray, shaking their heads in wonder.

"Time's up," Patsy announced at the end of sixty seconds, covering the tray with the fabric once again. "Now you have three minutes to write everything down."

Each woman retreated to her seat and began to scribble frantically, trying to recall every item that would be a requirement for an eventful wedding night.

"That's it, pencils down," Patsy called again as the second hand on her watch approached the twelve for the third time. "Now I'll read everything off, and you can check to see what you got right."

Consulting the list in her hand, she began, "Okay, first we've got the usual stuff: bubble bath, wine, grapes, *The Rubaiyat of Omar Khayyám*, candles, and incense. Then we've got the fun stuff: black bra and garter belt, handcuffs, flavored condoms, a copy of *Forum*, a dog collar and leash, a can of Crisco, a Twister game, *Debbie Does Dallas*, a pack of Lucky Strikes . . . am I going too fast for anyone?"

The women shook their heads, but none looked up from her pad of paper, each clearly intent on accurate scoring.

"By the way, Emma," Patsy interjected before continuing with her list, "Mindy and I do insist that you take the contents of this tray with you on your honeymoon. We'll wrap it up real nice for you."

"Uh, gee, thanks, Patsy," Emma mumbled with a sidelong glance at her future in-laws seated in a stiff row on the sofa. "That's awfully decent of you."

Patsy smiled. "Don't mention it. Now, on with the list. One bottle of cheap tequila—worm intact—one large salami, a blindfold, a bullwhip, a zucchini, a spatula . . ."

As it turned out, Adrienne was the winner of the

memory game, having identified and recalled each and every item that had been placed on the tray. She just barely edged out Virginia, who fell to second place because she hadn't recognized the French tickler. Francesca's expression had been indecipherable as she watched her youngest daughter collect her prize—something Patsy called a sea-monkey farm.

The shower lasted for the remainder of the afternoon. Once the games had been completed, the women turned to the opening of Emma's gifts for entertainment. Emma recalled then how her two cousins had looked at each other when they'd said in unison, "Personal shower." She should have realized no good would come of it.

Now, as Emma opened her gifts of piles of lace and satin and silk, with occasional sachets and toiletries thrown in for good measure, she wished she had asked for another kitchen shower instead. At least she probably would have used something like a carrot scraper or egg separator. Instead she found herself the new owner of what she was sure was the entire inventory of Victoria's Secret.

She had never much thought of herself as a lingerie aficionado, though she had to admit there was something peculiarly intriguing about the underthings she had received as gifts. Never in her wildest dreams would she have entertained the notion of wearing a garter belt and stockings, but when she opened the package from her cousin Deirdre to uncover such an ensemble nestled among the flowered, scented tissue paper, she found herself wondering if such garments would actually be comfortable. And that other thing Mindy had given her, Emma recalled, reaching for the box she'd opened before Deirdre's . . .

"What did you say this was called, Mindy?" she asked, holding up what appeared to be nothing more than a black bodice separated from what should have been a fuller garment.

Mindy looked up from the tray of mints she was passing around. "A merry widow," she said with a smile.

Emma had to admit it was a great name with which to endow a piece of lingerie. She was surprised to find herself growing more and more fascinated by every gift she opened. By the end of the afternoon, she had collected a very impressive assortment of lingerie, things she'd had no idea women actually wore, things she hadn't even realized were made anymore. There were teddies and camisoles and tap pants and chemises, words that had been virtually absent from Emma's vocabulary before today. And deep down inside, she had to confess she couldn't wait to get home and try them all on.

The afternoon had ended and the evening begun by the time most of the aunts and a number of the cousins had finished saying their good-byes. Emma began to gather up the boxes of underwear scattered about the floor near the chair of honor.

"Oh, no you don't. Stop that," Patsy said when she saw what Emma was doing. "You're not going anywhere."

"Why not?"

"Because the party's just beginning."

"What do you mean?"

"Just stick around," Patsy told her with a mysterious smile. "You're the guest of honor. So just have a seat for now, and let us take care of the rest."

Emma did as she was told, occupying herself with arranging and rearranging her gifts until each present was back in its original box and each box was stacked neatly in a pile beside the chair. As she performed her task, she noticed Patsy and Mindy were clearing the table of the soft pastel bridal shower trappings and gradually replacing them with bottles of bourbon, Scotch, gin, and vodka.

Mindy ejected from the stereo the chamber music cassette that had played during the shower and substituted it with the latest from the MTV buzz bin. Emma listened for a moment, then identified the band as Social Distortion. Although the crepe paper and decorations remained hanging, Patsy and Mindy shredded them until the whole house looked like the set for a bad music video. Then they turned to the others still present and shouted, "Let's do it!"

Emma looked around and saw that the only women who remained from the shower were her younger cousins, a few friends her sisters-in-law, Taylor's sisters, and her Aunt Virginia. Her mother and future mother-in-law, along with the other "adults" who had attended, were conveniently out of the way. And in their places, a number of Emma's friends had shown up, apparently through the back door, because she had seen none of them enter.

"Surprise!" a chorus of voices went up around her.

"Emma Hammelmann," Patsy said as she broke the seal on a bottle of white rum, "welcome to your bachelorette party."

"We women are alone tonight, our significant others all having been invited to Taylor's bachelor party," Mindy added. "And those guys will no doubt be going until dawn, so why shouldn't we?"

Emma laughed. Even if she'd wanted to, she knew there was no way this group would let her escape this party alive. And frankly, she didn't want to anyway. "You all are too much," she told them.

"Hey, Taylor and his buddies are going to be getting totally twisted tonight," Patsy said, "so why shouldn't we chicks have a deranged fling of our own?" She tipped the bottle of rum upside down and emptied its contents into the huge crystal punch bowl, which had until recently held lime sherbet punch. "Blue ocean waves, anyone?" she asked.

"Oh, God, no, Patsy," Emma pleaded, her stomach clenching at the mention. "Whatever you do, don't make blue ocean waves. You know what happened last time."

Patsy twisted the cap off of a bottle of blue curaçao

and tilted it over the punch bowl as well. "Yeah, we all got sick and puked blue. Wasn't it wild?"

Felicia frowned at that. "This stuff won't permanently stain the carpet, will it?"

Patsy peeled the tab away from a can of lemonade concentrate and plopped the still-frozen contents into the punch bowl along with a number of other ingredients, most of them alcoholic. "Relax, Felicia, will you?" she said as she began stirring. When the concoction seemed to be reaching the proper consistency, she looked up and intoned those immortal last words: "Trust me."

Felicia eyed Patsy closely, clearly unconvinced, but didn't press the matter further. Patsy began filling glasses with the blue mixture and passed them around to everyone. Then she lifted her own aloft.

"One week from tonight," she said gravely, "Emma and Taylor will be getting married. To Emma and Taylor."

"To Emma and Taylor!" the others cried.

Patsy thought for a moment, studying Emma as she tried to decide on just the right toast. "All the best to you in your connubial pursuits. May your copulations be many, your confrontations few."

"Hear, hear," the others agreed, lifting their glasses in salute before drinking heavily.

From then on, the evening slowly degenerated into socially questionable mayhem. About the time Patsy began to scrape bottom with the punch bowl ladle, three of Emma's friends from the local NOW chapter arrived toting cases of Bud. The party guests consumed those while Patsy made more blue ocean waves, but, unable to locate another bottle of rum, she was forced to use gin this time. However, because everyone's taste buds had been pretty well deadened by the effects of the first batch, no one seemed to notice the difference.

It was after midnight when the women decided it would be great fun for them all to try on Emma's gifts of exotic lingerie. It was twelve-thirty when they stumbled upon Eddie's imported cigars. And it was nearly one when Lobo, the male stripper, arrived with a cameraman in tow. He was extremely well oiled from calves to biceps and reeked of Brut, but no one seemed to mind.

And when Lobo stripped out of his rodeo wear down to a rawhide G-string and began his gyrations in front of a helplessly immobilized Emma to a rather raucous country-and-western rendition of "Wild Thing," everyone was more than happy to join in the fray. Dressed in little more than scraps of lace and silk and satin, clutching blue ocean waves in one hand, robustos in the other, Patsy, Mindy, Virginia, and all the others danced around the room as if disco had never died. By then Lobo was twirling his lasso with expert prowess, and had Emma in his sights for capture.

And that was how Taylor, Max, Eddie, and Vick found them all when they arrived shortly after two.

Taylor's bachelor party had been for the most part a civilized affair, something organized by Max and a few of his other friends and formally dubbed "The Last Supper." The group of twenty-two young men had arranged for a room at a local seafood restaurant, had ordered shrimp, scallops, mahi-mahi, and the like, had smoked Cohibas and imbibed good port, and then had swapped stories about the pros and cons of marriage and bachelorhood. Each had recalled stories from his own experience, and each had drawn his own conclusions. And Taylor's conclusion had been that nothing—nothing in the world—felt more right than being with Emma Hammelmann for the rest of his life.

Yet now as he watched a nearly naked, sweaty, muscular man yell "Yippee-ki-yay" and throw a rope around his scantily clad fiancée to pull her close, Taylor's conviction began to waver. He glanced at Max and Emma's brothers on each side of him to see if his companions were equally stunned by the chaos surrounding them, but the other three waded into the fracas with more enthusiasm than Taylor felt himself.

"What the hell is going on here?" he tried to shout above the loud music.

The only person who heard, unfortunately, was Lobo's cameraman, who turned quickly to get Taylor's reaction permanently on tape. And like an angry militant government official, Taylor snaked out a hand to cover the lens, effectively preventing further documentation of the event by an overzealous media.

"Emma!" he yelled over the din, taking several long strides across the room until he stood immediately beside her.

But Emma and Lobo were slow-dancing cheek to cheek with their eyes closed, and she seemed not to hear her fiancé's call. So Taylor grabbed Lobo by his upper arm—twice, because Lobo was so greasy that the first time Taylor made the attempt his fingers slipped off— and shoved the stripper away. Emma, gradually growing more and more aware that she was then dancing alone, opened her eyes little by little until she finally focused on Taylor. She smiled and tried to reach out for him, but her arms were pinned by Lobo's lasso. So intense did her concentration become on freeing herself that she completely forgot about Taylor's presence.

Taylor quickly loosed the rope from around his intended, then doubled his fists on his hips and glared at her.

"Thanks," Emma muttered as she stumbled out of the circle of rope pooled at her feet. She tripped, pitched forward, and landed in Taylor's arms. "Oh, hi, Taylor," she said against his chest when she finally recognized who he was.

Taylor pushed her away to arm's length and studied her closely. Her hair was a mess and matted down with Lobo oil, her eyes were closed, and she positively reeked of perspiration and some cheap cologne. And she was dressed . . . good God, she was dressed in a minuscule piece of black lace unlike anything he'd ever seen her wear before. Although, as Taylor studied Emma's attire more closely, he decided it wasn't such a bad little outfit, even incongruously coupled with blue jeans.

"What on earth are you wearing?" he asked her.

Emma glanced down at her body and then tipped her head back to stare at Taylor again. "Mindy says it's called a . . . a murray window . . . no, a wary minnow . . . no, wait . . . give me just a minute." She sighed again, and then replied slowly and carefully, "A merry widow."

Taylor couldn't help but smile. "Why, Emma," he said with a chuckle, "have you been drinking?"

Emma shook her head hard until it snapped forward against her chest. "Only a little," she confessed. "Patsy made blue ocean waves."

"Oh no," Taylor said. "Not again."

"Yup. You want one?"

"No way."

She seemed to remember something then, and went to great pains to articulate the question, "Why . . . why didn't . . . why aren't you at your . . . your bachelor party? What are you doing here?"

"My bachelor party ended almost an hour ago," he told her. "Eddie and Vick needed a ride home, so Max and I offered them a lift."

"Oh, that was so nice of you," Emma said as her eyes began to glaze over a little. "It's so far out of your way."

Taylor looked at Emma's little outfit again and smiled. "Yeah, but well worth the trip. Come on. I think it's about time someone made a pot of coffee."

"Oh, no, I don't need coffee," Emma insisted, stumbling again as she moved away from him.

"Well, I do."

Taylor tugged on her hand until she was following him into the kitchen. Once there, he did his best to place her carefully into a chair, but thanks to Emma's rather inebriated state, wound up fairly dumping her there instead. When he turned back from the coffeemaker as it began to brew, he found his fiancée watching him through narrowed eyes, as if she'd been staring at him for some time.

"You know," she finally said as she blew an errant strand of dark hair out of her eyes. "Even after all these years, I don't think I ever really noticed what a nice back you have."

"Oh, no?"

She shook her head several times, until she seemed to become dizzy, then lifted a hand to her forehead to stop the motion. "No. I've always liked your tush, though."

Taylor smiled. "Thanks. You've got a pretty nice tush yourself."

She smiled back. "Thanks."

Pushing herself away from the table, Emma made her way slowly across the kitchen until she stood before him. Taylor allowed himself the luxury of a slow perusal of her little outfit again, marveling at the way the black lace bustier was fitted to push her breasts up and out of their confinement. He'd never seen Emma wear anything beneath her clothes except practical cotton panties and undershirts, and found this newly uncovered side of her to be rather intriguing. He lifted a finger to trace the faint shadow between her breasts, feeling her heartbeat quicken beneath his fingertip.

"So, exactly what kind of shower did you have today?" he asked her.

"Personal," she said quietly as she untied his tie and began to unbutton his shirt.

"Oh, come on, you can tell me."

"No, I mean it was a personal shower."

When she had his buttons undone down to the center of his chest, she spread his collar open and dipped her head to nuzzle his neck. Taylor's own pulse skittered around a little at that.

"And what's a personal shower?" he managed to ask.

Emma kissed his throat, running the tip of her tongue along his jaw and over his earlobe. "It's where people give you lots and lots of underwear," she whispered near his ear.

"So, uh . . . so you got more stuff like this?"

He dropped his hands to her waist, where the merry widow ended in wispy black trim. Her bare torso below was warm to the touch, but Taylor raked his hands slowly over the soft fabric above, pressing his fingers into whalebone and lace until his hands completely covered her breasts. He squeezed them gently, running his thumbs over the peaks.

"Oh, lots more," Emma said with a sigh as she leaned into his touch. "You wouldn't believe some of the stuff I got."

"Oh, really?"

She nodded, skimming her hand up his thigh until she reached the apex of his legs. When she cupped him in her palm, she felt him grow stiff and full, and heard him emit a satisfied little sigh of his own.

"What kind of stuff?" he asked. "By any chance, did anyone give you a . . . a . . ."

She smiled and rubbed her palm more intimately against him. "A what?"

"Oh, God," he muttered, sucking in a ragged breath. When he trusted himself to speak coherently again, he said, "For some reason, Emma, I've always had this fantasy of making love to you while you're wearing . . ."

She ran her index finger along the length of him again. "Wearing what?"

The coffeemaker wheezed to a conclusion behind them, gasping out a cloud of steam. Taylor felt the damp heat against his back when Emma began to pull his shirt tail free from his pants.

"A garter belt and stockings," he told her. "And high heels. I know you don't own any high heels, Emma, but there's probably an all-night shoe stand *somewhere* in town. Maybe we could . . ."

Emma leaned back only far enough so that she could stare into his eyes. "You've been looking at *Playboy* again, haven't you?"

He colored faintly, but smiled. "Only for the articles. There was a very informative piece on the trade agreement with Mexico in this month's issue. Not to mention a short story by John Updike."

"And a centerfold who had really big hooters, too, I bet."

"Well, yeah, that too."

Emma studied him for a moment before revealing, "Actually, I did get a black garter belt and stockings from Mindy to match this. I don't think anyone's wearing them right now. And Felicia and I do wear the same shoe size. She has lots of high heels."

"Really?"

"She even has one pair with a leopard-print pattern."

"No kidding."

"I'm sure she wouldn't mind if I just slipped upstairs and borrowed them." After a moment she added, "But you wanted to have coffee, didn't you?"

"Oh," Taylor murmured as he slipped his arms around her waist, "I guess coffee could wait."

They quickly made their way back through the living room to the front door, never noticing that no one noticed their departure.

Lobo was now dancing with Virginia, who had opted for a more modest hot pink chemise. Eddie had gone in search of his wife, finally discovering her clad in a clingy red bodysuit and passed out on top of the piano. And Vick had discovered a rather nauseated Catherine in the bathroom splashing cold water on her face and down the front of a truly remarkable peekaboo nightie.

Max, shaking his head in wonder at all the sights to be seen, now went to the bar to help himself to a blue ocean wave. Just as he finished ladling a healthy portion into a glass, he felt a hand on his shoulder and turned to find Patsy Hammelmann wearing little more than a smile.

"Hi, Max," she greeted him in a sultry voice he scarcely recognized as hers.

Max's gaze slid over her body from head to toe, taking in the lush curves, the leopard-print garter belt, and the ample breasts straining against a matching bustier that looked like it was two sizes too small for her. She inhaled deeply on a cigar and blew the smoke directly in his face as she exhaled. It struck Max then that there was something incredibly erotic about the red stain from a woman's mouth encircling the tip of a cigar. When he slugged back his drink the ice shifted, causing him to dribble a good portion of blue onto his white dress shirt and tie.

"Hey, Patsy," he said, wiping his mouth fiercely on the back of his hand. "You, uh . . . you're looking good."

"Thanks. You're not so bad yourself." Patsy brushed at the stains on Max's tie, her fingers wandering higher until she reached the knot at his throat, which she loosened. Cocking an eyebrow suggestively, she enjoyed another puff from the cigar and asked, "You wanna dance?"

Max tipped back his drink and consumed it completely, then dipped his glass back into the punch bowl again, sloshing up blue around his cuff as he did so. He studied Patsy intently. "Yeah," he said. "Yeah, I'd love to dance."

Patsy tugged hard on his necktie until she'd pulled his body flush against hers, then circled his waist with her arms. As the two of them began to sway slowly to the fast heavy metal music blaring from the stereo, she let her hands wander lower until they covered Max's derriere.

"I don't think you realize this, Max," she whispered into his ear after nibbling the lobe, "but I have something that belongs to you . . ."

29

As her wedding day approaches, a bride will want to choose an opportunity to gather her bridesmaids together and thank them with a gift she has chosen as a memento of her wedding. If at all possible, Alison encourages you to host a brunch or luncheon for your bridesmaids. There is simply nothing more demure, more civil, more endearing to Alison, than a display of feminine repartee when the day is young.

—ALISON BRIGHAM

Emma's bridesmaids' luncheon was the following day. Desiree went all out to make the occasion a very special one and simply couldn't figure out why no one was enjoying herself very much. Although everyone had finally arrived—all of them more than a little bit late—no one seemed to be talking much.

Francesca, too, marveled at the lack of enthusiasm the younger women showed and especially wondered why Adrienne had worn dark glasses. Some new fashion thing, she supposed, knowing she would never fully understand the younger generation, not even her own daughter. At least Catherine looked nice, she decided as she surveyed her eldest. Well, for the most part. Perhaps there was a virus going around.

"Coffee, anyone?" Desiree asked when everyone was seated, holding up a fresh pot.

Everyone lifted her cup eagerly, but no one said a word.

"I've made something special for brunch today," Desiree went on as she poured.

"Bloody Marys?" Virginia asked hopefully, her elbows propped on the table, her head cradled in her hands.

"Oh, of course not, Virginia, shush," Desiree scolded. "Something Emma has always loved. Huevos rancheros, heavy on the onions, green peppers, and hot sauce."

Emma's stomach lurched at the mention of spicy food, and she felt the bile rising in her throat in a threat of nausea.

"And if you don't like Mexican food," Desiree went on with delight, "there's also fried ham, corn fritters, hash browns drizzled with bacon drippings . . ."

"Excuse me," Emma muttered, pushing her chair away from the table to make a mad dash for the bathroom.

"And later . . ." Desiree concluded, her eyes narrowing at her daughter's strange behavior as she watched Emma's retreat, " . . . after we've eaten, I have something even more special. Champagne!"

Her announcement was followed by a resonant scraping of chairs as several members of the party scooted themselves away from the table. Desiree watched in confusion as her guests ran off in various directions. When she looked at Francesca, the two women shrugged, and then Desiree returned to the kitchen to retrieve the heaping plates of food. By the time she returned, everyone except Patsy had returned to the table.

Emma lifted her nose to inhale the spicy aroma of food as each plate passed before her, and when she suffered no more ill effects as a result, helped herself to a small portion of each course, hoping her mother wouldn't notice if she did no more than push the morsels around on her plate. Virginia, on the other hand, ignored the food altogether, instead satisfying herself with an occasional munch of the celery stalk rising from the freshly prepared bloody Mary she'd brought with her when she returned to the table. Eventually Patsy came back to join the party once more, but upon seeing the food spread across the table, turned and fled again.

"What on earth is wrong with everyone today?" Desiree finally asked. "You all act like you got anorexia or something."

Emma lifted a bite of egg from her plate, stared at it for a moment, then let it drop back with a clatter. Virginia shoved her celery into her mouth bite by bite, consuming it without tasting it. Adrienne adjusted her sunglasses and said nothing. Catherine politely requested more coffee. When Patsy returned once again, it was with a pale face and watery eyes. But her hands shook only slightly as she lifted her coffee cup to her mouth.

The quiet mood remained as the women finished what they could of their meal. Desiree wound up making four more pots of coffee, something that surprised her because Emma and her friends had never seemed to be big coffee drinkers. And when it came time to pour the champagne, she and Francesca seemed to be the only ones who actually tasted it. Even when Desiree lifted her glass in a toast and wished her daughter and Taylor much love and devotion in the future—not to mention lots of healthy children—her good wishes were only feebly met with mumbles of "Good luck" and "God bless."

"And may the force be with you," Patsy added.

As silence settled over the table once again, Desiree elbowed her daughter and whispered, "Emma, don't you have something to give to your bridesmaids?"

Emma gazed at Desiree long and hard, making a very concerted effort to comprehend what her mother was saying over the loud buzz in her ears.

"You know," Desiree said, "the gifts you chose for them, to thank them for being in your wedding?"

Slowly her mother's words seeped into Emma's weary brain. "Oh, yeah." Turning to the others she said, "I have something for you. My bridesmaids, that is. Not that the rest of you don't mean a lot to me, too . . . Virginia . . . and Mrs. Rowan . . . and Mom. But this is the bridesmaids' luncheon after all," she reminded them unnecessarily. "Meant to honor those of you who were foolish enough to take me up on it when I asked you to be in my wedding."

Her announcement was met with quiet murmurs of acknowledgement and more requests for coffee.

Emma pushed her chair away from the table, gripping the armrests as she waited for her legs to steady, and then went to the buffet to collect a stack of brightly wrapped boxes. It took her a moment to focus on the names appearing on the cards, but eventually she managed to deliver each package to its proper recipient. Everyone smiled and murmured her thanks. Then each began to open her gift with about as much energy as she'd used to consume her breakfast.

Patsy was the first to reach the prize inside, and she chuckled as she held her gift aloft.

"A bowling shirt?" she asked with a genuine laugh.

The shirt was burgundy with a black collar, black trim, and black pleats in back—the color scheme of the wedding. "Patsy" was stitched over the left front pocket, and on the back was an elaborate design consisting of the wedding date, a multitiered cake, a bridal bouquet, and the words, "Team Hammelmann."

"Just a little memento for you all," Emma told them. "Taylor got the groomsmen Hawaiian shirts, so this just somehow seemed appropriate."

"Cool!" Adrienne cried, showing some emotion for the first time that day.

"How nice," Catherine added. "And you spelled my name correctly, too."

Desiree turned in her chair to gaze at her daughter with disappointment. "I thought you were going to get everyone earrings to wear in the ceremony."

Emma smiled. "I decided I wanted to do something a little different."

"Oh, bowling shirts are definitely different," Desiree said.

"Everybody gives earrings. I just figured they'd all get more use out of something like this." When Desiree continued to study her with silent disapproval, Emma added, "I actually had a couple made for you and Mrs. Rowan, too."

Desiree brightened. "You did?"

Emma nodded. "They're upstairs. Yours says 'Coach' on the back. Mrs. Rowan's says 'Manager.'"

Desiree smiled. "Well, that was very thoughtful of you, sweetie."

Emma shrugged a little self-consciously. "Hey, you're my mom. After everything you've done for me with the wedding, how could I forget about you?"

Desiree wadded up her napkin and tossed it onto the table beside her plate. Then she leaned over and hugged her daughter with all her might.

"You are such a good daughter," she said. "I'm such a lucky mother."

Emma grinned. "Mom," she said after a moment. "Mom, ease up . . . you're squeezing the life out of me."

When Desiree pulled back, Emma could see her mother's eyes misting up. Before she could say a word, two fat tears escaped and rolled down Desiree's cheeks, and Emma could only wonder what had generated this reaction.

"Mom, why are you crying?" she asked as she dabbed at her mother's face with her own napkin. "What did I say?"

Desiree reached for the napkin she had just discarded and blew her nose in the fine linen. "You don't have to

say anything," she said. "All you have to do is be you."
She pulled Emma close once again, her next words
offered quietly, for her daughter's ears alone.

"Oh, I'm just so happy for you, sweetie. You and Taylor are on your way to a wonderful life together . . . there's
so much waiting for you, such things that are going to
happen . . . I wish I could tell you. I wish I could prepare
you somehow . . ." She started to say more, then thought
better of it and pulled away, clasping Emma's hand in
both of her own. "But you'll find out. You and Taylor will
find out about all that together in the years to come. And
doing it together will just make it all that much more
special."

Desiree lifted a hand to brush back Emma's bangs, and
leaned forward to kiss her softly on her forehead. Then
she sat back in her chair and pondered her daughter with
eyes that were filled with love. "Be happy, Emma. You
and Taylor . . . you just be happy."

Emma smiled. "I will, Mom. We both will."

Desiree blew her nose one last time, then rose to make
an announcement. "We've still got cakes to eat," she
said, wiping her eyes with her napkin. "Little yellow tea
cakes with white frosting and pink roses on top. Laszlo's
sister-in-law Camellia made them—they're adorable.
And," she added with a knowing smile, "one of them has
a little prize inside. Whichever one of you lucky girls
finds the gold ring—not real gold of course, it might have
melted in the oven, who knows—but . . . whoever finds it
will be the next one to get married."

The women seated at the table looked at one another
anxiously as Desiree went to retrieve the silver tray upon
which was elaborately displayed ten tiny cakes, placing
the arrangement reverently in the center of the table.

"Go ahead," she encouraged them when no one
seemed inclined to sample one of the tempting-looking
treats. "I've had Camellia's tea cakes before, and I can
guarantee you that these will be delicious."

Yet they continued to sit motionless, all apparently uncertain whether they were willing to become the next bride.

"What's wrong?" Desiree asked. "You're not in the mood for sweets, either?"

Everyone mumbled an excuse, so Desiree took it upon herself to pass the cakes out to each of the women present. And when everyone only gazed suspiciously at the confection on her plate, Francesca decided it was up to her to be the first to uncover her fate. When she cut into her cake, she found it empty save a spongy yellow creation that fairly melted in her mouth.

"Well, that's only natural," Desiree said. "Because Francesca is already married. Now, who'll go next?"

"I might as well," Catherine muttered blandly. "Seeing as how I'm already saddled with the likes of Michael." She sighed when, like her mother, she found that her cake held little more than a treat.

One by one, the women began to gingerly slice into their desserts, eying the cakes cautiously as if they might explode. When Virginia's turn came, she swallowed with some difficulty, crossed herself ironically—ironic, because she wasn't Catholic—then inhaled a deep breath and lifted her knife with a surgeon's skill. Two single incisions—one lengthwise and one crosswise—revealed nothing. However, just to be sure, she snatched up her fork and mashed the four new pieces into an unsightly pile of yellow crumbs. Yellow but no gold, she noted. Yet instead of chuckling in delight to find she would remain a free woman, Virginia frowned and felt a little cheated. Choosing not to dwell on her confusing reaction, however, she turned to Patsy, who sat at her left.

"Your turn, kiddo," she told her niece.

Shunning the niceties of knife and fork, Patsy picked up her cake with both hands and split it in two. Then she stared in wonder at the circle of gold that leapt out from inside to fall in a seemingly endless arc of glittering light. Upon hitting the plate, it serenaded her with a song of *plink, plink, plink* and a circular dance on the fine china. Finally, it lay at the center of her plate, winking in the light of the overhead chandelier as if it were laughing at her.

"Wow," Patsy said softly. "It's going to be me. I'm going to be the next one who gets married."

"But you're not even dating anyone," Mindy said. She began to stab viciously at the cake on her own plate. "It's not fair. Bobby promised me a diamond for Christmas."

"Excuse me," Patsy said quickly as she felt another burst of nausea threatening. She shoved her chair away from the table and ran to the bathroom.

"What's got into Patsy?" Desiree asked.

"Got me," Emma said.

"Maybe it was something she ate," Virginia suggested.

"Not here," Desiree said. "Not today."

It was only then that Virginia recalled vaguely that Patsy hadn't been alone when she'd left the party the night before. She smiled wickedly as she asked Emma, "Is there something going on between Patsy and the boy who's going to be Taylor's best man?"

"Max and Patsy?" Emma asked, surprised by the question. For one thing, she hardly thought of Max as a boy, and for another, anything between him and Patsy existed only in her cousin's overly vivid imagination. At least, that's what Emma had always thought. "Not that I know of. Why?"

"Oh, no reason," Virginia answered, twisting a piece of hair around her finger. "Just that the two of them left the party together last night. And Patsy still had on your garter belt and bustier."

Emma felt her stomach turn again and knew the reaction had nothing to do with her hangover this time. "Max left with Patsy last night?" she asked in a very small voice.

"Frankly, I don't think leaving a party with a guy like Max would cause a woman to be sick the next morning," Mindy said. "Exhausted, maybe, but not sick."

Francesca smoothed her napkin across her lap and reached for her coffee cup. "If you ask me, I think there's something going around. Perhaps Patsy's caught it, too."

Emma looked over at her future mother-in-law to find Francesca staring at her intently. If she hadn't known better, she would have sworn Taylor's mother had meant that final comment for her.

"What's this party you all keep talking about?" Desiree asked. "Nobody told me about any party. And what was Patsy doing wearing Emma's lingerie?"

"It's a long story, Desi," Virginia said with a smile. "Emma, why don't you go check on Patsy while I explain to your mother and Francesca what happened last night."

Adrienne and Catherine looked up at Virginia's announcement, clearly as concerned as Emma over the new turn of events.

"Uh . . . if it's all the same to you, Aunt Virginia," Emma said, "I'd just as soon stay here and listen to what you tell . . . that is . . . what you say to Mom and Mrs. Rowan."

Catherine and Adrienne nodded and remained firmly seated, as well.

Virginia uttered a sound of disbelief at her niece's anxiety. "Oh, come on, Emma. Have you ever known me to incriminate anyone I love?"

"Well, yes, actually. There was that one time when you finked on Mindy and Patsy and me for smoking cigarettes we swiped from Aunt Claudia's purse."

"That was different," Virginia said. "You all were only twelve years old. Smoking can kill you. Fun can't. Now go check on Patsy."

"But—"

"Go."

Not quite able to shrug off her apprehension about

this new development where Max and Patsy were concerned, Emma scooted her chair away and went to check on her cousin. Surely Patsy was just still feeling the aftershocks of last night's revelries. A little club soda with bitters ought to fix her right up. It was the perfect hangover cure—worked wonders every time.

Unless of course, what Patsy was suffering from was something a lot more potent than a hangover.

30

Often the realization that a child is marrying may lead a parent to feel older and, perhaps, more melancholy. But these feelings are seldom overwhelming and tend to dissipate quickly. More likely, the parents of the bride and groom will experience an exhilaration that their children have taken that final step toward independence. As Alison can tell you, there is nothing more inspiriting than an opportunity to finally be alone with one's mate.

—ALISON BRIGHAM

Lionel Rowan pushed himself away from the dinner table and went in search of a smoke. He felt full and satisfied, Driscoll having completely outdone himself with this evening's dinner—lamb with honey mustard and rosemary, new potatoes with dill butter, lemon pepper asparagus, and that wonderful thing he did with squash. Francesca had missed a world-class chocolate souffle when she'd jumped up from the table before coffee had even been served so that she could . . .

What was it she'd said she needed to do? Lionel wondered. Oh, well, it didn't matter. All he wanted now was to relax in front of the fireplace with a good cigar and the latest issue of *The National Review*. Although it was only Thursday, and technically not yet the end of the work week, he would be taking the following day off because of tomorrow night's rehearsal dinner and any other last-minute wedding plans that might need his attention. Frankly, Lionel couldn't imagine any last-minute plans that would command his presence, but his wife had insisted he take Friday off, and so he would.

Despite the cold November wind gusting noisily against the windows outside, the library was very warm, thanks to the fire Margaret kept alive on days such as these. Lionel reached inside the cabinet bar beneath the world atlas. His fingers closed over the neck of a bottle, but what he withdrew was not the brandy for which he'd been searching, and was instead a bottle of wine. *Chianti?* he thought distastefully as he read the label. What the hell was that doing in there? Must have been a gift from someone, he thought as he replaced it.

When he finally located the bottle of cognac, he splashed a generous portion into a cut crystal snifter, fired up the last of his coronas, then made himself very comfortable in one of the leather wing chairs near the fireplace. He had just finished chuckling over Buckley's column on the national debt when a faint sound interrupted the silence. A strange sound, Lionel thought, unlike anything he could recall hearing in the house before. Music, surely, but not the kind of music to which he normally listened. Popular music, he realized with a frown. A man's melodious, mellifluous voice crooning something that vaguely resembled . . . "Chances Are?"

"Hello, Lionel."

Lionel turned with a start at the sound of a strange woman's voice. His mouth opened to demand her identity, but no words ever emerged. Because whoever the woman was, Lionel wasn't entirely certain he wanted her to leave.

She stood with her palms and forearms planted firmly against each side of the library doorjamb, a pose that gave Lionel the impression that the house remained standing only by virtue of her strength. Her hair spilled in a cascade of dark silk down her back and over her breasts, but her face and shoulders were in shadow. The light from the hallway behind her illuminated every luscious curve and valley on the most exquisite body Lionel had ever seen, and he could see quite a bit of it, thanks to the nearly nonexistent scrap of nothing she had on. The woman was exotic-looking, beautiful, and mesmerizing, the beads and feathers of her creamy gown making her seem ethereal and somehow unattainable. And of course that simply made Lionel want her all the more.

"Er . . ." he began.

The woman moved then, dropping her arms gracefully to her sides before striding into the room with all the leisure and delicacy of a swan. As she approached him, Lionel suddenly realized there was something distinctly familiar about the woman's walk, and a panic seized him like none he'd ever known.

"Jesus, what the hell are you doing dressed like that?" he demanded of his wife. "You'll catch your death."

Francesca seemed not to hear him, though, because she continued with her forward motion until she stood between him and the fireplace. Her position only made him realize that the gown he had thought translucent was in fact transparent, and deep down inside him, he felt the flicker of a tiny flame of something he hadn't felt for his wife in a very long time.

"You don't like this gown?" Francesca asked him. "I thought it was rather eye-catching myself."

Lionel inhaled a deep breath, counted slowly to ten, and then relaxed his lungs. "Well, it does have a certain . . . oh . . . unique appeal, I guess. If you like that kind of thing."

"And you don't?"

Oh, God, she was pouting now. Lionel didn't think he'd ever seen his wife pout before. He'd never noticed the pronounced curve of her lower lip, that fullness, that . . . that sensually arousing mystique that tugged at his very soul. "Don't what?" he asked, having completely forgotten what her question was.

"You don't like this kind of thing?"

And her voice. He'd never heard Francesca sound so . . . so . . . throaty . . . so intense . . . so . . . so incredibly erotic. "Well, yes, as a matter of fact, I do. But . . ." For some reason, he suddenly felt the need to stall. "But what if one of the servants sees you?" he whispered.

Francesca smiled seductively. "I've given Margaret and Driscoll the night off. They're going to a movie together. *Henry and June,* I think Margaret said."

"Margaret and Driscoll?" Lionel asked, weighing this new information. "Out on a date? Together?"

Francesca nodded. "Apparently they've developed a *grande passion* for each other over the past few months. Actually, they do make rather a nice couple, don't you think?"

Lionel shook his head in confusion. "First Taylor and Emma, then Brownie and that odd Hammelmann woman, now Margaret and Driscoll . . . my God, the wedding has everyone behaving strangely. Who'll be next?"

"I have an idea," Francesca said softly.

She reached out a hand to stroke back his hair, her fingers lingering in their task as she wound the white strands around her knuckles. Lionel tried to remain unmoved and simply stared straight ahead, an action that left him gazing wistfully at Francesca's breasts. They were beautiful beneath the sheer gown, turning from gold to yellow to orange to silver in the ever-changing light of the fire. Lionel itched to reach out and feel them in his hands, to steer them toward his mouth, but instead he curled his fingers into his palms and bit his lower lip. Yet when Francesca bent over to kiss the crown of his head, offering him a fuller view of her voluptuous figure, he could no longer tolerate the jolts of heat her strange caresses sent simmering throughout his body. He seized her hand and pressed it to his lips, tasting her palm with the tip of his tongue.

"How about a glass of wine?" Francesca asked suddenly, her pulse leaping to life at the thrill of fire his gentle touch ignited in the pit of her stomach. Carefully, she tugged her hand free from Lionel's so that she could go to the bar. Once she had retrieved the bottle of Chianti, she opened it, then poured two generous servings for them both. Cradling a glass in each hand, she rejoined her husband by the fire.

"I already have brandy," he said when she extended one glass toward him.

"You'll like this better," she told him.

He looked at her doubtfully, but smiled and accepted her offering. Lionel gazed at her as she handed him his glass, his eyes starting level with hers only to skim down the entire length of her body and back again. "Aren't you cold?" he asked softly.

Francesca shook her head. "Not in the least. Aren't you warm?"

As Lionel sipped his wine, his smile broadened. "Very."

She smiled back. "Good."

He swallowed more of his wine. "That certainly is some getup, Francesca," he remarked with a nervous grin, still studying the lines of her body beneath the gown. His gaze dipped lower to the lacy line of the panties that stretched across her hips. The next sip of his wine stuck somewhere in his throat when Lionel realized that a very significant part of those panties was conspicuously absent. He began to cough when he realized how strategically placed the triangular cutout was, and Francesca patted his back lightly to help him clear his lungs.

"Those . . . those panties . . ." he said with a gasp.

"Yes?" Francesca asked.

"They're . . . missing something, aren't they?"

She nodded. "Yes, they are. But if you'll notice, the manufacturer made up for that oversight by adding a little something extra."

When Lionel leaned in for a closer inspection, he was assailed by the warm, musky scent of her, and his body tightened accordingly. Lifting a hand, he traced his finger over a small object sewn at the satin apex. "A whistle?" he said incredulously. "What on earth is that for?"

"I guess there's only one way to find out, isn't there?" Francesca asked.

When Lionel looked up, she smiled down at him, a smile that held any number of libidinous suggestions. For a moment he could only stare at her, little by little recalling a time long ago when the two of them would leave the dinner table together in the middle of their meal and wind up making love someplace very unlikely—the stairwell, for example, or occasionally, when they were feeling particularly adventurous, outside on the balcony. That was back when they had lived in their Capitol Hill brownstone, when the servants had gone home at day's end, when it had been just the two of them at night. No children, no servants . . . no lovers clouding up the waters.

"You know, you haven't worn your hair down in years," Lionel said. "You even braid it at night before we go to bed nowadays."

Francesca raked her hands over her scalp, gathering her hair at her nape in two fists before releasing it, a gesture that had once been so familiar to him. "I didn't think you'd noticed."

Lionel nodded slowly. "I notice more than you think, Francesca. I know you probably find that hard to believe sometimes, but . . . honestly, I do."

She smiled at the way he said her name, wrapping his tongue around the syllables as if invoking an incantation.

Francesca dropped slowly to the carved Chinese rug before the fire, curling her legs beneath her, extending one hand toward Lionel in invitation. Immediately he joined her there, trying to fold his legs as she had, unable to quite manage the proper position.

"Bursitis," he mumbled as he extended his legs forward and crossed them at the ankle instead. "I'm not as young and agile as I used to be."

"I suppose that's true of us all, isn't it?" Francesca said. "The youth part anyway. As for agility . . ." She set her glass down on the hearth and leaned toward her husband, brushing her lips softly against his in a mere whisper of a kiss. Then she trailed a finger down his neck to his shirt collar and began to unfasten the buttons one by one.

Lionel's heart thumped wildly and his temperature soared as he watched her. He lifted his hand to curve over Francesca's breast, loving the soft firmness he encountered. "As for agility . . . ?" he asked her.

Francesca spread his shirt open wide, lifting herself from the rug to straddle his waist. She kissed him deeply as she pushed the soft fabric away from his shoulders, bringing her hips forward in a action that made Lionel groan. She groaned back when the hand on her breast tightened.

"As for agility," she whispered, "we can work on it together. And Lionel," she added a little breathlessly when he dipped his head between her breasts to nuzzle.

"Hmm?"

"If you need anything . . . just whistle."

31

*Your primary attendant, although someone you
have undoubtedly known for years, may surprise you at times. You may find that sharing a
meaningful experience—such as your wedding—
with the woman you choose for your maid or
matron of honor will bring you even closer than
you were before. And that, of course, is as it
should be.*

—Alison Brigham

The rehearsal dinner was to be a very civilized
affair in the Thoroughbred Room of a posh, five-star
Washington, D.C., hotel. Originally, when Emma and
Taylor had expressed their desire to host the event at a
small, intimate Dupont Circle restaurant that had a
room in back suitable for such a gathering, Francesca
had told them that would be impossible because she had
already made a deposit on the Thoroughbred Room.
When Emma and Taylor had tried to object, she had
told them further that the deposit was substantial—and
nonrefundable. So now Emma and Taylor and the rest
of the wedding party would be lifting their glasses in a
mahogany-paneled, wall-to-wall-carpeted, horse-paint-
ing-decorated hall beneath the biggest crystal chandelier

Emma had ever seen. She was rarely comfortable in such surroundings, and tonight would undoubtedly be no different.

"I don't know what to wear," Emma told Patsy as the two of them inspected her closet Friday afternoon.

"A dress," Patsy suggested.

"Thanks. Originally, I bought this to wear." She withdrew a short, red, slinky number that was nearly backless. "But now I don't know. I keep imagining Mrs. Rowan glaring at me and thinking I'm a tart."

"Oh, forget about her," Patsy said with a wave of her hand. "She's a big poop. Wear what you want."

"I don't know . . ."

Patsy began a quick survey of every dress hanging inside, finally extracting a white one reminiscent of a Victorian undergarment. Emma had lied when she'd told Max she'd given the dress away. She just hadn't worn it since the night the two of them had spent together.

"Okay, then, how about this?" Patsy suggested. "It's pretty virginal-looking."

"No, I don't think so."

"Why not? This is a beautiful dress."

"I know, but . . . but I'll be wearing white tomorrow."

Patsy nodded. "Yeah, I guess you're right." She started to put the dress back, but Emma stayed her hand.

"You can have that dress if you want it," Emma said impulsively.

Patsy studied the dress doubtfully. "We're not exactly the same size, you know."

"I know. But I bought that big, because I like to wear things loose sometimes."

Holding the dress up in front of her, Patsy said, "Okay. I'll give it a shot."

As Patsy began to change, Emma decided that maybe the red dress wasn't so bad after all. Patsy was right. Who cared what Taylor's mother thought? Her future mother-in-law would never approve of her anyway, so what difference did it make whether Emma tried to please her or not?

"Hey, it fits!" Patsy exclaimed when she had the white dress on. She spun around in a circle. "So what do you think? Think Max will go for me in this?"

"Max?" Emma asked, nearly choking on the one-syllable word.

Patsy's eyes fairly glowed with excitement. "I have a confession to make," she said in a conspiratorial whisper.

Confessions, Emma had decided a long time ago, were not things to be taken lightly. If Patsy had one to offer, Emma wasn't sure she wanted to hear it. Nevertheless, she couldn't help but ask, "What?"

Patsy sighed and seated herself on Emma's bed. "Will you French-braid my hair for me?" she asked.

Emma lifted her hairbrush from her dresser and went to sit behind Patsy, pulling her cousin's thick blond curls over her shoulders, drawing the brush through them in an effort to tame the unruly tresses. "Patsy, what confession?"

"Last Saturday night," her cousin began, "after your bachelorette party?"

"Mm-hmm?"

"Well, I don't know if you noticed me dancing with Max . . ."

"Patsy, after a few of your blue ocean waves, I didn't notice much of anything."

Patsy chuckled. "They were even more potent than the last time, weren't they? Which is probably why Max and I wound up . . ."

Emma slowed her brushing movement. "What happened?" she asked reluctantly.

"I'm not sure. It all went so fast. One minute, Max and I were dancing in the living room, then the next we were out in his car . . . you know . . . fogging up the windows."

"You and Max . . ." Emma began, unwilling to form the words.

Patsy nodded in resignation as she turned her head to

look at Emma sitting behind her. "Max and I did the nasty."

"Oh, Patsy . . . In Max's car?"

Patsy nodded again. "The first time, anyway."

"The first?" Emma asked before she could stop herself. "Just how many times did you two—"

"Oh, Emma, you're not mad at me, are you?" Patsy interrupted. "I'm just . . . I've been dying to tell you ever since it happened, but I was afraid you'd be mad at me."

"Why would I be mad at *you?* But I wouldn't mind getting my hands on Max . . ."

"See? Because of that. Because of Max."

"What do you mean?"

"Look, I know you've never actually been *involved* with Max, not emotionally, anyway. But I was afraid you might still . . . I don't know . . . feel *something* for him."

First Max, now Patsy, Emma thought. Who else was thinking that Emma was still involved with Max somehow? "No, Patsy, as much as Max would like to think I still feel something for him, I can safely assure you that I embrace absolutely no emotion for that sonofabitch. Except maybe a few homicidal tendencies."

Patsy turned around to stare at Emma. "What are you talking about?"

Emma pinched the bridge of her nose, then rubbed her forehead furiously. She felt a migraine coming on. "I'll be honest with you, Patsy. A few months ago, Max asked me to call off the wedding. He said it was because he was in love with me and wanted me to give him a second chance. Now all of a sudden he's trying to make time with you. The guy's a creep, Pats. I can't believe he did what he did—to both of us—but it's the truth."

Emma reluctantly turned to look at her cousin and was surprised to find her so clearly unconcerned about her announcement.

"I know Max is still carrying a torch for you," Patsy said.

"You do?"

"Sure."

"Did Max tell you that?"

Patsy shook her head. "No. Taylor did."

"*Taylor*? When?"

"Lots of times. He's always thought that."

"He has?" Well, that accounted for some of the strange things Taylor had said lately, Emma thought. But it didn't explain why he felt that way. She worried again about the possibility that Max had revealed something about the two of them to Taylor.

"Don't sweat it, Emma. Guys are always jealous like that."

"Taylor's never been jealous."

"Sure he has. He's just never shown it in front of you."

"But—"

Patsy seemed to sense how anxious her comments had made Emma. "Don't worry about it," she said softly.

"He doesn't know about me and Max sleeping together that night, does he?"

"No," Patsy replied immediately. "If he knew about you and Max, I'd know it. And I'd tell you. Trust me on that."

Patsy was right. There was no way Taylor could know about what had happened unless Max or Patsy told him. And had he discovered the truth, he certainly would have called Emma on it.

"But you know," Patsy added, picking up the brush Emma had tossed onto the bed. "You might want to . . . um . . . tell Taylor about what happened before the two of you get married."

Emma's head snapped up. "I thought we decided that wasn't such a good idea," she said.

"I don't recall deciding that. If memory serves, it seems to me that we—and more specifically, *you*—didn't decide one way or the other."

"I don't think I should."

Patsy stared at her cousin. "I'm not kidding, Emma.

It's not good to go into a marriage with a secret like that lurking between the two of you. What if Taylor does find out someday, from somebody besides you? Think about how that would make him feel. He might never forgive you. At least if you were the one who told him, he'd realize how honest you were—even if it was two years after the fact—and he'd be more likely to forgive you."

"More likely?" Emma repeated. "What if he doesn't forgive me at all?"

"Oh, Taylor's a fair guy, He'd forgive you. Probably."

Emma glared at her cousin.

"Eventually."

Emma rose from the bed and began to pace. "I don't think it's a good idea," she said again. "Especially since the wedding is tomorrow. This is something I'd need weeks, months even, to prepare for."

"If Max is serious about still being in love with you, he could tell Taylor about that night himself," Patsy said, reiterating Emma's greatest fear. "And time's a wastin', Emma. If Max is going to spill the beans, he's going to do it tonight at the rehearsal dinner or tomorrow at the wedding. He's a dramatic kind of guy. He'd thrive on that last-minute kind of crap."

Emma stopped her pacing and fell backward onto her bed. She studied a small crack in the ceiling that seemed to be growing bigger every day. Patsy was right. Deep down in her heart, Emma knew she should tell Taylor what had happened, and she should do it before the wedding. But what if he hated her after he found out? What if he wanted to call off the wedding?

"You don't hate me now, do you?" Patsy asked, her voice sounding to Emma as if it were coming from a million miles away. "For suggesting you tell the truth? Or for sleeping with Max? Please tell me you don't hate me."

"I don't hate you, Patsy," Emma told her cousin as she rose to a sitting position again. "You're not responsible for what went on two years ago. And of course I'm not mad at you for sleeping with Max. I don't love him. I love Taylor. Besides, as you said, it was a long time ago."

"So you're completely over Max?"

Emma made herself think about her cousin's question before she answered, and the discovery that she could reply so unequivocally when she did made her feel a little better. "I don't think there was ever anything to get over," she said. "I mean, I'd be lying if I told you I never found Max attractive. Because I did. And I guess, in a way, I still do. But whatever happened between us is over and done with." It felt good to finally voice her emotions out loud. "Anything I might have been feeling for Max over the past few months has been nothing but a leftover bit of nostalgia that needed to work its way out of my system." She smiled at Patsy. "And it has."

Emma put her arm around her cousin as she added, "My only concern now is that you're about to become involved with a real jerk."

Patsy laughed. "You don't think I know what kind of guy Max Bennett is?"

"Do you?"

"Sure. Charmer, womanizer, sweet-talker. But maybe a woman like me . . . arduous . . . enterprising . . . tenacious as hell . . . Maybe I'm exactly what a guy like Max needs. Know what I mean?"

Emma grinned, too. "So, uh . . . so what happened after you and Max did it in the car?" she asked her cousin in an effort to get them back to their original conversation, feeling much better in spite of the awkwardness of the situation.

Patsy stared down at her hands. "Well, after we . . . after we did it in Max's car, we drove naked back to his place."

"Naked?" Emma asked. "You drove through the streets of the nation's capital without any clothes on? What if a cop had pulled you over?"

Patsy was philosophical. "No one did. And Emma, I

have to tell you, there's nothing quite as exhilarating as driving around in a car in the middle of the night completely naked. It was unbelievable. Stopping at red lights was a major, major turn-on." She smiled. "Besides, our coats were in the back seat. We had to have something to wear from the car to the apartment." She smiled as if remembering a pleasant dream. "We didn't keep them on long once we got there, though."

"But Taylor was home that night, wasn't he?"

"Yeah. So?"

"So, Taylor and I never did it when Max was home."

"Oh, Max and I did," Patsy replied. "Three more times."

"*Four* times in one night?" Emma squeaked. "He could only manage two times with me." She clapped both hands over her mouth when she realized what she had said.

Patsy laughed, relieved that the tension surrounding them had evaporated. "Well, you guys were probably drinking a lot more than Max and I were."

"Not that much more," Emma was quick to point out. She began to laugh, too. "And not blue ocean waves, either. Those things are deadly."

"They're also a great aphrodisiac."

"Obviously."

The two of them laughed even harder at that, until they had to hold their sides and wipe away the tears streaming down their faces. When their laughter erupted into riotous howls, a knock came from outside Emma's bedroom door.

"Everything all right, girls?" Virginia asked as she poked her head inside.

"F-fine," Patsy sputtered.

"F-for the most p-part," Emma agreed, gasping for breath. Virginia withdrew, and Emma wiped a tear from her eye as she asked, "So, Patsy, what are you going to do about Max?"

Patsy sighed and tried to get a rein on her thoughts. "Oh, I don't know. The usual, I guess. Brand him and throw a rope around him and keep him tied up in the backyard. How about you, Emma? What are you going to do about Taylor?"

Emma sighed too and suddenly had no trouble at all keeping her jovial spirits under control. "I have no idea, Patsy," she said softly, feeling new, different tears spring quickly to life. "I really have no idea at all."

32

*The rehearsal dinner provides an opportunity
for everyone involved in the wedding to gather
for one final ovation for the bride and groom. It
is here that gestures of affection and appreciation often peak. Frequently we forget how
important friends and family have become to
us. But for one night prior to the wedding, we
can bask in the knowledge that we hold so many
so dear.*

—ALISON BRIGHAM

At seven-twenty that night, the rehearsal dinner
wasn't coming off quite as well as Emma had hoped it
would. The best man was late, Catherine and Michael
were fighting again, and Lionel and Francesca were making no secret that they did not approve of Adrienne's
date. In general, nothing seemed to be going right.

Worst of all, Taylor had been smiling at her all
evening as if nothing in the world were wrong.

Now as the two of them sat at the head of a U-
shaped table, surrounded by their families and closest
friends, Emma felt as if she were trapped in the worst
kind of prison with absolutely no chance of escape. She
had been thinking a lot about what Patsy had said ear-

lier and wondered if her cousin was right. Maybe she should tell Taylor about the night she'd spent with Max two years ago. And maybe she should do it before the wedding took place tomorrow. What she couldn't figure out was precisely how she was supposed to go about confessing.

Maybe it would be better to wait until after the ceremony after all, she thought. Like eighty years after the ceremony. Or better yet, during the ceremony. *I do. And by the way, Taylor, did you know I had sex with your best friend two years ago?*

Emma stifled a miserable groan. No, that wouldn't quite cut it. If she was going to tell Taylor the truth, then before the wedding was the time to do it. That way they could start married life together on the proper footing. Probably. She tried to smile back at her fiancé, knowing her effort fell short. Taylor covered her hand with his and squeezed affectionately, but Emma was unable to acknowledge his gesture. Instead she could only study a crease in the otherwise perfect linen tablecloth and rub her thumb across the flaw as if trying to heal it.

"Emma, what's wrong?" Taylor asked her quietly, ducking his head to look at her face.

She glanced up quickly, then down again. "Wrong? Nothing's wrong, Taylor. Why would you think something's wrong?"

"You've been awfully quiet tonight. You seem kind of . . . I don't know. Sad. It's the night before our wedding. I'd like to think you were a little excited about tomorrow."

Emma's fingers continued their back-and-forth motion along the tablecloth. "I'm just a little nervous, that's all."

A moment passed before Taylor said, "I get the feeling you're preoccupied about something."

His statement brought Emma's attention around in a hurry. When her eyes met his, she saw they were full of silent question.

"Is there something you want to talk about?" he asked. "Something you want to tell me?"

If you're going to do it, now's the time, Emma told herself. She took a deep breath and began slowly, "Well . . . yes, actually . . . there is something. Um, Taylor, I—"

"I'm here!"

Max's voice erupted from the other side of the room, and all heads turned to watch his entrance.

Emma started, mentally cursing Max for his lousy timing. Still, she thought, maybe it was better this way. She and Taylor did need to talk, but here in front of everyone was the last place she should be exposing her sins.

"Sorry I'm late," Max said as he approached the table and shook hands with Taylor. "Traffic is murder out there tonight. 'Skins game or something."

When he leaned over to kiss Emma on the cheek, he whispered softly, "I need to talk to you."

"Forget it," she whispered back.

"No, Emma, it's important."

"You'll be coming to my folks' house after dinner, won't you, Max?" Taylor asked him as his best man pulled away from Emma. "Mother and Dad want us all over for a nightcap."

"Sure, Taylor. Sounds great."

Emma smiled blandly. "Great."

"Hi, Max."

When Patsy came up from behind him, Max's expression changed drastically. Emma could have sworn he was embarrassed, flustered even. Clearly Patsy had him on the run. He spun around to greet her cousin.

"Patsy! Hi! What's up? Where are you sitting? Did you save me a seat?"

He hustled her away to two empty places at the most distant end of the table, pulling one chair out for Patsy before seating himself in the other.

Emma stared out at the remainder of the guests seated around the table, trying to discern who was having a good time and who was not. Her parents seemed to be their usual jovial selves, her father lifting his beer as he chuckled at something Joey was saying. Diane and Felicia had their heads bent toward each other in what appeared to be very serious conversation about the pattern on Diane's empty plate, while Eddie was inspecting the layout of his silverware. Catherine was ignoring her husband, who sat at her left, and chatting very avidly with Vick on her right, while Adrienne gazed in adoration at her date, a youth named Alex who seemed in Emma's opinion, generally pretty morose.

"Where did Virginia and Uncle Brownie go?" Taylor asked.

Emma shrugged. "They were here a minute ago."

Desiree, seated on Emma's left, told them, "They stepped out right after Lionel poured the wine, but Virginia said they would be back in plenty of time for dinner." She leaned in closer for Emma's ears alone as she added, "Don't tell anyone, but I saw Virginia put a little overnight bag in the trunk before we left. Just between you and me, I think the two of them are going to take advantage of the hotel's very nice weekend rate. You get two nights with breakfast, champagne, and health club facilities for only a hundred and fifty dollars. Now I think that's a real bargain."

Emma smiled, glad that at least one relationship seemed to be headed for a solid future. Aunt Virginia and Uncle Brownie, she marveled. Who would have thought?

"Quite a difference from the first time our families sat down to break bread together, isn't it?" Taylor asked.

Emma studied the guests again. "Oh, I don't know. Everybody still looks pretty uncomfortable together. Although our mothers seem to have made it past stiff civilities and are now gradually approaching the mild tolerance stage. And our fathers do at least smile at the same time now."

She neglected to mention the strange friendship Vick

and Catherine seemed to have struck, mainly because Emma wasn't so sure it was just a friendship anymore. Catherine had even bought a motorcycle, and Emma knew very well how Vick felt about women with Harleys. Someday, he hoped to organize them all on a calendar.

"All in all," Taylor said, "I'd say this isn't such a bad result. No blood's been spilled, no lives lost."

"You forget we still have almost twenty-four hours to get through before the wedding tomorrow night," Emma pointed out. "Why, there are any number of things that can still go wrong."

Taylor lifted her hand to his lips for a soft kiss. "Oh, come on. What could possibly go wrong?"

Emma pressed the fingers of her other hand against her lips, hoping to trap the hysterical laughter she felt threatening. When she trusted herself to speak again, she said, "Oh, I don't know. You can just never be too sure."

With the removal of the dinner plates, the waiters began to set up for dessert. Emma felt full and contented as she turned to smile at Taylor. He grinned back, lifting her hand to his lips again before tucking it beneath his own on his thigh. His skin was warm and hard below her fingertips, and Emma wished with all her heart that it was Saturday night instead of Friday. She and Taylor would be spending the night at the Four Seasons Hotel, then on Sunday they would fly to Miami to begin a two-week cruise. No more wedding plans, no meddling parents, nothing to stand between them but cool island breezes. Things would be settled between them by then, and everything would be fine. She hoped. Oh, how she hoped.

"Taylor, you and I need to talk about something."

He had been speaking to his father, who sat at his right, and turned to look at Emma with some distraction. "All right. About what?"

"But not here, not now. Could we maybe leave a little early and—"

"Taylor, I need to borrow your fiancée for a minute."

Emma and Taylor turned at the sound of Max's voice behind them.

"Why?" Taylor asked.

The question seemed to stump Max. He looked first at Emma, then back at Taylor. "Why? Because . . ." He smiled roguishly, then laughed as if in jest. "Because this is my last chance to talk her out of marrying you and into running away with me, you stupid geek, why do you think I want to talk to her? It's a surprise, all right? Jesus, you're so suspicious."

Taylor laughed, too, but only halfheartedly. "Don't be gone long," he said to Emma as he reluctantly released her hand.

"Don't worry, I won't." She kissed him quickly before following Max.

The moment they stepped into the hallway outside, Emma stopped and crossed her arms over her chest. "What do you want?" she asked him.

"There's something very important we need to talk about."

Max gripped Emma's wrist and silently urged her to follow him. Not again, she thought wearily. No way. She dug her heels into the plush carpet covering the long hallway.

"If you want to talk to me, you'll have to do it right here. I'm not going anywhere with you."

Max started to protest, then something over Emma's shoulder seemed to catch his attention. With a quick, deft maneuver, he spun her around, and suddenly the two of them were in a closet smelling of strong disinfectant and mildewed mops.

"Oh, gee, this is real romantic," Emma remarked. "You really know how to charm a girl. You take her to all the best closets in town."

"Very funny. It's the best I could do on short notice."

Emma sighed. "Doesn't this tell you something, Max? The fact that the two of us always wind up in some kind of illicit, sneaky situation where we're afraid of getting caught? Like maybe that we're just not meant to be together?"

"That's what we need to talk about."

"I know." She groped for a light fixture but found none. "Look, I wish you could see my face when I tell you this, because I only want to say it once, and I want to make sure you understand that I mean it."

She could hear Max sigh heavily, and when he shifted in the darkness she imagined him thrusting his hand through his hair in that impatient gesture of his. "Say what?"

"You know how you're always accusing me of having feelings for you?" she asked.

"Yes."

"Well, you're right. I do still have feelings for you."

"You do?"

His voice sounded odd, as if he were bothered by her admission. Emma somehow felt instinctively that despite his assurances to the contrary over the past several months, Max suddenly didn't want her to have feelings for him.

"Don't you want me to?" she asked.

"Well, sure . . . I mean no . . . I mean . . ." He sighed again. "Look, Emma, I don't know how to tell you this, but I . . . I've sort of met someone else . . ."

Emma couldn't believe her ears. The epic love for her Max had claimed to hold so dear had suddenly evaporated like so much steam. And she was certain she could name that someone new in five notes. Patsy Hammelmann. Emma started to chuckle, patting Max not so affectionately on the cheek.

"You've met someone else," she repeated. "Oh, Max, you're such a kidder. After months of tying me up in knots, swearing you love me and will have me back, threatening to expose our little indiscretion to Taylor, the night before the wedding you wanted me to sabotage, you come up and tell me you've met someone else. What a card. What a joker." She seized his chin in her hand and forced him to meet her gaze in the darkness. "What a creep."

"Listen, I know how you must feel about this."

"You have no idea how I feel," she said. "You've put me through hell for the past four months, and now you think you can make it all go away. Well, let me tell you something." Emma jabbed her index finger firmly against his breastbone. "I've got my eye on you, and if you do one thing to hurt Patsy, I'll find the biggest, sharpest, shiniest knife I can locate, and I'll emasculate you with one clean slice."

"Emma, don't you think you're overreacting?" She felt Max shift in the darkness again. "Besides, what makes you think it's Patsy?"

"Oh, I know it's Patsy," Emma said. "She told me all about it."

"She did?"

Emma nodded, then, realizing he couldn't see her in the darkness, murmured, "Mm-hm."

"So you're pretty mad, huh?"

"Yup."

"Because you still have feelings for me?" Max asked. "Gee, that's . . . that's so flattering, Emma. I'm touched, really I am, but—"

Emma sighed. Max was nothing if not egocentric to the last minute. "No, Max, that's not the reason I'm mad. I'm mad because I don't want you trifling with Patsy's affections. Like I said, you hurt her, and you'll be answering to me."

Max sobered then and pushed Emma's finger away from his chest. Then he lifted his hand to her cheek in a much more tender gesture. "I won't hurt Patsy, Emma, I promise. She's . . . I don't know. She's just completely unlike any woman I've ever met. I can't quite put my finger on what it is about her. She's great."

"Yes, she is."

"So then you're not going to hassle me about this?" he asked. "What about your feelings for me?"

"My feelings aren't what you think." Emma sighed again. In spite of everything, she still experienced a little twinge of wistfulness. "Look, I'll always have a tender spot in my heart for you. You gave me one night that was . . . Well, every woman should have one night like that to recall fondly in her old age. But I don't love you. I never loved you. I love Taylor, and he's who I want to be with for the rest of my life. This has got to be the end of it for us."

Max lifted his hand to brush back her bangs. "I'll never forget that one night we spent together, either. You're right, it was something to remember forever. But that's all it will be from now on, I promise. A memory."

He leaned forward to kiss her one final time, a soft, chaste brush of his lips against hers. It was a friendly kiss, a harmless kiss. A kiss that said goodbye.

Unfortunately, that wasn't how it looked to Taylor when he opened the closet door.

33

*Naturally, very few weddings come off without
some minor difficulties disrupting their rhythm.
Just remember that there's very little that cannot
be fixed with a few small adjustments, conces-
sions, or compromises. You and your groom will
no doubt find much to laugh about when looking
back on such incidents in the years to come.*

—ALISON BRIGHAM

"What the hell is going on here?"

Emma squinted at the sudden intrusion of light, then
widened her eyes in horror when she realized it was her
fiancé who was asking the question. Max still had one arm
circling her waist and a hand cupped over her jaw. Worse
than that, however, was Emma's realization that she had
placed her own hands on Max's waist while he had kissed
her. Now she jerked her hands away as if she'd suddenly
been burned, but not before Taylor had noted their position. For a long moment, no one said a word. Taylor
looked at Max. Max looked at Emma. Emma looked at
Taylor. Then they all switched, and Emma looked at Max
while Max looked at Taylor and Taylor looked at Emma.

Taylor was the first to move, placing his hands firmly
on each side of the doorjamb. When he finally spoke, his

words came out low and menacing. "Take your hands off her, Max."

"Taylor, this isn't what you're thinking," Emma said.

"Oh no?" He glared at her. "And just what is it I'm thinking? That my best friend is in a dark closet kissing the woman who's supposed to become my wife tomorrow? That my own fiancée—the woman who's supposed to be in love with me forever—is kissing him back?"

"I wasn't kissing him back."

Taylor's lips thinned in anger, and his hands clenched into fists. "But you were kissing him."

"No, he was kissing me," she insisted. "There's a big difference."

Taylor laughed, but there wasn't a trace of humor in the sound. "Not in my book, Emma."

Max, too, dropped his hands to his sides and turned to look at Taylor fully. "She's right, Taylor, this isn't what you think."

"I'm supposed to find your reassurance heartening, is that it, Max? You, the man who has made it a regular practice of telling me how great my girlfriend is? You, who swore up and down that given the slightest window of opportunity, you'd step in and take her away from me?"

"You actually told him that?" Emma asked Max.

"And more," Taylor added. "Max has told me quite a few things about you and him over the years, haven't you, Max?"

Emma paled. "Oh, Max, you didn't. You didn't tell Taylor about—"

"No," Max interjected, before Emma could do even more harm to the situation at hand. "I didn't tell him that."

"Tell me what?" Taylor demanded. "What did you mean by that, Emma?"

Emma's gaze ricocheted between the two men. "Uh . . . what did *you* mean, Taylor?"

Taylor eyed the couple warily, wondering what secret

parlay had just passed between them. When he spoke again, his voice was low and cautious. "He's told me about the night the two of you went out and got drunk together."

Emma closed her eyes against what was to come next. "Oh, Taylor, I can explain."

"Emma, don't—" Max warned her.

"It was only because you went out with Tina that night," she began. "I was so upset, so angry that you would go out with her behind my back. Max and I . . . we didn't plan any of it, we didn't mean for it to go as far as—"

"A kiss," Max finished for her. "We didn't mean for it to end in a kiss."

Emma glanced up at Max, but his face betrayed nothing.

"Max told me about the night you kissed him," Taylor said. "And I have to admit, it hurt like hell to hear about you doing something like that, but I guess I couldn't really blame you after what I did—going out with Tina, I mean. I guess I should be grateful it didn't go any further than a kiss." His face drew up in anger as he said, "Or maybe it did. After what I've seen here, who knows how often the two of you have slipped off to be alone together? How about it, Emma? Just what the hell has been going on between you and Max?"

Emma's head was spinning. She was growing more and more confused by the minute. Was she supposed to feel heartened by the fact that Max was helping her perpetuate a lie? This was her chance, she thought. If she wanted to expose her past with Max, this was the time to do it. Then again, would it really be smart to tell Taylor the truth now, given his present state of mind?

When Emma made no move to explain, Max stepped in to cover for her. "I told Taylor about the night you kissed me because I figured he'd find out about it eventually anyway. But this kiss tonight was different, Taylor," he continued, turning his attention to his buddy once again. "I was just telling Emma about how I was beginning to fall for Patsy, and she was just trying to reassure me that everything would be fine."

Taylor was skeptical. "Right. You two had to retreat to a closet right this minute to discuss your new affair with Patsy. And I almost forgot how Emma always kisses the guys who take an interest in her family members. Who will it be next, Emma? You want me to ask Uncle Brownie to come out here and join you in the closet?"

Emma frowned at him. "Of course, not, Taylor, you're being silly."

As if she'd known she was the topic of conversation, Patsy came up behind Taylor, looking very concerned.

"What's going on? Everyone's wondering where you all went. Emma? Max? Uh . . . what are you guys doing in the closet?"

"They claim to be talking about you," Taylor said.

That seemed to brighten Patsy's spirits. "Really? What were you saying?"

"Look, would you two step aside so we can get out of here?" Max said impatiently. "It's kind of crowded."

"I'll say," Taylor grumbled.

But he and Patsy allowed Emma and Max out of the closet. From the room nearby came the buzz of conversation where others were blissfully celebrating a union that was fast beginning to suffer a wide rift. Patsy studied her companions closely, wondering what she had missed. The tension between the other three was palpable, and she couldn't help but wonder if Emma had heeded her advice in revealing her brief encounter with Max.

"So, Taylor," Patsy began, "you look pretty steamed. Everything okay?"

Taylor's response was in reply to Patsy's question, but his eyes never left Emma and Max as he spoke. "Sure, Pats, everything is great. Just because I ran into my best friend kissing my fiancée in a dark closet the night before my wedding . . . what could I possibly have to be steamed about?"

Patsy's expression was crushed as she turned to stare at

the other couple. "You were kissing Max?" she asked Emma softly.

"Patsy, it wasn't like that . . . it wasn't what you think."

"But you said there was nothing between the two of you anymore, that the night you and Max—" She stopped abruptly when she realized what she had been about to reveal.

"It's all right, Patsy," Taylor told her sharply. "I know all about that night."

Patsy's eyes widened in surprise. "You do?" she asked.

Taylor nodded.

"Since when?"

"Since it happened."

"Patsy," Emma and Max began in unison.

Patsy stared at Taylor harder. "You're kidding! You've known about it for two years? How did you find out?"

"Patsy," Emma and Max tried again, a little more frantically this time.

But Patsy was watching Taylor, who shrugged and said, "Max told me. Can you believe it? And now here he is kissing my fiancée again, telling me it's not what I think."

"Maybe it's not," Patsy told him. "Just because they slept together two years ago doesn't mean they're going to go running off to some cheap motel again tonight. I, for one, have very good reason to know that Max—" She halted when she saw the drastic change in Taylor's expression. "What?" she asked. "What's the matter?"

"Oh, Patsy," Emma moaned, shaking her head.

Taylor heard Emma's plaintive groan, but continued to stare at Patsy. "They slept together?" he asked in a thin voice.

Patsy glanced at Emma and Max. Emma stood with her hands covering her face, and Max shook his head, staring at the ceiling. "I . . . uh . . . I thought you said you knew about that night," Patsy said.

Taylor turned to Emma and Max. "Is it true?" he asked. "Did the two of you actually sleep together that night?"

He sounded so forlorn, so sad, so utterly betrayed, that Emma felt tears stinging her eyes. She couldn't lie to him again, didn't want to lie anymore. But the look on his face was so shocked, so full of disbelief, she wished desperately that she could deny the charge.

"Oh, Taylor . . ." she said softly.

"Is it true?" he demanded again.

Emma nodded helplessly, her tears falling in earnest now. "I'm sorry," she whispered. "I'm so, so sorry."

She took a single step forward and reached for his hand, but Taylor crossed his arms over his chest, tucking both hands into his armpits before actually turning his back on her.

"Taylor, please. Just give me a chance to explain."

"There's nothing to explain," he said evenly. "You screwed my roommate and lied to me about it for two years. That's all that matters."

"Taylor, it wasn't like that. . . ."

Patsy, aware that she was the one responsible for the scene unfolding, slowly moved to stand behind Max, gripping the waistband of his pants fiercely. "Guess I'm in pretty deep doo-doo," she whispered.

Max stretched his arm behind him to drape over Patsy's shoulder and back. "This was bound to come out eventually," he told her. "Granted, this might not have been the best time in the world. . . ."

"Think we should leave them alone?"

Max shook his head. "Not just yet."

Taylor spun quickly around and pinned Emma with an accusing stare. "How could this have happened? I'm not surprised about Max. Hell, I half expected it of him, but *you*, Emma . . . I trusted you. How could you do that to me?"

"I was hurting, Taylor. I wasn't the only one who lied,

you know. You were out with another woman the night it happened. I went over to your apartment after Joanie called me from the party and told me you were there with Tina. I was so sure it was some awful joke, that you'd be home watching the game like you said you were going to do. But you weren't. And I got so upset. . . . I was crying and carrying on, and Max took me out to try and comfort me—"

"Oh, and he did a hell of a job at that, didn't he?"

Emma ignored the barb. "It was a mistake. We both knew it was a mistake. It never happened again. I'm sorry, Taylor. I wish it hadn't happened to begin with. But it was two years ago." She reached out a hand for him again, but he took a step back. Emma's heart sank further. "You can't let it ruin what we have together now."

"Can't I?"

Emma's breath caught in her throat. "What do you mean?"

Taylor shook his head. "I have to think about this. I need some time. I don't know what to do."

Despair filled every part of her body. "But, Taylor, we're supposed to get married in less than twenty-four hours. We just closed on a condo in Old Town, for God's sake!"

"I know what we're *supposed* to do," Taylor said. "I'm just not sure I can go through with this, knowing that you've not only been unfaithful to me, but that you've lied to me on top of it."

"Oh, Taylor," Emma whispered. She began to cry again. "Don't do this to me. Don't punish me this way. Remember what you told Reverend Ballard? You said you'd forgive me if you ever found out something like this had happened."

"I said I'd forgive you eventually, but that was before I knew you'd actually . . ." He shook his head slowly. "I still can't believe you did this to me."

"Taylor . . ."

"I need time to think," he repeated, turning away again.

Emma didn't know what to say. She couldn't believe he would let everything they'd built together crumble just like that, but she could also see how deeply her admission had hurt him. She turned to Patsy and Max for help, but they remained silent. Patsy looked terrified of what she'd caused, and Max was still shaking his head. Finally, just when Emma thought the silence surrounding them would deafen her, Max lifted his hands in front of his chest and slapped them loudly together.

He repeated the gesture a few more times, slowly, rhythmically, clap . . . clap . . . clap . . . Then gradually his clapping escalated to full-fledged applause, accompanied by an occasional cry of "bravo." Emma and Patsy stared at Max, and when Taylor turned around to meet his friend's eyes, it was with some suspicion.

"What's all that supposed to mean?" Taylor asked.

Max stopped applauding and dropped his hands to his sides. "Hell of a performance, Taylor," he said. "Oscar caliber. The scorned lover. You play it well."

Taylor narrowed his eyes. "Is there something you want to say to me, Max?"

Max shook his head. "Nothing that can't wait until we're alone together. Isn't there something you wanted to tell Emma?"

Taylor's expression was inscrutable, but Emma detected just the slightest tightening at the corners of his mouth.

"Tell me what?" she asked.

"Max." Taylor's voice was edged with warning. "What could I possibly have to tell Emma?"

Max only smiled and said, "Tell her, Taylor. Tell her, or I will."

"Tell me what?" Emma repeated more adamantly.

When Taylor only shook his head, Max looked at Emma and said, "You and I weren't the only two people getting a room at the Captain Willie B. Schmidt Motel that night."

"What do you mean?" Emma asked.

Max looked at Taylor one more time, pausing as if to give the other man one last chance. When Taylor still said nothing, Max continued. "You didn't notice it because you were too upset that night. But Taylor's car was parked in the parking lot of the Willie B. I knew it was his because he'd put the Triple-A sticker on the back bumper upside down."

Emma and Patsy turned to look at Taylor, too, but he glanced down at the rug and said nothing.

"Then, as I was closing the door behind us," Max went on, "I saw Taylor and Tina coming out of a room only a few doors down the way."

Taylor looked up then, angry at Max for revealing the truth, angry at Tina for ever entering his life in the first place, angry at himself for getting caught up in such a stupid farce. "Guess the Willie B. was pretty busy that night," he said.

"Oh, Taylor," Emma said. "How could *you?* At least I only went with Max because I was mad at you. You went with Tina just because you knew you could cheat on me and get away with it. You weren't going to tell me, were you? Even after I told you about me and Max, you were going to let me keep believing that you'd done nothing wrong."

"You didn't exactly tell me about you and Max of your own free will, Emma," Taylor said. "If Patsy hadn't blown it for you, you would have kept me in the dark, too, wouldn't you?"

Emma knew deep down that she couldn't honestly answer Taylor's question one way or the other. She wasn't sure whether she would have been able to tell him or not. "I don't know," she finally said. "I really don't."

"When Taylor came home that night," Max went on, "I wanted to call him on what I'd seen at the Willie B., but I didn't. So I told him the two of us had gone as far as a kiss to see how much he'd tell me about his own experi-

ences that night with Tina. I thought maybe if I offered
him an opening, he'd spill his guts about being unfaithful
to you and start crying and carrying on about how guilty
he felt." Max's voice softened some as he added, "The
way you did, Emma, after we . . ."

"After you what?" Taylor jeered.

"But then when he didn't," Max continued, ignoring
the question and shifting back to anger, "when Taylor
decided to keep his thing with Tina to himself, I figured
what they had was an ongoing thing. How about it, Taylor? As long as we're all being honest with each other, just
how many times did you and Tina get a room at the Willie
B. while you were supposed to be Emma's one and only?"

Emma and Patsy both watched Taylor intently. Emma
drew in a quiet breath and held it. "Well?" she finally
asked.

Taylor looked at his companions, then back down at
the floor. He sighed, started to say something, then
seemed to think better of it and shut his mouth again.
Finally, he did look up, but it was Max's eye he met
squarely, not Emma's. "Three times," he said.

"Three?" Emma repeated. "You were with Tina three
times while you and I were dating? Over how long a
period of time?"

Taylor struggled with his next answer. Keeping a lie
under wraps for two years had exhausted him, especially
over the last six months. His fear that Emma might discover what had been going on with Tina had nearly
overwhelmed him at times. On one or two occasions,
he'd come close to telling her the truth, but after their
session with the good reverend, after hearing Emma's
vow that she would leave him if she ever learned that he
was unfaithful, Taylor had reconsidered. However, had
he known about Emma and Max . . .

Then what? he wondered. Christ, what a mess they'd
made of an incredibly good relationship.

"The night you saw us there was the second time," he

finally said, opting for the truth. "There was one more time a few weeks later."

"Oh, Taylor," Emma said again. "How could you?"

"Emma, you have to understand. Tina and I dated for a long time before you entered the picture. We were very serious for a while there. And after you came into my life, she and I split pretty fast. We left a lot unsaid, a lot of loose ends. Although I loved you more than anything in the world, there was still a significant part of me that kept on caring for Tina. I guess a little part of me always will."

"Why didn't you tell me what was going on then?" Emma asked him. "Why didn't you tell me you and she had unfinished business? We could have tried to work through it together."

"Would you have understood?"

"I would have tried to."

This time it was Taylor who took a step forward, but Emma, still uncertain what to think about this new development, took a step back.

"I guess I deserve that," Taylor said of her retreat. "Emma, I'm sorry, too, about being with Tina. I know it was a big mistake now. I knew it back then. That's why it only happened three times. I finally told Tina that what she and I had was over. That I loved you and wanted to stay with you. You have to try and understand my position."

Emma tried, she really did. But at the moment, nothing much was making sense. The room had grown hot, and her stomach was reacting badly to something she'd eaten.

"And anyway," Taylor went on, his voice once more edged with anger, "none of this explains what you and Max were doing kissing in a dark closet tonight. At least what I had with Tina ended two years ago."

Max shook his head again, stepping between Taylor and Emma. "Then what was Tina doing in the apartment a couple of months ago?" he asked calmly. "Wearing one of your T-shirts, Taylor, and not much else."

"*What?*" Taylor and Emma asked in unison.

"Whoa," Patsy murmured. "This is getting good."

Max nodded. "Yeah, when I came home from work one afternoon, there she was in the middle of your bed. She looked real surprised to see me, said she thought I was supposed to be out of town, and then she said she was waiting for you. When I reminded her you were an engaged man, she mumbled something about it not being a permanent condition, got dressed, and left."

"Oh, God," Taylor mumbled. "I'll kill her."

"Oh, Taylor," Emma groaned.

"No, Emma, it's not what you think," Taylor rushed to assure her. "It's not what you think at all." He removed his glasses and rubbed his eyes furiously. "Ever since Tina heard you and I were engaged, she's gotten it into her head that she and I should get back together. I swear to God, Emma, I never encouraged her."

"Then how did she get into your apartment?" Emma asked. "And your bed?"

Taylor shook his head. "I don't know. She must still have the key I gave her when we were dating."

"And your bed?" Emma repeated.

"I guess she was planning some kind of ambush for me."

"An ambush." Emma nodded angrily. "I see."

"Look, Emma, I know you probably don't believe me, but it's true. Every time I saw Tina, I told her you and I were getting married and starting a family right away, and that there was no chance she and I could ever revive what we once had."

"That's why you've been so gung-ho about having kids all of a sudden?" Emma asked. Suddenly a lot of things were making sense. "To get Tina off your back?"

"Well I thought the image of me as a father might put her off. Maybe that's not the best reason to have kids, but . . ."

"Oh, Taylor."

"Emma . . ." He paused, not certain what he wanted to

say. "I guess we've both made a nice mess of things, haven't we?"

Emma stared at him for a long time, feeling stranger than she'd ever felt before. "I need some time," she said, an echo of Taylor's earlier statement. "To think. Patsy, will you take me home?"

"Emma, wait. We can't leave things like this. What about you and Max? What about you and me? What about the wedding?"

Patsy came to stand beside Emma and linked their arms together. Emma looked pale, sick, and frightened.

"There's nothing between me and Max," she said again. "As for me and you . . . as for the wedding . . . I don't know," Emma replied. "I need time to think. I just don't know."

34

It is not at all uncommon for tensions that have been escalating for some time to peak just prior to a wedding. For this reason, a bride should not be overly concerned about any little outbursts she or another member of the wedding party may experience at the last minute. She should simply remain calm and remind all concerned that each has a specific role to play in the wedding. Once responsibilities have been reiterated, everyone should be fine.

—ALISON BRIGHAM

A light snow had begun to fall by the time the party made it back to the Rowan home after the rehearsal dinner. The house was quiet when Francesca and Lionel entered, but Margaret was there to greet them.

"Stir up the fires, won't you, Margaret?" Francesca asked as she handed the housekeeper her coat.

"Yes, Mrs. Rowan."

"And I think it would be lovely if Driscoll could manage something hot for us to drink, don't you?"

"Yes, Mrs. Rowan."

The housekeeper began to turn away to see to her

duties when Francesca stopped her. "Oh, and, Margaret?"

"Yes, Mrs. Rowan?"

"Why don't you and Driscoll join us when you've seen to the others? The wedding is tomorrow, after all, and we want to wish Taylor and Emma well."

Margaret's eyebrows arched in surprise, but she smiled. "Yes, Mrs. Rowan," she said. "We'll be along shortly."

Francesca turned to find Lionel gazing at her hungrily. She hadn't seen that expression in his eyes for years—until last night, of course. She recalled the previous evening's escapades with a little smile. Now he couldn't seem to stop looking at her that way.

"Why did you have to invite everyone over tonight?" he demanded playfully. "I was hoping I'd have you all to myself."

Francesca brushed past him, patting his fanny as she went. "You will, darling, you will. Later."

Lionel whistled as he followed his wife into the living room.

As the others gradually arrived in small groups of two or three, they trickled into the living room where they were made comfortable with after-dinner refreshments and warm conversation. Only Emma, Taylor, and Max seemed to be absent, Francesca noted with a slight frown. Oh, yes, and that Patsy person who was to be Emma's maid of honor. The four of them had disappeared right after dinner without a trace. Francesca had assumed they would already be here, and she wondered now what could be holding them up.

"So, Francesca," Desiree said. "I noticed a Johnny Mathis CD over there in your collection. How'd it go?"

Francesca smiled, smoothing her hand carefully over her hair. "Quite well."

"Good. Now, Laszlo and I thought you and Lionel might want to come over for dinner some night next week. We could even go bowling afterward if you want. Gotta break in the new shirts, after all."

Francesca smiled. "I don't believe I've ever bowled before. Is it difficult?"

Desiree emitted a quick puff of air. "It's a darn sight easier than playing bridge, that's for sure. I never could see how anyone could get into that game."

"Then you must come with me to the club one Thursday afternoon," Francesca said. "And I'll teach you. We could be partners."

Desiree lifted her glass. "You got a deal, Francesca. So when do you want to bowl?"

"I'll have to check with Lionel." She looked around the room and saw her husband and Laszlo standing near the bar in deep conversation. "What do you suppose they're so wrapped up in discussing?" she asked Desiree.

"Knowing my husband, the new Nelson 732." When Francesca looked puzzled, Desiree amended, "The latest thing in circular saws."

Francesca nodded. "Knowing Lionel, it's something about some new case he's taken on."

Over by the bar, the two men were discussing neither.

"I tell you, Hammelmann, whatever it was she had on, it was absolutely transparent. With feathers and beads and . . . and . . . what do you call those little shiny things? About this big?"

"Sequins?"

"Yes, sequins." Lionel sighed and drank from his glass. "It was an amazing gown."

Laszlo recalled a number of times when his wife had surprised him in just such a way. "Desi's got quite a few of those. She really knows how to drive a man wild."

"Frankly, I never knew Francesca had it in her."

Laszlo grinned. "Yeah, they can sure surprise you sometimes. Wives are strange creatures. But who could live without 'em, know what I mean?"

Lionel nodded, surprised to find himself agreeing with Hammelmann about something. "Yes, actually, I do."

The small, impromptu party proceeded very nicely for

a short time, despite the ominous absence of the bride and groom and their primary attendants. Then Patsy and Emma came barreling into the house, Emma slamming the front door behind her.

"I told you I wanted to go home!" She shouted as they entered the den where the others had all ceased their conversation after the initial sound of impending turmoil. "Is this my home, Patsy? It doesn't look like my home."

"I know where you wanted to go, Emma," Patsy countered. "But all things considered, I think you and Taylor need to talk this thing out tonight."

"Taylor isn't even here."

"He will be," Patsy said.

"How do you know?"

"Max is making him come."

"Making him?" Emma asked. "And just how is Max supposed to make Taylor do something he doesn't want to do? They were about to beat the hell out of each other by the time we left."

Before anyone in the room had a chance to remark upon Emma's statement, Taylor and Max entered the house in much the same way Emma and Patsy had.

"Just who in the hell do you think you are?" Taylor shouted at Max, who followed behind him, shoving his roommate into the living room.

"I'm your best friend, you asshole, so shut up and get inside!"

"Best friend! You were pawing my fiancée in a dark closet less than an hour ago! Some best friend!"

"I explained all that! And after what's been going on between you and Tina, I'd think you'd be able to understand!"

Both men, who had been dressed so impeccably for the rehearsal dinner, now bore the clear marks of combat. Taylor's necktie was a tangle of striped silk around his neck, his shirttails were spilling out of his trousers, and the breast pocket of his jacket was dangling by a few precarious threads. His right eye was already swelling from what would soon be an impressive shiner. Max, whose nose and lip were stained with dark red, had completely lost his tie and jacket, and one sleeve of his white dress shirt was yanked free of its seam. All in all, the two men created quite a stark contrast to the two women they approached.

"What on earth is going on here?" Francesca finally asked. "Taylor? Max? Have you two been scuffling?"

Emma and Patsy stared at Taylor and Max, who naturally stared back at them. Yet no one offered an explanation.

"Girls?" Desiree tried, addressing her daughter and niece. "You want to tell us what this is all about?"

"Taylor and Emma had a fight," Patsy said.

"Looks to me like Taylor and Max had a fight," Laszlo interjected.

"Well, yeah, that, too, I guess," Patsy said. "But before that, at the dinner, Emma and Taylor got into one that was a real doozy."

Desiree and Francesca exchanged wary looks. "About what?" they asked in unison.

The foursome all looked at each other, at the floor, at the ceiling, and then back at each other again. Still, no one offered an explanation.

"It's a long story," Patsy finally said. "A real long story."

"Oh, I wouldn't say that, Patsy," Taylor piped up. "All we've got here is a failure to communicate. Emma and I want to call off the wedding tomorrow. It's as simple as that."

Desiree and Francesca gasped.

"Is that true, Emma?" Desiree asked.

All eyes fell on Emma, who studied a worn spot in the carpet with much interest and remained silent.

"Emma?" her mother prodded.

When she looked up, her gaze held Taylor's firmly. "Yes," she said softly. "Something's come up that we haven't quite been able to work out. So the wedding is off."

"But why?" Francesca asked. "How did this come about? Everything was going fine until a few minutes ago."

Taylor jerked himself free of Max's restraint, then spun around with his fists aloft when his friend grabbed hold of his jacket again.

"All right," Max said, releasing him. "I'll leave you alone."

"It doesn't matter why," Taylor told his mother as he relaxed his stance. "All that matters is that the wedding is off."

Francesca curled her hand beneath her chin, trying to hide the turmoil roiling around inside her. "And just when do the two of you plan to have the wedding on again?"

Taylor glanced back over his shoulder at Emma one final time, then at Max, then back at Emma. "I don't know," he said before turning to leave the room. "Maybe never."

Francesca noted how he looked at his fiancée and then his best friend. She recalled the engagement party three months ago and the way she had found Max and Emma at the foot of the stairs. One needn't be a genius to put two and two together. She watched her son's exit with some trepidation, then turned her attention to Emma.

"May I have a word with you? Alone?"

"Now, Francesca," Desiree began. "This isn't necessarily Emma's fault."

But Francesca was interested only in Emma for the moment. Without asking again, she approached her and encircled her wrist with firm fingers, then led her away from the group. She didn't stop tugging until the two of them had reached the library, where she closed the door behind them and gestured toward the couch.

Emma settled herself precariously at the very edge of the cushion, poised for flight should she find such an action necessary. God only knew what Taylor's mother had on her mind. Surely she would blame Emma for whatever had gone wrong tonight with Taylor, never thinking her son might have had something to do with the problem. The claret-colored leather of the wing chair creaked ominously as Francesca sat down, crossed her legs, and placed her hands primly over her knee.

"Now then," she said softly, fixing Emma with an interested expression. "I think the two of us are way overdue for a little chat."

Emma inhaled deeply, waiting for the ax to fall.

A long silence passed before Taylor's mother finally said, "Max is very attractive, isn't he?"

Emma started visibly in her seat, afraid to say anything. What did Taylor's mother know about her and Max? And how could she have found out? "I'm not sure I know what you mean," she said. "What does Max have to do with anything?"

"Oh, come now, Emma, I heard what Taylor said about you and Max just a moment ago. And I've seen you and Max together. At the engagement party, remember? I was coming down the stairs when the two of you were sharing a longing look."

"It wasn't what it must have looked like, Mrs. Rowan."

"Of course it wasn't, dear. But do you deny that there's never been a little . . . something . . . a little curiosity, perhaps, that's passed between you and Max at some point?"

Emma felt tears threatening and strove to contain them. This was ridiculous. Whatever had gone on with Max or Taylor or anyone else in her life was none of Mrs. Rowan's business. Yet Emma couldn't bring herself to do anything but be honest. "No," she replied. "I don't deny that. But it was never anything serious, and it's been over for a long time," she was quick to add. "I love Taylor."

"Emma, it's all right," Francesca assured her. "I know very well that you love my son. Any fool can see that."

Emma nodded.

"Then if Max isn't the problem, what on earth is?"

Emma swallowed with some difficulty, wishing she could simplify everything that had gone wrong. "I guess, in a way, maybe it is Max—at least, that's where it all began."

Deep down, she still felt responsible for what had happened. Maybe if she'd said something to Taylor sooner, he would have confided in her as well, and their problems would never have escalated to this point. "Taylor and I should have been honest with each other from the beginning. We should have . . ." Her voice trailed off as she shook her head.

The two women sat in silence for several moments. Francesca wanted to reassure Emma, but she wasn't quite certain how to do that. Finally she said, "It isn't a good idea to keep secrets, is it?"

Emma shook her head again, yet continued to stare at the floor.

"Not only do they generally wind up causing a lot of trouble, but they're absolute hell on one's conscience."

"Yeah," Emma agreed. "They are that."

Francesca paused for a minute before asking, "Would it bother you if I told you a little story?"

The question surprised Emma, but she nodded. Anything to take her mind off of Taylor and the wedding. Then again, why would Mrs. Rowan share anything personal with her unless it was to move closer to the topic Emma wanted so desperately to avoid?

Francesca drew in a deep breath and released it slowly before she began. "Some years ago, when Taylor and Adrienne were still in grammar school and Catherine was in high school, I found two plane tickets in one of Lionel's dresser drawers, round-trip to St. Croix. At first I was delighted, thinking Lionel was going to surprise me with a second honeymoon." She smiled at Emma, her expression softer than Emma could ever recall having seen it. "We hadn't been to the Caribbean since our first one, you see, and I considered his gesture terribly romantic."

Emma smiled back, and Francesca could feel the tension between them slowly begin to ease.

"However," Francesca went on, her words coming more quickly, "upon further inspection I realized, much to my dismay, that the name on the second ticket was not my own, but the name of a woman with whom Lionel had been working for months on a particularly difficult legal case."

Emma stared at her in wide-eyed surprise.

"Oh, yes," Francesca said, understanding full well what Emma was thinking. "I've known about Lionel's girlfriends nearly all along. And I confronted him with that knowledge from the beginning. I suppose Taylor told you about them."

"Well, actually . . ." Emma tried to stall. She felt trapped and nervous and had absolutely no idea what to say. How did one reply in a situation like this? she wondered. Although she racked her brain trying to remember, she couldn't recall a single chapter in Alison Brigham's guide that described how to react to one's future mother-in-law's announcement that one's future father-in-law was a lout.

"Naturally I experienced a number of reactions when I discovered the truth, but what was I to do? You must understand my position then. I had three children to think about, and I enjoyed my social status. Because I'd never graduated from college—I was majoring in art, anyway—I had absolutely no skills. And my father, who was also a man of numerous affairs, would never have supported me financially if I'd left my husband for something Daddy considered so inconsequential."

At this point Francesca rose and paced around the

room. Finally she came to a stop near the fireplace, pausing for a moment to rearrange the Staffordshire dogs. "Ultimately I saw no other alternative but to remain married to Lionel, in spite of his philandering. He wasn't obvious about it and was careful there was never any talk—at least none that was spoken to my face. I finally came to the conclusion that it would be better for all concerned if I suffered in silence and exacted revenge in my own quiet way."

Francesca returned to her chair beside Emma and gazed at her squarely as she said, "So I began an affair of my own. And it wasn't the only one."

Emma's mouth dropped open. "You're kidding," she said before she could stop herself.

"I'm not proud of what I've done in the past," Francesca continued. "And faced with the same situation again, knowing what I know now, I would have reacted differently. But times then were different from what they are now, and, I suppose, so was I."

Emma remained silent, waiting for Taylor's mother to go on. But when Francesca seemed lost in her memories, Emma asked quietly, "Mrs. Rowan, why are you telling me all this?"

Her question seemed to do the trick, because Francesca's eyes cleared of their melancholy shadows and met Emma's once again. "The reason I'm telling you all this, the point I'm trying to make is this—Max is a very sexy young man, and would doubtless be an exhausting lover. But ultimately, that's all he'll ever be to you, Emma. Exhausting. What you find with him won't be love."

Emma stared at Francesca for a long time, speechless. She couldn't believe what Taylor's mother had just confessed to her—not just because she was surprised by Francesca's behavior, but because the other woman had actually confided in her. Finally Emma shook her head and said, "I think you've misunderstood the situation,

Mrs. Rowan. Infidelity isn't the problem with me and Taylor. At least, it isn't now."

Francesca shook her head too. "Then I'm afraid I don't understand. What's gone wrong?"

Emma didn't reply right away. She was about to say that she wasn't quite sure what had gone wrong between her and Taylor, then she remembered. "Taylor and I discovered tonight that maybe the two of us simply aren't able to communicate the way two people should be when they want to devote the rest of their lives to each other."

"I'm afraid I still don't understand."

"We can't trust each other to tell the truth."

Francesca looked doubtful. "Since when?"

"Since two years ago."

"Two years," Francesca repeated. "That's not such a long time in the scheme of things." She reached over and covered Emma's hand with her own. "Listen to me, Emma. Things between Lionel and me are finally beginning to look up. But almost twenty years we could have enjoyed together are gone, never to be retrieved. Twenty years," she repeated. "Don't let that much time come between you and Taylor. Fix whatever is wrong now, while you're both still young and open-minded enough to do it."

Emma thought about what Taylor's mother was telling her, nodding as Francesca's words gradually began to register. Things between her and Taylor could be a lot worse, Emma thought. Here was a woman who had spent half of her married life being angry and unhappy, yet she was trying her best to hold on to someone she'd once cherished, trying her best to reestablish what the two of them had once had.

Taylor was the best thing that had ever happened to Emma. The relationship the two of them enjoyed was a once-in-a-lifetime possibility that most people never knew. In her heart, Emma was certain there wasn't another man alive she could love as she loved Taylor.

Did she really want to sacrifice all that for the sake of something that had happened two years ago? Did she really want to risk losing him for good?

"Actually, Mrs. Rowan, there really isn't all that much to fix," Emma said quietly, surprised to realize how true the statement was.

Francesca smiled. "Then you should have no trouble patching things up with my son."

"Maybe not . . . Thanks, Mrs. Rowan. For . . ." She shrugged. "For everything."

Francesca patted Emma's hand affectionately. She wasn't quite comfortable with the thought of embracing her future daughter-in-law just yet, but it was something the two of them could build up to in the years to come. "Don't mention it, dear."

Emma rose to leave and had reached the library door when Francesca called out to her again.

"And one more thing, Emma."

Emma turned. "Yes?"

"Do call me Francesca, won't you? Mrs. Rowan is the name of *my* mother-in-law. And she's a perfectly hideous woman."

Emma smiled. "All right. Thanks . . . Francesca."

"You're welcome, dear. Now go and find Taylor. I'm sure he must be looking for you."

Emma finally found Taylor in the garden behind the house. At first, she thought it was a strange place for him to be wandering around. The temperature had dipped below freezing after the sun went down, and a light snow was dusting what little was left standing in the Rowan garden. The few leaves remaining on the trees, long past their bursts of warm color, were now little more than clinging bits of dry, dead brown. The flower beds were black and vacant, and the rosebushes were cropped and skeletal and anything but beautiful. But as Emma gazed at

Taylor seated on a cold concrete bench, she began to understand why he had sought out this place after all. It perfectly reflected his crummy mood, which was probably pretty similar to her own right now.

For a long time she stood to the side watching him, then she bundled her coat more tightly around her and blew on her mittened hands as she walked over to stand beside him. At first she wasn't sure he even saw her there, because his gaze remained fixed on a single dead blossom dangling from one of the rosebushes. As Emma studied it, she realized there was another shriveled bloom like it hanging from another bush beside the first one. A cold wind rushed past her then, jostling both roses vigorously, and she held her breath, fearful that one or both might fall. Yet neither did. For some reason, she found their resistance encouraging.

"Why are we fighting like this?" Taylor asked her suddenly, still staring straight ahead. "We're supposed to be getting married tomorrow, and what we're arguing about happened two years ago."

Emma didn't respond right away, but she sat down beside him. The bench was cold and hard beneath her, penetrating the warmth and softness of her coat. "Maybe we're both just a little scared of what's to come," she said. "I mean, face it, we've pretty much sailed through all this wedding stuff until tonight."

Taylor stared at her incredulously. "You have got to be kidding. We've fought more in the last six months than we did for the five and a half years before them."

"Have we?" Emma asked. "Think about it. I used to tell everyone we never, ever fought, that there was nothing we disagreed on. But that's not true at all. We disagree about a lot of things, Taylor, sometimes to the point of shouting. We just always forget about our arguments once we've settled them. Which is maybe why we've stayed together for so long."

"Do you think we'll ever forget this one?"

"I don't know."

The quiet of the night enveloped them. The only illumination in the garden was a fat yellow rectangle of light that spilled out of a window to their right and was reflected halfheartedly off the sparsely falling snow. Emma's nose was cold, and she rubbed it with her mitten. She could even smell the cold, and she wished it were spring again. Back before anything had gone wrong.

"The first day I met you," Taylor said suddenly, "I knew there was going to be something special between us. I don't know how or why I felt that way, but I just *knew*. And then, the longer we went out, the more I fell in love with you. Maybe I loved you from day one. . . . I don't even remember exactly when *that* happened."

He turned his head to look at her in the faint light, and she could see that he was hurting. Probably as much as she hurt herself. Emma covered his hand with her own and squeezed hard. Her gesture must have encouraged him, because he smiled a little.

"What I had with Tina," he continued quietly, "it wasn't like what I have with you. I honestly thought I was in love with her at one time. But now, after feeling the things I've felt for you, I know I wasn't even close with her.

"Those times she and I were together while you and I were dating . . . I don't know. Maybe I was just trying to reassure myself that you were the right one. Or maybe I was afraid of how serious things were becoming between the two of us, and I was trying to find a way to pull back from you. But that's the point, Emma, I *couldn't* pull back. Try as I might to screw things up with you, I wound up ending things with Tina instead. I don't want her. I never wanted her the way I've wanted you. I don't want to lose you. Ever."

"And you never will," she tried to reassure him. "Taylor, what happened with me and Max was a mistake. I was furious with you for going out with Tina. But more than that, I was hurt. I felt like you were rejecting me, throwing me to the side. I was terrified I was about to lose you, too. And maybe I was trying to screw things up. Dump on you before you had the chance to dump on me. Does all that really matter anymore?

"Whatever happened between me and Max that night had nothing to do with love or forever after. And it never happened again. Max doesn't even want me anymore—he wants Patsy. That's what he was telling me tonight. Yes, he kissed me, I admit that. But he was kissing me goodbye. There's nothing to stand between you and me now unless we keep this stupid argument alive. As for me, this should be the end of it."

Taylor circled an arm around Emma's waist, pulling her close. "You've heard that old story about how when the world was young, there was only one gender of people walking the earth?"

Emma nodded and tilted her head to rest it on his shoulder. "And they were so happy that the gods got jealous and split everyone into two separate people—male and female."

"And now people are destined to spend their lives looking for their other halves," he concluded the tale. Inhaling deeply, he reached over her to link his hands together and hug her even closer to him. "That's what happened that day you stopped me outside the library, Emma. I found my other half. If anything ever happens to you, I'll never find another woman to take your place. You're it for me. You're the one. If I lose you, what's the point of walking the earth in search of something I'll never find?"

She nodded. "I feel that way, too."

He gestured toward the two rosebushes before them. "You know, these rosebushes are my two favorite things growing out in Mother's garden."

Emma smiled. "They don't seem to be growing much now."

"Oh, they may look dead, but they're still kicking. Just give them a little time. Just wait until spring."

Emma lifted her hand to trace her mitten gingerly over Taylor's eye. "I can't believe you and Max got into a fight."

When she came to a tender spot, Taylor jerked his head back with a quiet, "Ow."

"Sorry."

He smiled. "Me too."

Emma scooted a little closer, trying to draw upon Taylor's warmth. "So what kind of roses are they?" she asked.

Taylor shrugged and turned his attention back to the bushes. "I have no idea. But one's a white rosebush and one's a red rosebush. At least, that's what they used to be, a long time ago, when I was real little. But over the years, they've kind of cross-pollinated or something. The white one has gradually become light pink, and the red one's faded to kind of a fuchsia now. The colors are gorgeous. Each of the bushes has gotten more beautiful, thanks to the other."

He settled an arm over Emma's shoulder, pulling her close again. With his other hand, he reached down to grip hers fiercely. "I always kind of thought that's how you and I would become over the years. Two distinct people, but people who each improve because of the influences of the other. Does that make sense?"

Emma nodded.

"I've never wanted anyone to affect me or influence me. But being with you . . ." He stopped, not altogether certain what he wanted to say. "What you and I have together is so completely different from other married couples I know. It sounds like a cliché to say this, but what we have . . . it's special. And I don't want to blow it. Especially over something that happened two years ago."

"I'm sorry about what happened with Max," she said quietly.

"And I'm sorry about what happened with Tina."

They turned to look at each other. "Forget about it," they replied in unison. Then they both smiled.

"It's too bad the roses aren't blooming now," Emma said as she leaned her head on Taylor's shoulder. "I'd like to tuck one of each into my bridal bouquet."

Taylor rested his head on top of Emma's. "I guess we'll just have to find surrogates."

Emma snuggled closer to Taylor, hooking her arm through his. "Hey, Taylor," she said, "I'll be your rose if you'll be mine."

Taylor squeezed her hand tightly. "It's a deal. And what say later tonight, after everyone's gone home, you and I do a little cross-pollinating?"

Emma smiled. "Okay."

35

It may seem a long time in the making, but eventually your wedding day will arrive. And when it does . . . look out. Not surprisingly, to Alison, there is nothing on earth worth celebrating more than a wedding. And just because you and your groom are the focus of attention does not mean you should neglect having a good time yourselves. This is your day. Enjoy it. Revel in it. And save a little piece of cake for Alison, won't you?

—ALISON BRIGHAM

Johnson Memorial was packed the following evening. One hundred and eighty-eight invitations had been mailed to a total of four hundred and seven guests. And as Virginia glanced over her shoulder from her seat beside Eliot in the fourth pew on the bride's side, she decided that just about everyone must have made it to the wedding.

The church itself reminded Virginia of a huge Viking ship turned upside down, with arching walls that rose to a crest some fifty feet above her. Behind the altar, a huge, tear-drop-shaped stained glass window fashioned in abstract panes of cranberry, gold, and green reflected the light of hundreds of candles lit on the altar and at the end of each pew. The sanctuary was redolent with the fragrance of roses, carnations, and a number of other flowers, and Virginia couldn't help but smile as she leaned down to breathe deeply once again of the corsage fastened to her lapel. She'd been more than a little surprised when Desiree had told her Eliot was responsible for the extra corsage that had arrived with the other flowers for the wedding.

She glanced down at her watch to find that it was precisely seven o'clock, and waited for something to happen. Almost immediately, the four-piece brass combo playing something soft and melodious in the organ loft paused, then eased into what Virginia had heard often enough by now to distinguish as the "Promenade" from *Pictures at an Exhibition*. A door on the right side of the altar opened, and out came a procession of men, first Reverend Ballard, then Taylor and Max, followed by five groomsmen.

My, they were a handsome bunch, Virginia thought with a little sigh. Especially Taylor and Max. All in all, her nieces hadn't done too badly for themselves. She looked at Eliot beside her. Generally, where men were concerned, Virginia decided the Hammelmann women could usually pick the winners. Then something in the young men's faces caught Virginia's eye, and she leaned forward, to inspect the male members of the wedding party a little more closely.

"How do you think Taylor got that black eye, I wonder?" she whispered to Eliot. "And look at Max. I'm surprised he didn't need stitches for his lip." She turned to him. "I told you we should have gone to Francesca and Lionel's last night after the rehearsal dinner. It must have been one hell of a party."

"Shh," Eliot murmured. "We had other plans, remember?"

Virginia grew warm inside. "Of course I remember. Promise me you'll never shave off your moustache."

Eliot grinned at her. "I promise. Now hush."

As the bridesmaids entered one by one, Virginia decided her relatives had never looked so good. But when all six women stood before her, she narrowed her eyes once more and frowned.

"You know something?" she said softly, leaning toward Eliot again. "I never noticed how big Felicia's . . ." She paused before concluding, "I mean, that bow on her dress is in no way flattering."

"Shh," Eliot said.

"And Mindy . . . her back is breaking out again. That poor kid should see a good dermatologist. And look at Catherine. Have you ever noticed how short she is?"

"Shh," Eliot repeated. "Here comes the bride."

The music segued nicely from *Pictures at an Exhibition* to *Here Comes the Bride*, and everyone in the church was silent, even Virginia. Emma made her entrance, smiling when she saw Taylor silently mouth the word "Wow" upon her appearance.

Everything was perfect, Virginia thought. More than perfect. Absolutely wonderful. The church, the music, the flowers, the dresses . . . She sighed. Emma's wedding was the most beautiful one she had ever attended. But best of all, she realized with a little sniffle, even this grand spectacle in no way caused her to want one of her own.

Everything moved quickly after that. There were stories told, biblical passages read, vows and promises made, but all of it happened in such a blur that Virginia would have been hard pressed to remember most of it later. All too soon, the good reverend was announcing that Taylor and Emma were husband and wife, and then the music erupted again as the couple sped back down the aisle, this time a joyous rendition of the song Virginia only knew as the theme to "The Newlywed Game."

And then it was over. Three rows in front of Virginia, Desiree was dabbing furiously at her eyes with a lace hanky, her mascara flowing freely down her cheeks. Beside Desiree, Laszlo patted her back affectionately, but

Virginia could see that her brother, too, had been deeply affected by the ceremony. The couple was joined by Francesca and Lionel, who were obviously much better equipped to handle their emotions. But Virginia couldn't help noticing that Francesca reached into her purse for a fresh hanky to hand to Desiree, who promptly blew her nose into it.

"Thank you, Francesca," she heard her sister-in-law say as she handed the hanky back.

Francesca looked at the tiny square of white linen as if it were a big, wet fish and replied, "Why don't you hang on to it, Desiree? You might need it again later."

Desiree smiled and rubbed her nose with the handkerchief again.

Virginia started to rise to join the other members of her family, but Eliot stayed her action by placing his hand gently on her arm.

"They'll be a little while yet," he said. "They have to stay for photographs and well-wishers and the like. Why don't we just stay put for the time being?"

Virginia took her seat again, and they sat in silence as the other guests filed slowly out around them. Occasionally Virginia would identify one of her relatives to Eliot and then treat him to a story about that person's children or reveal some deep, dark family secret. Eliot would then respond in kind, choosing one of his in-laws for roasting. As the church gradually emptied, however, an awkward silence ensued.

When Virginia was no longer able to tolerate their lapses in communication, she gave Eliot her most dazzling smile and said, "It was a beautiful ceremony, wasn't it?"

He smiled back at her. "Yes, it was."

Another uneasy pause followed. "Emma looked beautiful, didn't she?"

"She was lovely."

"And the bridesmaids?" Virginia asked. "They were beautiful, too, weren't they?"

"Very."

"And the music? It was . . . beautiful."

Eliot nodded.

"And this church!" Virginia went on, spreading her arms wide. "Isn't it just absolutely beautiful? And all these flowers are just—"

"Beautiful," Eliot finished for her. "Yes, Ginnie, everything was beautiful."

Virginia nodded, suddenly feeling very nervous.

"Do you know what else is beautiful?" Eliot asked her.

She shook her head.

"You, Ginnie. You've outshone every woman here today, your niece included."

Virginia chuckled. "Yeah, sure."

"I mean it. I don't know what it is about you, but . . ."

Virginia couldn't meet his eyes as she asked, "But?"

He shook his head. "But I don't know. Suffice it to say you're wonderful to be around."

She smiled. "Thanks."

Eliot paused, as if weighing some issue of grave importance. "It makes me wonder, though . . . if you might not want to be around me a bit longer. Perhaps . . . permanently."

Virginia nibbled her lower lip. "What are you saying, Eliot?"

He studied her with a critical eye before beginning, "With all the beauty of the wedding you've just described . . ." He halted suddenly, then tried again. "What I'm trying to say is . . . it seems to me that the average woman, upon sitting through a ceremony such as this one, would spend much of her time there envisioning a wedding of her own. But I don't suppose you're one of those women, are you, Ginnie?"

She smiled again but this time felt anything but happy. "Are you accusing me of being average, Eliot?"

"Absolutely not. In fact, I suppose that's exactly the problem. You're not an average woman."

"Would you like me better if I were?"

He shook his head. "No. But if you were, it might be easier to ask you the question I want very much to ask."

Virginia's heart picked up its pace, and she wished there was some way she and Eliot could avoid this conversation. In a way, though, she supposed she'd been expecting it all along, and really, what was the point of prolonging something that was bound to rear its ugly head again? Why did it have to come down to marriage? Why couldn't there be some happy medium she and Eliot might reach together?

"You know by now what kind of woman I am, Eliot," Virginia said. "I'll be forty-nine in a few weeks, and although there's certainly nothing in the world I'm too old to do, there are a few things I'd like to avoid, simply because I'm so set in my ways. And, quite frankly, marriage is one of them." She smiled. "If any man could make me consider it, you would be the one. But marriage . . . it just isn't for me."

Eliot nodded, his eyes betraying the disappointment that he felt. "I see. And nothing I could say or do would change your mind?"

Virginia thought for a moment. "Well . . ."

"Aunt Virginia! Brownie!"

Emma and Taylor rushed up behind them then, Emma throwing her arms around her aunt from behind. "We did it!" she cried. "We're married!"

Virginia and Eliot rose to congratulate the couple, laughing and hugging and shaking hands.

"You're gorgeous, Emma," Virginia told her niece as she pulled away. "Who did your hair?"

Emma fingered her bangs, now a bouncing collection of loose curls. "Can you believe how nicely it turned out? Mr. Pierre, Mom's stylist did it. Who'd have thought he had a contemporary bone in his body?"

"What the devil happened to you?" Eliot asked Taylor, indicating the black eye.

"And Max?" Virginia added. "You guys look like you got mugged."

Taylor brushed his hand sheepishly over the wound. "Oh, you know Mother and her wild parties."

"Don't you two stray too far," Emma continued, "because we want you to be in the family pictures. Oh, there's the photographer. He wants us all right now." She took her aunt by the hand. "Come on. Let's get a good spot."

Virginia turned to offer Eliot one final, longing look. "But . . ." she began.

Emma, seeming to sense her train of thought, said, "Oh, Aunt Virginia, relax. You and Brownie will be sitting next to each other at the reception. You'll have all the time in the world to stare lovingly into each other's eyes. Now come on. We're getting our pictures made. Last one there's an old poot."

The Crosscreek Country club had never looked more festive. Thanks to the fast-approaching holiday season, the reception hall glittered with white Christmas lights, golden wreaths, and fragrant evergreen boughs. The band—a motley-looking group who called themselves Mondo Audio—claimed a repertoire ranging from rock to country to swing to jazz, and a vocalist with a big bouffant hairdo who did justice to them all. As a result, the dance floor was crowded with wedding guests.

At some point between picture-taking and their arrival at the reception, the groomsmen had shed their crisp, white tuxedo shirts in favor of the Hawaiian shirts Taylor had presented to them as gifts. To compensate for this behavior, and perhaps still hoping to hide their lesser assets, each of the bridesmaids had slipped on her bowling shirt over her dress. So when the band began a bluesy rendition of "Louie, Louie," everyone donned his or her sunglasses to affect the proper attitude and took the celebration to new heights.

Virginia watched their behavior from a table near the bar, wondering if she'd ever attend a party better than this one again.

"I never have understood what this song is about," Eliot said. Since their discussion at the church had ended so abruptly, the two of them had kept their conversation centered on more harmless subject matter.

"Me neither," Virginia said. "But it's great to dance to. How about it?"

Eliot nodded and rose from his chair, holding Virginia's for her as she got up. They threaded their way through the crowd until they were at some point in the middle of the dance floor, where he reached for her and pulled her close, his cheek settled affectionately against her hair.

"There's something I've wanted to tell you for some time now, Ginnie," he said loudly, trying to make sure she heard him over the noise of the band.

One of the groomsmen shouted something that sounded like "Gator!" and all the people surrounding them on the dance floor dropped onto their backs and began to shudder convulsively.

"Something to tell me?" Virginia murmured as she and Eliot continued to sway completely out of time with the music.

The other dancers slowly began to rise again, a writhing mass of bodies that reminded Eliot of a druidic ritual. "What on earth do they call that?"

"What?"

"That dance."

Virginia looked around them as if seeing the other dancers for the first time. "I think that's the 'Funky Cold Medina.'"

"I see. How . . . unusual."

"You said there something you wanted to tell me, Eliot?" Virginia asked, resting her head against his shoulder again.

"What?"

"You said there was something you wanted to tell me," she repeated over the din.

"Oh, yes. I love you."

Virginia pulled away from him only far enough to meet his gaze. "Oh, I wish you hadn't said that."

"Why?"

"Because now I have to say it back."

Eliot smiled at her. "You only have to say it back if that's how you feel."

Virginia continued to stare at him. "You know it's how I feel."

Eliot's smile broadened. "What's how you feel?"

Virginia inhaled deeply, blowing an errant curl out of her eyes as she exhaled. "Oh, dammit . . ." she muttered. "I love you, too. There, I hope you're satisfied."

Eliot pulled her close again, and the two began to dance some more. Neither said a word as one song ended and another began. They only continued to hold each other and sway slowly to the music that had picked up to an even more frenetic pace.

"That's a Nirvana song," Virginia told him. "Be careful. Everyone's going to start moshing in a minute."

"Moshing?" Eliot asked. "What's that?"

"It's like slam dancing."

"What's slam dancing?"

"Never mind, Eliot. Never mind."

As the people around them began to bounce up and down, Eliot pulled Virginia closer and asked, "So what are we going to do about this new development in our relationship?"

Virginia shook her head. "I don't know, Eliot. It's a mighty sticky situation, that's for sure. Just because we're in love, that doesn't change everything. I mean, for example, we're still totally different in our approach to things."

"Totally different."

"And neither one of us has any understanding of why we feel the way we do."

"None whatsoever."

"It could end as quickly as it all began."

"Yes, it could."

"And of course you realize your children hate my guts."

"Bugger my children."

"Eliot!"

"No, I mean it, Ginnie. I didn't approve of either one of the people they chose to marry. What should I care if they have a problem with you?"

"I never said I'd marry you, Eliot."

"And I don't recall asking you to."

Virginia nodded. "That's true. . . ."

He tucked her head beneath his chin and set them into rhythmic motion once again. Several more moments passed before he told her, "I've requested permission for a sabbatical next semester. I would have said something sooner, but I wasn't sure whether or not the university would grant it. And now they have."

"That's nice," Virginia said against his chest. "What does it mean?"

"It means I'm going to England the first of January. I'll be spending five months in London, Canterbury, Oxford, Cambridge, and a number of other cities. I don't suppose your adventures will find you in England any time soon, will they, Ginnie?"

Virginia smiled and snuggled more comfortably into Eliot's embrace. "How strange. I was just thinking not too long ago how much fun it might be to go to England again. Although I have to admit, I find Scotland and Wales a lot more fun."

"I'll be spending a good bit of my time in Wales," Eliot said.

"Really? How about Scotland?"

"I think I could probably manage a side trip or two."

They danced a bit more, then Eliot told her, "You know, there are a number of beautiful places in Great

Britain I could show you, all of them boasting great literary significance."

Virginia smiled. "There are some great pubs I could show you, all of them boasting some really first-rate public toilets."

Eliot spun her in a dramatic turn, then pulled her back into his arms and dipped her toward the dance floor. "I think there's quite a bit we could show each other," he told her as he pulled her into his arms again.

Virginia linked her fingers behind his back and squeezed hard. "That's true. But we could potentially wind up spending the rest of our lives doing it, too."

"Pity," Eliot told her without a bit of remorse.

"Isn't it just?"

"I suppose we'll just have to suffer through somehow."

Virginia sighed. "I suppose we will. Say, Eliot, have you ever thought about buying a boat?"

On the other side of the dance floor, Patsy spun Max in a turn similar to the one she'd seen her Aunt Virginia and Taylor's Uncle Brownie execute some moments ago. Max stumbled a bit as he came back, falling into Patsy's arms with a less-than-graceful landing, but he smiled nonetheless.

"You're a hell of a dancer, Patsy."

"Thanks, Max."

The band stopped playing abruptly, and the couple looked up to find that Desiree had commandeered the microphone.

"I got an announcement to make," she said, her voice echoing off the walls and ceiling of the cavernous room. "All you single girls out there, gather round. 'Cause Emma's ready to throw her bouquet!"

"Excuse me, will you, Max?" Patsy said. "This is kind of important."

Max released her, a thrill of foreboding crawling down his spine as Patsy joined the other single women. Not that he held any kind of faith in that bouquet-throwing business, but a man didn't like to mess with superstition if he didn't have to. He watched closely as Emma climbed the stairs at the opposite end of the room, and he shifted restlessly from one foot to the other as the photographer took his time in arranging her gown and coaching her on how to toss the bouquet just so. Max didn't realize he had been slowly approaching the scene himself until he stood just behind the group of excited women and heard Emma shout, "Here it comes!"

The bouquet arced up and up and over the crowd below Emma, a spiraling, spinning collection of white flowers and greenery, falling, falling ever so slowly, until Max realized too late that it was headed directly for him. The last thing he remembered thinking was that Emma would have made a hell of a basketball player, and then the bridal bouquet tumbled directly into his hands.

Every eye in the room fell upon him, each of the unattached women who had been vying for the trophy gazing at him with what Max could only liken to homicidal intent. Each of them, that was, except for one. If Patsy's smile had been any broader, her face would have split in two. She ran toward Max, throwing herself into his arms with enough force to send them both spinning backward. Max landed flat on his back with Patsy straddling him, kissing his face over and over again.

"I love you," she told him without a trace of shyness. "Let's go home and make love."

Max, having had the breath knocked out of him by the fall, was helpless to respond, a reaction Patsy mistook for his acquiescence. She stood up, helped him to his feet, then quickly bade Emma and the rest of the wedding party goodbye.

"My, but that was dramatic," Francesca remarked to her husband as they watched the couple leave. "What do you suppose all that was meant to indicate?"

Lionel circled his arm around his wife's waist and

shook his head. "Probably that it's time to shut down the bar."

"Oh, Francesca," Desiree sang out from behind the couple. She and Laszlo joined them near the buffet. "I have something for you. The directions to the Cupid's Arrow Motor Lodge. Can you believe it? It's still there."

"And just a stone's throw from Trump Plaza," Laszlo added. "That ought to be convenient."

"Actually, Hammelmann, I'm not much of a gambler," Lionel said.

Francesca took the slip of paper from Desiree and tucked it discreetly into the breast pocket of Lionel's tuxedo jacket. "He says that now. But just you wait."

Desiree laughed. "Then could you maybe get me a few souvenir chips while you're there?"

Francesca nodded. "Certainly. If we ever manage to make it to the casino."

"It should be nice to get out of town for a while after all this," Desiree said. "Weddings are terrific, but they can sure wear you out."

"How about the two of you?" Francesca asked. "Emma and Taylor will be going away on their honeymoon, Lionel and I are taking off for a few days. You two should escape to some secluded romantic rendezvous, too, now that the wedding is over."

"Nah," Laszlo told them. "We thought we'd just go home and have a sandwich."

Desiree nodded, elbowing her husband as she gave him her most beguiling smile. "Yeah. We been on our honeymoon for forty-two years."

"Mother! Daddy!"

The two couples turned abruptly at the sound of Adrienne's breathless cry. She ran toward them with a young man whom none of the others had ever seen before, both of them grinning.

"Mother, I have the most wonderful news," Adrienne said, gasping for breath. "I can't wait to tell you."

Francesca laid a hand gently on her daughter's shoulder, silently urging her to calm down. "Adrienne, what is it? What's happened?"

Adrienne pulled the young man to her side, beaming as she asked, "Remember Mickey? From Taylor and Emma's engagement party?"

Lionel and Francesca shook their heads. "No, dear," Francesca said, "I'm afraid we don't."

"Sure you do," Adrienne said. "He was one of the waiters you hired."

"Ah. I see." Francesca inclined her head toward him. "Hello, Mickey, how are you?"

"Great," the young man replied.

Adrienne looked as if she were about to burst as she announced loudly, "Mother, Daddy . . . Mickey and I are getting married! In June! Isn't that fabulous? Won't it be great?"

"Congratulations, sweetie!" Desiree exclaimed. "How wonderful for you both! Frances—" She stopped abruptly when she saw the other woman's expression. "Francesca? You okay?"

"Fine," Francesca said weakly. "Just . . . just fine. But I think I need to sit down. Lionel? Will you have one of the waiters fetch me a bourbon?"

"I already know which dress I want," Adrienne said. "And I want to get married outdoors . . . in the morning . . . at sunrise. . . ."

Lionel pushed a chair behind his wife and helped her down into it, pressing her drink into her hand.

"And a steel drum band," Adrienne went on. "There has to be a steel drum band. . . ."

From her place atop the stairs, Emma was joined by her new husband. As she and Taylor wove their hands together, she watched with a mixture of conflicting emotions the various exchanges below them.

"What are you thinking about?" Taylor asked her.

Emma rubbed her jaw. "About how much my mouth hurts after smiling for all those photographs."

Taylor laughed and pulled her closer. "Come on. You're looking pretty pensive. What gives?"

Emma shook her head. "Just that it's been such a long, strange road getting here. I feel so weird. For the last six months, this is the moment we've been building up to," she said softly. "And now it's over. Now it's done."

Taylor laughed and bent to kiss her. "Oh, Emma, that's not true at all. The wedding isn't what we've been leading up to. The wedding isn't the end."

Emma smiled and knew of course that he was right. The wedding wasn't the end of all the plans they'd been making for months. The wedding was just the beginning.

"Now what do you say we blow this joint?" he murmured. "And get on with the rest of our lives?"

Emma nodded and rose on tiptoe to kiss him back. As beginnings went, she decided, this one wasn't bad at all.

COMING NEXT MONTH

LORD OF THE NIGHT by Susan Wiggs
Much loved historical romance author Susan Wiggs turns to the rich, sensual atmosphere of sixteenth-century Venice for another enthralling, unforgettable romance. "Susan Wiggs is truly magical."—Laura Kinsale, bestselling author of *Flowers from the Storm*.

CHOICES by Marie Ferrarella
The compelling story of a woman from a powerful political family who courageously gives up a loveless marriage and pursues her own dreams, finding romance, heartbreak, and difficult choices along the way.

THE SECRET by Penelope Thomas
A long-buried secret overshadowed the love of an innocent governess and her master. Left with no family, Jessamy Lane agreed to move into Lord Wolfeburne's house and care for his young daughter. But when Jessamy suspected something sinister in his past, whom could she trust?

WILDCAT by Sharon Ihle
A fiery romance that brings the Old West back to life. When prim and proper Ann Marie Cannary went in search of her sister, Martha Jane, what she found instead was a hellion known as "Calamity Jane." Annie was powerless to change her sister's rough ways, but the small Dakota town of Deadwood changed Annie as she adapted to life in the Wild West and fell in love with a man who was full of surprises.

MURPHY'S RAINBOW by Carolyn Lampman
While traveling on the Oregon Trail, newly widowed Kate Murphy found herself stranded in a tiny town in Wyoming Territory. Handsome, enigmatic Jonathan Cantrell needed a housekeeper and nanny for his two sons. But living together in a small cabin on an isolated ranch soon became too close for comfort . . . and falling in love grew difficult to resist. Book I of the Cheyenne Trilogy.

TAME THE WIND by Katherine Kilgore
A sizzling story of forbidden love between a young Cherokee man and a Southern belle in antebellum Georgia. "Katherine Kilgore's passionate lovers and the struggles of the Cherokee nation are spellbinding. Pure enjoyment!"—Katherine Deauxville, bestselling author of *Daggers of Gold*.

*M*Harper **The Mark of Distinctive**
onogram **Women's Fiction**